EMERGENCY LANDING

Something flashed so bright that his eyes shut before he was aware of what had happened. The floor jerked up under him, impacting feet, jarring his body. He felt like he was traveling up, then stopped, hovered, floated. His eyes were open now, and all he could see was the dim lighting, the walls, the few controls, the compartment latches, and he knew, in that instant, that he was going to die.

He reached out for the reality control and hit the default toggle. There were several brief flashes as the computer took in the data from the external eyes and composited them. Then he was surrounded by night sky. Above him were three holes in the sky, three holes darker than the night itself, wavering with the breeze. The emergency parachutes.

He was drifting downward, and he had no idea where he was.

Books by Charles Oberndorf

SHELTERED LIVES
TESTING
FORAGERS

FORAGERS

Charles Oberndorf

For Frank—
You didn't make
the acknowledgements
for this novel, it
there was such a
thing for my life,
you'd be there—
Best,
Charlie O
15 April 96
U.S.

BANTAM BOOKS
New York • Toronto • London • Sydney • Auckland

FORAGERS

A Bantam Spectra Book/April 1996

ISBN 0-553-29695-7

Published simultaneously in the United States and Canada

Bantam Books are published by Bantam Books, a division of Bantam
Doubleday Dell Publishing Group, Inc. Its trademark, consisting of the
words "Bantam Books" and the portrayal of a rooster, is Registered in
U.S. Patent and Trademark Office and in other countries. Marca Reg-
istrada. Bantam Books, 1540 Broadway, New York, New York 10036.

PRINTED IN THE UNITED STATES OF AMERICA

OPM   0 9 8 7 6 5 4 3 2 1

For my grandparents
Lillian Oberndorf (1889–1956)
Walter Oberndorf (1888–1965)
Charles Gleason (1890–1956)
and
Mary Louise Vail,
who provides support
and a place to write each summer

And for the Hanover Wind Ensemble
(1981–1988),
my second family:
Gunnel Clark
Tony Geist
Paul Hecht
Roberto Mayoral
Abe Osheroff
John Wing

nature and nurture

Author's Note

Several characters in this novel speak a click language spoken by the Ju/'hoansi, who have been called the !Kung in the anthropological literature, and who are referred to here by the 1950s spelling, Ju/wasi. I have included some of the clicks for flavor. For those who enjoy such things, here is roughly how they sound:

/   is a dental click—the tongue is pulled away from the teeth as in "tsk, tsk."

≠   is an alveolar click—the tongue is pulled away from the ridge connecting upper teeth to gums.

!   is an alveopalatal—the tongue is pulled away from the roof of the mouth making a sound like that of a cork coming out of a bottle.

//   is a lateral click—the tongue is pulled away from the sides; in English this sound is sometimes used to urge on horses.

These soldiers are the owners of fighting. They fight even when they play, and I fear them. I won't let my children be soldiers, the experts at anger. The soldiers will bring the killing.

—≠oma Word, 1978

Lions eat alone, not people.

—Ju/wasi saying

Sentiment without action is the ruin of the soul.

—Edward Abbey

Introduction
to the
Second Alternative Edition

Two decades after its first appearance, it may be difficult to remember why *Foragers* was both reviled and celebrated in its time. The Human-Slazan War had entered its own second decade, and each meager attempt at negotiation had failed. One world, which had originally been shared by humans and slazans, had been obliterated. Human warships and slazan warships patrolled space, searching for enemy ships to destroy while seeking out the location of enemy installations, orbital colonies, and homeworlds.

The novel's author, Pauline Dikobe, was a little-known anthropologist and the only human to have had the opportunity to study any slazan culture for a substantial length of time. Three years before, a human-programmed exploration probe had discovered a lost colony of slazans. A warship was dispatched in secret, taking one lone anthropologist to study the solitary aliens far away from the war. She carried out her studies over the course of two hundred local days, working out of a diplomatic shuttle craft—complete with shower, bed, and working kitchen—that had been modified to carry some of the latest and some of the oldest kinds of equipment available to an ethnographer, everything from a spade to imaging pins.

After her time in the field had ended, Dikobe returned to the warship, expecting to spend her time during the journey home analyzing the wealth of data she had gathered. She found instead that the ship's intelligence had confiscated and sealed off all the collected data; even her own notebook was inaccessible. A recorded message notified her that the military required raw data presented with a minimum of interpretation. She was thanked for her efforts, reminded of the substantial pay she would receive, and removed from the project. "I was glad," she later said, "that the ship's captain hadn't been ordered to jettison me from the ship."

She was left with a four-month-long journey and time to kill. She first found out that even though her home planet, E-donya E-talta, was a freenet world, there were wartime laws that allowed the military to claim rightful ownership of the data she had collected. She didn't want the trip to disappear into secrecy, so she started writing a personal account of her six months on the planet. But with no field notes at hand, she believed such an account would be unreliable and unprofessional; furthermore, she ran the risk that the military might be able to claim ownership of this work, too. After days of hesitation and doubt, Dikobe found herself writing a novel in which she tried to dramatize the nature of slazan life through a series of highly dramatic events. She studied slazans for 200 days, but for unity of action, she has the novel take place over the course of 17 days, in which a human soldier attempts to find a missing anthropologist, whose name, ironically, is Pauline Dikobe.

Everyone who had followed the war knew there had been a secret mission to study a colony of slazans living in primitive conditions, and there was a hunger for some account of that voyage. *Foragers* filled that need. It did not matter that parts of the story were terribly fictionalized. It quickly became common knowledge, for instance, that Pauline Dikobe was the only person who had joined the warship's crew for this mission. The novel's human protagonist, the Ju/wa soldier who called himself Esoch al-Schouki, was Dikobe's invention, as were the four military scientists Dikobe included to make the fictional expedition appear more realistic.

Although it was clearly a work of fiction, readers were sure the novel contained a version of her own experiences. They saw in the fictional devices a well-intentioned subtext, and sometimes there was greater debate about the meaning of the subtext than about the anthropological detail itself. The reading public trusted Dikobe's anthropology: this was how the slazans really were, this was how they behaved, this was how they felt.

Literary historians have to go back several centuries to find a written fabrication such as hers that moved people to action. Those who were knowledgeable of such things compared *Forag-*

ers to *Oliver Twist, Uncle Tom's Cabin,* or *The Jungle,* works that both changed and charged public opinion. Each novel attacked oppressive social institutions by showing how human its victims were. In Dikobe's novel the enemy had been given a new face, and it had been given a heart. The socially accepted institution of the Human-Slazan War now seemed not only wasteful, but immoral.

Within two years a new, more extensive set of negotiations, led by General Muhammad ibn Haj, was begun, and an end finally came to a ghastly and costly war. Many credited the novel for playing a role in changing public opinion enough so that the military had to end the war. General ibn Haj, representing the military, argued to the contrary. Peace had been their goal all along, he said, and if Dikobe had been allowed to publish a monograph rather than a novel, the public image of slazans would not have been so happily changed.

Ten years after the novel was released, the military declassified most of the contents of the notebook Pauline Dikobe had kept during the expedition and made those sections of it available to scholars of the war. Fadl Sidnal and Yusuf Niws, of the Institute of Interspecies Conflict, edited an alternative edition of *Foragers*, one that included excerpts from Dikobe's notebook.

The notebook turned out to be a hodgepodge of musings and journal entries, which indicated that all along Dikobe had considered writing a personal account of the mission. Its contents surprised many. First, it became clear that she had been contemplating the idea of the novel during the off hours of her research. Second, the slazans she observed seemed very different from the ones she had invented. In the notebook entries, we see slazan actions but not the slazan heart, and the actions do not always create easy reader empathy.

Those who claimed that *Foragers* was propaganda when it was first released now believed they had the evidence to prove their case. Those who had lived and worked among the slazans were divided into two camps. One camp argued that Dikobe, with a novelist's eye for the truth, understood the slazans well; the other argued that she understood very little, that all she did was imbue slazan behaviors with human emotions.

Over time, however, it became clear that the alternative edition had been edited with an astute political eye. The editors included only sections of the notebook that highlighted the differences between the slazans Dikobe observed and the fictive ones she wrote about. A huge scholarly apparatus was used to point out how fictional the fiction was.

When other scholars read the original notebook, they discovered that Sidnal and Niws had omitted pertinent entries. All of Dikobe's musings about her novel and its relationship to truth were gone. Any incident that clearly inspired some moment in the novel was absent. The editors, in Dikobe's words, "made me look like a cheap propagandist."

In one interview Dikobe said, "I worked hard to make my fictional slazans as slazan-like as humanly possible. I took observed behavior and employed those behaviors in the narrative. A good part of the dialogue is lifted from conversations our eavesdropping devices recorded. If the military would declassify all the research tapes, you would see that the story is perhaps structured too much like a certain kind of human story, that perhaps the behavior of the slazan characters is determined by the way things go wrong in order for the story to be dramatic, but you would also see that what my fictive slazans say and do corresponds closely to what I saw real slazans saying and doing."

This new edition that you hold in your hands takes selections from Dikobe's attempted memoir and her notebooks to give a better sense of this process. With Pauline Dikobe's permission I have changed the name of the warship and the names of its crew to preserve their privacy at home. In each case, where possible, I substituted the name used in the novel.

For centuries now anthropologists have been of two minds as to whether anthropology is a scientific art that relies on understanding through empathy or if it is an artfully practiced science that achieves understanding through empirical data. *Foragers*—published with these excerpts from Pauline Dikobe's notebook—dramatizes that conflict well.

At the time of this writing, tensions are escalating on Tienah, the world where Pauline Dikobe made her fame by studying a small colony of slazans. The several slazan populations and the two large human settlements that once coexisted peacefully are now involved in several disputes over territory and trade. The recent imprisonment of three slazans, who were arrested for spying, and the retaliatory bombing of a human embassy building has only made matters worse. In light of this current tragedy, it is important to remember the role that empathy played at the end of the Human-Slazan War, a war that we hope historians will never have to write about with the use of a numerical qualifier.

—FAWIZA MUNEEF
Executive Director
Department of Slagan Culturos
Institute of Cultural Studies
E-donya E-talta

FORAGERS

by Pauline Dikobe

The following is taken from the notebook Pauline Dikobe kept during her 200 day study of the slazan foraging population on Tienah.

Day Eight

It is the third day that I am ill, on this planet that has no official name and no official number. I should be outside, but instead I lie here, in this converted shuttle craft, on my bed, reeking of sweat and sickness. There's something in the atmosphere that's working hard to find an ecological niche inside me, a secure haven where it can survive and prosper. Each morning, vaguely refreshed, my blood filtered and replenished with nutrients, I step outside the shuttle craft. I am dressed like a primal forager, wearing a leather pubic apron and sandals. The morning air is chilled, and my skin is hard with goose bumps.

Three quarters of the clearing is surrounded by a hill that curves around in a sweeping arc. Up to the crest the hillside is barren of brush; instead there are fresh grasses that glisten each morning with dew. Thick trees form a colorful wall along the crest of the hill. In the morning all the leaves are green, the same shades of green we have observed on Terra, Nueva España, E-donya, and long-gone New Hope. However, when the sun rises above the horizon and light strikes against the leaves, some chemical reaction is touched off; the leaves of different kinds of trees change to different colors. The thick, heavyset trees take on a deep red, the trees whose tops are pointed sharply become heavy with orange, and the spindly trees that sprout in among the others are ripe with yellow. A wave of color spreads across the clearing as the sun moves across the sky. In the afternoon, as brightness fades with a kind of stillness, the colors of the leaves fade too, and while evening grays deepen into night's blackness, the colors, too, are bleached away to their original verdant shadows. By morning everything is returned to green. By noon the next day the clearing is lush with reds, oranges, and yellows.

With the first fresh colors come the locals. They remain at the top of the hill. They stand behind the shadows of trees, watching. They are like ghosts, vague humanoid forms with leathery skin.

The shuttle craft's hull is covered with crystalline eyes, and the shuttle's intelligence magnifies the images on the screens inside. But the natives crouch behind colorful bushes and peer around thick, dark tree trunks, so we catch only glimpses: the tops of heads, the profile of a face, the reach of an arm, the swing of a body turning away, an infant grasping hold of a sagging breast, but we never see an entire body, we never make out individual faces.

The intelligence combines the data from the images, from motion sensors, from radar, and I get a readout on the number of slazans: anywhere from three to ten individuals may be up there. Each adult sits or crouches or stands a good five meters from another. If an adult is forced to step closer to a conspecific, as when returning to a path, both adults turn away: this is our leading cause of detectable motion. Several lactating females carry infants. We have made out two lactating females who carry an infant while a child stands by her side. Childless adults stand alone.

I vaguely wonder what each one thinks when she watches me totter about the clearing for a while, then half run, half stumble back into the shuttle, where, out of sight and out of sound, I throw up the meager meal I had taken in order to have something to throw up.

It had been assumed that the adaptation sickness would be mild. During the five months of travel that had brought me here, the warship's environment had been readjusted by increments so that during the last month of the trip I walked under the same gravity, read under the same lighting, breathed the same atmospheric composition, and paced out the same number of hours that I do on this nameless planet. If nothing else, I was supposed to be cheerier, since it's past the solstice: day is longer than night.

But all I can do is lie here in this tiny bed. I sleep restlessly. I awake holding on to the trace fragments of brutal dreams. I want to move. I want to get up and see how well these words have been transcribed. I want the comfort of the written word. I don't move. I feel as if I'm waiting for something, some rescue. I dream of a man with whom I shared a night five months ago, and I dream he's coming planetside, that he's making his way through the forest to rescue me. I don't need rescue. I just need to get better. Why do I yearn for someone whom I knew only for a few hours? Why do I feel that rescue is something I don't deserve?

From the *Way of God*, orbiting the skies above me, they talk to me. They speak kindly to me, and I respond with equal kindness. Their voices form an umbilical cord, from this solitary womb of a ship to their larger society above. When I fall asleep, when my mind is set adrift across this nausea, I long to relive the last five months, to say what I truly felt rather than pay attention like a good Muslim girl who was raised to nod and listen, and who later turned those polite skills to anthropology. I want to know what the voyage would have been like if I had traveled it honestly. Would I now be yearning for some masculine rescue from this lonely bed?

From the skies they monitor the medcomp's readout, they compare my condition now with my condition yesterday and the day before, and they tell me I'm doing better, that in a day or two I'll be fine. I know they're right, but it feels as if this condition will never end, that the fatigue and nausea and melancholia are mine forever.

Chapter One

The Fifth Day

After five days planetside, Pauline Dikobe—who was obviously suffering from adaptation sickness—finished planting a supply of imaging pins around a slazan living area and then half walked, half stumbled through the alien forest and back to the shuttle craft, her specially outfitted anthropological hut, where, without warning or clear motivation, she shut off all communication with the *Way of God* orbiting above. The enormity of the act was so astounding that the warship's captain, Alifa al-Shaykh, spent a few moments asking various people to confirm the conclusions the ship's intelligence had already laid out on her command screen in fine columns of Arabic script and numbers. The xenobotanist assigned to the mission confirmed that, yes, the lab was no longer receiving images from the shuttle's external cameras: the screens were blank. The engineer reported that she had sent her comrade-in-arms to do a personal systems check even though diagnostics showed that the ship's communications equipment was working perfectly. The AI handler had just finished trying to re-establish contact with the shuttle's own intelligence, but no luck, nothing.

Why had Dikobe done this?

The four women on the bridge, four veiled faces, turned to al-Shaykh as if she could understand the mental workings of this civilian whom they had carried with them for five months to this top-secret location light-years away from the war they should have been fighting. After spending her entire adult life with the military, two years of service with this particular crew, al-Shaykh could read their eyes: an expression that began behind a veil spread to the rest of the face: the raised cheeks or tightened skin around the eyes. She saw worry above their veils, a deep need for a ready answer. After five months of travel, how could everything unravel so easily?

"A little chemistry will do the anthropologist some good," she listened to herself say. "Things will be fine in the morning."

Al-Shaykh wanted to believe that the problem was just biology, that it was just adaptation sickness, that Dikobe's body was suffering from a difficult adjustment to an atmosphere full of micro- and macro-organisms that were testing this novel ecological niche for its food possibilities. She could see the anthropologist with her mind's eye. Dikobe, wearing nothing but a leather pubic apron, should be lying in the tiny bed, dark skin against the whiteness of the sheet, her arm strapped in and hooked up to the medical computer, the medcomp monitoring a careful recycling of her blood, balancing her systems with some cell modifications, leaving her body weak but functional by morning. Al-Shaykh could understand why Dikobe would want her solitude, why she would want the implant in her head quiet, why she wouldn't want every tremor and bout of vomiting recorded on a readout screen in a warship orbiting high above.

But that wasn't the Dikobe that al-Shaykh had come to know in the past few months. Instead, a different image forced its way into al-Shaykh's mind: Dikobe was pacing. Her lean legs measured out the four or five steps from acceleration couch to bed. Her compact body was caged in by the shuttle's narrow bulkhead, by the rows of lockers and equipment that had been built into the shuttle's interior. The curve of her quadragenarian belly pushed out against the pubic apron she was wearing. Sweat gathered on Dikobe's forehead. Her eyes were dark and mad. This was the Dikobe who had day by day become more strident, more solitary, who had stretched, then broken, any ties that she had formed during her first three months on the ship. As far as al-Shaykh was concerned, Dikobe could have the entire night to get over whatever was ailing her.

The call to evening prayer came as something of a relief. The corridor walls of the rest of the ship still bore the images of the dense alien greenery of the planet below, the ceiling's sky an off-color blue, and the floor and animal-trodden path that seemed too thin for even the ship's corridors. But outside the prayer room there was always the image of a mosque's courtyard whose virtual walls surrounded an actual fountain that sprinkled actual water into a pool, the calming sounds of water falling into water easing al-Shaykh's tension.

She performed her ritual ablutions at the fountain and tried to take some comfort in the thought that all things human fall apart; only God's work is full of glory. The interior of the mosque was cool and quiet. Verses of the Quran flowed across the walls, the ease and curve of the calligraphy a kind of stability. She looked to see who else had come for evening prayers, who had come with her comrade-in-arms, who had come alone. There was no rank here. They were equal before God's judgment. Like the others, she spread out her prayer mat toward the bow of the ship. The ship's aft was fictive north, making the ship's forward direction the metaphor for the direction Muhammad took when he left his exile in Medina and headed south to Mecca.

Alifa al-Shaykh bowed before God. She tried to concentrate on the words—"There is no god but God"—but the words became ritual and her heart remained cold. It was her mind that was alive, her thoughts heated and troublesome. What were they to do?

The alien landscape projected on the corridor walls came as something of a shock. A faint breeze carried the scent of a strange forest, and al-Shaykh suddenly felt nauseous.

Back in her cabin, al-Shaykh's comrade-in-arms, the executive officer, was dressing, preparing for her shift on the bridge. The ship's day was normally divided into three shifts, but during the five days Dikobe had been planetside, the two comrades-in-arms had alternated half-day shifts, with al-Shaykh eating dinner while the executive officer ate breakfast. Al-Shaykh rediscovered that she had trouble sleeping alone; she missed the heaviness of the executive officer's warmth, her back pressed against al-Shaykh's side. Al-Shaykh did not think she would sleep tonight, not until she heard Dikobe's voice again.

"Alifa?" the executive officer said. "Are you sure it's wise to wait until morning?"

"You want to send someone down." Al-Shaykh's words failed to sound neutral. What would Dikobe think? She had just spent five days getting the natives habituated to her presence after landing a shuttle craft near where a number of them lived.

"Land another ship, and the locals might get scared enough to move away."

"What if she's too sick to take care of herself?"

Al-Shaykh had considered this possibility and had wondered why it was so hard to order down one of the lifeships. She prayed to God, the merciful, the compassionate; where was her own compassion now? "She cut us off. If Dikobe needs help," she said, knowing she had to follow her line of thought, "she will have to open communications with us."

"What if she wasn't the one who shut them off?"

Al-Shaykh said nothing, waiting for the explanation first.

"While you were at prayers, I spoke with Jihad." The name of the AI handler was Rachel Stein, but she was called Jihad because of her zealous approach to everything. "She's still trying to reestablish contact between our intelligence and the shuttle's. The communication shut-down is thorough. As far as we can tell, it's virtually a complete electromagnetic shutdown."

The executive officer let the words have their effect. The enemy had developed a sophisticated ability to interfere with all electromagnetic systems, and humans had developed very sophisticated defenses. Except for a well-protected nuclear core, the shuttle craft had no defense against such an attack.

"The mapping satellites," al-Shaykh said. "What do they show us?"

"Nothing. Just the locals on the hillside."

"So Dikobe's not being attacked. It's more likely that she shut down things herself."

"Yes, but, Alifa, we can't come up with a motive for Dikobe to do this; she can't be that much at odds with us. Jihad's sure the war has followed us out here."

There were a number of good reasons to dismiss Jihad's worries. Over the past few months Dikobe had voiced her doubts to al-Shaykh, to Jihad, to anyone who would listen. It was easy to hear the growing bitterness in the anthropologist's voice as she became certain that this mission was immoral. But once she was planetside, she was in her element. For the first few days everything seemed fine until Dikobe became sick, then irritable. She had an implant in her head so that the ship could communicate important data to her whenever she was away from the shuttle. But Jihad had fallen in love with this mission, and she was always talking to Dikobe, her voice always in Dikobe's head, communicating every tiny detail: the temperature, the number of slazans nearby, their approximate distance from Dikobe, each of their movements, no matter how trivial. No one was surprised when Dikobe screamed out: "Leave me in peace. I'm sick enough without feeling like a madwoman who's always hearing voices. Just, please, shut up!" So it wasn't difficult to imagine a sickened, alienated Dikobe flicking a few switches and removing all human voices from her head. Al-Shaykh could see Dikobe planning this for hours as she wandered well-trod paths, the natives avoiding her so carefully that at times they went unseen.

And al-Shaykh would have dismissed Jihad's worries except for two incidents that had taken place six days before, just after they had begun orbiting the planet below. Twenty-three mapping satellites had been laid down in twenty-three geosynchronous orbits. Not long after, the ship's intelligence had detected, for the briefest of moments, an electromagnetic energy source on the planet's surface. Within an hour, three of the twenty-three mapping satellites had ceased to function. But when the three satellites were brought on board for examination, there was no sign of damage. Jihad had been certain the enemy was planetside. But the energy source was not detected again; it could just as easily have been a misreading made by their ancient ship's intelligence, who had mistranslated data once or twice before. Plus, there was no good reason for the enemy to knock out three satellites. Why not all of them? Why not the *Way of God* itself? So in the rush of the next five days—Dikobe's descent to the planet, her first glimpses of the locals, her bout of adaptation sickness—the earlier events were forgotten as anomalies, Jihad's worries filed away as youthful melodrama.

Now al-Shaykh was no longer so sure, and Jihad was called to meet the captain and the executive officer in their quarters. The executive officer, always the proper host, prepared coffee on the little machine each room had, and, after all three women had removed their veils, al-Shaykh and the executive officer sipped their coffee in quiet while Jihad talked, her heavy cheeks flushed with excitement, her dark eyes bright with energy, light glinting off the deep-black hair done up in a bun. The executive officer remained unusually quiet while al-Shaykh asked her usual array of pointed questions, playing devil's advocate to each response. Jihad tried hard to be deferential to the two superior officers, but her enthusiasm kept slipping out of her control. She answered questions that had only been half asked and contradicted anything with which she didn't agree.

And then Jihad stopped. Her flushed round cheeks, her

dark, intense eyes, held the silence. She leaned forward and said, "How about this? If Pauline is suffering from severe adaptation sickness, we want to get someone down to her in a way that won't disturb too many of the locals. That leaves out a lifeship or a one-man fighter. But if we do anything unusual, and if there is a contingent of the enemy down there, then we draw attention to ourselves, and perhaps we draw their fire as well. So we want to be on the safe side. We want to look like we're conducting business as usual. We want to act like we're on a research mission and suspect nothing." Jihad paused, and waited politely before recommending action.

The executive officer said, "Let's hear your proposal."

"Let's make the four scientists happy and send down their probes. The enemy, if he's there, won't know we're sending them down early. And along with the probes we'll send down a decoy probe."

Al-Shaykh hesitated, uncomfortable with the way the two women sat there silently as if they could watch her think. Al-Shaykh was still certain Dikobe had done the shutoff. But what if Jihad was right? They still had no idea why this colony of gathering and hunting slazans existed here light-years away from the war; perhaps some professional anxiety was in order. If you fought the paranoia of war too hard, you erred on the other side of judgment. And if they waited too long, Dikobe's condition could worsen; she could die.

Al-Shaykh nodded her assent before they went on to consider whom they would drop down in the decoy probe. Even though they tried out various names, the answer had been obvious from the start. Of all those qualified to go down, only one had the right thumbprint, one that when touched against the eyeplate would cause the shuttle door to open.

Still al-Shaykh hesitated. She didn't want to choose him for the wrong reasons; she didn't want to choose him because he appeared to be the most expendable person on the mission.

The truth was this: Once there had been a crew of thirty, of fifteen comrades-in-arms, plus a captain and her executive officer. The pairings had been made after extensive training and testing, after specialties had been selected and skills refined. The crew had been chosen on the basis of performance scores received on numerous tests, exercises, and simulations, until it was known, as well as it could be known when machines advised human decisions, that these thirty personalities drawn from disparate cultures, these fifteen different pairings and specialties, would make for an effective and honorable crew.

They had patrolled slazan space for a half year, had once almost died in battle. They had patrolled E-donya's stellar system for another half year, a standard rotation away from the war, to muster their courage to face six more months of battle before their tour of duty would end. Instead they had been chosen for this mission that would take up two years of their lives and take away the honor of combat. And this crew of thirty—selected and trained to work together as crew—had been reduced to eight in number. Four had been removed so four military scientists could be added to the roster. Two more had been removed to give a private cabin to the civilian anthropologist. And two hours before departure, at General ibn Haj's orders, another pair of comrades-in-arms, to provide a cabin for Lieutenant Esoch al-Schouki, Dikobe's newly-appointed aide.

The lieutenant was a small man, every part of him thin, but he moved with a kind of concentrated grace, like one who had grown up learning how to let the body consider its own steps. He was ill at ease among the crew members, his smiles deferential. He looked terribly isolated, having no comrade-in-arms and no apparent reason for being on board. He had no training in any of the Semitic religions, nor did he have the technical background for crewing a starship, since he had been trained in ground-level combat. Before being recruited for the war effort, he had lived on a reserve set aside for a group of gatherers and hunters whom Pauline Dikobe had studied to earn her doctorate. As the voyage progressed, some thought he had been assigned to the mission to advise Dikobe on the life of gatherers, but Dikobe, it turned out, was not one who took advice well. For the three months that he shared her quarters, it was said that *this* was his purpose: to provide Dikobe some fleshly company before she spent two hundred days alone on an alien planet.

But now, with Dikobe alone and perhaps dying, Lieutenant al-Schouki, it appeared, would have a purpose.

Currently, Lieutenant Esoch al-Schouki was asleep in the cabin that had been assigned to Hanan Salib, the mission's ethologist, and Amalia al-Farabi, the mission's xenobotanist. Amalia was currently in the lab with the two other scientists, purposefully giving Hanan and Esoch time to be alone. The cabin's two sleeping mats had been laid together, and Esoch was stretched out on his back on Amalia's mat. Lying next to him, her head propped up on her hand, was Hanan, who was wide-awake, almost mesmerized by the soft rise and fall of Esoch's chest, the peaceful way he breathed. Beyond him, on the far wall, was an enhanced image of the planet below: blue water, swaths of land, arabesques of cloud. God, the one god, the merciful and compassionate. all his worlds with life looked the same to the eyes of a generalist, the land cupped with blue and white, plants reaching up to the sun with (mostly) green leaves, animals traversing the slopes upon four legs, flying insects landing upon six. Who could not say there was a divine plan for the way the universe worked?

She was thinking that she should have shared her mat with him long ago, closer to the beginning of the voyage, before Dikobe had taken advantage of his loneliness. How betrayed and confused she had felt the night Esoch had first slept in Dikobe's cabin, his body resting peacefully next to hers, when, now, in current time, the door sounded. She assumed it was Amalia, leaving the shift in the lab early to fetch the two of them for dinner. Hanan called out to wait while she looked for something to put on.

Once the black abaya draped her naked body and the veil covered her face, she pressed the eyeplate to open the door. Standing on the other side was Sarah Karp, the ship's quartermaster, Jihad's comrade-in-arms, and the crew's chief gossip. Within a shift everyone would know why Hanan had not been at evening prayers. They would hear how Hanan had shown up at the door wearing the traditional dress of a married woman while her lover slept behind her.

Sarah Karp was apologizing for the intrusion. "But," she said, "the captain needs to speak with Lieutenant al-Schouki. It's urgent. Have you seen the lieutenant?"

Sarah Karp's voice was so kind, her manner so courteous, Hanan almost let herself believe that maybe the woman wouldn't tell anyone else. Because they had to get along for another year, Hanan let herself be deceived and let herself feel as friendly as she could when she told Sarah Karp that Esoch would report to the captain right away.

The door closed, and Hanan turned. Esoch was stretched out under the sheet, watching her expectantly, and she felt sullied by his presence. This was the first time since she had taken him to her bed two nights ago that Hanan had truly thought of her husband: how easily the body lets us betray the ones we love.

"You better bathe," she said, hearing the edge in her voice. "Captain al-Shaykh wants to see you."

They said nothing while he stood under the shower and drier, but she found it hard not to stare at him, at this body that had pressed so wondrously against hers. It wasn't so much his body as his penis that captured her attention. Semi-erect, like her child's penis when he had to pee badly, it lay atop his scrotum, rather than dangling like her husband's, or those of most men, she assumed, and she couldn't help but feel awe at the way it moved complacently with the movement of his body, or at the way its controlled energy recently had reached in and released so much within the core of her. Her husband's erections had become nothing more than a male habit and lovemaking a routine. She had forgotten how there had been a time when embraces were fresh and the penis, rising to its glory, merged both love and desire into the same feeling.

Esoch gone, she stood in the tiny cubicle and waited for the ration of water to be filtered and warmed, and she tried to avoid all the thoughts that came while waiting. She couldn't show up at the lab smelling of the early-evening's warmth. The water felt good. She imagined Esoch still there, watching her the way she had watched him. She turned her back to the doorway, surprised by how the sudden blush of desire made her feel ashamed.

She sipped coffee and fingered the fabric of her uniform and tried to face new anxieties. What would she do a year from now if she loved Esoch like this when they returned to E-donya? Of course, the strength of her desire might not be love at all. She was the ethologist, she had spent years comparing the mating habits of a variety of animals. She knew as well as anyone that what she felt could simply be the evolutionary, blind-to-contraception urge to produce children with strong genes, that she was attracted to his lithe body and the strength in his walk, that she was answering an inborn leaning toward variety: the epicanthic eyefolds, the yellow-brown skin, everything so different from the look of the crew, whose genes had been given a slight touch of cultural tailoring so that they all had olive skins, dark eyes, and aquiline noses conforming to someone's long-ago ideal of what an Arab should truly look like. But desire also leaned toward success and prestige, and that did not describe Esoch anymore. His presence on the ship was a solitary one. He had begun to socialize with the four scientists because he didn't fit in with the women who ran the ship, his rank of lieutenant having no true meaning in the ship's own hierarchy. He watched closely and learned, an anthropologist of sorts, the kind of person Dikobe would have been if she hadn't decided to try to teach a ship of soldiers to like the enemy, a crew of civilized monotheists to respect the primitive.

But there was something more that had drawn her to him. He talked like a good ethologist who displayed his knowledge of animal behavior through stories, and even though his people believed some odd things—such as snakes who tried to crawl into people's anuses—what Esoch knew about the ungulates he once hunted revealed a kind of sympathy she did not expect to hear from a hunter. His people talked, they told stories, they joked a lot in certain relationships, and she loved talking with him, loved hearing stories and jokes.

So maybe it was love. And after a year of it, when she was out of the military, with the combat pay that would help her husband and her father maintain the business they owned together, what then? Both her family and her husband's lived in the same village. When she had moved into her husband's home, he had moved into her father's office. There was a child, and the expectation of two more. There were cousins and aunts and uncles. How could she tell any of them? How could she tell Esoch there were forces more important than love?

Perhaps slazans were a successful species because they weren't torn in two by such contradictions. A species that preferred solitude to socializing must create fewer ties to confound their lives.

Hanan had finished putting on her uniform when the executive officer called on the comm and asked her to report at once to the loading dock.

Tamr and Maryam, head engineer and assistant, comrades-in-arms and fellow workers, were unloading the scientists' probes when Hanan entered the loading dock, in uniform and properly veiled. Tamr finished securing the emerging probe, then waved to Hanan. "All that veil will do is get in your way; hang it on one of those pegs over there." Hanan looked a bit surprised. She, like the other three scientists, was always surprised when Tamr didn't conform to her image of a devout believer. Tamr answered the call to prayer five times a day; she tried to make sure all believers showed for the evening prayer if they weren't on duty; she quoted the Quran when appropriate; but she also preferred the practical over the traditional, and she loved loud, bawdy jokes.

Hanan hung up her veil alongside those belonging to the three other scientists. She waved to Tamr, then joined her own comrade-in-arms—the Christian woman—and the two Hindu men. Surrounding them were the probes. Each one was large, ovular, and gray, scarred by straight lines and right angles, the only hint of the external openings from which emerged thrusters, stabilizing wings, and struts for landing, solar panels, waldoes, and camera eyes for planetside research. The scientists had hatched two of the probes, the egg split open, heavy internal hinges holding the top half perpendicular to the bottom.

Tamr watched while the younger of the two Hindu men spoke to Hanan in quiet tones. She looked confused at first, then distraught. The xenobotanist, the Christian woman, wrapped her arm through one of Hanan's. The young Hindu must be telling Hanan about Dikobe. Tamr felt for the young woman. She was sweet and well-meaning. Tamr also felt that Hanan had been led astray by her scientist friends. Early in the voyage Tamr had overheard the xenobotanist encourage Hanan to share her mat with the Ju/wa: "No one has fond memories of resisting temptation." The xenobotanist, Tamr had heard, was a woman who had joined the military to escape her family. Someone who flees a family was bound to talk that way.

The final probe to unload was the decoy. Tamr and Maryam both reached out for it, as if to guide the form, as if they could actually do anything with the heavy loads if the waldoes ceased functioning. Tamr watched Maryam's willowy form move with the decoy probe; she watched her thin fingers press against the probe's curved skin. Tamr's own thick hands were placed on the opposite side, doing the same. This is why they were such good comrades-in-arms.

At first glance the decoy probe looked the same as the others, but the lines for wing stabilizers and the location of thruster rockets were different. On the surface was a closed panel, like a door just large enough for a human body. A line ran across the middle of the door. Half slid up; half slid down.

Maryam did a personal override on the waldoes, then worked the controls herself, the mechanical arms reaching out to one end of the probe and pulling the coffin out of the decoy probe's center. The coffin was a rectangular object, its edges curved, its sides pimpled so the electronics inside could connect with the life-support mechanisms stored in the probe.

"They're so solemn," Viswam, the younger Hindu said, his

voice loud enough for Tamr and Maryam to hear, "you'd think someone had died."

Tamr looked away from her work and toward the scientists. Hanan had taken the older Hindu's arm. The old man held himself stiffly, but he patted the young woman's hand. Tamr could read Hanan's face: she had realized whom the coffin was for, that the Ju/wa was being sent planetside. And there was enough fear and concern in the look that Tamr was certain Hanan had finally given her heart to him.

The coffin was on the deck now. The top, section by section, slid open, until the bare insides were revealed. All of Lieutenant Esoch al-Schouki's vital and nonvital statistics were listed by the intelligence, and Tamr adjusted the insides for his small body. Tamr actually like Esoch. He was generous and unassuming. But she was uncomfortable with some primitive quality about him, his persistent rejection of civilized life. Even though Esoch had had a Muslim comrade-in-arms, he still had not bowed down to God. Esoch first had shared mats with Dikobe, and now, obviously, with a married woman. There was the primitive hunter in the man's blood; he was surely the best one to go planetside.

Everything was now ready. There was nothing to do but wait until the scientists were done; then she and Maryam would have to check everything over. An hour later Esoch appeared. Hanan was immediately by his side. They spoke quietly, Hanan looking more distraught, Esoch wearing a mask of uncertainty. What would he tell her? The executive officer had told Tamr that the Ju/wa would stay down with Dikobe for the remainder of the mission, for the whole two hundred days—that is, if Dikobe was still okay.

Amalia, the xenobotanist, the younger Hindu's lover, joined Hanan, urged her to the door, to leave with Esoch, which after some hesitation she did. Tamr watched the couple leave together, and she was surprised by how angry she felt.

"Don't be so hard," Maryam said softly. "He might not come back."

Tamr nodded. She hated the way the anger boiled in her when she watched people make the kinds of mistakes they had made since before Muhammad, since before Abraham. She had enjoyed talking with Dikobe, learning about anthropology and primitive life, and Dikobe had been more than happy to talk about the Quran and the war. Tamr had been sincere when she had wished the anthropologist well. "God willing, your work will help us defeat the slazan enemy."

Dikobe had exploded. "Is it God's will to wipe out thousands, maybe millions, of slazans?"

"If that is God's will, then that is what must happen. Humans must live safely in this galaxy."

"Perhaps," Dikobe had said, "that is why, right now, I'd rather be slazan than human."

So right now she was planetside, a human who'd gone slazan or a human who'd been attacked by slazans. Esoch had the blood of a primitive hunter. He'd have his primal fuck, and he'd be ready to go down and save Dikobe.

The Sixth Day

Rachel Stein—Jihad to her shipmates on the *Way of God*—had entered the university in the hope that after close study of the Torah and the Talmud she could one day comprehend the mind of God, only to discover that an artificial intelligence who thought at light-speed and chatted across light-years with others of its kind was the only vast intelligence she could hope to study and understand. But now, while she and the captain stood outside the loading-dock door and awaited Lieutenant Esoch al-Schouki, she felt some of that old faith pulling at her, asking her its ritual, unanswered questions about justice before God. The captain was following her counsel, and she wanted to believe she had counseled well. She wanted to believe this elaborate business with the probes was truly necessary.

But how likely was it that the enemy had followed them here? Jihad had gone through the calculations with the ship's intelligence. They had calculated how an enemy ship could have hidden behind one of the planet's two moons without being detected; they had calculated a flight path for it to leave the planet's surface and enter orbit without being detected until the last minute; they had programmed the weapons for just such contingencies; but they could not render it mathematically feasible that the alien ship had followed them out here; the flashes of light that accompanied their jumps into hyperspace spewed out photons that traveled at the speed of light and hence would take years to reach any alien astronomer; you would need a device that could look into the future to spot those flashes soon enough to follow them.

So maybe Jihad had said the wrong things in her desire always to be right, to be the one the captain turned to for advice. Maybe they should have dispatched a one-man fighter or a lifeship the instant Dikobe had broken contact. Because, now, if Dikobe was in trouble, or if she was dying from adaptation sickness, Jihad's elaborate designs would be responsible for her death.

The captain leaned against the corridor wall and the image of an alien tree. Jihad wanted to say something to her, but the courage of words seemed to come to her only during debate. Esoch finally appeared at the edge of a clearing that was projected where the corridor curved out of sight. He was properly veiled and alone, not with Hanan, which was what Jihad's comrade-in-arms had told her to expect. He carried two onesuits and a toilet kit. The captain nodded to Esoch, then faced Jihad while she placed her thumb alongside the eyeplate. The circles under the captain's eyes were dark, the eyes themselves darker.

The captain spoke. "There will be no honor lost if you change your mind now."

Jihad looked to the captain, and realized the captain was speaking to Esoch.

"I'm ready," he said.

The captain's thumb pressed against the eyeplate, and the door to the loading dock slid open. Cleared of everything—the shuttle launched, the probes all loaded within the last few hours—the loading dock seemed as expansive as the gym, and way too small to have held everything that once had filled its deck. To the rear of the dock rested one probe, and beside it, an open coffin.

On either side of the coffin stood Tamr and Maryam, their blue onesuits darkened with sweat under the arms. Maryam was fastening her veil; Tamr's veil was nowhere to be seen. The captain, who usually waited in silence until such matters were taken care of, simply said, "Are we ready?"

Tamr nodded. Jihad knew Tamr had rechecked everything several times; the head engineer put her faith in God, not in military design. For a moment Jihad remembered how the three of them—Tamr, Jihad, and Dikobe: the Muslim, the Jew, and the doubter—had time and again sat at the same table, had devoured hours arguing about the relationship between God and human, the words growing heated, the arguments losing their cleverness, and Dikobe never understanding that poor, devout Tamr was always arguing for her life. In the loading-dock silence, while standing near the coffin and the possibility of Dikobe's death, the heated words all felt so empty.

Esoch stepped up to the coffin and looked down. He tried to smile. Tamr took his things and passed them to Maryam, who loaded them in a regulation backpack. Tamr faced Esoch directly, clasped his shoulder, then gestured to the interior. Esoch nodded before stepping in and lying down.

Unsure of her own role in his send-off, Jihad knelt by the coffin and did a run-through of procedure. She barely heard her own words. Tamr and Maryam worked around her, readjusting the contours of the coffin's padding to match Esoch's small frame before strapping him in. Jihad couldn't help but notice how close the walls were on either side of him; bend the elbow a bit, a flick of the wrist, and his fingers could easily reach all the controls. There was no distance between floor and feet, and only because he was much shorter than the norm was there a significant space of air between his head and the ceiling. "Remember," she heard herself say, "the ship's intelligence guides all the probes down to their landing sites. That is normal procedure. You must maintain radio silence. The minute you open up communications, anyone who is listening in will know that yours is the decoy probe. Same when you get to the planet. We want no potential enemy to know where you are." And what if there is no enemy, thought Jihad, but our own paranoia? How close to death will Dikobe be when Esoch finds her?

"Esoch," said the captain, for the first time calling the lieutenant by his first name, "are you okay?" There was a weight to her voice, a trace of concern in the common words. Both the captain and Jihad had read Esoch's file. He had made four previous coffin drops during his military training: three had been reality simulations; the fourth had been an actual drop into E-donya's atmosphere, a run-through invasion of a slazan homeward.

"I'm fine, Captain," he said.

Tamr stowed the backpack in the compartment below his feet. Along with his onesuits, it contained rations, med-kit, tracking disc, pistol, and the five sections of a needle rifle. Dikobe had once told Jihad how members of certain pre-industrial cultures buried their dead along with things they would need for the afterlife.

Esoch looked at the sides of the coffin as if he saw the lighted panels for the first time. Jihad reached in and waved her hand across a series of meters. "These monitor your air supply," she said. Esoch's comrade-in-arms had died in that fourth drop when the coffin's air pump had malfunctioned.

"God is good," Tamr said. "We will hope for the best." She reached behind Esoch's head to unfasten his veil, which she folded and pocketed. She displayed a reality visor in her hands, then tenderly placed it over Esoch's eyes. Esoch reached back to fasten the strap around his head. Jihad had preset the visor's imagery. Esoch would be standing on the planet surface, rather than trapped in a box soon surrounded by the empty dark. The hatch slid over Esoch and clicked shut. The four women looked at each other; then Tamr turned to the controls. The coffin was slid into the ovular decoy probe, which in turn was loaded into the drop hatch. Soon he would be gone.

He'll be back in six months, Jihad told herself. If everything works out, he'll be back. She couldn't convince herself that she hadn't made a horrible mistake.

The cushion molded firmly to the curve of his back, the straps fit securely around his chest and thighs. A part of him sensed the closeness of the walls around him even though his eyes and ears, nourished by the reality visor, told him something different. He was still amazed by all the planet's shades of green, by the array of sounds. Breezes whispered among the leaves. Birds and flying reptiles sang and croaked out their territories. The land was so rich compared to the desert reserve where he had been a child and a young man. There were metallic sounds, clangs and pneumatic hisses, and he could trace in his mind the decoy probe's path into the drop hatch.

He wished he had taken one last look at the loading dock, at the captain and Jihad, at Tamr and Maryam, before the coffin hatch had slid shut above him. He wished Hanan had been there to see him off or that he had kissed her good-bye one last time.

Esoch inhaled; he tasted the sweet staleness of air that was being properly recycled. He breathed and he waited. They were going to drop three probes before his, and they assured him it wouldn't be that long. He breathed and waited. The alien sounds of the forest made him edgy. They were dropping him an hour before dawn lit up the clearing where Dikobe's shuttle craft had landed; the *Way of God*'s intelligence would guide the decoy probe to land in a clearing within ten kilometers; if she was still there, Esoch would find her early in the morning.

And if she wasn't?

Esoch subvocalized a reality switch, and now the visor presented a composite view drawn from the *Way of God*'s external monitors. Strapped into the coffin's contours, the ship's full gravity pulling him to the coffin's floor, he now had the illusion of standing below the warship's hull, surrounded by vast distances. Below him was the planet, unnamed and unnumbered. It was beautiful: brown and green and blue, mostly blue, beneath whorls of white. It was hardly ten days ago when Tamr and Esoch had shared tea while Tamr laid her palm against the holographic image of this planet and said, "We now know of six planets that look like this, and they all have plants and trees and fish and insects and reptiles and mammals—what further proof do you need of one god with one plan for life?"

Ghazwan, his dead comrade-in-arms, had once said the same thing. The words had such a ritual sameness to them that they had left Esoch unconvinced, but now the memory of those words, of Ghazwan's quiet, sincere devotion, overwhelmed him. Ghazwan had grown up in an orbital community, a Muslim utopian colony. He had been trained for the military on an orbital base. He had died in his first and only descent toward E-donya. He had died with no true blood on his hands. Ghazwan had killed only in simulated attacks, in military exercises, where the dead rose (never truly dead) after battle was over. Ghazwan had never taken a knife and jabbed it into someone's belly. He had never watched madness seep into another's eyes, so he had never fled the way Esoch had fled Dikobe's embrace, escaping the way an animal escapes a brush fire, to stand on some dune, nose twitching, to watch the burning, to feel relief at the escape, and to watch her make her solitary preparations, board the shuttle, and leave for planetside, where everything had gone wrong.

It shouldn't have been Ghazwan who had died.

Tiny numbers, the time, flashed in the lower right corner of Esoch's reality visor: 0324:58, 0324:59, 0325:00. Esoch watched the first probe drop, then trace a path parallel to the ship. The probe's metal reflected two different days, the light of the planet, the light of the sun; one third of the probe's curvature was cast into its own night. Invisible, soundless thrusters must have fired, countering the probe's orbital velocity, because now it appeared to be falling away, arcing downward. The air Esoch breathed tasted the same. If he removed the visor, he would see how close the walls were on either side of him. He knew he was manufacturing his own anxiety, that this drop would be fine. He found himself waiting for Jihad's voice to break the radio silence and tell him the mission had been canceled, that Dikobe had made contact.

The second probe dropped into view. The curve of the heat

shield, the rounded edges, would ease the turbulent slide into the atmosphere. He couldn't see, but he could imagine seeing, the outlines of the places where wings and solar panels and waldoes would emerge from the probe's surface.

The third probe dropped. This one came out night first, daylight sliding away as the *Way of God's* orbit carried it away from the sun, which now looked like a white explosion on the edge of the world. The third probe fell away and down.

The fourth probe was his. He felt a kind of internal lurch, stomach rising into throat, when full gravity became microgravity, his body startled, like that of a baby dropped, then caught, by its father. He felt as though he would float away, if not for the faint pressure of the straps across his chest and thighs, while at the same time his whole body registered the change with a kind of confusion, a dizzying disorientation, because his reality visor still showed him the view from the *Way of God:* his back was pressed against the acceleration couch, in the coffin, but his eyes watched the decoy probe that contained the coffin run parallel with the ship. Thrusters fired, a moment of acceleration pressed his body into the straps, and he saw his own probe fall away.

The coffin shuddered, then slowed when it slid into the atmosphere. If he had remained with the standard images, the coffin's tiny computer would have automatically shifted his visor to the image taken through an imaginary viewport. He would watch a faint whiteness gather round the decoy probe, then with the fall planetside it would heat to pink, then red, finally becoming a burning orange and red. Ghazwan must have been watching the flare of colors as his air ran thin.

But still Esoch had an external view from the *Way of God,* and the fifth probe was already dropping from the ship. He was mesmerized by the process. There was the glint of something in the distance, and he wondered if it was sunlight or planetlight that had caught a probe on its way down. Which probe would that have been?

The sixth probe fell away. He once again noticed the flash of metal and light, but it seemed farther away from the planet, not closer, as it should have been with the probes. Perhaps it was light reflected off one of the mapping satellites. But what he had seen suggested something bigger than a compact satellite. Could the ship's intelligence have miscalculated and sent the probe in at the wrong angle, causing it to bounce off the atmosphere and head away from the planet?

He forced his eyes to concentrate, to try to see the glint again. He wished he could break radio silence and ask Jihad what it was. The planet seemed to drift away, which, of course, it couldn't do, so the *Way of God* must have started to move away from the planet. Was it going into a wider orbit, or was it leaving the planet? This wasn't part of the plan.

He heard himself asking questions to the emptiness of the coffin, but he couldn't remember the words after he had said them. The planet was pulling him downward. He should have heard thruster fire, followed by the whine of stabilizing wings spreading into the air.

Then: everything was white.

Bright white.

Before he knew it, his eyes were squeezed shut, a painful afterimage exploding across closed eyelids. This wasn't supposed to happen. The coffin floor jerked up under him, impacting feet, jarring his body. He felt as if he was traveling up, then he stopped, hovered, floated. His eyes opened. The reality visor was cleared. All he could see was the coffin's dim lighting, the walls, the few controls, the compartment latches, and he knew, in that instant, that the *Way of God* had broken contact and that he was going to die. He reached out for the reality control and hit the default toggle. There were several brief flashes as the coffin's tiny computer took in the data from the external eyes and composited them. Then he was surrounded by night sky. Above him were three holes in the sky, three holes darker than the night itself, wavering with the breeze: the emergency parachutes. He was drifting landward, and he had no idea where he was.

He toggled off the surroundimage, and with his right hand he fingered the necessary keys to call up the data screens on his visor. The coffin was receiving no transmission from the ship, and he was under orders to maintain radio silence. The coffin's limited radar told him how far above the surface he was, and it estimated that he would be down within five minutes. The imaging showed him that the probe was heading toward the shore of a large freshwater lake, but there was no way to tell if he would touch down upon land or water.

The short minutes were too long for quick and scattered thoughts: the probe was buoyant, but he swam poorly; the land was hard, best to land on water, perhaps far away from shore, where the waves could overtake him, where everything he had done wrong in his life would no longer matter. But the truth was: he didn't want to die. He wanted to make it to the shuttle and find Dikobe. He saw how it would be. She was safe, hunched over a screen, going over data. Upon hearing him enter the shuttle, she turned. Her face was free of fever.

Her smile was tremendous when the decoy probe hit, and what it hit gave way with a resounding splash. Esoch felt his weight fall toward his feet, his head slapped against the headrest, then his body fell into the straps. The internal lights blinked, or he did. Esoch felt as if he were losing his balance, about to fall, and he realized that the probe was tumbling over, falling top down into the water. His body slammed again into the straps; his head snapped forward hard enough that he was surprised that it didn't hurt, that he could raise his head again. The probe rocked back and forth, then settled. Water lapped dully against the outside, making his breathing on the inside sound terribly empty. The contour couch was now the ceiling from which he hung, his slim weight pulling him into the straps. Every bruise created by impact was now being outlined by the restraints.

He undid the buckle of the restraint that held his right thigh in place. His foot dropped down, hit the opposite wall, and the probe rocked gently. He undid the left buckle, and even though he intended to lower the foot gently, it still fell. The chest harness pressed against his ribs, and he positioned his feet, flexed his knees, and pressed his butt back into the contour couch in order to relieve the pressure against his chest. The probe rocked a bit forward with the shift in weight.

Esoch felt sweat dripping down his face, from under his arms. He shouldn't be sweating this much. Breathing was becoming difficult. He was inhaling and exhaling too hard in too small a space. The recycler couldn't keep up with his breathing, or ... The thought overwhelmed him, and all he wanted to do was to get out of this thing. He undid the chest harness, and without the grace or delicacy that he had hoped for, he slid one arm out, then the next, and eased himself down onto the flat wall that was now the coffin's floor. With each movement the decoy probe tilted.

Against the sound of the lapping water outside, the six walls inside felt incredibly close. It was hard to inhale and feel like he'd taken in enough air, and he told himself it was just psychological, the air was fine. He reached out, played fingers over the right keys, and the graphs and numbers indicated a working air recycler. It had to be psychological. Or had the diagnostic broken down in tandem with the mechanism? Had Ghazwan fallen to his death thinking that it was anxiety and claustrophobia that were making it so hard to breathe?

He keyed up surrounding visuals and saw nothing. He punched out the command for short-range infrared, and all he saw was water, the vague stripes of the parachute, and the night sky. He couldn't tell where he was, how far out he was from land. If the recycler wasn't working, he didn't want to crouch here until he breathed up whatever oxygen was left.

His first thought was to tip the decoy probe, get it hatchside facing up. He rocked back and forth, he threw his body from one end to the other. The probe tipped each time, angled down, then abruptly righted itself. He lay there on the coffin hatch, breathing heavily, counting fresh bruises. There was one way out. He wondered if the lake contained carnivorous fish.

Esoch shifted onto his back. The flat metal of the hatch was cold. The rolling of the coffin felt like a secondary anxiety. He removed lightweight hikers. He unfastened his onesuit and withdrew arms, rolled the fabric off legs. He kicked the uniform aside. After removing the pack from its compartment, he checked through it. He'd stick to one set of clothes, to reduce weight. He added the hikers. He kept the food, and he kept the tracking disc. The rifle was heavy, too. He decided to keep the pistol. He hesitated with the med-kit, but it was heavy. If he made it to Dikobe's ship, there would be a whole diagnostic lab there.

He pulled the cords that tightened the pack's exterior, then slid his arms through the straps. He stowed the remaining gear, including the med-kit, in the compartment.

He was still breathing, still conscious. Maybe the recycler *was* working. If he stayed now, he might never decide again to leave.

Esoch placed his hand against the round plastic knob and turned. He heard the external hatch of the probe slide open. He touched the next knob. He pressed. Metal moved beneath him. A touch of water rose up, but the air inside the coffin kept the rest out. The hatch couldn't be stopped midway. It slid out from under him, and his body was in the water. Cold enveloped him. He reached up, grabbed hold of one of the restraints. The line where water met air circled his body like a thin band of ice. The air around him was warm, and he shivered. For a while he just hung there, the pack tugging on his bare shoulders. The pack was light compared to what he had been trained to carry. Leaving the med-kit behind was a mistake.

Two strokes, and he was by the compartment. But there was nothing there to take hold of. He had to tread water with one hand while he reached up and slid the compartment door open. It was harder to reach in than he expected, but he got his hand around the med-kit handle and brought it out. It had no buoyancy when it hit the water. The weight tugged at his fingers. His grip wasn't tight enough. The handle rushed by fingertips and was gone. Before he could go after it, the white box had wavered, shrunk, disappeared into the waters below.

He made his way back to one of the restraints and held on. He told himself he didn't really need the med-kit. And he took in five deep breaths. Eyes closed, he dropped down into the water, into the coldness, and found himself rising back up, pushing up along the curve of the probe, kicking his way along. He had hardly swum another stroke when something took hold of him, wrapped itself around his head.

Eyes snapped open. Air bubbled out of his mouth. He was surrounded by the striped silk of the parachute. He took hold of the material and tried to pull it away, but there was just more of it. This would be worse than suffocation. Don't panic. Don't panic. His lungs felt empty. How far up was the surface? The cold closed in on him. He couldn't feel toes or fingertips. Below him there was the faint glow from the coffin's lights. Everything else was parachute. He pulled at the silk, pushed it down, swung his arms up to grab more and push it down, away from him. He kicked hard. He wanted to open his mouth. He needed to breathe. His lungs felt like vacuum balloons that blew up with the absence of air. He kicked away at water and silk, he pulled silk, pushed through water. He forced his head upward, and his chest and shoulders hurt with the effort and with the water's deep chill, and he still thought he was going to die when his head broke surface.

He sucked in air and water with the first breath, choked, tilted his head back and trod water furiously, inhaling a second time, then a third. The water was impossibly cold. The way it closed around his skin made him aware of how vulnerable he was.

Once he had regained control of his breathing, he swam small, careful strokes until he found some of the parachute that was floating atop the water. He pulled himself along the fabric, feeling for the tugs that would give him a sense of where the decoy probe bobbed in the water. The sky was black and full of stars. One of the two moons hung upon a horizon etched with treetops. He couldn't tell how far away those trees were. But there was one of two moons. E-donya had one moon. Living in the desert, he had danced himself into trance under its brightness. This moon seemed tiny and far away, like the horizon. He reached the edge of the parachute. He could make out the dark curve of the probe, the faint glow below it in the water. He swam to it, and climbed atop.

He crouched there and shivered. He told himself dawn would not be long in coming. Sleep would be like a blanket to the cold. Sleep would be a salve to all the bruises, to the cramped calves and thighs. But he shivered and he fought against sleep. It would be so easy to slide back into the water.

He watched the sky go from deep blue to gray to pink. The early-morning noises were so alien that exhaustion filtered their individuality and blanketed his brain with the comfort of white noise. His eyes were half-closed with the first hint of dawn. The early-morning gray turned the horizon's shadows into an expanse of land spread out as beach and thickets and trees. Land was not more than two hundred meters away. He could swim two hundred meters.

Dawn flared orange, then red, and the landscape beyond the sand was green, unbelievably green and alive.

The following is excerpted from a draft of Pauline Dikobe's memoirs, a project she started and abandoned while the Way of God *made its return trip to E-donya E-talta.*

The return of the fourth Raman probe initiated a series of events that led to the moment when I joined the war effort.

The massive probe was essentially a small starship engine hooked to a large computer and populated by a variety of investigative drones. Scientists at the Amichai-Darwish Research Center had programmed the probe to chart the solar systems of several distant F- and G-type stars and to launch the drones to explore any planet that supported life or offered the possibility of commercial exploitation. The latter task was of the utmost importance, because most, if not all, of the project's funding had been provided by the Hindu-Muslim Investment Developers of the Northern Continent, who expected a return for their investment. The probe was launched four years before the war broke out.

While the Raman probe headed for its jump point at the edge of the solar system, I was working on my doctorate, doing my field research among the Ju/wasi, a group of primal utopians who earned their living gathering and hunting on a desert reserve that had been established four generations earlier. My research was funded by the Institute for Cultural Studies, which had sent out numerous ethnographers to examine the biosocial dimensions of the various utopian communities that had come into being as humanity spread itself across three humansafe worlds and too-many-to-count orbital colonies. We were using redefined Cosmides-Tooby culture-generation algorithms in order to examine further the dynamic of how individuals select, from a menu of nonconscious evolved behaviors, the specific behaviors that best match the current social environment. I was interested in the biological and social forces that shaped an individual's human nature. My schoolgirl's yearning devotion to God and my natural curiosity about humanity's place in a very large universe had diminished, and like all true loves, its fundamental energies were drained away by newer, smaller concerns. If I had read or heard anything about any of the Raman probes, I didn't remember it later.

I returned from the field, worked on a monograph, married, earned a doctorate, and gave birth to a son. When my son was weaned, when he could walk without amazement at his steps, I returned to the field to verify some of my data, and I returned to find both husband and son gone.

I had spent all my credit and had gone into debt searching for them when the war started. It was background noise to my private pain, distant news from a distant solar system.

For six years slazan and human had shared a world called New Hope, each species living more or less contentedly on its own continent. One day several human-made satellites and one orbital colony flew over different parts of the slazan-inhabited continent, and slazan missiles brought each one down. There were no diplomatic meetings, no lengthy explanations, no frantic negotiations. Human missiles struck slazan targets calculated to cause equal losses in credit and casualties, and then some, for added measure, as if destruction were a loan to be repaid with interest. Close up, it was anger and it was honor, it was avenging lost lives and lost capital. From light-decades away, on E-donya, in Wadi al-Uyoun, in the University district, where intellectuals could simultaneously balance lives like accountants and argue morality like priests, it all seemed so wasteful.

After New Hope was destroyed, the war expanded and continued until it seemed like nothing more than one long series of search-and-destroy missions. During the six years of prewar contact, both sides had worked hard never to turn over to the other anything with a chart, a map, or an image that would help one set of aliens learn the location of the other's homeworlds. The slazans knew of Earth, Nueva España, E donya, and the innumerable colonies that were perched on moons, embedded in asteroids, and encased in steel, but they did not know around which suns those worlds and satellites orbited.

So a ring of sentries was established in each stellar system in humanspace, and decoy bases and cities were built on uninhabitable planets, decoy colonies, full of explosives, orbited gas giants, all to draw slazan warships away from human habitations and into well-coordinated ambushes. We knew of two slazan homeworlds, and we knew they had built their own decoys and defenses in planet-bearing systems where no slazan lived. The rest was warships: heading out, probing defenses, trying to penetrate into systems, searching out enemy probes and warships, a perpetual hunt, the occasional flare of light followed by debris and empty space and the radiation of lost lives.

Of course, space exploration and redefined Cosmides-Tooby algorithms were forgotten. Raman probes remained on the drawing board, and a trip to the desert reserve was canceled. The Hindu-Muslim Investment Developers funded research into probes that sought out the enemy and charted his defenses, while the Amichai-Darwish Research Center remained committed to a science that tried to better understand God's designs—rather than one that tried to better fight humanity's wars—and in turn saw its numbers and its budget dwindle.

The Institute for Cultural Studies, on the other hand, prospered. A year into the war, it started its own department of slazan studies, which was held in high esteem by the government and by journalists, while at the same time it was held in contempt by other scientists. It takes hours and hours of observations to begin a proper study of a non-sapient animal. The history of ethology is filled with monographs about peaceful animals who, years later, were observed murdering their own kind, about monogamous animals who later turned out to be expert philanderers. Add sapience—add cultural diversity, add different histories and different symbols and different rules of etiquette—and you compound the problem. Send one anthropologist to live among a people, and you have a study. Send someone else two years later, and you have an argument. Send six simultaneously, and you have a vision. Send several more some other year, and you have endless controversy.

Prewar contact between human and slazan had been diplomatic and commercial. Humans weren't invited to live in slazan towns or cities. Slazan libraries weren't open to human readers. There were no hours of consistent observation to even start a decent debate. You got tales instead of research, you got wonderful stories told over dinner or coffee, the kind of thing that made Frazier's *Golden Bough* so fascinating for a century of literary scholars. Then you got the second kind of tale: the scientists explained the meaning of the first tales, each notion exquisitely argued, each conclusion supported by nothing more than an anecdote, an observation, a rumor. Hence the Institute, with its department of slazan studies, was dubbed the Kipling Institute, the department of Just-So Stories.

Worse, the Institute was tainted by its involvement with the war effort. Long ago, when anthropology struggled to be a meaningful science, governments gave friendly grants to anthropologists, feigning curiosity and craving facts. Dissidents, given pseudonyms in field reports, were rounded up. Rebel villages were targeted. Traditions that created a sense of community were disrupted, outlawed, done away with. As a result, anthropologists no longer commence studies that can be used against the people they study.

So the division of Just-So Stories was divisive. But what anthropologist did not want to understand slazans, did not have a heart that swam toward the lure of images and texts previously owned by private companies or classified by the government? What anthropologist could not be holier-than-thou when another fell to some prying temptation that had not yet teased him open? Those who could afford to be holy left the Institute for Cultural

Studies before finding other employment. Others left when they found employment. Others couldn't leave, but they stayed away from the Kiplingers.

I stayed in the Institute and stayed away from the Kiplingers until the fourth Raman probe returned.

When it re-entered the solar system, the sentry did not recognize it, even though the Raman probe sent out clearly stated messages in Arabic and Nostratic. Afterward a number of organizations argued—on the nets and before government inquiries—about who was responsible for the lapse in the sentry's programming, but at that point the sentry's stringent wartime protocol gave it no choice but to conclude that the Raman probe's message was a ruse, that the Raman probe must be a slazan scout or warship. The guardian sent its first message to the nearest military outpost, calling for a squadron of human-piloted warships. The second message was directed to the military base on E-donya's moon, where a general had to issue the appropriate orders, since no military action within the stellar system was allowed without a human command initiating it.

The women piloting the ships were eager for the encounter. A month before, six slazan warships had engaged the defenses around the system that contained Nueva España. One lone ship, piloted by one lone warrior, had made it through. There was a military outpost within the slazan's range, but instead it destroyed an orbital colony, ending the lives of five hundred worshipers of an arcane, isolationist religion. History would not be allowed to repeat itself: four human warships closed in on the intruder, ready for the kill.

But the captain of the flagship was uncomfortable with routine destruction, and the probe's ID broadcast was too esoteric to be a believable slazan ruse. She waited until they got a close look at what it was, and then her ship escorted it back to E-donya, where there was a well-publicized effort to find the probe's appropriate owner. Soon, within certain circles, there was nothing but talk about the scientific probe that had frightened the military.

It made for some good jokes.

It made for another kind of explanation as to why the war had dragged on for seven long years.

*   *   *

Before the war, when she had been assistant director of the Institute, Fawiza invited, with a fair degree of regularity, various researchers to her home for tea and informal chatter. After she created the Kipling division, she held the teas less often; fewer researchers would accept her invitations. Years later, the war still raging on in the distance, she is now director of the Institute, but few have forgiven Fawiza her breach of ethics. The teas are still small and infrequent.

I go when invited. I like most of the Kiplingers, and not one of their theories has caused a single slazan death. So I show up at her flat one late-summer afternoon, kiss the air next to Fawiza's cheeks, hang up my veil, and head to the living room to see who else has been invited. I don't recognize either of the men, and I feel myself blush. I want to turn and get my veil, but Fawiza has taken me by the elbow. "You are among friends," she says.

The two men, already unveiled, rise from the couch where they have been sitting. They say all the proper and polite things when we are introduced. There is nothing informal about their manner. I am not among friends.

Fawiza insists we have tea and get comfortable with each other. I listen to the three of them exchange niceties, and I watch the two men. General Muhammad ibn Haj, adjunct commander of local forces, is not in uniform, which is a wise move in the University district, but he does look awkward in civilian clothes. Or perhaps it's his height, his inability to do something graceful with his too-long legs. He has a certain charisma, a directed sense of energy, and I keep wanting to look to his face, to look to his eyes and see who he is. I also don't want to look to his eyes, so I keep averting my gaze to the man next to him. Dovid Ascherman—pudgy, unshaven, dark circles under his eyes, a yarmulke on his head—is the director of the Amichai-Darwish Research Center. He is well-known for several, perhaps unrelated, attributes. Although he lives in the Jewish district, he is married to

a Muslim woman. His grown son died over a year ago
during a search-and-destroy mission. And he has refused
to take on projects that would support the war effort,
preferring pure research and its requisite low funding,
which makes it odd to see him here, sitting by the general's side.

We are drinking our second cup of tea when ibn
Haj suggests that Ascherman begin.

"You know about the Raman probe?" Ascherman
asks me.

I nod.

"It charted three stellar systems. The third one has
a G-type star. The second planet from the sun looks to
be a humansafe world."

I try to take this in. I look to Fawiza. Why hasn't
this been made public?

"It also," he says, "supports sapient life."

I try to take this in, too. I try to understand why
they are telling this to me alone, this information that
should already be on the nets, that should be part of every new conversation. Ascherman has placed a case on
his lap and opened it, and he is now handing a flatscreen
to each of us. The first image is a bird's-eye view of a
winter landscape: bare trees and patches of something
analogous to pines. The second image is of the same
landscape at night. Fires glow. I glance at the scale at the
bottom of the screen, then at the fires. They are kilometers apart. The third image is a close-up of one fire. The
imaging makes clear that the one fire is actually three
fires. The magnification isn't clear enough to make out
the sapients sitting nearby. I can make out four individuals. They do not sit close together. In the reflection of
firelight and snow, on either side of the fires, are two
huts. A very tiny settlement for individuals dealing with
winter's pervasive cold.

I look up. Fawiza studies the image on her own
flatscreen, as if she has never seen it before. Ascherman
won't look at me. The general, ibn Haj, he offers me a
smile. He is letting me in on a secret. The tiny settlements are kilometers apart. A general is here. Fawiza,
the first Kiplinger, the Rudyard of the group, has invited
me here. I don't want to be part of this secret.

"The Raman probe," Ascherman continues, "sent

down a series of investigatory drones to take samples and collect images. Here's one image of interest."

Even though I vaguely know what I'll see, the drama of it has another effect. The image has this primal quality, as if we were stepping back to a species' evolutionary heritage. And the good Muslim girl in me can't help but think, yes, indeed, there is one God, and he works his compassionate evolutionary magic the same way on each living world.

There are the two feet: to stand upright, to walk, to run, to kick; the legs bent at the knees, the pelvis that holds up the rest of the body, and like the human pelvis, it is not the kind of structure that readily allows the passage of an infant head. Here must be the root of all courage—the strong, spread legs and the stoically accepted pain so another can make the difficult passage into life. The shape of the hips, the joining of legs to torso is obscured: a leather apron is wrapped around it. Alongside the apron, resting on the hips, are the two hands: to touch, to hold, to carry, to slap and to punch and to gather fruits and nuts, to dig for roots, to fashion a stick for digging, then, generations later, to shape a snare, to sharpen the point of an arrow or spear.

The slazan could have looked human, but for the proportions, but for the red leather skin, the dark thatch of fine hair atop the head, the wide mouth, the notched ears angled higher up on the head than human ears, and the nose. The nose is a slight protuberance with nostrils, the evolutionary movement away from smell, and the two very round eyes are flat up front for binocular vision, good but imperfect judges for scanning the distance, for gazing along a line of tracks, for singling out fruit from branches and leaves, for sensing the distances so hands can reach out and take hold.

The next image shows the same slazan returning. He approaches the small probe directly, so you can't make out what he wears on his back, but it seems that strapped over his shoulder, hanging behind him, is a quiver of arrows. I notice this time a small dark patch on either side of his throat. He is male. Those patches will fill out in the next year or so and look like heavy jowls extending from his chin. In his hand is a thick, heavy stick, a limb of some tree, which he now uses to bash the small drone deaf and blind.

Ibn Haj watches for my reaction to this act of aggression. I find I want to defend it, this attack against something odd and alien.

But Ascherman, hearing silence, continues. "We've done a census of the fires, we've made estimates about the land's carrying capacity. We think there are roughly a thousand of them. The population density is highest near the lake. About one slazan per every two square kilometers. About eighty klicks south of the lake, it has dropped to about one per every fifteen square kilometers. There is no visual evidence of farming. There are grassy clearings, but there are no fields. They must gather their food. We don't know if they scavenge or hunt for their meat. But the leather breechclout and the quiver full of arrows suggests a hunting population.

"And this we don't understand at all." The image shows a village of thatched huts, roughly thirty. The pathways look clear. A night image of the same landscape shows no fires. Other night images, taken other nights. No sign of fire, no sign of life. What kind of village is this? The huts are too close for slazans, who prefer solitude to sociability.

Ascherman sits back, and nothing is said for a moment. So this is why I'm here. They've found an isolated population of foragers. I've studied foragers. I know everyone else who's studied foragers. They're going to send a Kiplinger to study these slazan foragers, and they want to know who would be best suited. Jibril once accompanied me on my follow-up visit to the Ju/wasi, but all he ever saw of the rich life there was dry land and poverty. Bujra writes extensively on foraging lifestyles, but her knowledge comes from secondary sources.

Ibn Haj leans forward. I turn to him, drawn by his clear and easy confidence. "Dr. Dikobe," he says. "The location of this world is far away, but if you were to bisect this section of the galaxy into humanspace and slazan space, the planet is located on our side. It's isolated. As far as we can tell, the enemy doesn't know it's there. We would like to send an ethnographer to study them for half a year."

"Explain to her why," Fawiza says. It's a prompt. She wants something important said.

"Yes," said ibn Haj. "It was during our evolution in the Pleistocene, when humans gathered, scavenged, and hunted, that the basic institutions of all human societies were selected for. Language, kinship, marriage, and exchange ... well, you know the textbook examples better than I do. The point is, if we could watch a group of foraging slazans, we would gain insight into the basic institutions of slazan nature."

"No," I said. "This is a contemporary culture. You're not watching the slazan equivalent of *Homo habilis* or *Homo erectus* at work."

"Dr. Dikobe, I know we could entertain thirty or forty good scholarly caveats before we discuss any kind of project, but I have done my research. Before anthropologists carefully studied foraging cultures, the common opinion was that agriculture had been the salvation of human life. It was assumed that life before agriculture had been nasty, brutish, and short. The study of foragers changed all that. If a man and a woman each worked twenty hours a week in the Kalahari Desert, in southern Africa, they could usually gather and hunt enough food to provide an adequate diet. They spent most of their working hours maintaining the social system. By understanding these foragers, we found new ways to look at human behavior. We need new ways to look at slazan behavior."

To destroy more slazans, is what I want to say. Instead, "I'm not in slazan studies."

"You have studied human foragers. You have the expertise. What we know for sure about slazans you can learn in a day. We would like to give you two hundred days. We think you're the ethnographer who's best-qualified for this mission. Would you be interested?"

I want to say yes. "I don't know if I can."

Ibn Haj sits back, obviously frustrated. I now want to apologize, even though I have done nothing wrong.

"Muhammad," Fawiza says to him, "Pauline is obviously concerned with the ethics of this mission."

Ibn Haj looks as if he's just remembered something he foolishly forgot. He leans forward, as if to tell me a vital secret. I find myself leaning toward him. "Whatever you find out—it won't be responsible for a single slazan death. The strategy of this war for both sides is simple. It's search and destroy. Nothing you could learn about a group of foragers will change the way we fight the war. Which is why we need a capable ethnographer on this mission. Right now we are guarding eleven stellar systems. The slazans are guarding ten. Our resources are stretched thin. They've already made it through Nueva España's defenses. How long will it be until they can attack Nueva España itself? How long until they find Earth? Until they find E-donya? What happens when they find E-donya or Earth? What if they find both planets before we can locate and penetrate one of their home systems?

"I want you to think about this. You may be able to help us end this war."

Chapter Two

The First Day

The healer—who called herself I—was well respected among the ones who lived near the river, which she called Winding River, and which one or two called Lightfoot River. When she was young and her mother was the healer, I was like the other ones and was called more than one name. One woman or another called her Healer's Fingers because she had her mother's long, thin fingers that were considered good for playing the gzaet. One child or two had called her Boy Quiet because she didn't talk as much as other daughters did. The one woman and another who shared words with her mother always called her Healer's Daughter. After her mother had left, I was called Healer to her face, but when she wasn't within hearing, one or two called her Mating Close Who Doesn't Mate.

The healer, who had no children, was as tall as any woman. Her body was thin, except in the fall, when she ate as much as she could because there was little food during the cold months of late winter. Her cheeks were flat rather than puffy, giving her face a severe look. She once overheard a woman say that the healer's face matched her lack of kindness. Another disagreed. She said the healer was kind in deed, not in word, and as soon as the healer had a daughter, things would change for the better. The healer's hair was the bright color of the setting sun; like her mother, she ground up swamp tubers to make a paste that gave her hair this color of hot coals so that one who came from far away would know she was the healer.

Like her mother, I was well respected. A woman might come from as far away as the dunes or the dense southern woods to ask for help. She might have heard of the boy who had fallen from a tree, broken the bones in both legs, and who walked again the next spring. Another might have heard of the woman whose arm had swollen and bled white evil after a snakebite and who later returned to hunting, using the strength in that same arm to draw back the taut wire of a bow. Or a third might have heard of numerous children who one day thrashed with fever and who later calmly suckled their mothers' teats so they could grow with hopes of one day suckling a daughter of their own.

I's mother had taught her to behave as properly as a healer could. I always respected one's solitude. She touched another only when touching was necessary, and this she did with great respect and, if possible, when the sick one was asleep. When she played the gzaet well, its music drove away those spirits that didn't respect one's solitude.

Still, no one truly trusted the healer. There were many things said about her, though no one believed all of them were true. It was said that she had not mated for a number of years. It was said that she ate well when others went hungry. It was said that she spent entire days playing the gzaet, her eyes empty while her fingers touched the keys. It was said that she cut open the bodies of the dead.

And no one trusted the music, no matter how often it

healed. She may have sat at a good distance, the battered gzaet sitting upon the ground in front of her, her back straight, her eyes half-closed, but when her fingers reached out, when they pressed down keys, when they played songs that sounded much like the ones a mother might have sung, the sick one, the person lying there, would feel as if musical fingers were intruding upon the body, touching this part, soothing that part. Even though the healer sat at more than a respectful distance with her instrument, it still felt as if she used her music to get improperly close. This never bothered a son or a daughter who had yet to learn solitude, but it did bother each woman or man. One old man, at the season in life when he had too much love for solitude, found the music improper, if not frightening, and preferred illness to the healer's musical touch.

Because I shared words with one woman or another, she knew what things were said about her, how someone who was healed would leave a generous gift for her and then complain to another. I longed for the day when she could give birth to a daughter, whom she would raise and teach the musics. As her mother gave to her, I would give to the daughter the gzaet; she would give to the daughter the knife made of the same material as the gzaet; and she would give to the daughter the healing beads. And then I would be free to move away from the river. Once the color of the setting sun had drained from her hair, I would travel south and find a place where no one knew her as a healer. She would gather and hunt like any other woman, and each woman would respect I. She would be seen as an elder woman who kept the proper solitude, who touched only a child or a mate.

As a youth, she had lived during the spring and fall near her mother's hut, which had been built in a clearing that overlooked the distant lake. After her mother had left, I built hut and hearth near the Winding River, choosing a spot close enough to have water whenever she wanted, but not so close that she might cross paths with a thirsty nightskin or that the river, when it rose in the spring, would drown her fires.

Sour Plum had cleared the area. With his ax he had notched the bark, and several springs later the trees crashed down easily, wood ready to be fed into fires. He pulled up brush, removed heavy stones, and with smaller stones formed three circles: one for the fire inside the healer's hut, one for the healer's cooking fire, and one at the edge of the clearing for a waiting fire.

Roofer built her a large hut with one of his elaborate roofs.

The finished hut held up well to rain and wind, and there was enough room inside the hut so that on cold or rainy nights she could sleep on one side of the fire and a sick one could sleep on the other.

Soon after, when desire came, she mated first with Roofer, whose pollen had produced only boys; then, when the flower was ready for the pollen, she mated only with Sour Plum, whose pollen had given one woman and another daughters. I's belly had barely begun to bulge when the child came out in a rush of blood.

The first winter that I used her mother's gzaet to heal, she saved the life of Long Call, who never spoke, and in return he scraped out curves of dirt around where she lived so rainwater would run past on its way to the river. Long Call returned each spring and fall to dig out the gutters, which had filled with mud and debris, and he later laid flat rocks along the sides of each gutter in order to prolong its usefulness. Over the span of seasons the gutters had the carefully built look of the ones in the Many Huts.

Over the seasons the place where she lived had grown expansive as more trees had been toppled to feed up to three fires, and now there was enough open space that a chill wind or a burst of snow found an easy place to gather and swirl, making each winter harder than the last. During winter nights all I had was a fire and animal skins, and the winter wind slipped through the thatching easier than did the sun's light. On the coldest nights a woman who lived nearby sent her eldest son to I's hut. He was old enough that he wanted to prove his bravery to face the elements alone and young enough that he could lie against the healer as if she were also his mother.

When the weather was at its worst, when nights were so cold that the air tasted frozen or when snow blew between the trees like hard rain, a woman might seek out a man who had built her hut, carved her arrows, or mated with her, and take him into her hut for the warmth of the fire and her body. If it was cold enough, the man would remember what it was like when he had lived in his mother's hut, when warmth was more important than solitude. This last winter there had been a night when the wind had pulled down trees. I had huddled alone by the dying coals of her fire, listening to the sound the trees made as they bent to the wind, and she wished she had braved the afternoon cold to find someone to share her fire. Days and days later, after the snows had melted, a woman's eldest son found the remains of a man's leg buried beneath a fallen tree, and he found scattered bones nearby. I thought often of Long Call, who never spoke, who had built the gutters that kept her hut and hearth so dry, because no had seen him since that night.

Now it was spring. The early masculine rains, which raised the river and broke down flimsy huts, had for the most part ended and had been followed by the feminine rains that came so softly that the ground and leaves had time to drink in the sky's generosity. The leaves that faced the sun had taken on the colors of fire, so one woman and another had burned out the new brush to make way for grasses that attracted lightfoot and other meat animals. Fish swam away from the lake and up the river. Spring nuts were soft and chewy, and rock tubers could now be cut open and eaten. The days and nights were sometimes warm enough that fire was just for cooking food and keeping the night animals away.

But when summer came, there would be little to eat around this part of Winding River, and each woman and child would move away until the local berries ripened and the lightfoot and wetnoses returned to eat them. I would remain here so she could be easily found by those who needed her help. I did not know if she would find enough food on her own this summer or if she would have to wish for sickness so she could eat well. She would prefer to eat poorly rather than have such a reason to eat well.

One early morning, when these worries were so much in I's mind that she played the gzaet to comfort herself, a woman and her daughter arrived. They stood by the scorched ground where I maintained a waiting fire during the winter months and cold spring mornings. The daughter was naked and pudgy, while the mother was thin, as if she hadn't yet eaten her way out of winter's lean time. The mother wore a pubic apron and a kaross, which she had draped over her body so as to cover her teats. Even though I did not recognize them, she gestured them forward, and the daughter, already waist high, sat right next to I as if the healer were her mother. The mother sat at a more respectful distance. The folds of the kaross appeared empty of both fruit and child. I wondered who was caring for the infant the mother currently nursed.

The mother looked down at her feet and said, "Healer, my daughter and I used to live by the lake near the river's mouth. We kept our shelter the proper distance from other shelters. We respected the solitude of each man and each woman and child.

But by the lake there are one and two and three and four, and it was hard to show my respect and keep my distance. The daughter and I slept in a shelter built beside a springnut tree. I gave birth to a second daughter. After she died, my first daughter and I left the river's mouth to head south."

The mother looked away for a moment, then returned her gaze to the ground between her feet. "I speak too long," she said. "My daughter and I moved to a respectful distance from the river two or three days ago. During the first night, an almost-a-man left fruit and thatched roofing for our new shelter. The thatching was not very good, but it had been done. Before my daughter and I left that morning to gather food, I laid out a lightfoot hide for him. When we returned, the almost-a-man was there. He used his knife to cut the hide into a kaross for carrying things. It was a gift. I am from another place, but it is not respectful for a man to make my gift into his gift."

"That is also true here."

"But this one does not act like another almost-a-man. He embraced me even though there was no desire. He embraced my daughter even though we had not mated."

"One or two call him Hugger. He has lived as long as a man, but he has never grown into a man. He has too little solitude and hugs like a child. That is his way. Strike him several times, and he will leave."

"Those who live by the river's mouth do not strike."

"Hugger was mating close when he hugged you. Strike him, and he will keep a respectful distance."

"And my daughter?"

The mother was waiting to say more, which irritated I. Words flowed from her mouth like they did from the river into the lake. This huggable woman did not share a mother with I, but she talked like she did. I placed her fingers on the keys of the gzaet and played several musical patterns for her mind's ear, the concentration soothing the tension she felt within. She wondered if the kaross the mother wore was the one Hugger had made for her. It was a fine kaross, and Hugger did not make fine things.

"I have spoken too long," said the huggable woman. "I did not mean to be disrespectful. But I am a mother. I worry about my daughter."

"Why?"

"She embraces each woman she sees as if the woman were her mother. She says she likes the almost-a-man who embraced each of us, and she says she dreams about him. There is too little

solitude in her for one who is as high as my waist. I think the
man one or another call Hugger took away her solitude."

I looked away no. How could one person take away another's solitude? How could Hugger, who did not have one evil
bone in him? This woman seemed to be one who blamed another
rather than herself for the things she had taught her child. The
daughter had a sweet face and a smile that made I want to forfeit
her solitude. "If you return the day after tomorrow," said I to the
mother, "with four large fish, I will play some musics that might
return your daughter's solitude.'"

The mother thanked her and promised her eight large fish
and a basket of rootnuts. The daughter embraced I, and I, more
than ever, wanted a daughter to worry about and to raise properly.

With the woman gone, I felt more troubled than usual. So
she played the gzaet, listening carefully to the music and its resonances, working the music to distance herself from the world
around her. She had been playing for a while, and she was so involved in her playing that she was not quite sure when the sound
started. Her fingers stopped, the last resonances returned, and she
listened. She had never heard a sound like this before. Worse, it
became louder, like when one hears a waterfall far away, and the
crash and flow of water becomes louder as one draws nearer. But
I wasn't moving, and this sound filled up the silences, until it
was many waterfalls and I was scrambling into her shelter, until
it was the sound of a thousand rainstorms at once, and I was
wrapping her arms around the gzaet in her lap, enfolding it and
protecting it as if it were her newborn daughter. Then nothing.
Silence. Even the birds and the insects and the animals who
talked their way through the forest were silent.

I sat perfectly still, drawing no comfort from the gzaet in
her lap. The shelter would keep her dry except during the worst
masculine rain; currently it offered her no protection from the giant sound or the giant silence that followed. Her fear was terrible, and she did not remember ever having felt so unwomanly.
The fear that another might walk by and see her shaking
prompted her out of the shelter. The clearing, the fire, the
scorched land of the waiting fire, the clear, hard bodies of the
trees, the roof of leaves above, the sprinkle of light—none of this
had lost its everyday look. Insects, birds, animals: one by one the
familiar sounds returned. It became easier to act as if nothing
had happened.

Flatface called out her approach. Flatface and I's mother

had shared a mother, and Flatface was now as old as I's
mother had been when she had left the river. Flatface's skin
sagged with age, and her teats were withered with both her age
and the drying of her milk. By the end of summer the skin on her
chest would hang like the skin from her belly. Her face had inspired her name, but the creases, born of facing the sun and the
cold, made her face look rounder. Across one cheek was a long,
twisted scar. She was dressed in skins for a cooler morning, and
she wore her kaross draped around her shoulder and tied off
above her hips. Riding her shoulders was her knee-high daughter.
Walking behind her was her youngest son, who still climbed
trees with girls. Walking off the path, staring into the woods as
if no one were nearby, was the eldest son. He was almost as tall
as a woman and learning to enjoy his solitude. He was interested
enough in women's labia that he would soon be forced to leave
for another part of the river. Flatface's first child now had a child
of her own.

With four live children Flatface was no longer one who'd
wait by the waiting fire until I took proper notice. Today she
wasn't one to stop at a respectful distance, either. She took I by
the arm and pulled her along, all the while saying between heavy
breaths, "You have to come with me. There's something new in
the clearing. Many Wrinkles and Childless and Squawker are
there waiting for you."

I had lived the springs and falls of her childhood around this
clearing. She had helped her mother and Flatface burn away the
brush and leaves and had watched the grasses grow in their
place. She had gathered berries and dug up tubers. Before she
had grown to enjoy her solitude, I had played here with
Flatface's eldest daughter, who now had her own child. With the
eldest daughter I had run between and around the trees; she had
climbed the tallest trees to stare out at the way the land sloped
down to the distant lake; she had plucked leaves in the spring
and watched them slowly change back into the color they were
the rest of the year; she had snuck up on animals drinking from
the tiny stream that ran through the clearing; and she had hidden
behind trees when a nightskin had approached the stream to
drink its share of water.

One edge of the clearing overlooked the hills falling to the
lake, and the rest was bounded by hills. The trees along the hillside had all faced the sun and were now bright with color. The
slopes were bare of tree and brush, covered with grass, scarred

where animals and people had skidded down to the flat land of the clearing.

In the center of the clearing was something else. Something big. The ground around it was black and broken, like someone had burned a fire there until the grass became smoke and the land became so hard that it cracked open in tiny jagged lines. The thing itself, centered in the blackness, had the wet sheen of a rock recently pulled from the river. It was bigger than any rock she had ever seen. Behind it, the tiny stream whispered quietly as if nothing strange had happened.

Why was this thing here, in the place where she had been a child?

Each woman stood a proper distance from the other at the top of the hill. Each stood near a thick old tree in case there was a reason to hide. Squawker, who lived near the clearing, was telling again how she had heard it first, how she had come out to watch it fall from the sky. She was a squat woman with dark hair whose mother had been born far from the river. While she spoke, she held her infant daughter in her arms and let her nurse. Her son was clinging to her leg, his face turned toward the distant woods and its promise of safety. Squawker's eyes were fixed on the thing in the clearing, and she told them how she had seen it falling from the sky and how she had run into the forest with her son and daughter so they would be safe. While she told this, Squawker called the thing The Reason I Will Move Away.

Flatface had given it a different name. She called it the Sun Boulder, for the way you could see the sun and some of its brightness on the thing's surface. Childless Crooked, a thin woman whose skin was going soft again with approaching desire, called it the Slippery Hill because it looked like you would slip if you tried to climb it. Crooked said, "Someone has to touch it."

"I would leave it alone," said Squawker.

"You are leaving," said Childless Crooked. She leaned forward, probably to ease the pain in her back.

"No one should tell another one what to do," said Flatface, even though she, too, did not like Squawker.

The old woman whom Flatface called Many Wrinkles indeed had skin that sagged with the weight of too many seasons. I called the old woman Wisdom when she was there, and Talk Too Much when she was not. She liked to tell, at length, that she had been the first woman to build hut and hearth in this area.

Back then, she said, you were more likely to meet up with a sunskin than with another woman. But each woman knew that Wisdom had come to live near this part of Winding River with one woman and another who had shared her mother. One woman gave birth to I's mother and to Flatface, the other to Crooked's mother. Wisdom had given birth to three daughters who grew into women. Two had left together for the south, where there would be more lightfoot to hunt and more water berries to gather. The daughter who remained had a daughter who had daughters. Understandably, Wisdom was often tired. She had decided to sit against a tree. "If you drop a rock into the mud, it makes a hole in the ground. Mud flies everywhere. Why is the ground still flat? Why is it as black as meat you've left too long in the fire?"

"Because it is," said Squawker.

Wisdom did not even look at Squawker. "That sun boulder, that big rock, doesn't belong there. It fell from the sky, you say. But it must have landed softly. So maybe it can get up and leave."

Flatface looked to I, but I did not know what to say. She knew the thing wasn't leaving. She also knew that no one would do anything about it.

"It must be evil," said Childless Crooked. "It's burned up the grass. Fewer lightfoot will come here." Ever since the first time she had been pregnant, Childless Crooked's bones had ached like the bones of an old person. The child of that pregnancy and all that followed had been born too early and had died without breathing. She now saw evil in every accident and heard hatred in every joke.

"When it's hot, the lightfoot will come to drink," said I. "It's not a nightskin and it won't eat them."

"What will it do?" asked Childless Crooked.

"Sit there," said Flatface, "and scare you."

"Maybe it won't leave," said Wisdom. "Maybe it should be moved. Yes, maybe it should be pushed to the edge of the clearing and then down the hill where no one goes."

"And who will do that?" asked Squawker.

"One man and another and maybe another could move it."

"It's too big to move," said Childless Crooked.

"One woman and another," said Flatface, "will work as women. One man or two won't work as men. If it can be moved, women will have to do it."

"Young men before they leave their mothers will work as men," said Squawker. She patted her son's head.

"But not for long," said Flatface. "Old Sour Plum will surely come by. He'll get them to stop. He'll tell them their strength depends on solitude. No man wants to be called a woman."

"Old Sour Plum doesn't talk much anymore," said I. They had started calling Sour Plum old just before Flatface's youngest had been born. Flatface's eldest daughter in the flush of her first desire had tried to mate with Sour Plum. He had driven her away with loud words the first time she opened to him, and the second time as well. The third time he let her mount him and then bit off one of her fingers.

"What if a first soul is in there?" said Squawker's son, who now had one eye open, the other shut, and was staring at the thing in the clearing.

I looked at the thing again. It looked too solid to have anything inside it.

"Hush," said his mother. "Women are talking."

"If a first soul is in there," said Flatface, "we will have to move very far away."

"Why would a first soul be in there," said Wisdom, "when it has all the sky to roam? Here people have to get too close to each other; here living things die. And that thing . . . that thing is much too small for a first soul to live in."

"But if a first soul can become a wetnose or a tree," said Squawker's son, "can't it fit in a big rock, too?"

"Boys can be so smart," said Wisdom, "until they find their penises."

Squawker was not one to put up with words aimed toward a child of hers, so she reminded Wisdom of all the things the first souls had turned themselves into so that everything alive would have something to eat and air to breathe. Flatface had never heard a story about a first soul who became a tree so there would be enough air, and Childless Crooked laughed at the notion of breathing trees. Each was talking the way a child did when comparing mother-told stories with another woman's child.

"I will play music for it tomorrow," said I.

Each stopped talking and said what a good idea it was that the healer would play music for it tomorrow.

"Who will watch it during the night?" asked Childless Crooked. "It could do something while we sleep."

"It's a big rock," said Flatface. "We are behaving like our sons and daughters when Wisdom tells them her swamp story."

"I am not part of your we," said Squawker. "I will ask a man and another to watch this while we sleep. A man would like the solitude and bravery it will take."

"It's a rock," said Flatface. "It fell from the sky. It hasn't done anything else. It doesn't move."

"Go touch it, then," said Childless Crooked.

"Let's wait until the healer plays," said Flatface.

The healer barely slept that night. She spent the wakeful moments playing her gzaet, pressing each key slowly, drawing out each note, testing it, hearing it, listening to it carefully, separating what sounded healthy and what sounded ill the way her eyes would search out bushes for both berries and thorns. She then played rapidly, listening for each note, and slowing her fingers when the notes ran together like water, waiting until they were as distinct as drops of rain; then she played rapidly again.

And then she stopped, because the thoughts wouldn't. If she did sit down in front of the giant rock, and if she did play the gzaet, would the music tell her anything? If a first soul was inside, would the music bring it out? One first soul had dug rivers out of the flat land and piled the dirt onto hills so a woman could look at the hills and know from which water she and her daughters could drink without taking water from another woman. Did I want to meet such a powerful first soul?

And if she were to die tomorrow, there would be no daughter left behind to play the gzaet. This time, when the body craved touch, she would not mix her remedy of bitter herbs or play music to ease her desire; this time maybe she would mate with someone.

The Second Day

The next morning I arrived at the edge of the clearing in time to watch Roofer stride down to confront the boulder. Roofer had gathered his food along Winding River since he had been as tall as a woman. When he had first arrived, many springs ago, he had tried to get mating close to any woman who was ready, but each in turn would refuse him. He thatched roofs together as gifts, but he was still refused until he had grown as tall as a man and could issue the call that could be heard through the woods.

And here was Roofer, showing his bravery for I, the only

woman on the hill. He stepped out onto the clearing and walked until he was halfway between the bottom of the hill and the sweep of blackened ground. He stood there for a moment, facing the thing, and then walked calmly back as if nothing were there.

Not much later Old Sour Plum had to prove he was braver. He was a head taller than Roofer, his chest sagging with the extra weight that came with age, and he ponderously walked down to where Roofer had stopped and took three extra steps before returning and walking off into the forest.

Up in the woods, on the other side of the clearing, was Hugger, who had never outgrown his boyhood. He had shared Squawker's mother, and he had the same squat body and the same dark hair. Right now he paced back and forth, making lots of polite noise so no one would be surprised by him. When he wanted to hug someone, he could sneak up as quietly as a woman tracking a lightfoot.

I considered playing for the thing up here, on the top of the hill, near the woods. No one cared how brave she was. A child laughed in the distance. Through the trees she could make out Flatface carrying her youngest daughter, her waist-high son walking along beside them. Soon Childless Crooked would be here, as well as Wisdom and Squawker. She did not want anyone watching.

I faced the boulder and took careful steps down the slope, cradling the gzaet in her arms, the leather strap digging into her neck. Several times one foot or the other would slip, but she didn't lose her balance. She stopped halfway down. A woman has to be brave on the hunt. A woman has to be brave to give birth. A woman should be brave enough to get as close as Old Sour Plum did. She took several more steps until the slope flattened out, then several more to where the ground had been blackened. Nothing happened. She sat down and placed the heavy gzaet in front of her. Sunlight reflected off the boulder and forced her to squint. Maybe, she thought, it's less like a rock and more like water, which is soft.

She began to play, first the top two rows of keys, easing her mind, loosening her fingers, testing out the notes. Then she shifted her right hand to the lower keys, sending out music, waiting for the resonance, feeling it in the keys. The music played against the thing, and it was hard, hard as a rock, but there was still a resonance, a faint echo that rocks shouldn't have. The resonance was vaguely familiar; she'd felt it before. Sometimes she played her music against one thing, then another—a tree, a bush, then a dead sun-wings—to understand the full feeling of the music. She had felt a resonance like this when she'd played music against a shell or a hollow tree. If the boulder was hollow, was there something inside?

She stopped playing. She untied the gzaet's straps and stood up. She wanted to touch the boulder, see what it felt like. She had taken several steps forward before she was overtaken by the same fear that had left her huddled in her shelter, cradling the gzaet. She inhaled, listened to a music pattern with her mind's ear, exhaled, and took another few steps. Then a few more. Childless Crooked had said it looked slippery. Flatface had said it was just a rock. But it was a hollow rock. Along it were pieces of dull crystal, but each was as round as a melon, as tiny as a seed. I took four quick breaths, then touched the rock. She had never felt anything like it. She touched it again and slid her hand across the surface. It wasn't slippery the way a newborn child was slippery, but the palm of her hand slid over it as easily as it did a well-worn rock. She slapped it. It felt like the gzaet, only heavier. The sound was dull.

How could this thing be made of the same thing as the gzaet? She stepped back. The gzaet, her mother had said, had been made by people with magic no one had anymore. The idea of such magic had frightened I when she had been her mother's daughter, and that fear returned to her now. She ran to the gzaet, picked it up, and tied one strap around her neck, the other behind her back, and walked as fast as she could back to her shelter. She didn't care that Roofer or Hugger saw her. She didn't care that Flatface was watching. She wanted to be alone with her thoughts.

The following is excerpted from a draft of Pauline Dikobe's memoirs, a project she started and abandoned while the Way of God *made its return trip to E-donya E-talta.*

My answer should be no. I should say, I can't trust you. No one but university people talk about negotiating an end to this war. I have visited the town where I grew up. I watched my compassionate father seethe with anger when I said the galaxy was big enough for both human and slazan. I listened to my mother, who speaks like the angel of mercy even when swatting at flies, list the new kinds of weapons humans would deploy in the same tone she would talk about new methods of exterminating insects.

But General ibn Haj isn't my father. He isn't here to debate. He hears the silence and offers me several days to think about it.

Before he will leave, I have to thumbprint several documents. They've lent me secrets I've never requested, and they'll foreclose on my livelihood and reputation if I share them with anyone else. Nowadays, it seems, you sell your soul before you've accepted the prize.

Once they've left, once Fawiza and I are the only two sitting in her living room, our tea too cold and its taste of honey too sweet, I look to her and expect to hear why she lured me in, why she betrayed me like this. But she thinks that I'm overwhelmed by the enormity of the offer, that I'm only looking for comfort. She says kind things about Ascherman and ibn Haj, about how there are others who would respond very differently once they had found a colony of slazans. She knows I'm a nonpraticing Muslim, and she pours me a glass of wine, and she shows me more images the Raman probe had brought back.

I stay for the images, to see more of the slazans. I stay because it takes me an hour to find a polite way to leave, to get as far away as I can from what I've been asked to do.

Once outside, I know I cannot return to my tiny flat. I fasten my veil, cross to the female side of the street, and I walk. All I do is walk, past towers and domes, by institutes and centers, through parks, along footbridges. An occasional recruiting flyby glides above my head, flashing images of women who fly starships, who work in busy offices, who direct the organization of groups, and the words following the images ask me to help preserve the human community. The flybys come in pairs: the ones shooting over male pedestrians show infantrymen in training and simulations of future land battles and images of dark, smiling slazans; the words promise to train their strength, to enhance their endurance, so they can help humanity fight back the slazan enemy.

Parks, like libraries and temples, are classified as zones of contemplation, so flybys are prohibited. I head for the nearest one. I want to be away from reminders of battle. I want to think clearly about the foraging slazans who live so far away from the war. But the images Fawiza and ibn Haj and Ascherman showed me come back only as fragments of a vivid, fading dream.

I think of one image in particular. I try to concentrate and make it whole in my mind. There is one slazan. It is the size of a young adult. It does not have throat patches, so it is not an adult male. But it doesn't have breasts, either. Is it female? Her upper body is draped with an animal skin that is tied off at the waist and around the shoulder, much like the chi !kans worn by Ju/wa women. Along the fringes a series of curved lines are woven into the leather. Who made this? The chi !kan worn by Ju/wasi women are made by their husbands. Does this slazan use it the same way, to carry home the

fruits, nuts, and roots that have been gathered that day?
Do the females gather? Do males hunt? How do members of a solitary species go about sharing the fruits of
their labor? And why have these slazans decided to
gather and hunt in the forest rather than at the market?
Have these slazans settled here for the same reasons the
Ju/wasi settled in the desert reserve?

Several generations ago a group of men and women
from the University grew disillusioned with the conventional notion of utopia. Utopian colonies might design
their societies around extensive maps of human behaviors, but only the colonists saw their lives as utopian.
Ethnotechs from Nueva España might hire themselves
out to a community, they might redesign a culture or resolve some culture's internal contradiction, they might
alleviate some measure of pain, but in turn they plant
the seeds for some other problem that will be harvested
a decade later. Religions might use every social science
at their command to appeal, cajole, and coerce their congregations into better behavior, but for every devout person doing good, there was someone who employed
devout phrases to cloak less-than-devout behavior.

These disillusioned university men and women decided that utopia was impossible, that there were too
many contradictions in human nature. They wondered,
however, if there was a way of life that accommodated
human nature—one that encouraged the human propensity for friendship and sharing while fighting against the
equally human propensity for competition and greed.
They found the answer in simple foraging societies that
had once existed: they cooperatively shared the provisions of life; they had no true leaders and worked out
group decisions in a subtle form of consensus; other
than age and sex, there was little status or ranking, and
those who weren't kin could be made kin; among such
people wealth wasn't found in possessions or in freedom
from disease or in a quiet easing through of life; rather,
wealth was found in one's relations, it was earned
through daily encounters and exchanges, and it was
born when a child clenched his fist around a tiny share
of meat, as if to say *mine*, only to find the mother take
hold of his hand and say, *give*.

These University men and women, these primal utopians, chose a foraging group whose existence had been
well documented, whose blood had been drawn and
stored, whose genetic records still existed. They raised
funds and purchased an ideal spot of land on the Southern Continent. They terraformed the area so it looked
more like the Kalahari Desert of southern Africa than
the place they had found. They took centuries-old schol-
arship and images, and from those they designed and sat
through reality workshops to learn the language, to
learn which fruits to gather, to learn how to track meat
animals. Then they left the University and gave themselves the name of their spiritual ancestors: *Ju*, meaning
person, */wa*, meaning true, proper, pure, and *si* making
it plural. Their children were gene-tailored, given light
brown skin, a small bone structure, flat faces, so that
when their parents looked at their children, they might
see only the curve of a cheek, the corner of a smile, a
certain stubbornness, that told them, yes, this child is
mine.

So, like Ju/wasi, they live light upon the land. When
the season is dry, they come together in groups around
permanent waterholes; when it is wet, they spread out, a
family or two together, taking advantage of what is lush
and ripe. When weather is bad in one place, they visit
another, tied together by kinship and by marriage, by a
series of exchanged favors and gifts, by their shared
knowledge. So they walked from camp to camp, alert for
snakes and predators, gathering the right foods at the
right time, hunting large animals in small groups and di-
viding the meat up along proper lines of kinship and obligation, going through the days joking with the right
people and avoiding the right people, sitting around a
fire telling stories, recounting the day, making com-
plaints, discussing, arguing, and breaking up fights before someone got hotheaded enough to reach for his
arrows tipped with poison.

Could a group of slazans have done something similar? Could these slazans on this secret, distant world be
primal utopians?

In the distance, bells sound from the University's
highest tower. Other bells and chimes sound, an undulat-

ing wave carried through the streets and parks. Everything is cast orange with the sun's descent. Classes are ending, craftsmen are cleaning up, offices are closing. Soon Muslims will be called to prayer, Jews will head to temple, Christians will attend evensong, and nonbelievers in the University quarter will take advantage of the moment to beat the crowd to popular restaurants, bars, and cafés. There is meant to be relief or joy in the three distinct sabbaths, each respected in such different ways, but coming one right after the other that the entire end of the week is often called the sabbath.

I leave the park as the streets begin to fill with people. The number of flybys increase, advertising places to go after prayer, before curfew. I should feel a minor rush of excitement. There is the wealth of dress, the range of culture, the promise of the evening, but all I notice is the number of students who walk in public without veils, and the young, bare faces make me feel conservative, out of place.

The sun is setting when I make my way into the city's Muslim quarter, and now my dress feels too bright, its close cut immodest. In the desert town of my family, my clothes would be worse than immodest, the visible calves and arms, the glimpse of skin between breasts, too much an enticement.

A muezzin calls out from a nearby minaret. *God alone is great.* Not far away another man in another minaret calls out the same. Then farther away, the phrases repeating, the voices melding. *I testify there is no god but God.* All flybys have ceased. The moment has become sacred. I stop and look across the street at the tiny mosque. I consider crossing, I consider going in. *I testify that Muhammad is the messenger of God.* I like the muezzin's voice, the way it draws me back to my youth, when belief came so easily. *Come to prayer. Come to prayer. Come to success. Come to success.* It's been years since I answered that call. *God alone is great. There is no god but God.* But I am dirty and full of doubt and improperly dressed.

I walk on and look for public lavatories. All that tea and wine and no food. After relieving myself, I recognize my hunger. Flybys have resumed: this restaurant, that entertainment, the opportunity to help humanity. I walk through the heart of the city, past the closed gates of the market, past the giant mosque, past ornate fountains, where the sound of falling water eases something in me.

I should go home, to my solitary flat: the bright walls, the empty bed, the knickknacks I had accumulated while I lived in the desert reserve, the images of my departed son—and I remain in the Muslim quarter, forgetting every thought as soon as it's finished traveling through my mind.

It's past dark now. The calls from distant minarets sound again, until all sound is traffic and the call to prayer. I am light-headed from the walking, from the long afternoon's hunger. I find a late-night shop that sells food and prayer rugs. The owner is old and thin. I look at prayer rugs rather than food, and the owner asks where I'm from. I tell him, and he tries to look politely in my general direction, avoiding my eyes, avoiding the faint curve of visible breast. He tells me I should buy a second veil. "You are too immodest with your beauty." I feel ashamed for the way I dress, the way it must cause him such exaggerated thoughts about my chaste breasts.

The curfew is near. A former colleague lives in the Muslim quarter, so I go to see her. Judith greets me at the doorway, large and round, her smile as generous as her appetite until she gets a good look at me. "Pauline?"

"I can't bear my flat tonight," I say.

"Then you'll have to bear mine. Come on in."

She offers me food and wine, and I tell her I'm not hungry. We sit and Judith chats. She was the first to leave the Institute for Cultural Studies when the Kiplingers were formed, and since then she moved from her family's home in the Jewish quarter to this flat and produced one monograph after another about cultural purity and cultural mixing in the neighborhood and workplaces of Wadi al-Uyoun. I came here often just after my husband had departed for parts unknown with our son, and in those visits I found it hard to stop eating, as if there were some buried energy in me that had to be fed. Judith took me in, without qualm, even though we had mutual friends who would not talk to me because I had remained at the Institute and rubbed shoulders with Kiplingers. Now, years later, I have returned to her flat. Finally, after numerous offers of food, after an hour of pleasant chatter, she has to know. "How are things with Fawiza?"

I consider telling her. She will know the right thing to do. She will tell me why it's wrong of me to want to find answers to all my questions.

"Are things okay at the Institute?" she asks.

"They've been intense for the last few months. Ever since the slazan warrior destroyed that colony."

Judith says nothing for a while. The peace movement suffered after that attack. Recruiting rates had shot up immediately. The war had become real again. "You read al-Kharrat's piece, didn't you?"

I nodded.

My lack of response bothers her, provokes her to comment, to summarize for me what I've already read. It's the character flaw of those who teach: learning itself becomes its own religion, its own way to a better life. "Up until that point, the slazan strategy has been pure tit for tat. They have attacked only in response to our attacks. We must have successfully attacked a civilian population of theirs. Why else would they have destroyed a defenseless colony when there was a military target nearby?"

"Maybe the slazan warrior aimed for what was closest?" I say.

That only gets her going, and I regret having said anything at all. I'm tired of all the words. I wonder if there's some way to have a strong sense of morality that doesn't become encumbered by the accompanying rhetoric. And I realize that there's no way I can ask her advice. I already know the ethics of the whole thing. I know what she will say, and I know she will be right. By going I have made myself complicit in any immorality that follows from this research. By remaining silent I lend support to whatever happens.

But that night, feigning sleep in her guest bedroom, I carry on the conversation with the Judith who lives in my mind, who has become part of my conscience. I tell her that I am not the executioner who ignores the blood on his hands while he claims that someone else would have done it. *But the execution looks the same, no matter who lowers the blade.* The research is shaped by the researcher. If I don't go, someone else will go. What if it's a person who sees the war the same way as my parents? Who sees it the same way as most people on this world see it? My own imaginary Judith is honest to the real one snoring loudly in her own bedroom: *This thinking is the way of madness. It's not the research, it's who reads the research. Those who don't want to see what's good won't see it.* I tell her she's wrong. I think of ibn Haj and tell Judith that there are people who want this war to end; they need to know how to negotiate its settlement. *You'd be better off screwing this general of yours, and once that's out of your system, you can think about history, about how these things really happen.*

I want to talk with the real Judith. But I've thumb-printed away my voice. So I shift in bed, slip in and out of sleep, until I'm no longer sure if the dawn call to prayer is a dream or not. *There is no god but God. Prayer is better than sleep.*

I shower completely. For a while my hunger feels healthy, my body alive. I have freed myself of the city's dirt. In the guest-room closet is the old black abaya I had left here after my husband had left me. I expect it to bring back memories, but the musty fabric is comforting in the way it covers everything between ankles, wrist, and neck.

Because this is a flat built in the Muslim quarter, each room has a tiny niche in the wall directing the devout toward Mecca. When E-donya was charted and mapped, they unraveled the prime meridian and wrapped its invisible thread around the world, tightening it along a line that would make it possible for a spot in one of the world's deserts to bear the same coordinates as Mecca on Earth. There they painstakingly built a facsimile of the city's heart so pilgrims could walk seven times around the Ka'ba and traverse the distance between the sacred columns of Sfa and Marwa. That a desert existed at the right latitude for this to happen made it possible for the devout to transpose a religion and a people to this world with the geographic certainty that the move was part of God's design.

It is this certainty I want to feel once again when I stand facing the niche, facing Mecca, facing the Ka'ba. I declare the greatness of God. I recite the first chapter of the Quran, the words coming readily to my lips. It's as if time has been erased. I have returned to my devout adolescence, when fresh hormones opened my body to all the wonders and pains of the world, when the absence of righteousness and the presence of God were as self-evident as hunger and bread. I bow down, I declare there is no god but God and Muhammad is his messenger, but in my submission, in my prostration before God, I feel nothing. There is no one listening, there are no answers.

All I know is the hunger in my belly. All I feel is a yearning for the bed I left too early. I write Judith a note of thanks and leave, wearing abaya and veil, the prayer rug hanging from a strap over my shoulder.

I walk from one end of the quarter to the other. I walk through the main market. I stare at food, and I listen to women hawk their wares. I try to envision the fine balances between religion, law, and custom that keep us connected to the men and women in markets since men built the first cities in lands like these light-years from here, that cluster of people digging in, refusing to move ever again with the seasons, marking a break in human affairs, a rift between when life was local history and a time when life was world history.

A man in Siberia could shape a necklace and give it to his lover, and perhaps his wife would recognize the style of his craft hanging from another woman's body, and perhaps this might affect how her family and his family dealt with each other for years to come. But no one who lived along the Mediterranean would be touched by this event, have their lives and alliances altered, and the only trace of this distant history might be found around the neck of a woman who generations later is given an odd but sturdy necklace that has changed hands numerous times. Something well made, with luck, might travel across a continent, but human actions, long ago, never had equal force. Now they can ask a woman to travel many light-years to a distant planet where she will live among an alien people, and they tell her what she finds out could affect the lives of billions of people she's never known. She tells herself that this war has little effect on our daily lives, that we sense it only in increased taxes, in news of faraway deaths. There are so many humans that it is possible to keep death a stranger, keep war at a distance so that everyone accepts its reasonable costs.

The midday call to prayer. I follow the muezzin's voice to the nearest mosque. In the courtyard are two fountains. I join the women, splash water on feet, forearms and hands, face and head. Inside the mosque I stand with the women, who stand behind the men. We face the mihrab, we face Mecca. We bow down twice. An imam rises in front. He recites from the Quran. His voice carries through the mosque. It is a lovely voice. I find it hard to fix my attention to the words. I hear just the voice. My hunger betrays me. He then offers a sermon. I try hard to attend to what he says. Each of us, he says, takes part in an individual holy struggle, each wages jihad with the worst of ourselves, to make ourselves worthy of God. Each of us prays alone. But we pray together. We answer the call to prayer. We recite the same verses of the Quran in the same language. On Fridays we gather as Muslims to bow down to God together.

But has each of us taken an equal part in the holy struggle to make the universe safe for humanity? Has each of us done more than offer a prayer for the men and women who fight the enemy? A slazan is alone, too, just like a human. But a slazan will only touch another slazan when mating. (*That's wrong, I hear myself think.*) A slazan will not stand with another in prayer. A slazan will not bow down to God. A slazan cannot be righteous. A slazan destroys without provocation. (*Liar.*) Each of us must do more than pray. Each of us must commit ourselves to the struggle, or God will allow the slazan to win, for humanity cannot win when it's weak, when it avoids moral struggle.

He goes on and on, and the slazans he talks about are not the slazans in the images I saw yesterday afternoon, nor are they the slazans who shared a world with humans for six years. Liar, liar, is the banal refrain in my head, my own form of useless prayer. He recites with such beauty and knows nothing. How can that be?

He finishes, we bow twice to God, and on our knees wish peace to each other. The contradiction of the moment is appalling. I should stand up, shout something, demand that he retract such evil words. I file out with the rest, continue my walk. Judith is wrong, I think. I have to go.

So why do I keep walking? Why don't I return to my flat to contact ibn Haj?

Because I know so much has been written about the slazan, and none of it has made its way to the imam's lips.

I am in a park when I hear the afternoon call to prayer. Several mothers are showing their children how to perform the ritual ablutions from the separate fountain built here for that purpose. One points to me in my black abaya and says to her daughter, "Watch the married woman. See how properly she does it."

Before the evening call to prayer, I make my way to the Jewish quarter. For a moment I am taken aback by how everything is the same, the same kinds of buildings, the same messages on the flybys, the same segregated sidewalks. Only the synagogues are built differently from the mosques: there is no courtyard, just a simple dome over a simple building, each one oriented toward the center of the quarter where flat, cleared space represents the space in Jerusalem where the holy Temple once stood.

I don't go into one of the synagogues, but I stand outside and listen for the sound of prayer. Later I watch people leave and head to their homes, where women step up to windows and light candles. The women shut their eyes as they speak the blessing, and then they open their eyes to the sabbath light. Judith once told me each Jew receives two souls on the sabbath to hold all the joy. I want to keep this thought, but all I can think of is the family around the table, the ritual words, and the bread they share.

I find a bench on which to rest. Walking has become a chore. I am awakened by an elderly man. He has a long beard. I imagine it's Abraham, but this Abraham speaks with a raspy voice. "Are you okay?"

I sit up. What does he think of this woman in her black abaya whom he found lying unconscious on a Jewish bench?

"It's almost curfew. You will be arrested."

Is this what I want? To be arrested? This way I

won't have to make a choice. Ibn Haj will have to find someone else.

Someone else says, "She's a bum."

I try to focus my eyes. There's another man, about Abraham's size, wearing the same kind of beard. He's standing on the other side of the street.

Abraham says, "Ignore my brother. Do you have somewhere to stay? Where do you live?"

I tell him. I recite my address.

"You do not look well. Are you sick? Do you need help?"

"I'm fasting. For the sabbath."

"Are you Jewish?" He sounds upset with himself, as if he had been wrong to think differently.

"No. Yes. I don't know. I'm fasting for all three sabbaths."

He stands there for a moment. I expect derision. Instead he takes my arm. "The police will not let you fast. My brother and I do not have much, but we do have a sofa. A pilgrim such as yourself should not have to sleep in a lockup."

The couch is too short, but the morning shower is warm, cleansing. The light-headedness, the weariness, is a whole part of me. Abraham's brother offers me food. He grins as if he expects me to bow into hunger. I shake my head. Abraham, whose real name is Judah, says, "There is enough temptation without our adding to her burden."

I thank them both and leave. I can't stand for long. I walk and have to rest. I enter a synagogue, something I haven't done since I entered the University, an uncertain young woman, who wandered from synagogue to church to mosque, translator in ear, to listen to priests and rabbis and imams speak with sonorous certainty. I am handed a disposable ear translator and a yarmulke. At the lectern stands an adolescent girl, a white cloak draped over her shoulders, and she reads from the prayer book. She tells me in Hebrew, while the translator whispers Arabic in my ear, that prayer will not bring rains to a dried-out field or rebuild a ruined city, but prayer can cure the thirst of a parched soul and heal the wounds of a broken heart.

I should have left then, but later, when it is time for

her personal remarks, she says how still she mourns for the five hundred who died in the slazan attack. "I say this because my sister is not here now. She is in training. I am proud of her. I am proud that she is committed to peace and to justice. If we are still fighting this war when I am her age, I hope I also have the same courage and faith."

I return to the street. All I can see is the bright face of that adolescent girl. If I stay here—if I don't go on ibn Haj's mission—I will have done nothing to change her view of justice, whereas now, because of her sister's life, she can only rejoice at slazan death.

I'm listless. People stare at me. I wait for something to happen, for someone to come get me. Instead, I run into three former students. Two are wearing yarmulkes. These two are young female versions of Abraham. They look concerned. They want to know if I am sick, if I need help. The third, Maryam, looks uncomfortable. She never expected to see her professor in this state.

"I'm fasting," I say.

"For how long?"

"Until the Christian sabbath is over." I tell them how I will go to stay in the Christian quarter this evening. Maryam wants to know where I'll stay. I shrug, shake my head, and she offers me her flat, which she is secretly sharing with a young man. The two other students giggle.

I stay there that night. The walls are thin. I hear them make love, even though they try to be quiet, and I find myself yearning for touch. I imagine myself with the general, and I force my mind to go blank, to deny myself that kind of desire.

At breakfast her lover is embarrassed by my presence. I watch them eat. I tempt and test myself. She must see the look in my eyes, and she kindly offers to make me something. "She's got a day left," he says. "Don't ruin it." He's an anthropological historian. He's studying pre-Contact cultures, how they lived just before Europe's people touched every part of the globe, before world history ended all local histories. He wants to try out his learning. He asks me all sorts of questions. He wants to know if what I'm doing is like a vision quest. Am I starving myself, going out into a metaphorical wilderness alone until I see some kind of totem to guide me? I have to disappoint him. "I'm doing penance," I tell him.

We walk out together. They kiss before fastening their veils. She gives him a shy wave, and he crosses the street. I offer thanks and farewell, and I watch them walk away, each one now and then glancing across the street to the other, the other always knowing when to look back. What in love makes such timing possible?

I make my way to the giant cathedral that was built in Wadi al-Uyoun's early days. Inside, a line of people kneel up front, their mouths open, the priest laying the host upon each of their tongues. The wafer is such meager food, quickly dissolved and gone. I don't want to hear the priest's sermon. I have heard hatred in the guise of holiness, and hatred in the guise of justice. I don't want to hear it in the guise of love.

So I stand alone on an empty street beneath an empty sky. All I have is hunger. Why do I cling to this? I try to walk. I refuse to sit down. I can sense how my body weaves even though I imagine my course is straight. I frown at those who stare at me. I finally sit, and I take pleasure in forcing myself to walk again. Every restaurant yields smells I can taste. I dine on such smells. I yearn. I keep walking. My throat is dry. I dream of beer, a good Christian beverage. The spring sun is warming. The sweat breaking out on me dries when I rest, forming layers of sweat for future archaeologists to dig through.

Perhaps Maryam's lover is right. Perhaps I await the hallucination, the one from inside, the vision that will tell me what to do. I should have left the city, headed for the wilderness, risked snakes rather than cars, because the only vision I see is that of a lonely anthropologist with adequate talents who has produced one well-received monograph and a series of articles, one who has only mildly bored her students and who now can be known for decades because she studied the right people at the right time and has never had the nerve to join either side of the ideological battle. But do you say no when they offer you such a moment, do you say no when you believe in knowledge, when you believe the right words could remove the hatred from their hearts;

or do you acknowledge that words are just words, that no matter what you do, this war will drag on until too many have died and too much has been spent, or until one side gets the proper advantage over the other; or do you spend days without food and water, finding some way to say you that makes you whole, that gives you moral cause?

On the way home I walk through a small Hindu enclave that houses scientists and businessmen from the northern continent. A woman stands outside her door and scatters rice grains in front of her. She speaks in Hindi. I know a textbook version of what she might be saying. "May the ants, worms, insects, and whoever are hungry, receive this food offered by me." She looks up and smiles warmly to me. She asks in stilted Arabic if I'm okay. Does she later go in and wish death to slazans?

I return to my flat. Everything about it is so familiar that it's ugly. I sit at my desk. There are two images of my son. There's the young boy, the old infant actually, the cheeks still pudgy with the last of baby fat, dark hair, the smile that caused his eyes to light up; we never got a shot of that stubborn frown, the upper teeth biting lower lip when something didn't work the way he wanted, the frustration hardening into anger. The other image is a projection: how he might look now. Each day, when I remember, more often at the end of week, I read into his file the food he would have eaten, the major physical and emotional experiences he might have had at home or at school, and the computer, starting with genotype, calculates the shape of experience and projects phenotype: his smooth, thin face, the dark skin, the serious set of the lips, the determination in his eyes. I know if I ever see him again, the projection will be a lie, but I tell myself this lie is no worse than any other projection a mother has forced upon a son.

I expect to start crying, but I am too sick and exhausted. I lie down in bed and stare at the ceiling, the white paint a road map of familiar cracks.

My husband and I met at the University. He lived in the Christian district with his agnostic parents. He converted to Islam so my father would approve the marriage. When I was away studying the Ju/wasi, he read extensively about Hinduism. After I became pregnant, he was circumcised and studied the Torah. When our son was born, my husband was baptized and found a life in Christ. My small doubts were a threat to his one very large doubt, which in turn became a threat to our son. During a one-month trip I made to the reserve, my husband sat down my son and told him that I had been accidentally struck by a poisoned arrow and that they couldn't get me to a medic in time. My son grieved, and his father explained how they'd start a new life somewhere else. He left me a note—the first thing to light up my screen when I got home and turned on my console— and then left for some religious commune on some orbital in some other stellar system, disappearing in a maze of digitized trails full of different names, different ID numbers, all for my son's own good.

So I am frozen in time with my son, who's still at the point where words are becoming sentences, where he can walk by my side, my outstretched hand resting so easily on his head.

We share so little. We speak Arabic. We veil ourselves in public. Women walk on one side of the street and men on the other. We pray to the same God, but we read to him from different books. We return home to our flats and speak with different friends, plug into different networks, and walk along our individual paths until not even love can hold us together.

I yearn for the desert reserve. I yearn for the steady struggle with life itself. To move about with the seasons, spreading out when the desert is lush with life, coming together in the dry days when cooperation is the same thing as survival. When the things that bring us together are clear and certain, so that on certain nights we will dance together under the night sky, and as the women clap and sing, men with n/um summon the boiling energy within them and reach out to heal everyone.

Here in Wadi all-Uyoun, on E-donya, all we have in common is the war.

No wonder a group of diverse people left for the desert and turned themselves into Ju/wasi, to have one life, one language, one shared daily struggle to take them through life's routine failures. Did a group of slazans do the same? Did they tire of the compromises that civilization imposes on their nature: the larger groups, the lesser solitude? Did they fly far away from where any slazan lived in order to start again, to be truly themselves?

The next morning, a new week begun, all sabbaths over, I shower and break my fast. I meet with ibn Haj at Fawiza's flat, and I accept. Ibn Haj is ecstatic. He plies me with food and coffee as quickly as Fawiza can prepare it. He laughs heartily and eats as much as he offers. He grows drunk on excitement and food and caffeine. He tells me how we will find the best-trained crew to fly the mission to this secret world. He tells me how we'll pick the best four scientists in the military to carry out research on the planet itself, to take down its natural history. He asks me how we could perhaps find a Ju/wa man or woman to accompany us, a true forager to interpret the behavior of other foragers. All this will happen once the general who ranks above ibn Haj approves his budget and his plan. The mission will make scientific history as well as peace. Ibn Haj's smile is as generous as his vision.

My fast has taken its toll. All this food, and hunger still gnaws at me.

Chapter Three

The Sixth Day

Among the people of the desert reserve, where Esoch had lived as a child, the sun was considered a death thing. After the rains ended, the sun drank the water from the summer pans, from the inside of berries and fruits, from the roots hidden beneath the ground. The sun drank so much that leaves turned brown, then shriveled, and human flesh wrinkled and withered before a man had stopped hunting or a woman had stopped bearing children. In space, where he had been trained, the sun was also a death thing. Its light may well have lit up outstretched solar cells and ignited the chlorophyll in the orbital farms, but its radiation toyed with the insides of cells and cut at the strands of double helix within.

But here, on this planet so distant from anything Esoch had known, the sun was a giver of life. It sparkled across the tiny waves that hushed each other when they ran up the beach where he crouched; it warmed his bruised and chilled body, naked now that he'd discarded his soiled briefs; and it drew out of the distant leaves bold colors rising from the trees' dark trunks. The sky's blue was deep, but he could no longer remember what kind of blue stretched over the veldt where he had lived his youth.

He stared at the sun a moment, and its brightness stung his eyes, left them glowing with a red afterimage that pulsated against black every time he closed them, and then he knew that this sun was the same kind of thing as the different sun that had sucked his life dry.

Alone, without comrade-in-arms, he crouched on the deserted beach, the same way he had crouched on the curved metal probe, cold water washing over his ankles with each wave: his thighs resting upon calves, his bottom almost touching his heels. The beach stretched out and curved away, until all that was in front of him was water of such depth that its presence here seemed permanent compared to the short-lived existence of the summer pans. Behind him the beach sloped upward, turned gray, grew long reeds, then shrubs, until finally, almost like an extensive wall, were the first trees of an endless forest, the reds, the oranges, and the yellows more imposing, more alien, than the twisted trunks of impossibly shaped trees would ever be. Several hundred meters to the west, the form of a hut, presumably empty, rose from the sand. In the other direction, barely visible, was another. Esoch had swum ashore, his strokes poorly learned and incompetent, more struggle than stroke, made worse because he lifted his head clear out of water to exhale and suck in new air and to look for the inhabitant of either hut, who he had been sure would come out to await him, spear in hand.

Nothing of the sort had happened.

Which only emphasized how alone he was.

Only once before in his life had he been this alone: when he had hiked out of the desert reserve, walking one night and one day, expecting to be devoured by a lion and, instead, arriving dehydrated and delirious at a small village full of people like himself, people who had left the reserve for some other kind of life.

How much longer was he going to wait? He had waited for the sun to rise above the horizon before he swam to shore, and he had waited for his skin to dry before he ate his rations. Now he waited for good measure before he unsealed the pack once again and pulled out what he needed. He dressed in supporter and onesuit, strapped wrist and ankle cuffs tight, pulled on the lightweight hikers, slipped the pistol onto one waisthook, the torch onto the second, the palmtalk onto the third, and the tracking disc onto the fourth.

He faced the water one last time. The decoy probe was drifting westward and toward the distant shore. The silk chutes had long ago filled with water and sunk from sight. The sun was high in the sky, and the morning breeze had warmed to the point where he could no longer feel it. Waves brought in the fresh smell of water, as if the air could surround and clean his personal scent of fear and exhaustion. Some kind of flying reptile circled above and flew on. A fish—at least he assumed it was a fish— leaped from the water and returned with a splash. Far off, a dark quadruped emerged from the brush and made its way to the lake to drink.

Esoch turned to confront the forest. Red, orange, yellow, and within, everything dark and green.

Somewhere, at least thirty kilometers in, was Pauline Dikobe's shuttle craft. He raised the palmtalk to his lips. Just to speak for a moment, to know if she was still alive. But there had been that flash of light, the disconnect, the abruptness of the parachutes. If there *was* a slazan warrior, he could pick up the transmission, locate Esoch, locate Pauline, if he didn't already know where she was. The captain had ordered radio silence. Jihad had assured him that she would make contact if Dikobe had reopened communications, if everything was all right. Jihad's voice had yet to sound in Esoch's ears.

He replaced the palmtalk on the waisthook and picked up the tracking disc.

It fit snugly in his hand, and he held it for a while, its screen blank. The maps he called up could take many forms, and their images had been derived from many sources. A topographical map flashed onto the screen. The landscape was white, and the thinnest of black lines outlined the slope of the hills. Thick blue lines, like veins on the back of a hand, branched off into thinner blue lines and spread across the screen: the river and its tributaries. Red lines wove along and through the black topographical ovals: possible pathways. All this data had been provided from images collected by the Raman probe. When it had flown overhead two years before, it had been winter, the ground visible enough for computers to estimate the contours of land hidden by shadow and snow. A touch of a switch, and a transparent layer of green—the forest canopy as recorded several mornings ago by the mapping satellites—overlay the other lines.

Near the top edge of the screen was the length of shore, split apart where the mouth of the river emptied into the lake. Near the bottom edge of the screen, a small dot represented Dikobe's shuttle. The dot was fluorescent green, brighter than the greens of the forest. The dot stood out in its solitude. Just before she had left the *Way of God*, when Esoch had tried to apologize for the bad feeling between them, Dikobe had faced him, her eyes dark and hard: "This is what I want," she had said. "I want to be as solitary as a slazan."

Now all Esoch needed was to make quick contact with the three mapping satellites above the horizon to triangulate his own position. If Jihad had been right, if a slazan warrior existed, if he had attacked and destroyed the *Way of God*, then surely he would have destroyed the remaining human-made satellites. If the satellites were gone, the current display wouldn't change.

His thumb pressed the tiny switch. A green dot appeared on the tiny screen's beach. A straight white line cut over beach, grass, trees, angling southwest to the fluorescent-green dot. The tiny readout window presented the measurement: 41.52 klicks.

Two things occurred to Esoch at once. One thought was this: at least three mapping satellites were still in place. What had created the blinding flash? If the *Way of God* still existed, was it out there now, playing a game of cat and mouse with a slazan warrior, maintaining radio silence to protect Esoch and his mission? Was Hanan still alive?

His second thought overlay and complicated the first: if things had gone as Jihad had originally planned them, the decoy probe would have landed within ten klicks of the shuttle, and he would have been there hours ago. Now he had a several-day hike through a forest he didn't know.

Yesterday, when he had been called in to be briefed by the captain, she had assured him that she thought Dikobe had shut things down, that the adaptation sickness had compounded her previous feelings. But Jihad respectfully disagreed. "The slazans have developed a rather sophisticated device for shutting down all electromagnetic transmissions. It works only for a moment; our backups take over right away. But you know, Lieutenant, it was enough for them to get to the colony in the Nueva España system. It might have been enough to shut down Pauline so someone could take over the shuttle."

Esoch thought Jihad was getting carried away. Like the captain, Esoch had been sure that Dikobe had shut down the shuttle. So sure, that he had barely thought of her when he and Hanan had shared a last meal, when Hanan had led him back to her cabin, when he had pulled Hanan close and told her how badly he wanted to stay with her. But now he began to wonder if Jihad had been right, if a slazan had made it to Dikobe. Or if the sickness had gotten progressively worse and had left Dikobe alone and dying. He was already beginning to think of Dikobe in the past tense, and now he wished he had loved her better.

*   *   *

The geography was simple. Five klicks west of where Esoch stood a wide river fed into the lake. Less than five meters from Dikobe's shuttle a tiny stream cut through the clearing, ran down a steep hill, nursed a tiny river that meandered northeast, which in turn flowed into the main river.

He called for a close-up of the area surrounding the green dot that represented his position. The tracking disc immediately overlaid the screen with scrawls of red. But the detail on the tiny screen was so dense that he couldn't make out the different pathways. He could follow the red lines through the forest until he hit the main river. If he could follow the paths, he would stick to them. If not, he would follow the river. It would take longer, perhaps, but even with the tracking disc he feared that he would end up walking in circles.

Esoch set the tracking disc to beep a warning if it detected a discrete motion within one hundred meters, and he set off. He cut across beach and across grassland, his feet slipping with the sand, forcing him to walk a touch harder to build his momentum, to take him through scrub and wood.

But the forest itself stopped him. He stood on its edge, and it towered above him, full of shadows within. It smelled cool, damp, and alive. Whatever surge of adrenaline had brought him here, whatever boost he had received from the glucose and sucrose in his rations, had all disappeared. Exhaustion and the new world overwhelmed him.

Insects might have six legs here and mammals had four and flying creatures had two, and the look of some of those animals might have analogs back on E-donya and Earth and Nueva España and long-dead New Hope, but larynxes, tongues, vocal cords, mouths and beaks and snouts were shaped to different proportions—the roars, the croaks, chirps, songs, gurgles, distant buzzings, were, taken together, so different from anything he had ever heard before that he could no longer remember how things should sound in the world he once knew.

He should have a comrade-in-arms at his side. Every training exercise, every simulation: he and Ghazwan, side by side, back to back, working together. If your comrade-in-arms was killed, you joined with someone else. Those who fought alone, died alone.

All he had was a tracking disc and a pistol. All that existed between him and Dikobe was this forest. The sun was high in the sky; it was midday. The forest canopy filtered out that light; inside was dark and cool. He started walking.

He pushed brush and branches aside. An abrupt rustling

startled Esoch. Next, a pocket of quiet. He waited for a moment. Everything was tight around him. There were so many places a slazan could hide, so many places from which he could launch an ambush. If the slazans had a contingent of warriors here, they could easily have laid mines.

He didn't believe there were mines, even though the fear persisted. He pressed forward, pushing away at branches and brush until he stepped out onto a path. He looked at the tracking disc. He couldn't get this path to correspond to a red line on a screen. He followed the path for a moment, but it took him east rather than southwest, where he wanted to intersect with the river.

He cut through the woods again. He told himself that there were no slazans waiting in ambush, that he was better off making as much noise as possible, that he didn't want to startle anything with jaws. Small animals scurried up trees, and birds or flying reptiles called out and flapped away. He looked up and could barely see traces of sky. Some treetops swayed with the breeze, but all was quiet where he stood. His green dot was closer to the river.

There was less brush now under the canopy. But soon he came upon a network of trails, and he walked through a number of clearings where the brush returned, reds and oranges and yellows and greens stretching out toward the sun.

In one clearing he stopped to examine a tree. Around the waist the tree had been notched, bark and tree carved out. Esoch looked up. The leaves were withered and pale. This tree was obviously dying. Scattered ash covered the ground.

The tree next to it hadn't been notched, but its branches and its trunk were full of tiny holes. He touched one of the holes, and something stung him. He was holding his finger while he looked. A tiny brown insect darted out one hole; a second from another; then a third. He tapped his boot against the bottom of the trunk. Suddenly there were several insects on his foot. He kicked his toe into the ground until they were off. Tree protectors. The tree must keep them well fed.

As he walked, he saw few protected trees, but he noticed more notched trees around clearings, more scattered ash, more and more grasses growing in the clearings, poking up through the nutrient gray. In a larger clearing sun poured in like water, giving the space a park-like effect: grassy areas surrounded by trees lush with color, and no brush.

He remembered the desert reserve: the fires walking toward

the horizon like a slow wind, burning up nettles and thorns, and from those ashes fresh grasses and berry plants grew, drawing the meat animals to food. He tried to imagine these slazans working in groups to set such fires, and he couldn't.

One large clearing stank of mildew and decay. At its edge was a shelter much like the ones on the beach, but it was collapsing, its reeds dark and rotting. Behind it, farther in the woods, was the former inhabitant's middens, separate piles for refuse and shit. There were bones in the refuse. The bones he could see had been cracked open, the marrow gone. Whoever lived here had eaten well.

He walked carefully, looked constantly, and tried to take in everything. He landmarked each spot of interest on the tracking disc with a small violet dot. He rehearsed in his mind the things he would tell Dikobe. If she was alive and well, if the *Way of God* still existed, he wanted to have this data as a peace offering, a way to shape their relationship for the next two hundred days, to make himself something more than Dikobe's aide, or, as he had once overheard: Dikobe's boy.

But the doubts were as persistent as insects. He couldn't communicate with Dikobe. He hadn't heard from Jihad. And it became harder and harder to keep an eye on everything in the forest. When he had walked through the desert reserve, plucking berries or gathering nuts with others in a //gxa grove, or stalking a kudu with his father and a cousin, or simply moving with family from one encampment to another, he had walked with secure knowledge: he'd known which bushes had thorns and which snakes looked like branches; he'd known how to avoid lions and jackals and where to find water when the heat became impossible.

But what did he know about this forest? Had the dark animal that drank from the lake been a predator? Did it take an interest in bipeds? What insects liked to land or crawl onto slazans and take a bite? Which plants released irritating oils, which ones protected themselves with thistle and thorns, and which ones leaked juices that might ease the bite of a wound? The landscape became too much for him, and a kind of sleepy autopilot kept trying to take over.

His green dot had almost met the blue line of the river when he came to another clearing. At the edge was a quiet shelter, and in front were two separate fires, both with blackened logs and wisps of white rising into the air. Someone lived here. A tiny beep sounded in his head: motion detected by the tracking disc.

Esoch gazed about, saw nothing. He watched the shelter. Was someone inside? He imagined the slazan crouched there, something sharp in his hands, ready to spring.

He gave the clearing a wide berth as he walked around it. The tracking disc didn't sound again. No one came for him. If Esoch had been the slazan, he would have hidden, he would have hoped danger would have passed by. Why had he expected something different from the actual slazan?

Three hundred meters away was the river. The water was wide and moved with the ease of its width. It was dark green and sparkled where the sun touched it. Up ahead the river tumbled and fell over a line of rocks, and the sound of water rushing, falling upon water, eased a tension that had become so common that he had forgotten it was tension.

He walked until he felt he was far enough away from the last shelter before settling against a nearby tree. It was then he noticed the scratches on his hand, felt their minor stings. He opened his pack to remove his dinner: one ration and a drink packet. Eating rations here, by the river, made him feel like it was a training exercise, that all this would end. He missed Ghazwan, the talk, the teasing. He longed for company. With someone at his side he would have walked farther, feared less. If he had been a slazan, this hike would have been easy.

He was still thirsty, and the flow of nearby water accentuated the need. His back against the tree, leaning into his own exhaustion, Esoch remembered past thirsts. His older sister crouching on stone, her hands lowering the hollowed ostrich egg into the small waterhole, the bubbles of air rising to the surface. His father leaning over the hollow of a broad //gxa tree, cupping water, bringing it to his lips. His mother handing him a bitter root; the air was hot, and the wetness of the fiber spread across his dry tongue.

There were other memories, and he didn't want them called forth. He knelt by the river and rinsed his hands in the water, splashed the sweat off his face, and resisted the temptation to drink. He checked his tracking disc. The straight white line that connected the two green dots now measured 31.5 klicks. He reshouldered his pack and moved on, this time staying close to the river.

During the last month of the voyage, when he had returned to sleeping in his own cabin, Esoch often wound up in the converted armory that served as an observation lab. He found it easier to talk with the scientists than with the ship's crew, and he liked to sit next to Hanan and watch her at work.

He really had nothing much else to do, since he had no role on the ship other than as Dikobe's aide, and she had given him only one task. The general had provided her with a tanned antelope hide so she could emerge from the shuttle dressed more like a native than an astronaut. She wanted him to fashion a pubic apron, then a chi !kan, one she could fasten around shoulder and waist and use to gather like any Ju/wa woman. "Make one," she said, "as good as the one you would have made for your wife." The only time she had called him back to the loading dock and the shuttle was to help her with the final inventory.

In the mornings he sat on the metallic floor of his cabin and with metal adze and knife gave shape to the chi !kan. Against the bulkhead a mat was unrolled, and there lay Ghazwan, his pockmarked face at rest, his breathing raising and lowering the blanket with a gentle ease. He had turned the image back on when he'd returned to sleep on his own mat.

In the afternoons he could often be found in the lab, sitting by Hanan's workstation, and he had been sitting in that spot when the first images from the shuttle's eyes had been transmitted to the lab screens. On the second day he and the four scientists watched quietly, in awe, when one large slazan male entered the clearing, then turned away. Dikobe ID'ed him, and the four turned to Esoch for an explanation when a Ju/wa name appeared on the screen: Hxome. "I knew two men with that name," he said. "Pauline's probably thinking of the one who was called Hxome Lion because he once took meat away from a lion." The second slazan who came down was a veritable giant, and he ambled into the clearing, glared at the shuttle, then ambled away. Dikobe named him //koshe. "His visits were always short," Esoch said. "He was always boasting, and everyone found him insufferable."

Then a third slazan male came down. Except for the lack of throat patches, he was a smaller, younger version of the first two. His hair was colored bright red. ("It must be a dye," came Dikobe's voice over the speaker. "No one's seen a slazan with red hair.") This slazan walked down the hill with a large metallic object cradled in his arms, a strap around his neck taking some of the weight. "There are no throat patches," Dikobe said. "This slazan's female." The name *N!ai* appeared on the screen.

"Who's Nai?" Hanan asked, pronouncing the name without a click.

"It's a woman's name."

"Is something wrong, Esoch?"

"No," he said, hating the lie. "Pauline's just using the names of everyone I used to know."

The slazan stopped several meters from the shuttle, unstrapped the object, and placed it upon the blackened ground. The object was obviously battered, its metal surface pockmarked and discolored. It looked like a giant version of the thumb piano Esoch had played as a youth, except this one had three rows of keys, which the slazan —Esoch was sure he was male—began to play. The music sounded awful, and Esoch couldn't hear any logic in the progression of notes. Dikobe, her voice still coming from the speaker, was talking with Jihad on the bridge. The instrument must be something that the original colonists had brought with them, but why had a portable piano been allowed to survive the generations whereas everything else the locals carried was native to the environment? Jihad had the ship's intelligence do a library search of known slazan instruments; she also had it analyze the music, listen for tonal quality, for the mathematical structure of the relationship between the notes.

Esoch lost track of the conversation. He was listening more and more to the music, which began to jar at his nerves, making him anxious, irritable. But at the same time he was in awe of what this red-haired musician was doing. Something large and impossible had landed in the middle of this man's life, and he was playing music to it.

That night Hanan sipped wine, and he drank tea in the tiny ship's café, and he told her how he had come to own a sleek, tiny tin piano. He had been as tall as his father's chest the day they both had gone to track a wildebeest his father had shot the day before. They had found the animal lying upon the ground, and he had gotten too close. It kicked out, cutting a gash across his leg. After a day or so the gash began to bleed white, and the healers had danced hard, had called up the n/um within them, but the white blood remained. His father finally hiked alone to the edge of the reserve and brought back a medico, his skin turned red by the sun. The medico did not think the young man would live, and then several days later, when the heat burned through him and clean sweat cooled his clammy skin, the medico gifted him with a thumb piano that had been made outside the reserve, its metal smooth like all things made by the reds, the notes evenly spaced, having a sound unlike that of thumb pianos people had made of wood, bone, and animal sinew. Esoch told

Hanan how much he had loved playing that thumb piano, how its music had comforted him on nights when he'd felt overwhelmed by being with others and doing everything you had to do to keep everyone else happy.

Afterward Esoch walked Hanan back to her cabin, and they stood their in the night-lit corridor and said nothing. The wall projected a full moon rising above a minaret. He wanted to lean forward to kiss her; he knew she had a husband and a child awaiting her return, and he didn't know how to interpret her silence, the look in her eyes. Months ago he had stood here just like this, and he had stepped back and said good night. This night she looked to him with the same eyes and took his hand and led him into her cabin.

Her kisses were warm; there was none of Pauline's urgency. She called him Esoch, not ≠oma, and he told himself that in a day or two he would tell Hanan who N!ai was. When they were naked, Hanan did not ask about the deep blue lines along his chest and arms and beneath his left shoulder blade; instead she traced the length of the scar along his leg.

Did the *Way of God* still even exist?

He walked and he walked, and his mind established its own pace. He followed the river, wove his way around trees, climbed over fallen trunks, walked thin trails between tall bushes, and he remembered that time he had almost kissed Hanan and had decided not to; he remembered the nights that followed, the longing he could feel in his skin, the way she laughed but no longer reached out to touch his hand, and the night Dikobe had come to his cabin, how they had talked, how her palm against his cheek, the simple longed-for touch, made it easy to lean toward her.

But it was no longer Dikobe's face he saw, but N!ai's. She was smiling. His fingers touched the deep-blue tattoos, the zebra lines across each side of her face, the bold line cutting down across her forehead. They alone were in a //gxa grove, the low trees shading them from the sun; her chi !kan, now lying on the ground, was full of the trees' nuts; his leather bag, which lay nearby, was bloated with them. N!ai giggled, averted her eyes, then removed her pubic apron. This was the first time she had gone gathering with him alone, and her sister had joked with both of them about what kind of food they'd really be eating, and her female cousin had joked, loud enough for him to hear, about how they must be in search of wild honey. Some older women laughed loudly, and he had been afraid that N!ai would change her mind.

The river thinned out, and water rushed loudly over rocks, a sound much like that of a distant fountain. He did not want to think about N!ai, that part of his life was gone; even though then and now were separated by a year and some months, his time with N!ai was as distant as his childhood.

Now, crossing through an open clearing, where everything was cast orange with the setting sun, then moving under trees, where everything took on a cool grayness, he couldn't understand what had happened, how the anger had taken hold of him, how if he had given the thumb piano away, if he had stopped believing that its keys were meant for his fingers alone, then he would still be on the reserve, N!ai might have a child, and someone else would worry about Hanan on the *Way of God* and Dikobe in her shuttle.

Exhaustion tugged at him. Looking ahead, he could see the way the land sloped in fits and starts, but as he'd followed the river, the uphill gradient had been invisible except to his calves and thighs. He wanted to rest for a moment, but when he stopped, the world wavered.

He started to walk again to put an end to the dizziness. Something large crashed through the forest. Far off, he heard the long call of a slazan male: starting low, increasing to a quavering bellow, then fading. Esoch felt a palpable chill, as if a cold wind had slipped down his spine. He had to move on, but even with the torch, how far would he get? He had to be sensible. If he didn't rest, he'd collapse.

But where to sleep? If he stayed on the ground, he was at the mercy of anything that slithered, crawled, or walked. He could build a fire, which would keep away some of these potential guests, but he didn't want to invite the attention of any local slazans when he was at his most vulnerable.

He almost walked past the nest, but it was too big not to register. He turned to have another look. It was about as high off the ground as a man is tall. The nest appeared empty.

He could always sleep in a tree. Human evolution, Dikobe had told him in one of her many postcoital ramblings, was the movement out of the trees and onto the ground: nests under the bottom were replaced by roofs over the head. He might as well go from primal to primate.

Esoch stepped closer. The nest was shaped of vines and some kind of reed that had been bundled tightly into thick rope.

The two materials were interwoven in such an intricate way that he couldn't help but raise his finger to trace the patterns through the air. The shelter near the river had been built with equal care. Ju/wa shelters were built quickly, if at all. During dry seasons sometimes a large stick was pounded into the ground to declare an area as home and to divide the male and female sides of the fire. The more elaborate huts, made to withstand the rainy season, could be built in a day and would be abandoned within weeks.

This nest had been built in days, not hours; it had been built to last, or it had been built to impress. Who had built it? Who lived in it? It curved gently, like two hands cupped together. Did a woman and her infant reside here, safe from nighttime predators prowling the ground? Would the owner return tonight? Esoch didn't want to find out.

He found a thick, sturdy tree twenty or so meters away, and after breaking off a section of a shrub and using it to brush away the debris, he sat down and waited. He became aware of the sweat coating his body, clogging his pores, of the dirt in his onesuit. The exhaustion was tremendous, but so was the need to keep moving. He had to make it to Dikobe's ship. To sit here, to contemplate sleep, was . . .

He opened his eyes with a start, and he could not see a thing. There was this beeping in his head, and he did not know where he was. His back was against a tree, its roots pressing into his bottom, and his palms and fingers could make out the moist ground. Had he sleepwalked away from the face of the huts? Hadn't N!ai noticed him leaving? Hadn't anyone noticed? There was always someone up, like Debe talking with Old Gau or //khuga plucking at the five strings of her //gwashi to ease her constant sadness. But the beeper was getting more incessant, and he became Esoch again, and he knew something was getting closer. He fumbled for the torch hanging from a waisthook. He panned from right to left, the torchlight illuminating tree trunks, leaves and skeletons of new bushes, and the hint of water from the nearby river, and then, eyes. In the light they reflected back as deep red, which for the barest moment caused him to think that the eyes belonged to a //gangwasi, a spirit of the dead, his father, perhaps, here to take him, but the light shone on the rest of the animal, a sleek creature, dark as the night, its snout long and pointed. The animal was crouched, low to the ground, and Esoch knew it would pounce before he could reach for his pistol.

But instead the animal backed away a few steps, then ran off into the forest, the leaves whispering after its body.

The nest, some twenty meters away, now appeared a more attractive place to sleep. Torchlight showed it to be empty. The light also revealed something he hadn't noticed before. Four spikes of wood had been driven into the tree trunk. Esoch planted his foot on the lowest spike. There was room enough for just one foot. He grasped the third spike with his hand and pulled himself up. For a moment his head spun. He wasn't quite sure where to put his other foot or his other hand: the spikes were spread out awkwardly.

He finally made it to the top and sat down upon the closest branch. He flicked on the torch. The ground seemed farther away than it should. The dizziness returned; his head felt like it would float away from his body. All he wanted to do was sleep.

He scanned the nest with the light. It looked like a broad, thatched bowl. He could already see himself curled up inside it, fast asleep. He lowered his foot into it. The thatching whispered against his weight. A line of thatching moved. He shifted the light, caught the movement. It looked like a snake. Its colors, differing shades of brown, blended well with the thatching.

His vision wavered with exhaustion. He wondered how many shots it would take before he hit the creature. It seemed a whole lot simpler to grab it by the tail, flick it away, and let the force of the gesture carry the snake head and the fangs away from him. All he wanted was for the snake to be out of the nest. All he wanted to do was sleep. Before considering if this was the wisest move, Esoch already had grasped the snake's tail. He did not bend his wrist the right way, or did not throw his arm out fast enough, because fangs caught hold of the onesuit fabric near his stomach. Everything happened so fast that he first dropped the torch, and then, disoriented, he reached up to grasp the middle of the snake to tug harder.

It wasn't quite a snake. It had tiny legs, with sharpened ends that could dig in for purchase. The pain in his hand was immense. He stumbled back, hit the cusp of the nest, slid down. There was a pain, like something clasping shut, in his belly. His free hand, before his brain could consider the wisdom of the move, grabbed at the head biting into belly, laid fingers under jaw, and pressed thumb into brain. He squeezed until the jaws let loose. Then he swung his arm away, in an arc, letting the creature go, hearing it slide through the brush and strike softly against the ground.

He lay there in the nest, stunned, breathing heavily, the torchlight illuminating the thatching opposite him. He retrieved the light and examined his wounds. A line of blood creased his palm. There was blood and torn skin on his belly. He remembered watching his mother take a club to a black mamba, pounding against the ground until the snake moved only when the club struck the ground. He remembered his uncle blind for days after a cobra had spit venom in his eyes. He stared at the purpled swelling, the blood dripping two tiny rivers. How could he have been so stupid?

Esoch lay back against the rim of the nest. The shape of it cupped the curve of his back. He wondered how the creature had made its way up into the nest; then, if it was poisonous. If the snake's venom was toxic, then he needed the creature itself for the antivenin. The creature was down there, and he was up here. He should be worried. He should be missing the med-kit. He should be telling himself that a venom evolved to kill animals on this planet might not poison him at all.

Instead, Esoch fell asleep wondering how long it would take him to die so that Dikobe could have the solitude she'd said she wanted.

The following is excerpted from a draft of Pauline Dikobe's memoirs, a project she started and abandoned while the Way of God *made its return trip to E-donya E-talta.*

During the week that follows my decision, I am a divided soul. At work, among people, I am at a loss. I don't know what to say in class, so I fall back on the perfunctory clichés of the discipline. In a series of meetings, I stare at walls rather than look at graphs and charts while several colleagues work to finish a paper on the cultural genetics of isolated utopian groups. In the streets I try to look straight ahead, like I'm deep in thought.

There were three of us during the prewar days. Judith, Lila, and I. I have lunch with Judith because we share lunch once a week. She wants to know what's wrong. She wants to know what drove me to her flat last week. I lie. I tell her I'm tired of solitude and celibacy. I have tea twice that week with Lila. She wants to hear about people at the Institute, what their latest research is like, if they're sleeping with anyone. After she left the Institute, Lila didn't talk to me for years, and for years I felt like she'd betrayed me. She should have trusted me to do good work at the Institute without violating any of the ethical guidelines. Now, staring at a cup of chamomile tea, hoping it will ease the grinding in my stomach, I tell Lila all the gossip, even though I can't tell her the juiciest piece of news around. I tell myself I've done nothing wrong, but I feel like I've betrayed her.

But once I'm alone in my flat, I come alive. I make lists of questions about subsistence, social structure, leadership, kinship. On my desk I have an image of the first two generations of the Ju/wasi. African, Arab, Hindu adults, wearing breechclouts or chi !kans, and among them, small, golden-skinned children, naked, eager to run. I keep looking up at them as I map out a schedule for the two hundred days, and I tell the Judith who lives within me that she's wrong, that this can be made to work.

On the day of the Christian sabbath, ibn Haj arrives unannounced at my door. I veil myself before letting him in, and we drink our coffee gingerly, both well mannered enough to know how to drink without wetting our veils or revealing our lips. It's awkward. No other person has ever sat before in my flat with a veil on, but I don't want his smile; I want the courtesy that exists in a public space. I don't want his easy charm to take me in.

He handles inconsequential pleasantries with great skill. He knows where my parents live and asks how they are; he must know about my errant husband and son, because he asks no questions that could lead there. He never hints about being more informal, about how uncomfortable we both must be wearing these veils. I wonder if his honor is that of an honorable man, or that of a skilled manipulator who knows that honor has its place in winning the hearts of others.

He finally gets to the heart of the matter. "The General who oversees special projects has considered everything with great care." He speaks the words so carefully that I am sure he will tell me the project has been canceled. I am relieved. "He considers such research to be vitally important, but he is not convinced that the strategic outcome would be as momentous as we had concluded. He wants the mission to go ahead, but he doesn't want to fund it as extensively as we had hoped. He wants to insure that whatever efforts we make do not detract from the goals of the war effort."

"He's not interested in negotiation," I say. I want this general's attitude explained. I know ibn Haj will tell me nothing that would make his superior look less than sensitive, less than intelligent.

"He is interested in negotiating from a position of strength."

"He wants the slazans to surrender."

Ibn Haj says nothing for a moment. He's uncomfortable. He can't save this moment with a smile. "The General"—he uses the title like a name—"prefers a settlement that works to our advantage, that is true. But he does want data at hand if slazan and human decide to build a table and dine together."

And to make sure we know our table manners for such dining, the General has done the following. He has requisitioned a warship that does not have an outstanding war record. He has approved limited but substantial funding to convert a diplomatic shuttle into an anthropological hut equipped with all the necessary devices. He has allocated moneys to design and land four scientific probes on the planet's surface in lieu of sending four military scientists and converting the armory into a rather expensive laboratory. He has agreed to send one civilian ethnographer and provide her a private cabin as long as the pair of crew members removed from the ship are those with the lowest recorded scores for social adaptability, and as long as the qualified anthropologist has never participated in any publication, symposium, or public activity that aimed to demoralize the war effort. The General granted Ibn Haj the courtesy to make a counter-proposal, but it did no good. The General didn't believe there was anything an anthropologist could find out that would make a difference one way or another in the way the war was fought.

Ibn Haj waits a long while before he asks if I still want to go. He lets the anger simmer. He lets the thoughts percolate. He waits until I too despise the General, until I too want to convince the General of how wrong he is.

We plan the research during the next week. Fawiza arranges for several colleagues to cover my classes; she was vague about why I wouldn't be in. I leave messages for three of my colleagues; they'll have to work on the data without me. I contact Judith's and Lila's computers at times I know they'll be in class or in conference, and I tell them I won't be able to meet for lunch or tea.

The planning sessions are held in my flat in the University quarter. The building is full of scholars, who live their days in classrooms, offices, and cafés, whose children and spouses have school and work to attend, leaving the building virtually empty. Ibn Haj does not want to be seen much around the Institute or Fawiza's flat; he does not want me to be seen near any government building; he does not want easy rumors to start. At first the secrecy disturbs me. Closed doors hide sin, my mother used to say. Then the secrecy thrills me. Closed drapes prevent a neighbor's gossip. It all depends on the metaphor you choose.

I expect us to discuss context on the first day. Who are these foragers? Where did they come from? What challenges are posed to foragers living in a woodland environment? But ibn Haj is a practical man. We have only one week for planning. I will have over 150 days to refine these plans. He spreads a clear screen out on my kitchen table, the only table in the flat, and hooks it up. Soon we are looking at computer-generated maps of the regions where the slazans burned their fires. Ibn Haj wants to know where I want to land the shuttle.

"Away from the population. I can hike back and forth."

Ascherman disagrees. He wants me to land near the lake, where the population is densest. "I would assume the tensions over resources would be greatest. We would see how conflicts start and how they are resolved."

I start to argue, but Fawiza raises a hand for silence. She is looking closely at the maps, calling up actual images, calling up topographical pictograms of the area, then going back to the map itself. She says, "I see no clearings for Pauline to land close to the shore, and the beach is out of the question. As access to water and fish, it's prime real estate, and we won't want to disturb it."

Ibn Haj suggests a compromise. I land about thirty klicks from the coast. The population is sparser there, but not as scattered as on the fringes.

"You can't land a shuttle right in the middle of where they live," I say. "These are a population of sapients. They will see this giant thing come from the sky and land in their territory. Out will step a kind of creature they've never seen before. They will have to adjust their entire worldview to accommodate the shuttle's presence. What we see will have more to do with a change in worldview than in how they normally live their lives."

"Again, won't that work to our advantage?" asks Ascherman. "If they arc under stress, won't we see more of conflict and, hence, won't we get a better look at how they resolve those conflicts?"

I want to say vicious things. I look at my hands and force my voice to sound even, to sound flat. "This is not the kind of anthropology you asked me to do."

"Pauline's right," says ibn Haj. He then goes on at length about why I am right. I expect Ascherman to shake his head, but instead he listens to ibn Haj as if the man were a font of wisdom. I don't listen as carefully. I know the purpose of such praise; the word *but* will soon follow all the kind words. But, ibn Haj explains, sounding appropriately mournful, there is the shuttle craft itself. The hull will be covered with a multitude of sensors. The lockers will be filled with the kind of devices an ethnographer dreams about. The shuttle's small intelligence will be led through some very expensive simulations that will give it the ethnographic experience it needs to organize and classify all the incoming data that the devices and hull sensors will collect.

I repeat myself. I argue against it. I feel my face heat up. Ibn Haj listens attentively and apologizes profusely. The General wants substantial hard data, collected by diverse instrumentation, to supplement and substantiate whatever data I collect. "You are right, of course," he says, "but we have to live with other people's decisions. You, however, should decide where the best place to land the shuttle will be."

So I choose an empty clearing with a tiny stream that runs through it, one that appears to overlook the hills leading down to the lake. Everyone thinks it's a splendid location. It's a hollow victory.

That night I turn off the phone because I know Judith will call. She leaves a message on my computer: Is everything okay?

*   *   *

The next day we discuss contact.

An ethnographer goes into the field with permission. You go with the permission of the government who claims sovereignty over the area, and you conduct work with permission of those among whom you live, those whose secrets you will scatter to the academic winds.

"Permission," ibn Haj says, "is not the issue. You will be new. First they have to get used to something new sitting in one of their clearings. Then they have to get used to a new resident."

The whole morning is spent on habituation. Animals being observed by an ethologist have to learn the habit of accepting the new observer as an innocuous part of the environment. They then continue with their routine lives. But these slazans will have their own curiosities. They will want to know what I am. "The worldview thing you were talking about," says ibn Haj.

"Perhaps," Fawiza suggests, "she should step out naked."

I expect both men to leer.

Ibn Haj says, "If they have any standards of modesty, such a display may be an unnecessary offense."

"Well," I say, "why don't we bring along a male ethnographer, and we can show the slazans everything they might like to know." My smile is forced, my face is warm, flushed.

Ascherman looks away. Fawiza concentrates on her flatscreen. Ibn Haj smiles. "The General is devout, and very conservative. He wouldn't approve."

Alone that night, I try to imagine ibn Haj standing before the General. I try to imagine how his air of authority—even when he defers to me, he does so with an air of easy command—transmutes into some other quality when he speaks with his superior. Does he change his tone when trying to convince? Does he smile and avert his eyes more often? Does he wear his veil? And when the General, in very polite language, tells ibn Haj he is wrong, does my general return to his quarters and seethe with anger?

The next day is endless and awful.

On my computer are five messages from Judith. She called every hour on the hour. No one has seen you.

Please call. I want to know that you are fine. There's one
message from Lila: I heard a great tidbit about Fawiza
Muneef's new love—a military man. Let's drink some
tea and have some laughs.

Ibn Haj brings coffee and pastry for the morning
and specially prepared saffron chicken for lunch. He
pours us coffee while he talks to me. "I've arranged the
workshop couch, and we've requisitioned the necessary
tapes so you can learn pan-slazan. When do you think
you'll want to make verbal contact with the natives?"

"I suppose when someone is close enough that I
don't have to shout."

Fawiza asks, "What will you do if no one in this
population speaks pan-slazan?"

At this point it becomes obvious how little ibn Haj
truly knows, how much of his working knowledge came
out of sitting through several workshops on human evolution and ethnography. He says, "Won't they speak
pan-slazan? Their language is hardwired into the brain,
isn't it?"

Everything in Ascherman's face that had been held
taut and alert for each of ibn Haj's words now drops
away. Ibn Haj's words reveal a popular misconception,
one that Ascherman must have thought the general was
beyond.

"Isn't pan-slazan like Nostratic?" he asks. "It's
their first language, but it hasn't changed into many
other languages."

"The generalized structure of language," I say, "is
structured by biology. Vocabulary can't be. Even birds
have to learn the songs they sing."

I think this will be enough. Ibn Haj is nodding. But
Ascherman has to explain that Nostratic is not really the
first language; that notion is a centuries-old fiction;
Nostratic is a language created from both the sounds all
languages have in common and the concepts that all cultures have in common; that it starts with root ideas from
foraging cultures, adds on agricultural notions, then
industrial, then informational, until you have a pan-
human language useful for all intercultural communication. Fawiza then has to add on: No human has ever
been to one of the slazan homeworlds; who's to say there
aren't dozens of slazan languages?

We go on like this all day because, of course, Fawiza's very good question is unanswerable. I will learn pan-slazan and hope there's enough structure and similar vocabulary that I can learn whatever the natives are speaking.

"There's a lot we can learn from just watching," Fawiza says.

"Is that true with sapients?" Ascherman asks. "Isn't half of human life based on how we interpret others' actions?"

I recite, "There's the action and there's the intent; there's the interpretation of the recipient of the action, and there's the interpretation of the audience, and finally there's the response to the action, all of which is influenced by the context of the previous relationships of every actor involved." I shake my head wearily, dramatizing my exhaustion with all this talk. "I'm hungry. Can we go out for dinner?"

Ibn Haj decides both that it's inappropriate for us all to be seen together and that if I was to be seen with anyone, it would raise fewer questions if I was seen with Ascherman. The two of us go into the Christian quarter to a Latino restaurant, which in keeping with our mood is dimly lit. Ascherman is concerned what his wife will think if he is seen dining alone with an attractive woman. He looks disconcerted by the cliché but doesn't know how to recover. I don't say anything, but I, too, don't want to be seen by anyone. I don't know what I'd say to Judith or Lila if they were to see me here. But Judith works on her research at night, and Lila works on her husband. I find I miss their conversation. Ascherman and I have little to say, for the only thing that binds us together can't be discussed in public.

The next three days in my flat go better. I call up the notes I took from the previous week, and we start going through the various issues. I want to chart out subsistence. A solitary animal can provide for its own subsistence if it is vegetarian. But slazans, like humans, are poorly designed to compete with lions and jackals. Survival requires cooperation.

Among the Ju/wasi, marriage is the central agreement of cooperation. The majority of the calories are provided by the wife, who gathers for the members of her nuclear family and any visitors to her fire. The meat is provided by the husband, who hunts large animals in small groups, taking advantage of the shared knowledge of men. A newly wed husband will live with his wife's family until several children are born. He will prove he is a good enough hunter to provide for their daughter, and he will provide a share of meat, which his father-in-law can share among his kin, reinforcing bonds with his many family members.

We know that although slazans prefer their solitude, they can work cooperatively; otherwise, there would not be the rambling cities they build, nor the spaceships, nor the lengthy war they fight so well. But how do they go about insuring such cooperation? Who gathers the fruit and tubers? Who hunts the meat? Who tans the skins and who makes such fine designs on them? Who gathers the wood and builds the fire? Is there division of labor by sex? What reinforces it? What is exchanged? What does the individual provide for herself? Where do they establish residence? Most foraging populations have to move through an area during the course of the year: how do we identify individuals and follow their movement? Do we offer gifts marked with isotopes and see how often those gifts, if they are accepted, change hands over the study period?

"What about leadership?" asks ibn Haj.

"Simple foragers tend to be pretty egalitarian," I say. "Leadership is ad hoc. They listen to whose opinion they trust. But they spend a lot of time teasing each other mercilessly. No one's allowed to rise above anyone else. You get leaders with intensification: you need to do something big—build a large weir, chase animals off a cliff, organize a war party—and a single coordinator becomes necessary. It usually happens when the population is denser, when you have to get more out of the territory you inhabit."

"Perhaps," Ascherman says, "a good reason to land near the shore, where the population is densest."

"We have to remember," Fawiza says, "that these are slazans. They are not Ju/wasi in alien skin. They are not humans with a different language. We know of no slazan word for *marriage*. We know of no slazan word for *father*. We know little about child rearing, except

that it seems to be the mother's task. And the words for
leadership in pan-slazan are ambiguously translated at
best. Let's make sure we schedule the research so Pauline is open to new questions. If she's over-scheduled,
she'll tend to see along the biases of the research plan.
Anthropologists who look for leaders find leaders. Anthropologists who look for dominance hierarchy can always find it. After she gets habituated, Pauline will have
less than two hundred days for her actual study. We
want her to find what is really there."

I continue to have dinner with Ascherman because
I need to be free of my flat's confines. We talk theory.
We talk about the Raman probes. We talk about what
it's like being a Jew married to a Muslim. He tells me
stories about occasions when both sides of the family are
brought together. I wish Judith were here; she'd love
Ascherman's stories of casual misunderstandings, covert
animosities, and unexpected friendships. I tell him of my
parents living in the village where my father grew up, of
my brothers who live in the same village, and of my sisters who are married and living where their husbands
were children. "How out of place you must feel," he
says, "when you go home."

"Oh, no," I say. "I love going home. It's a great life
they live, as long as I don't have to live it."

At night I look at experiential programs for the
shuttle's intelligence. We are going to be collecting so
many images that the intelligence will have to be adept
at classifying, sorting, and analyzing, but the day when
Fawiza and I started talking about multivariate analysis
of variance and discriminate analysis and cluster analysis, ibn Haj threw up his hands and told us he'd trust
our decision. So after saying good night to Ascherman, I
go through reviews, preview simulations, and the like,
trying to sleep at night, but sleep is impossible. There
are too many things to think about, to consider. I want
the research impeccable. I want it done right. I want to
produce an ethnography that no one can misuse.

I don't check my computer for messages.

On the Muslim sabbath ibn Haj leaves us for over
an hour to go to the mosque. Fawiza and I argue extensively about which programs to choose for the shuttle's

intelligence. Ascherman is at a loss as to what to say. Fawiza and I have done so much research that we're committed to our choices. Each system has its failings, and we despise the failings belonging to the systems the other has chosen.

When ibn Haj returns, he asks if we can take all the systems. When he finds they're incompatible, produced by rival firms who don't want you to meld various versions, he says, "Let's go with what Pauline wants. She has to use the system for the duration of her stay."

Fawiza sulks after that, a surprising reaction for one with so much prestige. Our discussions falter because they're all about specific research plans, and Fawiza is the one who has guided dozens of ethnographers into hundreds of different field situations. A pall is cast over the entire day. We've been in the same room for far too long. There are huge gaps of silence. We stare at the long itineraries and charts we've devised. The last two months still have to be accounted for.

The pounding at the door doesn't come as a surprise. It fits in with the tone of the day. Ibn Haj switches off the clear screen on the kitchen table and goes into the bathroom. I open the door. It's Judith. I don't know what to say. I don't know how to keep her out. She's hugging me, talking about how worried she's been. There had been that upset two weeks ago, and last week I had looked so depressed, and no one had seen me this week ... well, she had expected the worst ... and then she stops. She sees Ascherman—"Hello, Dovid"—and then she sees Fawiza, and then she turns to me. "I guess I don't quite fit in here."

Ascherman has to be with his family that night for the sabbath. Fawiza has to catch up on work at the Institute. Ibn Haj offers to stay, and I almost say yes. The solitude of the flat closes in on me, and I call Judith.

She doesn't say hello. "Are you a Kiplinger now?"

I don't know what to say.

"Don't lie to me," she says.

I nod. The screen goes blank. I should have lied.

Ascherman isn't there the next day out of respect for the sabbath. Ibn Haj asks me a lot about Judith. He sounds solicitous and concerned. He knows how horrible it is to break with a friend. But he asks far too many questions. Then, as we get back to work, he begins to defer to my opinion. The next two months of research begin to look exactly as I want them. I start to hear Judith's voice: *This is how he eases your doubts, this is how he hooks you in.* Ibn Haj doesn't understand Fawiza's very esoteric but very good objections. I'm tired of objections, even good ones, especially good ones. "I'm weeks behind on Institute work," Fawiza finally says. "Do you really need me here?"

On the Christian sabbath Ascherman returns. He looks awful. His skin is pale. There are dark circles under his eyes. He hasn't shaved. Ibn Haj conducts business as if everything's fine. I want to ask Ascherman what's wrong. I expect to hear that his wife is upset about the hours he's been keeping.

We go over the final plans. Tomorrow I go up to a military orbital while the last of the requisitions are made. Fawiza will announce a last-minute grant that will send me to do some studies on As-Sabr and a Christian utopian community orbiting Earth.

There are several clear weeks left in the schedule. I want to hike out to the empty village. I want to do a thorough inventory. I want to know if these slazans were a group of primal utopians.

"What does it matter how they started?" Ascherman asks. "They're there and trying to live out their lives. What else matters?"

Ibn Haj looks to Ascherman as if his face will reveal the source of such a strange question. After a moment the general once again okays my plans.

It is my last night in Wadi al-Uyoun. Ibn Haj is off finalizing plans for my departure. Fawiza hugs me good-bye and wishes me luck. Ascherman takes me to the Latino restaurant in the Christian quarter. "I guess this is your farewell party," he says.

It isn't much of a party. Dovid drinks too much wine and tells me what a mistake he's made. He was the one years ago who convinced the Muslim-Hindu Investment Developers to fund this Raman probe. When the probe came back, he didn't have the funds to analyze the data, so he created a secret budget, siphoned off funds from other projects. When he found a humansafe world with a colony of slazans, he hid the knowledge from the investors, who had a legal right to it, and instead spent days looking into the reputation of various generals to see who would use this data in the best way.

"They confiscated the data yesterday," he says. "The Muslim-Hindu Investment Developers gave it to the military in return for several key contracts. It's all locked away. No one at our center has access to a bit of it."

"That's not surprising. This whole operation has been classified."

"You're a scholar, Pauline. You know what it means when no one has access to data. No one believes it if it isn't accessible on the net. As far as the world is concerned, these one thousand slazans don't exist. If ibn Haj ordered them to be exterminated, no one would know, because only a handful of people know about their existence. And without direct evidence, no one will believe any of us if the military does something wrong."

"Why would they exterminate them, Dovid?"

"Because it's a humansafe world. If the slazans don't know about it, it's our world. If we win the war, it's our world. But if the peace is negotiated, then a world with slazans on it becomes part of the settlement."

"You're overreacting," I say, even though his doubts take hold of my imagination.

He starts to go on about the one thousand slazans. When did we once think about them? Why didn't we once say it would be better if they lived out their lives without ever seeing a single human being? He wishes he'd blown up the Research Center and destroyed all the data. But then there would have been lives lost, careers destroyed. He couldn't have done that to his family.

I want to hear the voice of justice; I want him to be one of the rabbis I listened to once in my youth, the voice calm, the logic measured, the wisdom steeped in millennia of tradition, but Ascherman's voice is blurred by alcohol, his hands around my hand, warm and sweaty, his gaze that of a man whose seduction has failed and who hopes that sympathy will do the same work as desire. I look at him and imagine the man who, at the start of his career, had been energetic, full of charisma and enthusiasm, who had attracted a Muslim wife, and who now had discovered that what was right was not what society wanted. There is no potency here, as there is with ibn Haj, who keeps his prestige and dignity because what he works for is in accord with what is socially valued.

I don't let Ascherman walk me home because I don't have the heart to say no. He embraces me tightly and wishes me luck.

In bed that night I am restless. I can't get Ascherman's questions out of my mind.

An ethnographer learns through trust. I will be asking a number of slazans to trust me, to let me tell their stories to others, to ones who hate their kind. But I won't have landed with ibn Haj and the General above him. Neither has asked for the same trust, and so neither will be honor-bound to respect it.

I start to hear Judith's voice all night long.

I tell her this is the only way. The minute others can read about slazans, can see how they live, view how they struggle to survive like everyone else, then the hatred will dissipate. Hate grows from fiction. To hate well, you have to transform a person into someone unreal, someone less complex. You can't hate well someone you understand.

Maybe, Judith says. She sounds dubious. *But they will listen well only if they trust your goals. Only if they want to trust what you have to say.*

Chapter Four

The Third Day

The second morning after the boulder had appeared in the clearing, the land was covered with damp fog the color of stone. When I emerged from her hut, Huggable and her daughter were waiting for her by the scorched ground of the winter fire, the trees beyond them black shadows amid the fog. Before the trees sat a basket of nuts. Hanging from a limb were strips of meat. Huggable was hushing her daughter, telling her that the healer would take care of her when the time was right. "I like my dreams," said the daughter. Huggable's hand swung out, ready to strike, but before I's gaze the mother converted the gesture into a caress and stroked her daughter's cheek. I pitied the daughter who dreamed of embraces, but I no longer felt any kindness for the mother. It was easy to say, "Come back in two days."

"I brought meat, not fish. It's good meat. A woman who one or another call Childless Crooked watched my daughter so I could track the lightfoot, and she wanted half the meat. I do not know enough women to hunt often here by the river. My daughter embraced Crooked too many times, and Crooked struck her. My daughter needs your help. I can bring more meat. You can have my entire share of the meat."

I hesitated. The woman should have brought fish. She should be offering the rest of the meat to those who lived nearby. She was selfish or she was desperate if she was to offer all the meat to the healer. Perhaps I should stay. The boulder was not going to leave, and a girl the size of Huggable's daughter should not be so full of embraces. But I strapped on the gzaet. "Come back this afternoon," she said. "For now, I accept the basket of nuts." She left them behind and made her way through the mist.

She reached the edge of the clearing, the world nothing but trees and fog and the faint colors of a fire that had almost burned itself out. The boulder was invisible, and she was straining to make out the blackened ground around it when she heard an odd sound, like someone humming. It was a tuneless hum, and so brief that it was eerie. I stopped and held still. She told herself she was hunting, that there was a lightfoot nearby and she didn't want to scare it off. From where the boulder should have been, she heard the very quiet, far too quiet, sound of footsteps. Then nothing but the usual forest sounds. The mist cleared. Sunlight cut it apart and cleared it from the ground so everything could be seen.

Standing in front of the thing was an animal that stood like any man or woman stood. Its skin was the color of the clay that Old Sour Plum had used to make pots when he had been younger. The hair on the animal's head was the color of night, the texture of root moss. And it was modestly dressed around the waist like anyone who could walk off into the bushes should be dressed. It had two teats, but there was no infant to be seen, unless it was now sleeping inside the giant rock, for the rock now had an opening, shaped very much like the opening of a hut. The inside was dark.

I wanted to run, but there was no reason to run. The clay-colored animal with teats just stood in the same spot. Every now and then it turned its head like it was waiting for someone to appear. Soon it started to hug itself, as if its body was cold.

Farther along the hillside, Hugger stepped out from behind a thickbark tree, and, clumsy as a man, he stepped on something that made a small crunching noise. The animal looked up in Hugger's direction, and its glance must have scared him because he stepped back once, then twice, and returned to hide behind the thickbark tree.

The sun had burned off the mist when one woman after another joined I. First came Wisdom, also called Talk Too Much, who had nothing to say when she saw the animal. Standing as tall as the bone-pains would let her, Wisdom stepped back until she stood near an arrowpoint tree. Childless Crooked found her own tree to stand near. Both Wisdom and Crooked stared at the animal for the longest time. The animal remained standing. Finally Crooked reached into her shoulder bag and took out two strips of smoked lightfoot meat, which she offered to each woman. "It will spoil unless eaten," said Crooked after I's first refusal.

The animal looked in their direction, its eyes wide, as if trying to understand what each woman might be saying. Then it did something an animal—one that was intent on understanding what was going on—wouldn't do; it looked down at the cracked ground, as if examining the blackened lines. It was as if the animal knew it had stared too long at them, as if it were aware of its improper behavior.

I remarked upon this to Crooked and Wisdom, making her voice louder than usual, trying to attract the animal's attention. Crooked laughed at the idea; there was fear in the laughter. Wisdom looked at I with her sad eyes, as if the healer were hopelessly naive.

"Hey, animal!" shouted I.

The animal continued to ponder the ground. An animal—whether it had hooves or paws—would have looked up at the sudden shout. Crooked was asking I what she thought she was doing, but I barely heard the words. I felt suddenly very alive and aware, the same way she felt when she tracked a meat animal for most of a day and found it nibbling leaves in a clearing, or when she found the right music to drive away the spirit that had sickened a child. She was certain: this animal was not an animal.

But she couldn't believe it was a first soul. A first soul wouldn't act so much like . . . like a stranger to the world it had helped create.

After a while the animal returned to the boulder, and the opening to the thing disappeared. Gone, like it had never existed. Maybe it was a first soul.

Hugger came out from behind his tree and took several steps down the hill. "Iamhere!" he shouted, but of course nothing happened.

After a while, when it was clear the animal was not going to come back out, Wisdom and Crooked stepped away from their trees. Wisdom talked for a while about what the animal could be. Crooked said, "I don't care what it is. I want to know when it will leave."

The sun had barely moved in the sky before the opening appeared again and the animal stepped out. This time it wore a kaross, and one of its teats was covered by the fabric. Wisdom and Crooked remained where they were seated, but I could tell that each one wanted to head back to the safety of a tree. But the animal stood still again, and soon Wisdom spoke in hushed whispers about the animal's kaross. The animal looked up. Wisdom stopped talking. The animal looked away, and Wisdom began to speak again. The color of the kaross was darker than any animal skin Wisdom had ever seen, and she wondered what kind of man would make a kaross so dark and why he would make a gift of something so plain. Wisdom finally grew restless with her own words and left to gather some food.

Roofer came to the hillside and stared hard at the animal. The animal ignored Roofer, and he walked away. When Crooked told Squawker that the animal never moved, Squawker sat down to nurse her daughter, her son pacing back and forth behind her. The animal looked up for a moment, her eyes on mother and child, and then looked away.

I looked at Squawker's teats, then at the animal's. The skin on Squawker's was so rough, while the animal's was smooth. Squawker's infant daughter cried whenever she stopped nursing, so Squawker left, even though her son insisted that they stay. What would the son say if the animal walked up the hill right toward him?

The animal returned to the boulder. The sun rose until the boulder cast a shadow so thin that it was hardly a shadow. I knew that it had to come out again; if nothing else, it would need to look for food. If it didn't have food, then it couldn't provide milk for its child. What kind of child would such a creature have?

I wanted to stay, but she stood up and walked back to hut and hearth. Huggable and her daughter were sitting by the remains of I's waiting fire. "I brought more strips of meat," said Huggable. "I came earlier, but you weren't here."

"I'm here now." I accepted the meat and told them they were much too generous; her abilities with the music would make her seem stingy. She walked into the hut, and they followed. I sat on one side of the fire; mother and daughter sat on the other. I added wood to the fire until its warmth created a sense of respectful distance between the two of them and the healer. "The body best hears the music when there is no skin over the body's skin."

The daughter was already standing to remove her pubic

apron when Huggable grasped her hand to stop her. "When I lived by the river's mouth, no woman would ask such a thing."

The music was meant to be respectful, but I wanted each one to be uncomfortable, especially the mother. "I have not eaten the nuts. I have not touched the meat." I gestured to the food, and Huggable's eyes followed the motion of her hand.

Huggable let go of the daughter's hand and rose. She removed the kaross first, then the pubic skirt that modestly covered buttocks and pubis. Standing naked in the firelight, her shape highlighted by shadow and shifting light, it became obvious how large Huggable's teats were for a woman with a waist-high daughter. As the woman sat, I, whose eyes should have been averted to show the proper respect, glimpsed Huggable's labia. One woman or three liked to joke that the ones by the river's mouth had long penises or long labia, but there was a thickness to Huggable's labia that suggested the onset of desire. And she was still nursing her first daughter. Why did a woman like this have to move here?

"Now," said I, "would the mother sit with her legs open and the daughter sit with her back to the mother's belly and chest?"

"This is the kind of behavior I want to stop."

"The music works with the behavior," said I, "and changes it. You should embrace her."

Huggable averted her eyes, and her chin quivered, as she sat there hugging her daughter tight to her. I knew she was being cruel, but a woman who nursed her waist-high daughter needed a measure of cruelty to get her thinking properly. The daughter smiled at I, but it was an anxious smile. She had the daughter's trust and she had the generous gift of meat and nuts, and it made I feel as if she were lying. The music might not be needed at all. If this was indeed her time, Huggable would mate, have another child—a daughter, if lucky—and the first daughter would have to stop nursing and learn to favor her solitude. But what if Huggable was too fond of nursing and did not mate?

I closed her eyes and began to play. She focused on the daughter, sent out the music, felt for its resonance. There was a tightness in the way the daughter held herself, a bounded energy. I touched her fingers to the upper keys until she played a soft song she liked, a child's song, one her mother had sung to her; then with the lower keys she started another music, one to relax the daughter, to ease each muscle in her body. The daughter's smile had changed; it was the smile of someone asleep. I changed the song, played a hunt song, something a little more jarring. The daughter opened her eyes, squirmed in her mother's grip, pushed away her arms.

"Don't push," said the mother. "The healer wants me to hold you like this."

The daughter kept pushing.

"You did want your daughter to reject your hugs," said I.

Huggable was confused. She let go and her naked daughter stepped away. "Come back and pick up your apron to cover yourself," said Huggable.

I said, "If you take a bitter root, mash it to paste, and spread it on your nipples, your daughter will no longer be eager to nurse."

"She no longer nurses," said Huggable. "My teats are filled with milk that had been meant for my second daughter."

It was an obvious lie. Huggable's teats should have been thinning out after the infant's death. They would not be heavy with milk unless she was suckling the first daughter. I felt great anger, but she said nothing. Huggable dressed and walked away, her daughter following.

I cooked the meat Huggable had brought. She ate two strips. Two pieces of wood had been driven into the ground on either side of the hearth; they held a long piece of wood that had been carved by a man whom I had cured of a spring sickness. Over that wood I hung a portion of the meat to dry it and preserve it, and to keep the meat out of the reach of scavengers. Another portion she cut into bits, which she scattered far in the woods to offer thanks to those animals who avoided her hut and hearth. She placed other portions into her carry bag, made for her by a man who had lost his arm to a nightskin, and set off into the woods.

She listened for the call of Roofer's "Iamhere. Stayaway." When she came close enough that she could hear him snap a branch, she called to him and said she had meat. She later found Old Sour Plum and also gave him meat in return for staying away. She found Wisdom at her hut and hearth and gave her a larger portion.

I was on a trail leading to the clearing when she found Flatface, her knee-high daughter, and her waist-high son returning to hut and hearth. I gave Flatface an even larger portion because Flatface and I's mother had shared a mother. In turn Flatface offered to hunt with I soon. She also told about what she had seen this afternoon. "The animal started to walk. It walked back and forth in front of the rock, but it never left the black ground. Its head hung low, and it kept sitting down. My eldest daughter thinks it is sick. Crooked said that if the animal was sick, then it couldn't be a first soul. I think Crooked is right."

With a few portions of meat left in her carry bag, I made her way to the clearing. When night came, she built herself a small fire and sat in front of it to watch the rock. Hugger came and stood behind her. Every now and then he came close to add a piece of wood to the fire, and once he wrapped his arms around I in a quick embrace, withdrawing into the night before I could strike out at him. The night dragged on, the animal remained in the rock, and exhaustion crept up on I like a nightskin. I dreamed she was mating, her mate taking her from behind, and the dream was pleasant. But she woke up and found that Hugger, still modestly dressed, had nestled up to her and had fallen asleep. She was about to yell at him when she heard the short, toneless hum.

She could hear the animal's soft footsteps as it emerged from its boulder. It stood there and looked first in her direction, then up at the sky. I disengaged herself from Hugger's embrace and took several steps closer to the edge of the woods to get a better look. The first moon was out and full tonight, and it was easy to make out the animal's basic form, the way her neck twisted back so her face could confront the sky. The animal was always alone. Where was the child who suckled from those teats? Was it in the boulder? Or had it died, like Huggable's second daughter?

The animal had turned and was now looking up at I. I knew that she was a shadow standing several paces in front of a fire, but she felt like the animal could see her clearly. It was hard to be brave when there was no daughter to feed, but I stood there and stared back. There was too much dark and too much distance to see more than the animal's face, and I so much wanted to look into those eyes, to see what kind of animal it was that could live for three days in a rock without once coming out for food. The animal returned to the boulder, and the opening closed.

Hugger still slept by the fire as if nothing had happened. I tried to sleep on the other side, but she found that sleep wouldn't come. The first moon was setting and the second was rising, so it was easy to make her way down into the clearing. She looked up into the night sky to try to see what the animal had seen. But the sky looked like the sky always did. The true bodies shone clearly against the night's darkness—many of them—tiny bright motes that had positioned themselves the way they did each spring to remind a woman to eat more fish than meat, to gather nuts rather than to pluck the fruit before it had grown large and ripe. And beyond the true bodies were faint clouds where it was said that the first souls roamed, each in her solitude, free and unseen.

And this animal, staring up into the night sky, could she be a first soul? Could she be looking up there and longing for her distant home?

The Fourth Day

The animal did not come out right away the next morning. Before she stepped out of the boulder, one person after another came to the hillside. Flatface came first and found a place to sit, her knee-high daughter sitting beside her. Her waist-high son and her almost-a-man son were farther back in the woods, chasing each other in and around the trees. I was glad to see the eldest son playing; he had reached the age where every now and then he eyed respectful women as if their labia were showing. Flatface's eldest daughter, who carried her own infant son in her kaross, sat a respectable distance from her mother.

I watched the eldest daughter for a moment, the easy way she moved so as not to wake her sleeping infant. She and I had been born around the same time and had played together in this clearing before each had found her solitude. I remembered long ago how they had played the solitude game, how they would hold each other close and stare into each other's eyes until one smiled, looked away, or, when they were older, pushed her way out of the embrace. I had looked into the other's eyes and saw herself, a small reflection in a small round spring of water. I used to call her Clear Eyes; now each rarely spoke to the other. After I's mother had moved south, I began to visit Flatface and to share words and food with her, as I's mother had done before she had left.

Hugger had left I's fire at the appearance of the first woman, and with each new woman he moved farther away, following the curve of the hillside, until he now stood across the way, on the other side of the clearing. A long call sounded in the distance; it was Roofer, announcing his approach to the clearing. Hugger immediately climbed the nearest tree as if he were still a boy. Roofer ambled around the hillside and stopped below the arrowpoint tree where Hugger hid. He didn't look up.

"If Old Sour Plum shows up," said Flatface, "Roofer will climb the very same tree as Hugger."

"That's all we need," said her eldest daughter, "is more men and more noise. The animal will never come out."

Childless Crooked arrived, her skin looking soft, almost as smooth as that of the animal. Crooked would soon feel her desire, she would soon try again to have a daughter, so it wasn't surprising that an almost-a-man whom no one had ever seen appeared on the hillside. He was about as tall as Hugger, but his throat patches were dark, baggy. By next spring he would be as tall as any man. He didn't look at any of the women except Crooked.

Flatface's almost-a-man son had stopped chasing the waist-high son. He stood rooted to the ground, staring at the Newcomer as if he were a rival. I looked to Flatface, but she was purposefully watching the silent boulder. The almost-a-man Newcomer did not react to the eldest son's stares; he was more concerned with Roofer. He could not know that Crooked's children would never live, that Roofer would have no interest in her. He did not notice how well worn was Crooked's kaross, how frayed were the edges of her shoulder bag. He must think too much with his penis; otherwise, he would wonder why no man made gifts for Crooked. So he stared at Roofer like a rival, and later looked surprised when Roofer walked off. By then Flatface's almost-a-man son had returned to chasing the waist-high son through the forest.

Newcomer now made several attempts to get close to Crooked, but each time she turned on him and hissed until he backed away. He cast his face down, looking hurt. Crooked ignored him; she just watched the boulder. Newcomer's face took on a harder quality as he stared at Crooked's back. I became certain that this almost-a-man would have tried to force one woman or another if he'd been big enough. Poor Crooked. I glared at him, as did Flatface, as did Flatface's eldest daughter. He had to know he risked a stone-throwing if he tried anything, so he walked a bit into the woods, found some flatleaves, pulled them off the branch, and nibbled on them.

I walked away into the woods so she couldn't be seen. She reached into her carry bag for a slice of meat, and she ate it quickly, barely tasting it. She was no longer sure when she would have time to hunt again, and she regretted being so generous with the meat Huggable had given her. She found an old clearing and the remains of an abandoned hut and sought out an appropriate spot to urinate. She was heading back when Flatface's voice called out, "Healer, Long Fingers."

When I reached the clearing, everyone else on the hillside was quiet. The opening had appeared, and the animal had stepped out, wearing pubic apron and kaross. Newcomer stopped nibbling and turned to the animal. Flatface's eldest daughter leaned forward; her mother's story had not prepared her for the strangeness of what she now saw.

The animal's walk was slow. She looked up at the ones on the hill for a brief moment, then looked away. She walked around the boulder, crossed the tiny creek, and walked up the opposite hill, where she stopped to lean against a sharpleaf tree. Not very far away from where she stood was the arrowpoint tree that Hugger had climbed. I wondered if the animal had seen Hugger up there. The animal pushed herself away from the sharpleaf tree and took several more uphill steps before stopping again. She lifted up her kaross, undid her pubic apron, and squatted. There was no bush to hide behind. All the brush had been burned away earlier this spring. I was disturbed that she herself did not turn her head away, which would be the proper thing to do, but that instead, like the other ones, she watched the animal first urinate, then defecate.

"Is this the first time she's done this?" asked Flatface's eldest daughter.

"Maybe," said Crooked, "she's done it in the boulder and the stink is too much for her."

Newcomer said, "She could have walked farther away."

"You can walk farther away," responded Flatface's almost-a-man son, who was now standing at a respectful distance behind his mother.

Newcomer glared at him, and he glared back. Then Flatface's son looked away, and it was like nothing had happened.

The animal retied the public apron and adjusted the kaross and hadn't taken several steps away when Hugger scrambled down the arrowpoint tree. Was Hugger scared by the animal and trying to run? The animal had been definitely scared by Hugger's sudden presence. She stopped dead where she was, obviously uncertain as to what to do while Hugger ambled toward her, an almost-a-man trying to walk with the confident gait of a man. If she had been a first soul, she would have been able to do something, but the animal stood as if planted there. Her eyes met Hugger's, and Hugger stopped. He stared at her. Was he going to embrace her? Why didn't she leave? What was she trying to encourage? Hugger reached out and touched one of her teats. I wished she had been closer to see the animal's reaction, but from here it looked like she hadn't moved at all. She faced Hugger and allowed the tips of his fingers to rest on her teat. No one said a thing. Each watched the animal watch Hugger. It must have been too much for Hugger. He looked away, and knowing he had lost, he dropped his hand to his side. He walked off into the woods until he was out of sight.

If that wasn't enough, once the animal got back to the creek, rather than crossing over, it once again removed the kaross then the pubic apron. It stepped naked into the creek, then crouched until the cold water covered its knees and thighs. I wanted to be closer, to be able to study the way foot was joined at ankle, the set of curves below the knee, the set above, the way the hips were wider than the torso, the clear curvature of the teats and the nipples large enough for nursing, the sets of curves connecting shoulder to elbow, elbow to hand. The odd, flattened features of the head, the thin eyes, like someone always squinting. There was a patch of hair covering the labia, and I wondered how big they were, if this animal could bear the children of people. The idea of a person mating with this clay-skinned animal was both revolting and intriguing. Why didn't the creature have the modesty to bathe when no one was here? Or perhaps this was the creature's way of demanding the solitude no one would give her. The animal cupped her hands and splashed water all across her body. Each one watched.

There must have been something provocative about it, because in spite of her teats, Newcomer called out to the animal, "Do you want to mate?"

Crooked hissed at Newcomer. The animal's eyes fixed on him just for a moment, as if she had understood his words; then her gestures became more rapid. She splashed water on her face, along her arms, then rose and gathered kaross and pubic apron to her chest before she ran and stumbled into the boulder. The opening disappeared.

That afternoon a woman came to the hillside and built herself a fire. Her skin sagged like Flatface's, but there were no signs of a child. Across her chest were dark scars, which marked her as a woman who lived along the lake. When a woman brought down her first lightfoot, scars were cut into her body. The woman with the chest scars did not look at anyone in particular, but she asked to the air, "Does a woman gather her food from these trees and bushes?"

"A woman does," said Flatface. She told Chest Scars how to find Squawker's hut and hearth.

Night had begun to steal light from day when a woman, who said she was from the south, arrived with a leg-hugging daughter. Her belly was wide with another. She walked a respectful distance from Chest Scars' fire and built her own. She too asked if a woman gathered from these trees and bushes.

"If more people come," said Crooked, "and if more people will build fires, there will be little wood on the ground for Squawker to warm herself."

"If more people come," said Flatface's eldest daughter, "she will have to move. Everyone will eat her food."

"The next place to gather is where Crooked gathers," said Flatface.

"Maybe more won't come," said Crooked.

"Maybe we should say no," said Flatface's eldest daughter,

"Yes," said Crooked. "Tell each one no. Then no one will be here. Maybe the boulder will leave."

"Say no?" said Flatface. "And when the berries are sour and the tubers are dry, who will say yes to you?" She didn't give Crooked time to respond. "It will be dark soon. There's no reason to stay. The animal is too ashamed of its improper behavior to come back out."

Flatface left, followed by each child. Crooked left. Newcomer trailed after her. Only I and the woman with the big belly and the leg-hugging daughter remained. Not much later Chest Scars returned from her visit to Squawker's hut and hearth. She had flatleaves and springnuts in her kaross. She left some by I's fire and some by Big Belly's. Each woman ate quietly.

When the first moon had risen above the trees, Big Belly and her daughter were asleep. Chest Scars stood on the opposite side of I's fire. "I am here," she said. "I have some dried meat."

"I am here," said I. "And I have nothing."

"I still have meat, if you have words to share."

I gestured for Chest Scars to sit. Chest Scars placed several pieces of meat between herself and the healer. I took half of them. The meat was old and tough. She said it was good.

"No," said Chest Scars. "The meat is stale. But I have eaten mostly fish. Fish does not travel as well as meat."

"What words did you want to share?"

Chest Scars wanted to know about the boulder. One woman

had told another, and she had heard about it. I told her that Squawker had seen it fall from the sky, that the music I played had done nothing, that the animal inside it had smooth skin, teats, and no infant.

After a moment of respectful silence, Chest Scars said, "I want to share with you something that happened several winters ago. The snow fell till it covered our knees, and the winds off the lake froze sweat into ice. I spoke to the one woman and another who shared my mother. We decided to leave for the sturdy hut and hearth I had built in a ravine where the winds are not so terrible. I have given birth to one son who lived and who is now a man. The next woman had one son and another. The youngest had no children that lived. Each of us bore the lack of solitude and shared our warmth until one day when there was a sound like the wind. But it was a wind that echoed only through one set of trees. Each was scared. The sound was over, but the youngest and I tracked it down. In a nearby clearing we found something that looked like a rock with legs. The rock was large, but not so large that a woman couldn't pick it up. It was made of the same kind of rock as this boulder."

"Did the rock have an animal in it?"

"No. A man took a heavy stick to it and broke it apart. It was full of strange lines and light. The man hit it again, and sparks the color of true bodies flew out of it. Then all its light was gone. I dug a hole and buried it. When we returned to the river's mouth, I told one or another, but no one believed me. It was a good winter story. Anyone who sees this boulder will have to believe about our rock with legs."

I looked to Chest Scars, whose eyes were filled with the fire's glow. She sounded like a woman who wanted to impress another woman, and I did not know if she should believe the story about the rock with legs.

The Fifth Day

I woke up several times that night, but was too tired to sit up and enjoy the wakefulness. She later remembered hearing one woman sing a song I's mother had never sung and later listening to the soft patter of rain that walked atop the leaves but never fell through. What woke her in the morning was less the dim brightness of a cloudy day and more the sounds of Squawker's son shouting at Squawker's infant daughter, who laughed in reply. I opened her eyes to see a woman sitting on the other side of the fire, presenting her back to I, allowing the healer a degree of solitude. The woman's back was a fine one, and her arms curved like those of a hunter.

I sat up and announced she was awake and listening.

The woman repositioned herself to present the side of her body to I. Her belly was tremendous, and I remembered musing the night before why a woman so close to delivering would walk north from Small Lake all the way to this clearing. Big Belly said, "The woman with a daughter and a son"—she nodded toward Squawker—"told me you healed with music. Would you play for me?"

I looked down into the clearing. Everything looked different when the sun walked behind the clouds. There was a kind of bright darkness illuminating the boulder and the blackened land around it. The boulder's opening had not appeared.

Big Belly waited without speaking. I could not refuse her request, so she left for hut and hearth, Big Belly and her daughter following from a respectful distance. Mother and daughter sat by the blackened spot of the winter-waiting fire while I lit the fire in her hut, fed it wood, and played the gzaet until her fingers moved comfortably on the keys. She then gestured that Big Belly should come.

The woman left her daughter at the waiting fire and approached I, remaining outside the hut until I gestured her in, remaining standing until I gestured her to sit, and then sitting on the opposite side of the fire, respectfully looking away from both the fire and the healer. I began to think that Big Belly was the wrong kind of name for a woman whose manners were full of respect. "What does your mother call you?" she asked.

"Right now she calls me Moon Belly"—and she patted the stretched skin—"because it looks as large and round as a moon."

"And before that?"

"Lightfoot Watcher. I like to track lightfoot and watch them. I shoot them only when I'm meat hungry."

One and another child were called Watcher by a mother because a child did like to watch something: a bushytail hunting for nuts, a flathead slithering through the brush, water dripping from leaves, fire consuming a log. I's mother had called her Maker of Parts because she used to pull legs and wings off insects and then try to put the parts back together again.

Lightfoot Watcher set her kaross aside and leaned back on her strong arms so the music could touch the completed curve of her belly and reach into her and touch the readying child. I

played the music, and she enjoyed replaying the pattern of welcome songs her mother had sung and played for each pregnant
woman who had come to her. Soon she played the lower keys,
reaching out with the most private of touches, to discover what
Lightfoot Watcher must have known all along. The belly was
big, but not because the belly protected the child with lots of water. I stopped playing the gzaei. Lightfoot Watcher opened her
eyes and sat up.

I faced the woman. "A woman once told a woman who told
me about the healer who lives near the Tall Hills. It is said that
she is good."

The woman nodded.

"No woman who carries a child within should walk one day
and another to the Winding River when she could walk a little
less than a day to Tall Hills." I stared at the woman because she
wanted this to be a confrontation.

Lightfoot Watcher looked away. She said, "I have heard
what a woman told a woman about Small Winding River: there
is a woman who has no children and would like one."

The woman shifted her gaze to face I, and I looked away to
show the proper respect. When twins are born, the first one out
of the womb, it was said, was the second one put in the womb;
that was the one to be buried before it breathed, before anyone
spoke the word "child." "Forgive me," said the woman. "I don't
know how to ask." She edged her body away, draped it with the
kaross, hunching her body over in embarrassment.

I was both angry and proud that she had been asked to handle such a delicate matter, but she did not know how to ask this
of poor Crooked, who was almost ready to take a man, who believed that this time she would give birth to something large
enough to breathe in a true body. I could ask Crooked to take the
first twin, and Crooked would refuse. Then, in autumn, when
she buried something too small to live, she would cry out into
the night for everyone along the river to hear about her grief,
and, this time, about her regret that she had not accepted the offer of someone else's child to be her own.

I did not want to say this about Crooked, so instead she told
Lightfoot Watcher, "A woman without a child will have no milk
for an infant. The infant will die, anyway."

"A woman cannot gather enough to nurse one infant and
another, and a woman with an infant who always wants to suck
rarely hunts and eats only meat that is another woman's gift. But
a woman has two teats after she has given birth, and each child

can have one if there is another woman who hunts enough so that there will be enough milk, and if this other woman is well gifted, the child then has blankets to keep her warm and baskets for her to carry nuts and fruit."

Lightfoot Watcher spoke these words to the ground so that the healer had the solitude necessary to react honestly. The healer did not know how to react. The woman was not offering one of the twins to Crooked; no man made gifts for Crooked. Lightfoot Watcher was offering the twin to I.

"I need a daughter to learn the music," said I.

"And if the first out is not a girl?"

"I cannot take it."

"And if the second is also not a girl?"

I could not find the heart to say the words. If the first was a boy, then so most likely would be the second. When the first one breathed, a true body filled the child's chest and body, and the child would breathe for as long as the true body wanted it to. When the second child came out, a true body would be pursed on its lips, eager because it had been waiting since the first one took breath. If the second one never drew breath, the true body would not return to the night sky. It would be trapped on the world, and it would fill itself with anger; its anger would take away its sense; it would not wait for another newborn's breath to take it in; it would remain with the mother and the firstborn, and it would trouble mother and child until each had stopped breathing.

This mother, this watcher of lightfoot, loved one child and the other before they were yet children. I once had carried a boy within her, and when she lost it, she too felt like she had loved something that had not yet breathed. She wished this woman from somewhere else had not offered her the chance to have a child, because it had made I see how cruel and heartless she could be.

I continued to play the gzaet, and she hoped that Big Belly would get up and leave. The music sounded like the river after the first rain of spring, a rush over rocks and fallen limbs, a torrent along the banks, and she played the music like the sun and the ground and the softer feminine rains, easing the river to its tranquil downstream flow. Lightfoot Watcher left the hut and sat by her daughter and the empty black ground of the winter fire. She adjusted her kaross and directed her gaze into the woods. I realized that she most likely did not know the way back to the clearing.

It was past midday when Lightfoot Watcher and her daughter and I reached the clearing. There were one or two more hearths built along the hillside, and more people. A child and two or more were climbing trees and shouting to each other, or were they shouting to the women on the hillside? "I don't see it!" shouted one. "It's not near here!" shouted another.

Chest Scars was standing by her fire, and standing on the opposite side of the same fire was another woman. This woman had the same thin build, but the scars were along the tops of her arms. She had teats full with milk and a knee-high son standing by her side. Wisdom and Squawker were standing at the bottom of the hill, and Flatface had walked up to where the ground had been burned to the color of night. The boulder's opening had appeared, and the sunlight made the darkness inside look even darker. The animal was nowhere to be seen.

Lightfoot Watcher and her daughter remained on the hillside. I headed down and stopped at the burned ground, standing at a respectful distance from Flatface.

"The animal has gone," said Flatface. "One or another want to track it and make sure it does nothing harmful."

"Track the animal?"

"My son came and called for you."

"No. I haven't seen your son."

Flatface looked up the hill. Crooked and the Newcomer were nowhere to be seen.

I said, "When did the animal come out?"

"It came out when the sun was overhead. It followed the creek out of the clearing. Perhaps it is hungry. One or another wanted to follow."

"Did someone follow?"

"No."

Squawker stepped forward. "The healer played the music. The next day the animal came out. The healer should track the animal."

Chest Scars must have heard. She said, "What if the animal is a first soul?"

Wisdom said, "If a first soul came back as a woman, she would have both teats and child, not just teats. Nor would she come back with skin like the color of clay and eyes that are half-closed."

Chest Scars took several steps down the hill and faced I.

"One first soul became a sunskin and another became a many-legs. You can't track a first soul like you track a lightfoot."

"The healer played the music," said Squawker.

I asked, "Where's Hugger?"

"Squawker doesn't know," said Flatface. "And I don't know where my son is."

"Your son," said Squawker, "is probably following some woman."

"If the healer played the music," said Arm Scars, her voice like an accusation, "and if the animal came out because the healer played the music, then perhaps the healer should find the animal."

Wisdom had come closer. "Maybe each one here should try to find the animal."

Chest Scars said, "A first soul would not find that respectful. We cannot hunt the animal like it was starvation time. We cannot act like we are trying to drive a lightfoot out of the forest."

"It's not a first soul," said Wisdom. She told the story about the first soul who became a woman and the first soul who became a man and why the man grew larger than a woman. I could see the impatience on each woman's face, but each one gave the story the respect it deserved. When it was over, I said, "I will find the animal. If it harms anyone, then each of us can notch an arrow and find it."

Without further thought or words, I stepped away from the women and onto the hard, dark ground. She approached the boulder. There was the opening. She could go into the boulder and see how the animal lived. Fear made her want to stop, but each woman watched her back. She crouched low to the burnt ground, which carried as many tracks as a rock.

She walked to the creek and followed it upstream to where the water fell through the clefts in the hillside. She knelt here, worked her eyes, and found the animal's footprints. She placed her fingertip along the rim of one and traced it, its contours so much like a person's foot and yet not at all like a person's foot. She reached forward to trace the next one, to examine the depth of it. The soil here was soft, yielding easily to the animal's weight, and I guessed from the indentation that the animal weighed about the same as a woman the size of Crooked. I stepped forward to look at the next track, then the one after that. The stride was uneven, not the measured, purposeful stride of a healthy creature.

I rose and followed the spoor into the forest, stopping and squatting each time the trail changed. At one point the prints edged into the ground at an angle, suggesting the animal had been leaning against a nearby sapling. If the animal was tired, why had she walked out into the forest? What would she have done if one and another woman had followed her?

Two well-used trails met, and the prints stopped, shifted, then chose a path. After several places where paths met, I noticed something. The spoor approached a tree, and there was a weight upon the balls of the feet as if the animal had been squatting. But the area was clean; there was no sign of vomit or stool.

Up ahead the tracks found their way into an area of tall brush that should have been burned away this spring. Several sunset fruit trees grew here, and with all the brush and prickers, it would be difficult to get at the fruit when it ripened late in the summer. Squawker had been asked to burn this area away, but she had refused. She had told I that she was always asked to do too much because her mother had been born near Three Ponds and not along Winding River.

Through the brush I heard the animal say something. It didn't sound like the hiss of a nightskin or the growl of a sunskin; it sounded like the animal had said one or two words no one else had ever heard. The sounds frightened I, and she stood rooted for a moment, before crouching and toe-stepping forward as if she were hunting a nearby lightfoot. She found one thin path through the brush, and parting stalks and leaves with her hands, she stepped forward.

Within the brush someone had cleared enough land for hut and hearth. Who would want a hidden hut and hearth that one could stumble onto by accident? And who would build it right beneath a sunset fruit tree? No one would come and ask to gather fruit here with a hut so close by. She wanted to get closer, to look at the thatching, to see what man might have helped this rude, greedy woman. She would tell Flatface and Crooked and Wisdom and Wisdom's daughter with daughters, and, of course, she would tell Squawker, and no woman would hunt for such a man, nor would any mate with him.

But I couldn't get any closer to the hut, because the animal who had spoken the odd words was inside it, and she listened intently to the sounds of the forest and hoped to hear any sound coming from within the hut. The animal soon emerged. She was wearing the kaross, but she was also wearing a carry bag made from the same kind of skin as her kaross. In her hand was something round and smooth as a water-worn rock the color of night. The animal looked at the dark thing, then looked at the brush before finding another thin path that led back to the normal path where the brush had been burned away.

A sound whispered through the grass. Then forests sounds. Then another whisper. The animal was moving slowly, as if tracking something. Had the animal seen I? She crouched closer to the ground and held herself perfectly still. A third whisper, then the animal was standing on the cleared path. She looked in all directions, but a bit too quickly, as if she didn't expect to see anything there. Old Sour Plum's distant call caught her attention for a moment: she looked in the direction of the noise, but before the echo had faded, the animal had knelt down by the root of the tree, its useless teats hanging free. The animal reached into her leather bag and pulled out a piece of wood, a finely whittled stick with a pointed tip. She placed the tip against the ground; there was the noise of insects, and the stick slipped right out of her hand into the dirt. It either did that or it disappeared into thin air—it happened too fast to tell. The animal stood up, looked at the thing the color of night that she held in her hand, and walked off in the direction of the boulder.

I remained as still as if she were stalking a lightfoot who might turn around and see her. She waited until she could no longer see or hear the animal. Then she walked over to the spot of ground between the tree roots and searched for the stick, first with her eyes then with the tips of her fingers. She found something stranger. Poking up from the ground was something round and tiny. It looked like a nighttime drop of water made visible by moonlight. She held it between two fingers and pulled. The thing came right out of the ground. The stick underneath the water drop had been the color of a stick, but the minute it was out of the ground, the color changed to the color of leaves and bark mixed together.

I couldn't help but drop it, and she couldn't help but step back several times and watch it from a distance. I looked at the hand that had touched the stick. Her fingers and thumb still could curl one by one to fold within her palm. Her skin was the same color as before. Her heart was beating faster, but that was fear. The stick was now the color of the ground, and if the dark droplet hadn't been attached, she wouldn't have been able to find it.

With thumb and forefinger, she picked it up and held it against a leaf. The stick changed color. She held it against a tree trunk. The stick changed color. She placed the point of the stick against the tree trunk, and it made the sound of insects and slipped right through her fingers and into the tree. Only the tiny waterdrop, pressed against the bark, remained visible. The rest was in the tree. She wanted to pull the stick back out, but each time she pulled on the waterdrop, her fingers slipped off.

She was going to look for a rock when she heard a girl's voice in the distance. It was Huggable's daughter, and Huggable said something in reply. The voices were coming from the direction of the hidden hut and hearth. So Huggable was the hut's owner. Who had built it for her? The voices were getting closer, and she didn't want to be seen. So she followed after the animal's spoor to see what she was doing now.

The animal had double-backed on its tracks, and soon I found herself wondering how the animal managed to follow the exact same trails. Except for the uneven stride, and the prints that edged into the dirt whenever she leaned against a tree, there was no sign that the animal stopped and crouched to re-examine its own prints. Unless she was a first soul, she had never been in these woods before, and the woods must have changed much since the first souls had left for their rightful solitude. So how could the animal make its way back to the boulder with such ease? What kind of magic did she have to go along with those tiny sticks that changed color?

The animal walked slowly, stopping to rest often enough that it was easy to catch up. Then I stayed off the paths, keeping herself behind trees and the occasional bush, moving forward almost as if she were tracking an animal she wished to shoot.

The animal stopped though, and turned, and looked right in I's direction. I crouched there, uncertain what to do. She had hunted these woods often enough to know she had been quiet. How could the animal have known where she was? The animal grabbed at the leather bag, and now I wished she had brought her quiver and bow, even though an arrow might not be enough against the animal's magic. But all the animal did was turn away and stride off at a faster pace, breaking into a run.

It wasn't difficult to keep up with her. The animal couldn't run very fast, and after many steps she would stop, turn, look back, right at I, then walk on, stumble forward, and start to run again. How could an animal with so much magic run frightened, the leather bag slapping at her side, her teats bouncing? If I had wanted to drive the animal to exhaustion, she couldn't have thought of a better way.

The animal ran into the clearing, and the sudden light must have disoriented her because she spun, tripped, and fell. I looked toward the boulder and the opening. Maybe the animal would remain on the ground and sleep; maybe I would get the chance to go in and see exactly how this creature lived. But the animal was up on hands and feet, then regaining enough poise to walk into her smoothly shaped hut. The opening disappeared.

Each woman sat on the hillside, close enough to listen to the healer, each trying to remain at a respectable distance from another. Squawker did not believe the story of the stick. She asked Chest Scars if such sticks had ever been seen near the river's mouth. She asked Arm Scars if such an animal had been seen near the river's mouth. Arm Scars, whose chest-high son had joined the knee-high son at her side, told about the small rock with legs and about the man who destroyed it. One woman or another had questions, but Squawker wanted to talk more about the sticks. She asked Lightfoot Watcher if any woman who lived near Small Lake had seen such sticks. Squawker said the healer was making up the story about the stick. "You want us to think it was dangerous to follow the animal."

"You," said Flatface, never looking at Squawker, "can follow the animal tomorrow."

"Maybe," said Arm Scars, "someone should hunt the animal."

"You mean," said Lightfoot Watcher, "someone should kill it?"

"It is an animal," said Squawker.

"You say that," said Flatface, "because Hugger touched its teats."

"Watches Everything," which is what Squawker called Hugger, "was brave enough to see what her teats were like. The teats are not used to suckle any child. There is something very wrong about this animal."

"But you said it wasn't dangerous," said Wisdom. "You said the healer made up the story about the sticks to make it look dangerous."

Squawker said nothing. She looked at Arm Scars, then Chest Scars. They looked away. Lightfoot Watcher was already staring at the ground. There were no words for a long time. Roofer's long call was easy to hear. The light was fading, and he announced that he was walking to his nest. Each woman who lived near the river soon got up to leave, and each woman from another place gifted them with some fish they had pulled from the river or tubers they had gathered with Squawker's permission.

Night came. Chest Scars and Arm Scars shared a mother, and so they shared a fire. From their hearth each one answered Lightfoot Watcher's questions about the rock with legs. I just listened respectfully even though she wanted to know why a man, and not a woman, had destroyed it. Later, when each child had fallen asleep and the hillside was quiet, Lightfoot Watcher looked over to I as if she were waiting to offer a word, but I sat motionless by her own fire and looked away. Later I tried to sleep, but couldn't. She thought about the rock in the clearing and about the animal inside. She thought about what Lightfoot Watcher had asked her to do.

She was only half-asleep, and the familiar hum woke her instantly. She sat up. She was the only one awake. Arm Scars was lying with her children on one side of the fire; Chest Scars was alone on the other. Lightfoot Watcher's daughter was learning her solitude, and she slept on the opposite side of her mother's fire. It was the time of night after one moon had set and the other was just rising, so it was hard to make out the shape of the animal as it stepped out into the clearing. I took several steps down the hill so that the distracting light of the fires was behind her. The animal ignored any sound she might have made. She was staring up into the night sky. I walked forward, out of the trees, and looked up to see what the animal might see.

In the sky a true body had turned the color of sunset and had started to grow larger. A second one did the same. Then another. The first had turned the color of the sky and was shrinking. The light hurt her eyes even though it wasn't bright, and she had to look away. When she looked up again, the true bodies were gone. Shafts of light, the color of the other true bodies in the sky, cut across the night.

The animal fell to her knees and screamed out at the sky. The sounds it made caused a chill cooler than the night air. The sunskin would roar so each would know to stay away, that it would kill anything that came near, but these loud screams were more like those of a mother whose breathing child had died. Behind her, each woman was roused to see what it was. Arm Scars gave suck to her knee-high son to quiet his concern and hushed her chest-high son. Lightfoot Watcher must have thought the screams were a death wail, because like any pregnant woman who hears a death wail, she left the area, the terror of the sound worse than the terror of meeting a nightskin out on a dark path.

The animal did not seem to hear a sound from the hillside. She screamed and she pounded her fists upon the ground, and then she lifted her fists toward the sky and screamed even louder. Finally the screams stopped, and the animal curled up on the ground and made sounds like sobs and fell asleep. The opening to the boulder was darker than the night, forbidding. And the animal was lying there with no fire to ward off a nightskin, so I watched the animal, knowing she should feel fearful of a creature who had appeared in a hut that had fallen from the sky, that had brought lights in the sky no one had ever seen before. But curled up and lying there, she looked no more harmful than a sleeping pointed-ears. A sleeping nightskin never looked harmless.

The following is excerpted from a draft of Pauline Dikobe's memoirs, a project she started and abandoned while the Way of God *made its return trip to E'donya e talia. This is the last version she wrote before she abandoned the project and decided to write the novel,* Foragers. *The Ju/wa soldier featured in this section was the basis for the character of Esoch al-Schouki. His name, and all the names of the* Way of God's *crew, have been changed to match their counterparts in the novel.*

On board the military space station, I know I am bound to become an alien.

Wadi al-Uyoun traces its heritage back to a rich time, to a Golden Age, when Muslim, Jew, and Christian lived together, when the great works of Greece and Rome and Persia were translated into Arabic (and from Arabic into Latin for a few interested minds in the north), when music as well as medicine were sciences, when great treatises were written about the relationship of man to man and of man to God while at the same time Shahrazad prolonged her wedding night, the last night of her life, into one thousand and one nights as she told the jealous caliph her wondrous stories of djinns and barbers and kings.

With the notion of efficiency through harmony, this orbital is populated by Arabs, who relive these same past glories and see only Arab faces, not the white-faced Iberian, the dark-faced Indian, or the deep-hued African, all who played their roles in the world medieval Arabs knew. I look nothing like an Arab.

*   *   *

Ibn Haj escorts me aboard the orbital, proud of the itinerary, of the things he will show me. I am to meet the captain of the warship that will take me on the mission we planned within a week, and later I will dine with the General who approved the mission. But I don't meet the captain. She is busy. Everything is behind schedule. The warship's engines are still being overhauled in preparation, officially, for a return to the war zone. The revisions of the shuttle have at least another day to go. The new programming for the shuttle's intelligence has not arrived, nor has the ordered shipment of antelope skins.

Ibn Haj is all kindness and wit. He leads me around the orbital, impresses me with its efficient layout, the devotion of its design to the sanity of those who live there. He shows me the large mosque and the smaller church and the even smaller synagogue. We walk the insides of the spider legs, long, hollow tubes that connect the orbital to various spacecraft. We look in on the expansive dining halls where the enlisted eat, the more intimate dining room for officers, and the small gorgeous room where we will dine with the General. We walk through the dormitories, and he leaves me in a tiny cabin where I can wash and change for dinner.

The General does not look like a general. He looks like my youngest sister's husband, and after a few moments it becomes clear that the General, like my brother-in-law, lost his charm at an early age. He pats my hand rather than shaking it and tells me how glad he is to meet the anthropologist who will bring peace. He is happy to hear that I am a Muslim and not some pagan. He wants to hear about life as a forager, but once I use the word "egalitarian," he interrupts. "I dread that word, Professor Dikobe," he says. "Egalitarianism can be such a destructive idea. No society can survive it. Accomplishment needs hierarchy. We'd lose this war if we had to fight it by consensus. Great buildings would never be finished. The poor would never be fed. Great masses of people couldn't be moved from one planet to another. The betters must rule over the lessers. I presume even a good hunter must lord it over a poor hunter."

"Among the people I studied, sir, it's exactly the opposite. A good hunter will always talk like he's a poor hunter. He will always come back after a large kill and say he's found nothing. And then he'll admit to having killed something worthless. And when others go to help him butcher the meat, they'll all say that the animal's nothing but skin and bones, hardly worth the effort to butcher it."

The General's eyes widen. "They do this with a large kill? They have no respect for an individual's abilities and accomplishments?"

"Oh, they do. One Ju/wa explained it to me like this. He said, 'When a young man kills much meat, he comes to think of himself as a chief or a big man, and he thinks of the rest of us as his servants or inferiors. We can't accept this. We refuse the one who boasts, for someday his pride will make him kill somebody. So we always speak of his meat as worthless. This way we cool his heart and make him gentle.' "

The General does not say anything for a moment. He looks like he's taking this in, trying to look for an ulterior motive. Ibn Haj's eyes have lit up, but his face becomes instantaneously serious the moment the General looks to him. The General says to me, "Well, you are the expert on primitives, but I think it's a shame that a good hunter cannot live off his goodness. But, you know," he says, the tone of his voice switching with the subject, "we aren't at war with primitive slazans. We are fighting a dangerous, resourceful, and very proud bunch. Each of their very effective warships is piloted by only one slazan. What could be prouder than that—to go out alone and destroy a civilian outpost all on your own? The slazan enemy is ruthless. And I don't want you confusing some primitives with the ruthless warriors we are fighting. We must fight this war. We must win it. We must confine the slazan to only one or two worlds if we are to make life safe for human expansion."

I look to ibn Haj, who says nothing, who does not contradict the General. "But," I say, "there's a third world with slazans on it."

The General nods. "Yes, and you will document the obvious. It's a failed colony that has no contact with rest of the slazan species."

"Failed? They might be rather successful at the way they live their lives."

"Maybe, but look around you. Compared to this, how can you call a group of primitives with bows and arrows successful?"

"So what will happen to them?"

"If God wills it, and we win this war, then we will ship them to a slazan homeworld."

"But they are on their homeworld."

The General looks to ibn Haj rather than to me. "We are spending a substantial sum to show that they do not belong on that world. God willing, that planet will be settled by humans when the war is over." The General looks to me, his voice generous, not a trace of cynicism. "Your outstanding research is what will help make that possible."

After dinner ibn Haj is wise enough not to ask what's wrong. He tells me there's one café that serves wine during select hours after the last call to prayer. The café is small, and one perpetual candle lights each table. Only a few tables are occupied, but each tiny group leaves the moment they've finished drinking, each casting a covert glance or two to ibn Haj in his general's uniform.

There are no waiters or servers. Ibn Haj punches in a code, and a glass of wine is presented. I am surprised by its quality. While I sip the wine, looking forward to its mild effect, ibn Haj tells me not to worry about the General.

"You lied to the General," I say, surprised by how easily honesty comes. "Or you lied to me. You told the General this mission would help claim a world for humanity. You told me it would help us negotiate peace. Which is it?"

"What I told you."

I say nothing.

"Look, Pauline, we aren't going to win this war. We aren't going to drive the slazans back. They fight too effectively."

"In fact," I say, "they're winning the war. They've broken into one of our systems."

"They're not winning. We've found one of their

home systems. We think we got one missile through their defenses."

"This was before their attack?"

"Yes. We want to hit a military target first before we announce we've hit a civilian target."

I'm thinking: *The article by al-Kharrat was right. Judith was right. Their attack on the civilian outpost was retaliation, tit for tat.*

Ibn Haj misreads my reaction. "Look, the General is overly optimistic because of one missile. He's not right. And, besides, he's not a very good general. He rose to his current position because of family connections. But, look, he hasn't been close to the war for over three years."

Ibn Haj waits for me to pick up on the significance of this. The standard military rotation is a half year in the war zone, a half year patrolling a human-controlled stellar system, then a final half year back in the war zone. It's expected of every able-bodied person, enlisted or officer. It indeed does not speak well for the General if he's been kept here on one pretext or another for three years. I smile faintly.

"You see? If you do good research ... if you can show us how the slazans resolve conflicts, how they establish leadership, how they work out territory and possession, you might give us enough to help negotiate a real peace. If we can't make sure that slazan and human are discussing similar values, no peace can be settled. Knowledge can't conquer. It can only convince. But if we don't have the knowledge, we can't convince anyone."

I want to be swept along by his charm and conviction. "But does it really matter what we know to be true? No matter how inept he is, he is in charge of the project, and he outranks you."

The next shift—morning as far as my stomach is concerned—ibn Haj escorts me to medical for surgery. They place the implant in my skull and microphone studs in each earlobe to record what's around me. Ibn Haj returns after I have recovered. "Your ship will be ready in two days, but I want you to meet the captain and crew now."

Seen from the wall-viewers, the *Way of God* is enormous, but most of its enormity is engine, water, and food storage. The corridors are slim, the cabins tiny, the shared washroom dismal. Captain al-Shaykh is a thin, severe woman, but a well-mannered host, who offers coffee and makes me feel welcomed. The cabin she shares with her comrade-in-arms, the executive officer, is more spacious and has its own tiny washroom. She and the general lead me on a tour of the ship, and everyone is courteous and dignified around the captain and the general.

Ibn Haj sets me free for the afternoon. There is so much to attend to. "I'm sure an anthropologist will see enough in a few hours to keep herself amused."

So I walk the station and feel terribly out of place. I am the age of the officers, and the bulk of the inhabitants are the age of those I teach. My skin doesn't have the same lively sheen, nor do I have their well-sculpted muscles. I watch them march the corridors in pairs, their faces veiled, the women in uniforms of ship's crew, office personnel, or orbital organizers, the men wearing the clothing of high rank, of infantry, of security personnel. But they all seem to move with the same hard, dull energy, and I am unable to tell if they walk with purpose or if they are pacing away off-duty hours, awaiting some new posting that would take them far away to where warships patrol the stars and occasionally battle the enemy.

At least a third have had cultural tailoring, all of these youths with shiny black hair, dark eyes, and cheekbones angled like the wings of birds. But even with the variation—the fair skin, the light hair, and the hazel eyes—there is no one with a face as dark as mine.

They stare at me all the time. In the dining halls, the cafés, the mosque, heads turn when I enter, and eyes watch with curiosity. It doesn't matter that I wear a uniform that attaches me to a warship. There is no meanness or hatred; they are curious; they want to know why someone—who possesses neither Arab roots nor impressive rank—is on board an Arab station.

I think of the ship I will be boarding, its wealth of Semitic faces, its crew trained in pairs, having served together for almost a year. There will be no place in their little society where I will easily fit. I will be with them for a year of voyage. I will be alone, planetside, by myself for two hundred days. I begin to wonder at the wisdom of my choice. Not because of the mission's moral ambiguity, not because of the General, but because I don't know if the human psyche has evolved to cope with so much solitude.

At dinner ibn Haj and I dine with several majors and a general who is scheduled to return to the war zone. Ibn Haj wants me to see how readily he can talk with them, how easily they listen to his point of view. Fearing my future solitude, I am easily impressed. I allow myself to be drawn in by his prestige, by the strength he carries so readily, by his promises of peace.

I let him serve me wine in his quarters. I let him sit as close as he wants. And I lean forward just enough so he knows to kiss me. I hint between kisses at how long it has been, and the desire on his face is softened further by a new tenderness. I tell him because I want to be a chaste prize, I want something that will be warm and lasting.

The Ju/wasi say that hunger for sex, like hunger for food, can kill people. Sex is called doing work, eating meat, drinking fat. *Tain*, the Ju/wa word for wild honey, is also the word for orgasm. Just when ibn Haj takes me into his full embrace do I feel the accumulated years of hunger, and I pull him to me with the same urgency a starved man may break his fast.

Afterward I feel both sated and empty. The bed is warm, but I find I don't want to be lying next to him, to have his arm around my shoulders. I speak into the darkness, wanting some kind of shared secrecy, some kind of intimacy that justifies his skin pressing against mine after all the desire is gone. "Muhammad?"

"Hmmmmmm."

"What happens if we don't make it back? What if the *Way of God* becomes a statistic? What if we are lost in hyperspace, or hit by a meteor, or . . . whatever?"

He says nothing for a moment.

"Well? Do you send a rescue team? Or a follow-up mission?"

"The rescue team would be too late. And there's no money for a follow-up mission."

"So what happens?"

"You get what you want. The slazans on that planet get left alone for a long time. All the data is in one place. If you're missing and assumed lost, I'll inform the intelligence that guards the data. If I follow the protocol I've established, all the data will be wiped out. It will be as if we never knew the slazans were there."

I roll onto my side to try to get a better look at him. "It's all gone?"

"It will be if you don't come back. Your slazans will be left alone."

"Won't you get court-martialed?" I say it with admiration. I've begun to feel differently, to reevaluate everything I've thought.

"No. The General approves. If we negotiate a peace, a record of this planet's existence can cause us problems, more problems than it's worth without your study. The slazans might exert a claim once they know of its existence. Human space is located between slazan space and this world. It's better to sign a treaty that includes its stellar system in our sphere of influence. We know where the Raman probe went. It wouldn't take too long to rediscover the planet once the peace was stable. But that's a good decade or two or three that your slazans will have on their own. With no war going on, they'll probably get a reserve just like your Ju/wasi did."

My Ju/wasi did not get a reserve. A group of Arabs, Hindus, and Africans purchased a reserve and turned themselves and their children into Ju/wasi. The Ju/wasi on Earth lost their land, piece by piece, first to the Dutch, then to government planning, and finally to Bantu pastoralists, until there was so little land that only handfuls of people could gather enough food to survive. No one provided needed land for the Terran Ju/wasi. Who would ever buy these slazans a reserve?

The next shift, after we breakfast, ibn Haj presents me two gifts, two packages that had been delivered to his quarters while we were out. I think, the first is for last night, the second is for tonight. Last night's reward is a knife and its sheath. The sheath is made of finely tanned leather, inscribed with pan-slazan lettering. I remove the knife. The blade is sharp, curves nicely. The hilt is black.

I hold it in my hand, let it respond to my warmth, re-form itself to the shape of my grip. I can't help but smile, and I can't help but hug him. The slazan knives had entered the market months before the war started, just a year before New Hope was burned from planet into rock.

"I can't take this," I say.

"Take it as a talisman," he says. "It was made by slazan hands—well, by slazan technology, actually—and you will be studying slazans."

"And the second gift?"

The second gift is Ju/wa clothing meant for a woman. "Try it on," he says.

I feel suddenly shy, but I will be wearing these in front of alien strangers soon enough. The pubic apron, decorated with beads, brushes against my thighs; another apron of plain leather rubs lightly against my behind. I lift up the chi !kan, fashioned most likely from a gemsbok hide. I rub my hand over the red-brown leather and think of the work that has gone into it—the sun-drying, the scraping, the tanning, the hard rubbing that gave this skin the soft texture of suede. I tie one end over my shoulder then use a thong to tie the other end around my waist, more leather draping my backside, a pouch around me, where I can place what I gather. "Is this from the reserve?" I ask. The trust law requires that no Ju/wa craft be made for sale.

"No. It was made here."

"By who?"

"His name is Esoch al-Schouki. He's a lieutenant in the infantry."

I consider the name. *Al-Schouki* is the name of a noted poet. *Esoch* has no meaning in Arabic or Ju/wasi. "How did he come by such a name? How did he know to make a chi !kan?"

"He chose his own name. The garments he made himself. He grew up on the reserve."

"He's Ju/wa?"

"Yes. He was recruited after he left the reserve. We shipped him the supplies; he finished making these yesterday. He did good work, especially since he had no idea why he was asked to make them."

I stand before ibn Haj, bare legs, naked breasts,

and I feel on display. "You know," I say, "Ju/wa men make these for their wives."

"He must have been married once. The work looks good."

Ibn Haj leaves me to spend the day wandering. Final shipments have come in, the overhaul is almost done, and he must tie together the final strings of our plans to insure the mission will leave the next day. I walk the station, speak with no one, and take notes in my head as a way to feel in place and useful. Just before we are to meet for dinner, ibn Haj sends me a message that he will be up during the entire next shift tying off too many knots. I dine alone. I wander. After the final call for prayer, I go to the café that serves wine. I am not a general, so no one leaves.

I find myself sitting near a man who looks equally out of place. He has all the features of the Ju/wasi—the short stature, the flat cheekbones, the epi eye folds, the peppercorn hair—and I ask him if he is Lieutenant Esoch al-Schouki.

He is surprised. I tell him who I am. He does not seem to recognize my name or face, but he is more than happy to have someone to talk with. His Arabic is good, hardly the trace of an accent, but I want to speak in the tongue of all my romantic ideals of human sharing. I ask him his name.

"≠oma."

"There are a lot of ≠oma's. Did they call you anything else?"

He hesitates, and in his hesitation I see the adult face of a Ju/wa boy I once knew, and desiring that fondness, I wait for this grown man to offer another name, Owner of Music. What he says, almost too soft to hear is, "No. Just ≠oma."

He is alone in the café because his comrade-in-arms died in a war-games accident several months ago. He just returned from compassionate leave, and he is awaiting reassignment and retraining with a new comrade. He explains in Arabic, his tone matter-of-fact, devoid of self-pity. I feel like I see a deeper emotion in his eyes.

I switch back to Ju/wa for conversation, and we

share stories. I tell him research stories. He tells me
hunting stories. He doesn't want to talk about his family
or where he grew up. But he tells his stories well, and I
am drawn to him. He is as out of place as I am, because
once he starts speaking in our shared language, he gains
a kind of energy that belies the wine and the late-night
hours. I take him to my cabin that night, and there is
more tenderness than pleasure. After making love we
sleep like a Ju/wa couple, his chest, belly, and thighs
pressed to my back, and I don't sleep for hours, just sa-
voring the warm touch of human skin against mine,
shoring up this memory for the solitude of the next two
years. In the morning I awake with him inside me, his
arms wrapped around my belly, and he calls me his wife
when he reaches his moment, leaving a dull edge of desire where his body had once been.

On board the *Way of God*, I keep thinking of him.
We accelerate away from the sun toward our jump
point. The walls of the corridor bear images of Wadi al-
Uyoun streets, and the gravity and air composition
match those of the University quarter. But rather than
nostalgia for my scholarly flat, large in comparison to
my cabin, or for my colleagues; rather than dream upon
ibn Haj's handsome form, or Ascherman's failed honor,
I think of the Ju/wa infantry man.

And I think of his Ju/wa name, ≠oma, and in my
mind I compare him with the boy who was called by the
same name. I conjure up the adult face and compare it
with a youthful face that bore similar lines and curves.
The younger ≠oma was at the border between boyhood
and puberty when I came to live among the people at the
Dobe waterhole. He had been a pleasant boy, eager to
please, already going out with his father on the occasional hunting expedition. He was anxious to kill his first
male antelope, which would be the first part of his initi-
ation into manhood, and as modest as the rest of them
try to be, he told me how poor a hunter he was and how
he would never catch anything and have to grow old and
never marry. He said it with a sly smile. When he shot
arrows into one of the giant anthills, they always sank in
around the same spot.

But there was already trouble. He had been injured

once, and the reserve medico, taken in by him, had gifted ≠oma with a wonderful eight-keyed thumb piano. A music company on the Northern Continent had developed and sold such thumb pianos for those moderns who liked Ju/wa music, which was fashionable for a very brief time. These thumb pianos are more durable, their sound more assured and professional, than those made from traded metal and wood that the Ju/wasi build themselves and that reserve charter forbids them to sell.

Little ≠oma loved that thumb piano. And he played it every night, and he steadfastly refused to give it away in the extensive gift-giving network that ties the Ju/wasi together. There were at least two arguments when I was there, and once his family was forced to move to another waterhole where his uncle lived until things cooled down. When they called him Owner of Music, it was both envy and insult: he played so well; he shared so poorly, as if he could own music itself.

The older ≠oma, the one who called himself Esoch, did not tell me why he had left his people. He said he had lived for some time in a settlement camp called Chum!kwe, located near a dried-up waterhole on the northern edge of the reserve. The north is the driest part of the reserve. There are more people than the land can carry, and occasional Ju/wa migrate out, hoping to find another source of sustenance. But the entire region is depressed. So those who come to Chum!kwe stay there and live on government rations of mealie-meal and work odd jobs paid for in local scrip. Nutrition is low, a tuberculosis analog is on the rise, and anger is everywhere. I stayed there one week, among the disheveled huts and the dust. There are too many people, and when angers flare, there's nowhere to move. As many people have been murdered here in five years as in the entire reserve over five decades.

The government provides two ways out. For those with a qualifying talent, there are training programs for primal peoples who want to rejoin and contribute to contemporary societies. For the young and strong, there is the military.

≠oma said he had gotten in a fight with a man and afterward joined the mili. He thought he would use his anger well in war but was surprised to find how frightening the simulations were. He hoped they never found a slazan homeworld for the infantry to invade.

More and more I visualize his serious face, lay its image over that of the twelve-year-old ≠oma Owner of Music, and I remember the sly youthful smile. When I am planetside, when I am laid out flat by adaptation sickness, I will dream of him making his way through alien forest and coming to my rescue. I will lie there, sweaty and miserable, and feel unworthy of rescue. And the real Esoch al-Schouki will be on a military base that orbits E-donya, he will be assigned a new comrade-in-arms, and together they will await a new assignment.

Chapter Five

The Seventh Day

Esoch didn't die of snakebite that night. He dozed off readily, dreamed, remembered, until some sound, or the shape of the nest—which hadn't been designed for a human body, and perhaps wasn't well designed for a slazan body, either—kept waking him. Each time, he opened his eyes to the darkness, then let them shut again, curling up, on the edge of sleep, a victim of his wandering mind.

He kept seeing Hanan, her black hair, the gentle curve of her cheek, the way her black eyes stayed with you when you spoke, and his mind kept intruding with Dikobe's face. And later he dreamed he was on the reserve. Dikobe was wearing her pu-

bic apron and chi !kan. She was sweating with sickness and leaning against Hanan. He started to dance while someone he
couldn't see clapped out the rhythm; his feet pounded the sand
until the n/um began to boil within him, his stomach tightening,
everything around wavering until he could see the //gangwasi,
the spirits of the dead, out in the night, beyond the fire. There
was his father, his body thin and frail, having spent the last years
of his life coughing and coughing. He was walking toward
Dikobe, and Esoch implored, "Don't take her. She's got so much
work left to do." But his father didn't touch Dikobe. "You're the
one," he said, "You're the one I've missed for so long. You're
the one I want to see."

And his father stopped there, so he could dream it all over
again, dancing his way into !kia, until he felt the pain in his
belly, the energy boiling through his body, then he reached forward to pull the arrows of sickness out of Dikobe, and always
his father, walking toward him, until it started to rain on them
all, the water drenching their bodies, soaking their clothes, his
father about to speak when something exploded, once, then
twice, and the water poured in, washing Dikobe away, and Esoch
was a kid again, running in the rain, the other kids, none his age,
running through the chu/o—the face of the huts—dodging
hearths and logs, fires sizzling into gray and black because the
rains were washing the heat away and soon everything would
grow, greens sprouting from the ground, from the limbs of trees,
flowers opening with the season's ripeness, but here everything
was black, and Esoch could only feel the rain: heavy drops—he
imagined—sliding through the canopy, sounding almost like
waves lapping against the shore, then cascading down, rustling
leaf after leaf. The rain was cold, and he lay there, unable to see
a thing, muscles cramped, an edge of the thatching sticking into
his lower back. His hand touched the center of the nest; a small
puddle was collecting there. He wasn't sure how long he remained curled up, miserable, listening to and feeling the cold
rain, before he sat up. This rain pounded against the ground; he
could hear it like tiny footsteps, not the snake hissing he'd heard
in his youth when the sand eagerly drank in the falling water.

The torchlight, a bright tunnel against the darkness, made
the rain look as if it were suspended, just a series of elongated
drops that hung there without falling, but then he shined the light
upon the ground, watched in amazement the way the ground refused the water, the way tiny brown rivers rolled downhill, forming the tiny tributaries to the long thin streams, all rushing

headlong. If the rain weren't so loud, he imagined, he would hear the nearby river swelling and frothing. He sat there, eyes open, his onesuit drenched and sticking to his body. He shone the light on his wounds. Each was swollen and dark. The rain had washed the blood away.

Dawn was invisible in the forest, but as soon as the gray light made it possible to see without a torch, Esoch consumed a ration and clambered out of the nest and down the tree. The white line connecting his green dot to Dikobe's had been reduced to 25.1 kilometers. He headed off, following the curves of the river. He had walked over three kilometers when he remembered that he had wanted to retrieve the dead snake, to save it for its antivenin. He rechecked the tracking disc; the white line connecting him to Dikobe had been reduced by a little more than a kilometer. So much walking, and he was hardly any closer. He didn't have time to turn back.

He continued on, following any path that stayed close to the river. He passed through areas where the ground had been burned clean and where fresh grass and bushes grew. He passed through old cleared areas wild with brush. The sky above remained heavy with gray. Leaves everywhere remained green, and the lack of color seemed foreboding. It smelled as if it would rain again, but he didn't trust his senses.

The forest thinned out: fresh grasses and fewer trees, gray light filling up a hole in the distance. Esoch found himself drawn away from the river and toward the light.

The clearing was large, and in the clearing was a village. Standing at the edge of the clearing, hidden behind the brush, Esoch could see shelters as elaborately designed as the nest in which he had spent the night. Paths wove around all the huts, each path bordered by elaborate thin ditches, half-filled with sluggish water. The village paths were littered with leaves and branches, fresh from the storm, but there was no sign of other debris. There were no hearths. No black smudges left by fire. No sign of life. The only sounds came from the forest, giving the village a haunted quiet.

Who would build a village so carefully, who would maintain its paths and drainage ditches and shelters, and then leave it empty?

Even under gray skies the thatching had a golden glow. It then occurred to him: the shelters were close together, too close together for a slazan village. And such carefully structured villages suggested a people rooted in place by the plants they cultivated. But there were no signs of fields, nor had the forest been picked bare by a concentrated populace. He was reminded of empty mosques between calls to prayer, the quiet hush of sacred places.

Pauline would want to see this place. He marked it on the tracking disc—a dark violet blip. He felt as if he were marking the future, a way of insisting that there would be a Pauline, that she would later want to see this place.

Esoch retraced his path, and not much later he came to a fork in the river. One branch was the main river itself, the other a tributary. Was this the tributary that would take him near to Dikobe's clearing? He couldn't make sense of all the lines of the tracking-disc screen—the blues, the blacks, the reds. The skills he'd learned in training had diminished with his increasing exhaustion. He'd grown up without flatscreen maps; the knowledge of landscape had been built upon years of experience: everything was pictures in your head, not drawings upon a screen.

He sat down. He ate his second-to-last ration. He drank from his third-to-last packet. He wished Ghazwan were here; during simulations Ghazwan only had to glance at that tracking disc to know which way to go. Esoch studied the map several times with several different overlays. He decided this tributary wasn't the one, he had to go farther southeast.

He wondered how the locals crossed the river, but he saw no signs of bridges, no nearby fallen trunks, no rocks to form a stepping path. From their waisthooks Esoch removed pistol, then torch, then tracking disc, then palmtalk (which he held on to for just a moment while he considered breaking radio silence, contacting Pauline, but there was the *Way of God* leaving orbit, the flash of light, the possibility that the enemy could be listening in), and he sealed the four items in his pack. He carefully lowered himself into the river, dirt and small stones digging into his palms, then waded through the water, which rushed up to his chest. As he groped to climb the opposite bank, mud splattered over his chest, smeared across his knees, and covered his hands.

His wounds now stung. He rinsed his wounded hand clean, but a thin layer of dirt had been etched into the broken skin. He couldn't get to the wound on his belly without removing his onesuit, something he briefly considered doing.

He emptied the water from his boots, returned everything to the waisthooks, and set off again. A kind of hunger worked through his body. He felt removed from everything, his limbs weak. The occasional gust of wind, or the accidental run-in with a bush, rustled the leaves like last night's storm and showered down a proportionate amount of rain. His skin was cold, clammy, and he felt he would never be dry again. The pain in his hand remained. The onesuit fabric rubbed against the wound on his belly.

Clearings where slazans had cut away wood were fewer, but none was bathed in sunlight: overhead loomed gray, darkening clouds, and by midmorning the rains resumed.

The rain, he told himself, was safety: predator and prey would be hiding; neither would be out seeking food. Slazans would be huddled in shelters or under trees, and no one would be seeking him. And Dikobe? Was she safe and warm inside the shuttle? Or was she out in the wilderness, sick and dying?

He waded through a second tributary, the water speckled by rain, ripples of water overwhelmed by the river's flow. This time the water rose to his waist. Someone had carefully placed a log over the third tributary, and he crawled along it so he wouldn't slip. Whoever had found or placed it there had carved elaborate designs into the wood. He marked his tracking disc for Pauline.

He stopped to lean against a tree. Water dripped from his hair, ran cold down across his eyes, along cheeks, over ears, down the back of his neck. He bent his legs, then stretched, but the tension in the back of his thighs would not be eased away. He longed for a familiar landscape: the wide spread of yellowing grass and dull-green bushes, an occasional tree rising up and spreading out its limbs, all of it merging in the distance like a low wall. And when the rains fell, they didn't fall forever like this. They often fell over distant land. He once stopped at the edge of the reserve and turned to look in the direction he had come. His attention was held by the dark, faraway clouds, and— his throat dry, the land where he stood parched—he watched the rain's hair falling from cloud to land.

The rains died slowly, but afterward tiny brown streams still carved their way through the growth, washing down to the river, and trees still showered down sudden bursts of water. Esoch ate his last ration and drank from the second-to-last drinking packet. He was still hungry, still thirsty. Sounds returned: birdsongs, trills, garbles, croaks, a distant roar. Rain-sparkled green and reds and yellows began to glow, and up above, thin cracked lines of blue outlined the highest leaves and branches.

As the afternoon progressed, so did his sense of weakness.

It became harder to walk. The wound in his hand was darker, the swollen skin harder. The pain along his belly was its own separate fire. He came to a tributary, a wedge of hillside where the two waters met, the waters a momentary rush of turbulence, the air carrying a scent of cool water, as fresh as last night's rain. He was sure this tributary would take him to Dikobe. The red lines on the tracking disc seemed to waver. The white line measured 10.8 kilometers. He was close. He should feel something. He followed the new stream of water.

After a while all he wanted to do was curl up and lie down. He drank from the last packet. The light-headedness wasn't abated. He took no more than five steps before he dropped to his knees and vomited a liquid, rank bile. He continued heaving. If this was adaptation sickness, if this was his body adjusting to everything new in the atmosphere, then he could see why Dikobe's behavior had become erratic, why she had snapped at Jihad, why she had shut off all transmission just to be alone. All Esoch wanted to do was curl up and let his body somehow live through this moment.

He remembered Chum!kwe: the dust, the too many people, the government-built shelters, the gray recruiting station, the long lines leading to where they distributed the mealie-meal, the crowded, pockmarked clinic with the sallow-faced medico who had no medicines but who could diagnose anything, the man who gave you minor jobs and paid you in blue slips of paper, the fat woman at the bottle shop who took the blue slips in return for bitter whiskey, and Bo—long legs and hard eyes—who shared the whiskey with him, and the morning he had found himself lying alone in the mud, his body curled in pain. How could he have kept drinking after what he had done to Bo?

He'd been trying to end a life then; but now he'd been entrusted with a life. Somehow, he stood up. Somehow, he walked, following paths that curved in and around areas, staying close as he could to the winding river. He walked three kilometers to get one kilometer closer to Pauline, another three to get a little less than two. He kept looking down at the black disc in his palm, at the tiny numbers on the readout screen. The numbers held his attention. The numbers helped him stay upright and ignore the pain, because the white line between his green dot and Dikobe's green dot kept getting shorter and shorter.

A beeping started in his head, becoming background noise with all the other noises. By the time he heard the rustle of leaves, the sound was close enough for him to realize that something was running toward him. He stopped and listened. He hardly heard the beeping. Instead he heard footsteps. Running footsteps. Two sets. They sounded so human. His wounded hand was already at the waisthook, already lifting the pistol, already switching the safety off.

The first one emerged ten meters in front of him and stopped. The slazan child couldn't have been higher than Esoch's chest. It stood there, naked, semi-erect penis between legs, and this very human part of its body enhanced the alien quality of the rest of him. A slazan girl stopped right beside him. Her head was even with the boy's shoulders. She too was naked. She too stared at him with eyes equally wide. Surprise? Wonderment? Fear? Why didn't they turn to run?

A voice sounded in the woods. He hadn't heard any kinds of words in so long that he found himself turning to face the speaker even while his grip on the pistol tightened, the metal pressed against his swollen palm. An adult slazan, not too much taller than the boy, stepped in front of the two children. Esoch couldn't tell if it was a woman or a man. The skin of the breasts looked withered, like those of an old man. A pubic skirt hung from a waist band. Looped over the shoulders and tied at the waist was a huge skin that was shaped much like a chi !kan a Ju/wa woman wears to carry food, to transport ostrich eggshells full of water, much like the one he had made Dikobe, but this one had elaborate designs all along the edges. The chi !kan made Esoch decide this was a woman, a gatherer, but, then, what was she doing with that quiver full of arrows? The arrow the slazan woman withdrew from the quiver and notched in her bow was impressive: the shaft was thicker, longer, than anything a Ju/wa would use, the arrowhead large enough to do substantial damage.

Here was the enemy, preparing to kill him. It would be so easy to fire the pistol. The burning in his hand distracted him. The harder he gripped the pistol, the more it hurt. The adult slazan took no notice of the gun. Why should she? She wouldn't recognize it. So why hadn't she let loose the arrow? He was the enemy. She should kill him, he thought, and, at the same time: she's only protecting her children.

Even though she held bow and arrow, and even though Esoch had always associated arrows with men and with hunting, he found it easy to think of this slazan as a woman, as a mother, and he found it easy to step back, once, then twice, then three times.

The two children watched him. The arrowhead remained

steady. He took one more step, then another. The farther away, the lesser the target. But a kind of controlled anger replaced the fear. What was to stop him from raising the pistol and demonstrating his strength? Esoch hated himself for the thought, for the way it came to him so readily the more he retreated into safety. This woman's face, these children's faces, belonged to the face of the enemy, and he felt like a coward, he felt like he must shoot them. What was brave in shooting them? The idea was alien to him. Until he'd joined the mili, bravery and murder had had nothing to do with each other. Murder was sudden anger, and he had no reason to be angry.

Now he was a good ten meters away, the intervening trees and brush making him a poor target for bow and arrow. He still held the pistol, and the swollen wound still stung. What was one more death? They weren't human.

He ran until he couldn't run, until breathing became impossible. He wrapped an arm around a tree to hold himself up. His heart beat against the inside of his chest. His body was bathed in sweat; his damp onesuit clung to his skin. Perspiration rolled into his eyes, and he blinked. He gulped in breaths of air, and he felt like he was drowning.

When he recovered, he found that he had lost the tracking disc.

The dark ground was moist, and it was easy to follow his own spoor: the sole and heel of his boots made clear indentations. Accustomed to reading tracks in the sand, he was surprised how readily he could interpret the impressions in dark, wet soil. The deep, heavy tracks of his running, the zigzag of his exhaustion. Each time he crouched, each time he tilted his head to read the ground, nausea swam through him. But one clearing was slick with mud, and it was hard to find himself in the splattered impressions he had left. The nausea became unbearable, and he found himself on hands and knees heaving up air, noticing the terrible, muddied pain in his hand only when he rose to his feet. He considered giving up, just following the river without the tracking disc, but how would he ever find the tiny stream that ran through Dikobe's clearing?

He finally found the spot where he had started running. Here was the trail of back-steps he had taken away from the mother's steady aim. Then he found where he had stood when the children had burst forth, where the woman had found them.

Nothing in the tiny clearing looked familiar. It was as if he'd never been here at all.

By now light was fading; it was early evening. He used the torch, scourged the whole area, but he couldn't find the tracking disc. If he hadn't dropped it here, where had he lost it? Did he have it with him when he heard the two children rushing through the brush? He remembered using it every time he stood up. But the time he had fallen asleep? Most definitely. He had used the disc to reorient himself.

The ground of the clearing was clouded with his prints now. He tried to re-see the whole moment: the boy, the girl, the woman. What exactly had he done? He heard himself step back, he heard the soft whisper of the disc hitting the ground, but he didn't know if that was memory or a memory he'd just invented.

He left his own spoor for theirs. The tracks here were clear. By the size of the feet, by the depth of the impression, he made out the boy, the girl, the woman. He could follow this to wherever they would camp tonight. But would they have the tracking disc? And if they did, how would he get it back? They had no language in common, no sure gesture he could make to assure them of his peaceful intent. And if he had to shoot the woman to get the disc? Dikobe hadn't wanted a single slazan life to be harmed because of her presence here.

He heard voices in the distance, feet running, an occasional shout. He assumed the two children were playing. He didn't hear the waggle of leaves and the fall of rain, so he guessed they were playing in a clearing, staying away from the forest and its potential threats. He listened harder, heard a faint sizzling: fire and wet wood. Whatever role they had assigned to him, they hadn't considered him a hunter, someone who had the skills to follow them.

He waited for night, crouched on his haunches, dull pain radiating from his hand, from his belly, every muscle aching. He should go in now, use the pistol, and get the disc. Pauline was depending on him. But he couldn't move. His heart was pounding, but his eyelids kept drooping, shutting. He yearned for sleep, lots of sleep. It was as if his body were trying to turn itself off so he wouldn't have to commit the crime he feared.

Bo, his whiskey-drinking partner at Chum!kwe, had been older than he, had a brother living at Mahopa whose name was ≠oma, so Bo called him tsin, younger sibling, and he called Bo, !ko, older brother, even though ≠oma had been the oldest of four children. So the two brothers by name shared their time at

Chum!kwe eating mealie-meal, drinking, and avoiding the military recruiters.

So one night it had been Bo and ≠oma—!ko and tsin, older brother and younger sibling—drinking and sharing stories. Nothing grew in Mahopa, the waterholes were dried out, Bo's family had gone to live with cousins, with uncles, and Bo came here, out of the reserve. ≠oma told only part of the story: how he had fought with his wife's father, how he had shouted at his wife's mother, how he couldn't bear to stay after the horrible things anger made him say. He told Bo how he had walked across the desert and hoped a lion would eat him and end his misery. But there was much that ≠oma didn't tell Bo. He didn't tell Bo about the thumb piano or the things his wife's mother had said to him. He didn't tell Bo that when he had walked across the desert toward Chum!kwe, he had often stopped and looked back in the direction of /gausha. He could imagine N!ai's face. He longed to return to her. He considered facing the endless teasing, hearing again and again about the things he had done wrong, to cool his heart, to make him less stingy and more generous, and how even in Chum!kwe, among the gray shelters, he sometimes stared off into the distance, in the direction he had come, and considered heading back. Perhaps if he had said that, perhaps then Bo wouldn't have made the jokes a brother can make. Bo said that N!ai must be alone and cold at night, that Bo could maybe keep her warm, and ≠oma resented those words and Bo's laughter and how his laughter joined in because they called each other !ko and tsin. Bo said that N!ai must be hungry with no one to hunt for her, and ≠oma could have teased Bo about his lack of a wife in Mahopa, but he said nothing because what Bo said was true, which made the resentment harden into anger. Bo said how hungry he was and how maybe he would leave Chum!kwe to eat the food his tsin, his little brother, didn't want.

A knife that had known only the blood of animals was in Bo's gut before ≠oma understood what had happened, how quickly the anger had boiled, how quickly it had caused his hand to act.

It didn't matter that there had been an infirmary and a medico; all that mattered was this: if it had been at /gausha, if his anger had burned his heart, he would have grabbed an arrow, and nothing would have cooled the poison on its tip, and Bo would have died within a day. Lying on the infirmary bed, eyes half-opened, Bo saw ≠oma approach, and Bo turned his head away.

Later that day ≠oma went to the gray recruiting station. He couldn't think of a better place for a killer.

When he had been assigned a comrade-in-arms, he had wondered: how long before he turned on this friend, too?

The night was cold. Esoch shivered in his wet onesuit. He had to concentrate to keep his teeth from chattering. The caked mud on his palm was a compress of dull pain, and he was dizzy from hunger. For an hour all he had heard was the sputtering and crackling of the campfire. He dimmed the torchlight enough to make out the trail, and he made his way toward the camp, surprised that he could walk rather than stumble.

At the edge of the clearing he stopped. In the center was a shelter, and in front of that, one large fire. The woman was wrapped in her chi !kan and slept on one side of the fire. The two children slept on the other side. Each was wrapped in animal skins. The smaller body, the girl's, was closest to the fire. Near the shelter stood one sapling. Various items hung from its branches, including the quiver of arrows and the bow. Whatever the woman had thought of his presence, it hadn't made her anxious enough to place weapons close at hand. The woman was sleeping soundly.

Esoch wanted the comfort of the pistol in his hand. He left it on its waisthook. He crouched and stared until he was accustomed to the fire's light and his own anxieties, and it was on his third or fourth visual scan of the camp that he noticed it, the firelight dancing red across its black surface: the tracking disc. It rested, face down, near the girl's sleeping body. If they all slept soundly, it should be no trouble to walk across the smooth surface of the ground and retrieve it. All his worrying for nothing. He didn't need the pistol. No one had to die.

One step, and the way his clothes slid against his body made more noise that he had expected. The second step was quieter; the night sounds of the forest were louder than any motion he was making. With the third step he remembered that their hearing would be filtering out the common sounds of the night, their subconscious open to the unique sounds, the ones that could accompany a threat. But he took his fourth step: he was even with the woman's body, and the three slazans hadn't moved. He took a fifth step: was the slazan woman awake, holding her body still, calculating what action to take? Sixth step: would she make a run for her weapons if she awoke? Seventh step, and he was almost there. The warmth of the fire was inviting. He shook his head, as if that would make the dizziness go away. How long had he been standing there, staring at the fire? The next step, and he was standing over the girl. There was nothing sweet and soft about her alien face, but there was something tender in the way she held the animal skin around her, her body curled, the cold night damp against her back.

It was when Esoch crouched down that her eyes snapped open. She screamed. Both the boy and his mother were up, the mother tangled in the animal hide. Esoch bent over, the nausea back, the dizziness worse, but he had the tracking disc in his grasp, except that it slipped out, bounced once, then twice along the dirt. The boy was just standing there. The daughter was scampering away. And the mother wasn't heading for her arrows, she was coming straight for him.

He stepped after the tracking disc. His hand closed on the smooth black surface; he had it and he was rising, ready to run, when the mother's body collided with his. He heard his own body hit the ground. He wanted to get up—he knew what would happen next—but his body gave out on him. He lay there, unable to move, waiting for the inevitable jab of pain. He waited until he forgot what he was waiting for. He heard distant voices, felt the ground scrape his body and the warmth of the fire. When he opened his eyes, he expected to see his father crouching by his side and Ghazwan kneeling opposite him. And would Hanan be there, too, among the //gangwasi, perhaps standing there with Dikobe at her side?

He saw no reason to stay awake.

The Eighth Day

He was lying flat on his belly, the ground rough against his cheek, and he wasn't sure where he was. Had he drunk too much last night and decided to sleep in the street? It was a wonder he wasn't dead.

But the ground was too soft, and he heard the crackle and felt the faint heat of dying coals. The sun was warm upon his face, but it didn't seem to touch the rest of his body. He was tired, lying there, wondering why the sun was up and the women were too lazy to start up the fires, and where was N!ai, who should be pressing her toes against his side, followed by her voice, kept low so her father wouldn't hear, the tone playful, asking him how he could lie there all night and all morning, what kind of husband was so lazy that he could lie there hungry and not think about getting up and hunting?—and then she would giggle, because she was young and amused by the idea that she could talk to him the same way she had heard her mother talk to her father.

He rolled onto his back, and the sun was warm against his eyelids, a soft brightness upon his eyes. He remembered lying like this when he was a child, as high as his mother's waist, and he had opened his eyes to look up her, and she, sitting beside him, had looked down and smiled. His older sister, Kwoba, was sitting by their mother on the female side of the fire, and she was clapping her hands, softly singing a song the women had sung last night during the dance.

"Can I marry Kwoba instead of N!ai?" he asked.

His mother laughed. "You can't marry your sister."

"I mean the Kwoba who lives at /xai/xai."

"No. She has the same name as your sister. I won't have my child become my daughter-in-law."

"Can I marry N≠isa?"

"No. Her father is my brother."

"Can I marry /wa?"

"No. She has the same name as your father's sister."

He asked again and again, and always there was a reason why he couldn't marry any of the girls he named. But he didn't want to marry N!ai. They had just visited /gausha, where N!ai's parents and his parents gave to each other gifts they had made: ostrich-eggshell beads, a knife, a musical bow, and a blanket. Little N!ai—she was as high as his chest—either ran around her parents or clung to her mother's arm while the gifts were given. He liked her father's voice and the easy, joking way he had with his own father, and though he did not look at her mother's face—his own mother had told him to be very respectful with the mother—he did like the sound of her laughter. But he didn't like N!ai, the way she kept running, her face always dirty, or the way she kept sticking her tongue out at him.

He didn't want these memories, he didn't want to remember what it was like living at /gausha, the things N!ai's mother had said about him the day he'd finally left. But he didn't want to open his eyes. His body preferred to lie here in the dirt, listening to the fizzling of dying embers, waiting for the downpour of sun to flood the rest of his body with warmth. He'd just stay here like this and listen to the sound of something moving toward him.

So he had to open his eyes. There was a creature as big as a porcupine, bloated big with dull-colored feathers rather than quills. It had crawled right up in front of him, and its jaw held a loosely wrapped bundle of leather. Before he knew he had the energy to do it, Esoch had rolled away from the creature and jumped to his feet. The creature, frightened by the larger creature's sudden size, scurried backward, but it let go of its bundle, which began to unravel, chunks of food spilling onto the ground and rolling a bit before settling. The creature returned to the woods trailing a banner of animal hide.

Esoch stood there, recovering his breath, in the center of an empty camp. Except for the tumbled food, the ground was empty. No, not quite: the tracking disc was lying on the ground, right near where the wrapped bundle of food had been. But that was it. No weapons hung from the trees. The shelter was empty. Except for three sets of slazan footprints, there was no sign that anyone currently lived here.

Why had they left him alive? Why had they left him the tracking disc and the package of food? He collected up what turned out to be three pieces of fruit, something that looked like a tuber, and five pieces of cooked meat. Was this a gift of some sort? Could they be watching him from the forest to see what he would do?

There was some kind of meaning to the food. And the meaning depended on how the slazan woman had defined his role. Anyone who was invited to live with the Ju/wasi was given a Ju/wa name; Pauline had been named Hwan//a, after a Hwan//a whose husband's name was ≠oma. When she'd come to Dobe, she, being older, had called him little husband, and he had finally called her old wife. He had been a child; it had been a joke.

How had the slazan mother identified Esoch? Or had the gift been a kind of experiment: had she left the food in hopes that the gesture would be interpreted positively?

He took the piece of meat and hesitated. The food could make him sicker. But Jihad had yet to talk to him. He hadn't made it to Dikobe's ship. He had no food of his own. The meat tasted like meat, but like no meat he had ever had before. There was a sweet, crisp edge to the flavor. He ate it slowly. It had been so long since he had eaten meat. The bright-red fruit and the tuber had tasted so bitter than he discreetly spit the pulp into his hand and wiped them on the ground. He was sure the hunted meat carried more prestige than the gathered fruit, but he placed the remainder of the fruit and tuber into his pack to present the illusion of saving them. The two other pieces of fruit had a cloying sweetness to them, but he finished them both. He found where they threw their garbage, and left the pits there; he found where they defecated and did so nearby. He stood, breathed, and found himself weak, but no longer on the edge of delirium.

The slazan mother had given him a place to rest and food to eat. This was the enemy, he told himself. And he was still alive. And the tracking disc still worked. The white line measured 5.8 kilometers on the readout screen. If he hadn't lost the disc, he could have made it there last night.

There were several paths leading away from the camp. He chose the one that curved in the direction of the river, and he followed it, thinking again and again, I'm almost there, I'm almost there, everything should be fine. But still the paths wove in and out of the white line, distance accumulating, the uphill gradient all too soon bringing back the exhaustion and tedium.

More and more he could see the continuities of the land, the way green leaves lifted, twirled, and grew toward the sun, the flashes of red and orange and yellow where the sun shone into open clearing, the way certain animals bore the dull colors of their surroundings and the way others flashed brightly to attract the proper kind of attention.

The more familiar the landscape, the more Esoch's mind turned to other things. He found himself thinking back on Dikobe's talks, on his chats over tea with Hanan, on his parents, and on that tiny thumb piano he had loved too much. He remembered what they had called him. Everyone had nicknames, in part because a number of people had the same names; Dikobe had told him there had been over twenty-five ≠omas and over fifteen N!ai's when she had done her own research. There was N!ai Short Face, and there was his N!ai, N!ai Water, for the way she loved to bathe. There was ≠oma Word, for the way he spoke, and ≠oma Wildebeest, for when he had hunted and killed six wildebeest the day after his marriage, and ≠oma Big Feet, his grandfather, his old name. And they had called him ≠oma Owner of Music for the way he was always playing his thumb piano, early in the morning while children ran between the huts, under a tree when it was too hot to do anything, late at night when he couldn't sleep. They called him Owner of Music, and they told him his testicles would grow into the sand if he kept playing all the time. They told him his wife would never have enough meat. They told him the thumb piano would be a nice gift. He didn't want to think about that, no, not at all.

Esoch would soon be at Dikobe's clearing, he would soon have access to her medicine and her computers, and he would soon know why the *Way of God* had left orbit and why it hadn't returned.

It was late afternoon when he followed a series of tiny waterfalls, no wider than his two hands placed side by side, up a graded hill, his breathing hard, his boots slipping against the mud as he made his way up to the top and finally stepped onto the flattened landscape surrounded by a colorful wall of forest. There was the shuttle craft, all bright and smooth in the sun. The door was open. The clearing was deathly silent. He felt that the forest itself had seen him and hushed in surprise.

"Dikobe!" he called out. His voice sounded harsh, awful, terribly accented.

"Pauline!" He yelled it, but his mind remembered long ago when he had whispered it loudly, again and again, as he struggled for a moment of pleasure.

He hesitated, wanted a voice that sounded right, without the accent and memory. "Hwan//a!"

But no answer. He ran for the shuttle craft, for the open door, then stopped. The ground around the shuttle had been burnt black. The black flatness had been broken up by tiny rivulets from streams that must have formed during yesterday's rain—or was it the day before yesterday?—and had been marred by footprints. But the ground was mostly black, except for an area alongside the ship. There was a swelling of dirt, longer than wide, the dirt fresh, not rained upon, brown flecked by black. Someone had dug a hole and had filled it back up. The hole was long enough to hold a body.

The shuttle door was open, and it was far too quiet. He reached to the waisthook, flicked the fastener aside, and raised the pistol. The safety was off before the pistol was aimed at the doorway. He sidestepped several times, then rushed to the hull of the shuttle. Now he was out of sight of anyone inside. He looked up the hillside. Was he being watched? Was he vulnerable? There was no reason they should recognize a pistol, or was there?

He slid one foot forward. Was this how it was done? He pressed his back so hard against the hull that it hurt. His pistol was leveled straight forward.

No sound came from the inside of the shuttle: no shuffling, no heavy breathing. Was it only empty, like his worst fears, or was someone waiting? What if he leaped in, saw movement, and fired his pistol, and the movement turned out to have belonged to a sick and exhausted Dikobe, rising from the bed where she had been sleeping? What if it belonged to some exploring child, too scared by his approach to do anything but wait?

He was at the edge of the doorway. All he had to do was step up, jump forward, pistol aimed, ready to scan and fire. "Pauline!" he shouted.

No answer. So quiet.

He leaped in, spun around once inside, spun twice before feeling empty and foolish. The cabin was empty.

The following is taken from the notebook Pauline Dikobe kept while traveling to Tienah on the Way of God.

Day Two
   I already want to cry.

   I like the way the neat lines of Arabic script travel across the page as I speak out. I like the way the program adjusts for the infelicities of spoken speech, the same way the mind adjusts to the uneven contours of our spoken sentences, a number of which would read as barely literate if written out word for word, sound for sound.
   I am calmer now. I can sort out my ideas.
   I am not welcome here. The respect and honor I received when I toured the ship with ibn Haj are now absent. There is common courtesy. There are manners. No one will get up from a table when I sit down, but rarely am I joined when I sit down by myself. I can exercise in the tiny gym, but no one invites me to play free-ball. It sounds like self-pity when you find you won't be included. But inclusion is a human expectation; exclusion is the great changer of behavior to all but the most asocial.
   The captain told me this morning that there was little I could do but remain polite and wait it out. The crew is upset. Two crewmates were transferred off the ship so I would have a place to live. The crew credits the two with saving the ship when it came under slazan attack in

the war zone. Everyone was primed to return to the war zone. Their half year of keeping E-donya safe was over. They expected another shot at honor and glory, not a two-year mission far away from the war.

Day Three

The captain or the executive officer sit with me during my meals. They tell me about military routine and what it's like patrolling the war zone and what it's like patrolling around E-donya. They ask me about my religious upbringing and my life in the University.

The captain, in her cabin, over coffee, explains that they sit with me to demonstrate their support. It feels more like protective custody.

Day Four

A routine has formed.

It took two days for the captain and me to work it out.

During the morning shift, when I am most alert, I go over all the research materials the Division of Slazan Studies could provide. There are plenty of images. There are plenty of anecdotes. There are plenty of theories. You could probably print a pamphlet on what we know for sure.

In the afternoon I work with various members of the crew. The ship's intelligence translator teaches me to work with the shuttle's intelligence, and she goes over my daily research plans to look for logistical problems. The engineer demonstrates the working of the shuttle and the equipment. The executive officer teaches me the piloting system because the regulations require it.

I don't see how we're going to fill up five months of travel before I go crazy.

Day Five

I'm still not used to wearing a veil so often. Like all social rules, there are a number of exceptions. The exceptions, I am sure, make sound cultural sense, but they aren't easily enumerated in any conscious rule book.

In the town where I grew up, you wore a veil in public and at home when nonkin were visiting, a tradition that stretches back to the Mediterranean, where honor and modesty were once predominate values. But certain distant kin, and certain less distant male kin, weren't considered close enough, and the veil remained on. Certain friends were so much like family that the veil was removed.

In Wadi al-Uyoun you wore a veil in public places and for formal occasions. In your home and in informal gatherings you removed the veil. In the University, where it's unclear what's formal and informal—a student arguing a point is part of an informal conversation, but the setting, between professor and student, is formal—you saw different people take on different habits.

I expected never to have to wear a veil again once I boarded the *Way of God*. And for the first several days I thought that they kept their veils on only because a civilian stranger was aboard. But, no, you wear veils in the corridors, in the gym, in the dining hall. Even in the washroom the veil stays on until just before you step into the shower. The veil comes off in your cabin, and when someone invites you to their cabin. And during meals veils come off while people eat. During intense conversations, the veil comes off. And in the mosque, on the sabbath, bowing before God, the veil comes off.

Wearing the veil is a way of preserving dignity and privacy, as all thirty-one of us are so cramped together. I think of a group of Ju/wasi, five, or ten, or twenty together, always jabbering at each other, always telling stories, or arguing about a gift, or planning for the next day, or teasing someone else, and only at night do you get some rest from the proximity and the constant companionship and the constant surveillance. Maybe veils make sense, a way to maintain your solitude in a crowded ship.

One of the key slazan words is *solitude*, but slazans don't wear veils. You almost think they would.

Day Six

I like working with Jihad. I like her intense zeal. Her thoroughness is impeccable. Today she had one thousand and one questions about aspects of the anthropological programming we've loaded into the shuttle's intelligence. She wants to know the difference between discriminate analysis and cluster analysis. She wants to know in case the intelligence needs any coaxing. "Intelligences always get confused the first time they do anything really complex. Their inexperience shows."

When we go over the logistics of the research, her zeal takes another turn. Every time I step outside the shuttle, whether it be to stand in the clearing or to go out into the forest to plant imaging pins, Jihad wants to know what I'll do in case of attack. She's sure some slazan at some time will come after me, more likely sooner than later.

I try to explain to her why she shouldn't worry. Attack is a possibility, but it isn't the norm. I give her all sorts of examples, from chimps who dart into the woods, to gorillas who shake branches, to humans who await gifts and money. Attack was the risk you took when dealing with the dullest of animals, like sharks, or with populations who had been previously attacked. We are sitting in Jihad's cabin. Her comrade-in-arms has just served us coffee. Jihad is shaking her head. "We're not talking animals or humans. We're talking slazans."

Day Ten

Tonight I sit alone in the tiny café. It serves wine. Because I am alone, no nearby believer to offend, I have the mixer pour me a glass, and I take it to a table. I can't bear to face the solitude of my cabin. I can't bear to face my solitude among the crew.

Tamr comes in, and I am embarrassed. The engineer is the most devout of the crew. But she asks the mixer for a glass of wine and joins me. "Only drunks and nonbelievers drink alone," she says.

I don't know how to react. She's the same way when we work in the shuttle. She asks me where my prayer rug is when she doesn't see it, she asks me where I've been when I don't show up to the mosque for the afternoon call to prayer, she quotes the Quran when it comes time for wisdom. At the same time, she jokes about the stretch marks she has gained from fattening up during shore leave, and she makes ribald commentary about any equipment that has anything vaguely sexual about its nature. She's a large, imposing woman, charismatic when she's not domineering. She's the last person on the ship I'd expect to see drinking wine.

We sit quietly for a while. She finally asks, "Are you a believer?"

I am tempted to be honest; I am tempted to lie. I settle for compromise. "I am a doubter."

"Were you a doubter before you entered the University?"

"No."

"Do you know a lot about the slazans?"

"I know some. We don't know a lot."

"Will this trip of ours help us know enough to win the war?"

I shake my head. "It might give us enough to know how to negotiate a peace."

Tamr stops drinking. "We can't do that."

"Why not?"

"Negotiating peace, it would make our struggle meaningless. You don't fight seven years against evil and then tire of the fight."

"The slazans aren't evil."

"Then you don't know much about slazans. You haven't paid attention to how they've fought this war. Maybe you'll learn something important on that planet once we get there. I just hope they don't kill you before we can get you back."

I want to tell her what I think of everything she has just said. But what will honesty do but make the voyage even more difficult? I have sat here, in my cabin, for the past hour trying to believe that, trying to convince myself I'm not a social coward.

Day Fifteen

Tonight, after dinner, Jihad invites me back to her cabin, and we sip tea and chat. We start talking about nightmares. Jihad tells me about the nightmare she had about a slazan. One warship, with one slazan warrior, outsmarts the *Way of God*'s intelligence, outsmarts her, and destroys the ship. Jihad's comrade-in-arms, who seems to be the ship's gossip, tells me about other crew members, about their nightmares filled with slazans. As I listen, as I hear again and again about the slazan warrior who travels alone, in the night, or across the night sky, and does his damage, I begin to wonder if these nightmares are the product of group empathy, or of military training.

But the slazans they talk about are nothing like the slazans I know from text and image. How are these people going to feel when I try to befriend the enemy, when I try to find some role where I can live near one's campfire and try to play some minor part in their lives?

"But these are nightmares you are talking about," I say to the two of them.

Jlhad says, "I'm sure the real slazans will be worse."

The following is an excerpt from "What We Know About Slazans," a small pamphlet that Pauline Dikobe put together along with visual imagery and left in the Way of God's *dining hall on the twentieth day of the voyage. Only five copies were taken. Someone disposed of the rest.*

What we have: we have lots of images, we have a slazan vocabulary including words for all anatomical parts, we have records and images from a few dissections (the recovery of slazan bodies is a genre of storytelling all its own). We know nothing of the slazan fossil record. We know nothing of other species within the same animal order, their primates, so to speak. There are hundreds of theories born from examining slazan DNA, but without populations to watch, behaviors to observe, all the theories are just words.

When human and slazan shared New Hope, human and slazan representatives negotiated interstellar trade routes and exploration protocols. From the discussions it became clear that there were two stellar systems that contained slazan populations, but no human has visited a world that was exclusively populated by slazans. Because we don't know the slazan homeworld or its ancestral history, we do not know the environment of evolutionary adaptiveness that revised some previous animal's design until you have the current design of the slazan body and slazan behavior.

Biology: slazans have the same general anatomical features and organs of mammals everywhere. We know they prefer solitary activity over social activity. We don't know the biological roots of their solitude, or the benefits the solitude conferred on their ancestors.

Language: there is, as far as we know, one pan-species language. How do slazans, with their emphasis on solitude, readily learn language without continual social input? It has been hypothesized that a social construct such as language might well have to be hardwired into their brains—syntax and vocabulary both passed on through the genes, but the theory isn't very convincing, nor is such a language very adaptive: words and meanings have to be able to change when the natural or cultural environment changes. Perhaps, others have theorized, slazans have better retentive memory when it comes to pronunciation, definition, and syntax: making language change possible but less likely.

While the slazans on New Hope were reticent to share much in the way of knowledge about slazan life and history, they were more than willing to share their language, first to prevent any unnecessary misunderstanding and second, during the several-year drought, to secure adequate trade agreements. Using the language-reality workshops—so a diplomat can learn Nostratic or an anthropologist can learn Ju/wa—they created a workshop for humans to learn pan-slazan. From that we know the word for *elbow*, and the word for *penis*. We know there are two ways of saying *my sister*: one means the girl who shares my mother; the other, the woman who shares my mother. We know there is a genderless word for *newborn*, for *infant*, for *child*, but once you hit adolescence, there are different words with different roots for male and female; however, there is a word for *son* and a word for *daughter*, neither word associated with a word for "age." The words hint, but never directly describe, the sexual dimorphism, the way the adult men shoot up in size until they're almost twice as large as the adult women. We have a word, transliterated as *gza*, which means both music and medicine, but we have no idea why slazans have associated the two ideas.

Technology: they have an advanced technology, comparable to ours. The social systems that make such cooperation possible are unclear. We know they prefer organic technology—fabrics and medicines derived from

living materials—but they are adept at using metals and
plastics.

Social Customs: adults maintain a personal space of
at least a meter, they look you in the eye only when they
want to emphasize the words they are using, they look
off in the distance when they mean no, and, oddly, they
nod a very human nod when they mean yes. They speak
of sharing words, but they have never offered to share
an actual thing with a human. Their society and indus-
try is built around computers—what better way to preserve personal space?—but they refuse to negotiate or
finalize deals unless it is in person. When asked about
how they organize their society, each slazan has looked
away, off into the distance: no.

We have images of large older males, and so we
have heard their loud calls; we have never seen these
males on the same streets where humans were permitted
to walk. Other than the few buildings where humans
were permitted to stay, we have not seen the internal arrangement of slazan homes, and the language workshop
imagery focuses on the images of the things being
learned and turns everything else as opaque as an old
memory. The workshop, like the human ones, starts you
off as the initial language learner, the child, so we have
seen that mothers, when no longer lactating, lose their
breasts and, aside from their hips, look almost the same
as men of equal stature. Many of our dealings were with
young men, but a number of slazans on New Hope wore
tunics or robes that hid their necks. It's not clear from
the accounts if all our dealings were with men.

But kinship? economics? politics? law? They offered to tell us nothing. They told each human with
whom they had business the name of the person to contact, but never the reason why. No one came with a title
or a role—it was as if slazans had in mind a larger social
map that did not require them to name roles and positions, to verbally parse their lives into understandable
spheres in order to know how to deal with each other.
What does this social map—if it exists—tell them? How
does it help them conduct their lives as a social group?
If group decisions are made, who makes those decisions?
If they are rarely together, how do slazans living on separate worlds negotiate the conduct of a war? If individ-

ual slazans avoid each other, how does violence ever happen?

Chapter Six

The Sixth Day

Just before the sun rose, when everything had the color of smoke, Roofer began to walk the woods. His long call echoed among the empty spaces, and the specific words, stretched out like long-held notes, were hard to understand at first. She didn't hear anger at a rival or the harsh warning off of others; instead she heard the music of astonishment, the kind of sound you heard from sons but not from men. Roofer had watched the night sky from his nest. He had seen true bodies grow large and change color. He had seen true bodies disappear from the sky. Where had they gone?

Chest Scars sat up to listen. On the opposite side of the same fire, Arm Scars was nursing her knee-high son. Her older son walked to stand among the trees and listen to Roofer's long call. Lightfoot Watcher's daughter sat by the dying embers of her fire; her mother had not come back yet.

The animal lifted its head from the ground as if to listen to what was being said. Her eyes found the healer's, and I felt like she should explain something to the animal. But an animal would not understand. She pushed herself up and rose from the ground. She wore only her pubic apron, so she stood there, looking up into the woods and at the people watching her. She stood there with the pride of a woman who had just brought down a large male lightfoot. She then turned and walked back to the darkness within the boulder, and the opening disappeared.

I stared at the boulder for the longest time. Most of the time she didn't see the boulder at all. She was thinking about last night's sky. She had watched it intently after the animal had fallen asleep upon the ground. All the true bodies still seemed to be in their proper position. But what else in the sky could have changed colors and disappeared but true bodies?

Chest Scars called to her. "Healer, did you see the same thing as the long caller saw?"

"Yes."

"Could the animal have caused that?"

"An animal who could cause that is not an animal."

Each woman who lived along Winding River returned to the hillside and heard about the lights in the sky. Crooked said that the animal must be a first soul who had been cast from the sky because of trouble she had caused. Squawker was sure it was an animal, but she agreed that its presence would cause trouble, since no one knew the habits of such a creature. Flatface said if there was at least one or another to watch it, the animal could not cause trouble. Wisdom said the same thing for a very long time. Arm Scars wanted to talk about the true bodies that had disappeared. Lightfoot Watcher, who had returned, said when the true bodies have shined away who they are, they are fresh and waiting for a child to breathe them in. Maybe so many children were born last night that several true bodies had to shine away who they were so quickly that the effort lit up the sky.

"Why, then," asked Crooked, "would the first soul grieve the way that creature did last night?"

"It's an animal," said Squawker. "It cried from fear."

Wisdom said, "When a smoke-ears sees a nightskin, the smoke-ears doesn't cry. It tries to hop away. The lightfoot runs away when it sees the nightskin. No meat animal cries in fear when it is hunted."

"A person cries in fear," said Flatface's waist-high son.

"A boy *would* say that," said Flatface.

The talk back and forth lasted all morning because no one could sit still at a fire. There were too many people, and so one or another would get up to walk into the woods to defecate or to find some solitude. All the fallen tree limbs, loose sticks, and the remains of winter-fallen trees had been used up for fires, so sons and daughters had to be sent farther away to bring back wood, and mothers accompanied them because you also had to walk farther to find something to eat. Returning for the second time, this time with wood, I noticed that Chest Scars and Arm Scars, who lived by the river's mouth, had not left their fires all morning, and she wondered how each one could stand having so many people nearby.

The third time I left, she went to check out a nearby tree that should be full of ripe fruitnuts, a tree only a woman who'd grown up near the river would find. But when she got to the fruitnut tree, she discovered that there no nuts within easy reach. However, there were rounded pieces of wood that had been driven into the side of the tree. Many years ago, a man had carved the pegs and hammered them in, but every time he tried to mate with a woman, Sour Plum drove him away until he left the river for some other place. I clambered up to the second set of branches and plucked every fruitnut that felt soft enough to eat. She soon realized she would not have enough to give each woman by the clearing a handful, so she ate her fill while listening to Sour Plum long call his way through the woods. She saved a portion of fruitnuts to leave on a trail for Sour Plum to find.

The old man, however, found her first. He stood away from the tree as she climbed down, and he ignored the nuts she laid out for him. Standing on the ground, not that far away, Old Sour Plum loomed over I, and she was both impressed and frightened by how large he had grown in his old age.

Old Sour Plum said, "I saw the night sky, too. The boulder came, and it happened."

I waited for his next words.

"The animal's dangerous," he said. "If enough individuals ask, I will throw rocks at it until it leaves or dies."

"We do not do that to a nightskin," said I.

"It is not a nightskin."

"She has harmed no one."

"She will," said Sour Plum, and the old man ambled off, carrying his tremendous weight and strength.

I stood alone, but she was not comfortable with her solitude. Off in the distance a long call wafted through the forest, the tone pitched low going high. The voice was deep, a man's voice, and it was not at all familiar.

When I returned to the hillside, the animal was still inside the boulder, and today's new arrival was a man. He was at the point in his life where a man seemed to grow larger every day.

Now he was a shade taller than a woman, his skin slightly darkened, and the pouches on either side of his throat puffed out, but they were not yet the size to make the kind of long call that I had heard before returning. The man had reached the size when a woman in desire would open up for him, and so he might well be looking for a woman who was unimpressed by the men who wandered near her hut.

It looked like this Tall Enough man had taken an interest in Crooked. Crooked was seated by her fire, staring down at the boulder as if that were the only thing of interest. Sitting not too far behind her was Newcomer, who, as far as I could tell, had not left Crooked's side. I had never seen such a patient almost-a-man. Usually an almost-a-man was so eager with his penis that he would try, with the slightest provocation, to find his way into a woman. Tall Enough was still in the woods, walking back and forth, but he liked to veer in, get close to Newcomer, and see if the almost-a-man would quiver, get frightened, run off.

Newcomer was frightened. He held his body taut, as if he expected Tall Enough to get mating close and deliver a blow to the back of the head or the side of the face. Down the way, Flatface's almost-a-man son was playing a toss game with the other son and daughter who shared his mother, but every time he held the hollowed melon, he stopped to watch Tall Enough, then Newcomer, and then to cast an eye on Crooked.

Crooked was woman enough to act like none of this was going on. The wrong look could give a man the wrong ideas, and Tall Enough was just large enough in stature that he would be hard to resist once he thought a woman was open to him. Crooked was also anxious enough that she paid no attention to any other woman. Arm Scars and Chest Scars, who were talking like young girls who still lived with their mother, looked over at Crooked to see what was going on. Lightfoot Watcher was cooking fish at her fire, but she had started to watch I watch Crooked. Wisdom must have left to fish or to check her snares. Squawker was on the other side of the clearing, her back turned, her daughter nursing, her son running circles around them, his outstretched hand every now and then shoving his mother's shoulder while he announced that he, too, wanted to nurse.

It was all too much for I. She walked down the hill, moving as far away as possible from the others while remaining in the shade of the trees, and sat down to watch the boulder. Voices carried, and she wished she had the gzaet.

The sun had walked high above them when dark clouds

drifted in the distance, and I could smell a difference in the air. By tonight it would rain.

The sun seemed directly above the boulder when Old Sour Plum strode onto the hillside. His long call had alerted everyone to his approach, and he stopped just at the edge of the woods. He seemed astounded to see so many others. Still he strode forward. Chest Scars and Arm Scars scooted away from their fires as he passed by. He walked down into the clearing and stopped right where the ground became black. He called to the animal. He told it to leave. He said the same things several times in several ways. Nothing happened. Was the animal scared? Was she curled up and cowering inside? Old Sour Plum called one more time, but what could he say? He was accustomed to threatening boys and men, not animals, not women. He walked to the edge of the clearing and seemed to stare off to the distant lake. After a moment he clambered down the hill and disappeared from sight.

The sun was still high when one woman, then another, came to the hillside. The first was a tiny woman, smaller than Flatface's eldest son, who came alone, watched the boulder, and shared no words. The second woman was as large as the other was small. She had the bulk of a man who had just started to outgrow a woman, and along her neck were faint splotches of gray, almost impossible to see from a distance, like those of a boy just before he began to grow. I *would* have thought this person was a man, but for the kaross she wore, the hunter's scars cut into her arms from shoulder to wrist, the quiver of arrows slung over her shoulder, and the large, powerful bow she carried in her hand.

And this woman, this Far Hunter, lacked the habit of solitude that I would have expected of any man this size. She called an "I am here" to Arm Scars and Chest Scars, and they called back. She sat between the two women, their heads as high off the ground as her shoulders. Arm Scars' knee-high son, who had been afraid of everyone else, appeared unconcerned by the presence of this large woman. I looked away so as not to stare improperly.

Dark clouds drifted in the distance, and I could feel a shift in the breeze. Dust bugs had begun to chase each other in the air. By tonight it would rain. Huggable appeared, her kaross tied oddly so that it covered her teats and was useless for carrying anything. Beside her was her daughter, wearing a pubic skirt, leggings, and vest, as if she were dressed for the chill of early spring. The daughter saw I, and her face opened with a smile.

She almost ran from her mother, who was holding her daughter's hand, her attention held by something else.

I looked to find the source of Huggable's concern. She was looking in the direction of the three women from the river's mouth. Far Hunter still wore her quiver of arrows, and across her lap was the bow.

Chest Scars was the first to notice Huggable, and she said something to Arm Scars and Far Hunter. The other two looked up, but once they saw Huggable, they did not look away. They continued to stare. Huggable took several steps toward them and stopped. The three continued to stare. Huggable turned away, glanced about as if searching for a new direction in which to walk.

The stare did not stop. Their eyes followed Huggable, and every time she turned her head to check on them, she found their eyes still gazing upon her. The encounter was strange enough that it created a kind of silence on the hill. One by one, a woman noticed and gave it her attention. Flatface picked up her knee-high daughter and walked to a space between the three women and Huggable. She faced Far Hunter with her own full stare. "Do you come to hunt?"

Far Hunter was respectful of Flatface and looked away. "I came to see the rock and the animal in it."

"Then why the bow on the lap? Why the quiver on the back?"

"I thought that I would hunt if one woman or another wanted to track a lightfoot with me. I would share meat with any woman who lives near the river and lets me sit where I sit and eat fruit from any tree."

I approached Flatface, who turned to her and said, "She must live near the river's mouth. She likes to talk."

Far Hunter pointed at Huggable. "That one, too, lived for a time by the river's mouth. Ask her why she is here, and not there."

Huggable's daughter stood as still as a lightfoot listening for an approaching predator. Huggable tugged at her arm and walked her daughter away, heading in the direction of the sunset fruit tree where she had built hut and hearth.

Far Hunter's gaze followed Huggable's back. "I have arrows." Far Hunter said it to Huggable, but she spoke her words loud enough so that probably the animal in the boulder could have heard them.

"For hunting animals," said Flatface.

"For hunting animals," said Far Hunter, with a new meaning added to the word animal.

"For hunting animals that a hunter eats," said Flatface.

"Does she live near Winding River?" said Far Hunter.

"Yes," said I. "She lives near the river."

"She once lived near the river's mouth. Before that she lived beyond the dunes. She came with her daughter. Even though she still nursed her daughter, it became time for her to mate. The almost-a-man who shares my mother mated with her. She mated only with him. The daughter did not live long enough to taste the milk of life." Far Hunter stood up, walked to another part of the hillside. Alone, she began to clear the area for a new fire.

Meanwhile, a newly arrived woman, who had come south from near the waterfalls, had tied two corners of her kaross to two young trees. She was now trying to break a rather straight limb off a nearby tree, probably to drive it into the ground and use it and another like it to attach the other corners of the kaross. The storm clouds were closer perhaps. The air smelled cleaner, cooler. A spread-out kaross would not keep out the hard, masculine rain that fell from such dark clouds; her daughters would get as wet as any other woman on the hill.

I looked to the boulder. The animal would probably stay inside while it rained. Sour Plum was nowhere to be seen. His voice could not be heard. Flatface sat across the fire from her eldest daughter. Wisdom had appeared and was resting against an old, thick tree. And there was Far Hunter building her fire, Chest Scars eating some fruit, and Arm Scars watching the boulder. There were too many in so small a space.

I left. It was too much for her. But the thoughts stayed with her. Why had Far Hunter been so upset about an infant that was not her own? Newborns died and mothers had to bury them. Could Huggable have buried hers before it breathed in its true body so she could continue nursing her daughter?

Back at her shelter, alone, she uncovered the gzaet, took it to where the coals of the ritual fire had turned to the color of ash, and she played, wanting to lose herself in the music, to recover a proper sense of solitude. She stopped because things felt different. The light was dimmer, and dustbugs drifted about like dust caught in a shaft of sunlight. She looked up to see the clouds above the canopy of leaves.

There was movement behind her. It was Lightfoot Watcher. She was sitting near the black circle of the waiting fire. Her daughter sat between her legs and leaned against her mother's big belly.

I picked up the gzaet and entered her shelter. She ate from the basket of nuts Huggable had left her. Hanging above the dead cooking fire was the smoked lightfoot meat; she didn't want to go out to get any. If she did, she'd have to share some with Lightfoot Watcher and her daughter. If she gave them all of it, they would feel compelled to leave, but then she would have no meat. In the distance, wood snapped. Later Lightfoot Watcher's daughter carefully laid the wood out by I's cooking fire. Unlike Huggable's daughter, this girl took care to show proper respect. Not once did she look toward the healer's hut as she put down the wood, laid it out by size, and walked away.

I did not want to accept the gift, but fire kept the night animals away. She walked out and made the fire without looking once at them. She pulled down four strips of meat and left them on the ground. Back in the shelter, she made a tiny fire to help keep her warm. Roofer had made an opening in the top and had made a wooden cover attached to a long, curved piece of wood so that the cover could be moved. I expected it to rain, so she left the roof cover on. She played music until the tiny wisps of smoke stung her eyes, and then she slept.

She heard the thunder first in a dream she wouldn't remember; the second clap of thunder shook the ground and the air. Her eyes were open, she was sitting up, and fear held her body taut. The rain tapped against the ground with the sound of running animals. Water made a whispery rush as it slid along the gutters that dead Long Call had built. Outside, a girl cried, her words lost among her sobs and the rain. A few coals burned among the night's black, but they produced no warmth I could feel. In the distance the river churned with the weight of added water. Lightfoot Watcher was saying soft things to her daughter, comforting her.

I stood in the doorway of her shelter and looked out toward the voices, but the night was black. All fires had been washed out. The rain was cold and made her shiver. "Come into my shelter," she said to them. "It is better to be warm than to be alone."

Lightfoot Watcher politely refused, and I insisted, repeating her invitation. She heard the two approach, stumbling in the darkness. In the dim sunset light of the shelter's coals, they were no more than shadows.

She added the remaining dry wood to the fire. Lightfoot Watcher's daughter complained that she was cold, that she was wet, that the fire wasn't warm enough. I had two darkfur hides, each given to her after her music had saved a life, and she handed them directly to Lightfoot Watcher's daughter. Her mother insisted that she refuse the gift. I insisted that mother and daughter accept. The daughter was already wrapping her body in the animal warmth. "Take off your wet clothes," said Lightfoot Watcher.

Mother and daughter finally slept together on one side of the fire while I tried to sleep on the other. She had been given other animal hides, but she had given those as stay-away gifts to one man and another. She wrapped her kaross, which was really too small to offer much warmth, around her body and stared at the slowly shrinking fire. At some point the wind changed direction and did something rare; it swept right through the opening, bringing in a nighttime chill and the splash of rain. The fire sizzled; the flames wavered with uncertain life. The cold slipped through skin and sank into bone. She curled up into a ball, but no warmth came. She listened to her teeth chatter; she felt the way her jaws moved. Lightfoot Watcher whispered something to her daughter, and then mother, followed by daughter, joined I on her side of the fire. Lightfoot Watcher's back pressed against her back; the daughter's back against her belly. The hides stretched over the three bodies. It took forever for the warmth to find its way back to her body; she couldn't help but keep shivering even though her body was warm. Her hand lightly touched the hair atop the daughter's head, then caressed the girl's forehead and cheek. There would be comfort in having a daughter.

The Seventh Day

The healer woke up first; Lightfoot Watcher and her daughter were still fast asleep. The light was dim in the early-morning haze, and there was only a vague hint of the day's warmth. The voices of insects and animals, silent during the storm, now filled the air. I walked far behind the hut, near to where she tossed all the leftover parts of animals and fruits, and near there, but not too close, she emptied her body. At the river, its newly rushing water cold to the touch, she washed up. She watched fish swim by, but she didn't have the patience to catch any.

The strips of meat she had left hanging over her cooking fire were tasteless. If Lightfoot Watcher and her daughter had not been sitting outside her camp, intruding upon her solitude, she would have remembered to take them in. She ate a second strip.

She left out six strips hanging for when they awoke. The remaining strips she placed in her kaross.

On her way to the clearing she chose a thin animal trail that would take her by some snowmelt bushes that should be fresh in bloom. The snowmelt turned out to be empty. Broken fruit, lined white with mold, was scattered around the path. I left the trail for the brush, walking carefully, for every touched tree limb or shrub brought a short, sudden downpour of last night's rain. She eyed the ground carefully, avoiding crawlers and itch moss, and she finally found the springleaves. She pulled up several plants, plucked the leaves, dusted the dirt off the tubers, and ate the bitter food.

By the time she had reached the clearing, it had started to drizzle. The darkened ground was scarred the color of mud where water had rushed through it toward the brook. But the boulder didn't look wet at all, not the way rock and ground would darken with water. The water ran straight off it, splashing light musical notes into puddles that lengthened away from the boulder. The animal was probably as dry as a nightskin inside a cave. Maybe dryer. I envied the animal its perfect solitude and dryness.

At the bottom of the hill slept Roofer, curled up by the remains of a fire doused by the rain. Old Sour Plum and Hugger were nowhere to be seen. She made sure she walked toward him just loud enough to awake him. He sat up and positioned himself to watch the boulder as if he had been watching it all night. He smelled of wet hair and damp skin.

"Are you protecting us?" she asked after some thought. Too much talking, like too little distance, made Roofer very nervous.

"No. I want to see the animal before Old Sour Plum does."

I walked to a respectful distance from Roofer and sat down. The ground was soft and wet, soaking into her pubic skirt. She did not look over at Roofer once.

"Old Sour Plum," said Roofer, "is so solitary that he no longer hungers for knowing. I think he will kill the animal next time it comes out, and I think that is why the animal stays in there."

Although Roofer was nowhere near as strong as the old man, Sour Plum would avoid fighting with a man from the area. "Have you been here all night?" I asked.

"Yes. And the night before."

"Are you hungry?"

"Childless brought me fish, but I did not eat it."

"Would you like some meat?"

"Yes. I am tired of berries and nuts and roots.".

"I have meat but it has no taste."

"It is still meat."

She handed him one strip at a time. "This is for watching. This is for respecting my solitude. And this is a gift because the roof you made kept me dry last night."

Roofer showed his respect by saying nothing and by sitting still while I stood so close to him. Once he had grasped all three strips of meat, I stepped back to a respectful distance and looked away from him.

The dampness had sunk deep into I's bones, and she couldn't imagine ever feeling comfortable again. The ones who had come from the river's mouth and the ones who had come from elsewhere looked equally miserable. They wrapped themselves in sodden hides and waited for the sun to become generous. Another almost-a-man, this one with scars along one arm stretching from elbow to wrist, paced back and forth, keeping near to the ashen remains of the fire which Far Hunter had built. Nearby Chest Scars and Arm Scars were huddled by their fire. Arm Scars' two sons and Far Hunter were nowhere to be seen.

Later in the morning the sun appeared, but it was stingy with its warmth. A mother with scars across her shoulders and her waist-high son stood at the crest of the hill. While the mother leaned against a tree, the son walked to the edge of the woods, yelled at the boulder, then ran back to his mother's side, his feet sometimes slipping upon the muddy ground. Wisdom was sitting against the same old thickbark tree, and she told I that earlier that same morning Childless Crooked had passed by, and she was being ardently followed by the almost-a-man I called Newcomer and by Flatface's almost-a-man son. "Now, what does her son want to do with Childless?"

Chest Scars approached I. "I am here," the woman from the river's mouth said.

"I am here," said I. "I have no food to share."

"I have some words to share." She told I the animal had not come out of the boulder to see the rains or to see the sunrise.

They shared some more words until I felt comfortable enough to ask about the almost-a-man who had scars that went from elbow to wrist on one of his arms.

"One or another call him Clever Fingers. There was a man who no woman wanted to live near the river's mouth, and Clever

Fingers fought off the man. The scars are to mark that he could be as brave as a woman."

The idea was unsettling. I did not like the idea of a man fighting another man at a woman's bidding. Nor did she like the idea of praising brave men, as if brave men were needed to make karosses and build huts.

I left and returned that afternoon. Roofer was pacing back and forth farther back in the woods. Off near where the stream cut through the woods, Hugger was also pacing. Each worked hard to ignore each other. Along the hillside the woman with the knee-high son still leaned against a tree. Her son was curled up by her feet, napping upon her kaross. I could now see the angled scars along her shoulders; she, too, must live near the river's mouth. Chest Scars and Arm Scars sat by their fire. Clever Fingers now walked back and forth behind them. Wisdom was sitting against her thickbark tree. Lightfoot Watcher and her daughter were sitting by the hearth they had built two nights ago. I tried to ignore them, but every time she looked, the daughter was watching her, eyes wide and warm.

Later there was shouting that could be heard from where the clearing overlooked the lake. The shouting came closer, belonged to two voices, one man and another, who called to each other to stay away, not to come too close. Each came over the crest of the hill and stood in the clearing. The first one looked like a man who had just started to grow, with darker skin and pouches on his neck. The second one, who topped the hill a bit later, looked just the same. Only the way the mud had splattered on their legs looked different. I's mother had told her a story of a mother who had given birth to twin sons and who did not bury the first child. The first always wanted the same as the second; the second always wanted the same as the first. They reached for the same thing at the same time, and they always ended up mating close and angry. One day each was so angry at the other that they each took the knife they used to cut and fashion a kaross or a carry bag and stabbed the other in the heart. Now, seeing twins for the first time, I was astounded, and a bit scared. What if they came to blows here? I kept her back to Lightfoot Watcher.

The twins looked at the boulder for a bit, then looked at each other. After a few whispered words, they walked to different sides of the boulder, called to it, demanded that the animal come out, pounded on its sides, the slaps resounding in the woods. I couldn't help but be impressed; no man who lived near Winding River had walked this close to the boulder, no man had touched it. They walked around it, calling to each other to stay away, the call becoming a screech the one time they came around the boulder from opposite directions and almost walked right into each other. The sun had become generous, and sweat shone on their skins. The twins finally left the way they'd come, heading down the hill and out of sight, each one's voice calling to the other to come along but stay away.

With the two men now gone, Lean Against Tree's waist-high son started once again to run to the clearing and yell at the animal inside the boulder before running back to his mother. She was once again leaning against a tree and watching.

Huggable's daughter arrived. She ran to a respectful distance from I, stopped, averted her eyes, and said, "Has anything happened yet?"

"Nothing has happened," said Lean Against Tree. "I walked two days to watch my son run back and forth."

Huggable had reappeared too. She still wore her kaross so that it covered both her teats, and over her shoulder hung a quiver full of arrows and a light bow. Standing by her daughter's side, she said to Lean Against Tree, "I am here."

Lean Against Tree looked away. "I am here," she said, the words hard and carrying no respect.

Huggable looked to Chest Scars and Arm Scars. "I am here."

Neither woman answered; neither woman looked in her direction.

Far Hunter was heard before seen, calling out in her loud female voice that she had food. With her came Flatface's eldest daughter and Squawker. Along their shoulders was a long pole of wood, huge flanks of meat hanging over it. Flatface soon followed with an infant on each hip, both reaching for her withering teats. The other children followed, running around trees, screaming out that there was meat, fresh meat, that the woman from the river's mouth was the best hunter ever.

Far Hunter was the one to cut up the meat and divide it, and I and each woman watched her carefully. The first cut went to Wisdom, of all people, the second to Flatface. Flatface said something to Far Hunter, and an even larger portion was handed to I, who had no children or men to pass it on to. She cut off for herself what would be filling, and she carried the rest to Lightfoot Watcher in hopes that after such a gift the woman would not be able to ask another favor of her.

After Far Hunter had given portions to each woman who

lived near the river, she gave portions to each woman who came from the lake, then to each remaining woman. Each woman gave portions to each child, and every now and then an older child would be sent off with a portion to some man who was walking through the woods, calling out softly, keeping each one aware of his presence.

As the meat was cooked, as it was eaten, there was the feeling of happiness, of nourishment, and there were jokes and mother's stories retold, but there was also an air of tension. One should be sitting by her cooking fire with another woman, perhaps a chest-high boy running off with a girl who shared his mother to give a portion of meat to someone farther off. Here there were too many people, and only because of the boulder. A kill this size would be shared across an area, with enough meat left over to smoke and to eat later. Here it was hard to keep your distance, to show respect.

There was a yelp, a few words shouted, and a crying boy ran to his mother. He had stepped too close to an older man. Maybe Old Sour Plum had been right, but not in the way he had meant to be right. The animal in this boulder was harmless. It was her presence here that caused the harm.

"I deserve a portion of meat."

It was Huggable's voice. She faced Far Hunter from a respectable distance, her teats still covered, the quiver and bow still slung over her shoulder. Huggable's daughter was sitting next to Lightfoot Watcher's daughter, and she was chewing on some meat and laughing.

"I am the only one who did not get a portion of meat."

"Give her some," a woman yelled.

"I have some," said Lightfoot Watcher.

"She has some," said Far Hunter.

"I want you to give me a portion."

"Your daughter is being fed."

"You divided the meat. You gave me none."

"You do not share a mother with anyone who lives near the river. And you do not share a mother with anyone who lives along the river's mouth."

Huggable gestured toward Lightfoot Watcher.

"Neither does she."

"The healer gave her that meat."

"I once lived by the lake. I once lived at the river's mouth. You once gave food to me."

Arm Scars and Chest Scars looked away.

Far Hunter said, "You have done nothing to deserve the meat. I am tired of talking." Far Watcher sat down by her fire. Clever Fingers, the almost-a-man with scars from elbow to wrist on one arm, stood behind Far Hunter and chewed on some meat she must have handed him.

I considered returning to her hut to get her gzaet and bring it back. Perhaps some music carefully played would ease what was wrong here.

But she didn't leave. She stayed on because another child got too close to another adult and was slapped away. Squawker took offense at something Lean Against Tree had said, and Flatface did her best to separate the two, to get them talking so much that they would prefer to walk away rather than let their anger take them mating close. Huggable remained in the spot where she had argued with Far Hunter, and she stared hard at the woman from the river's mouth, who worked hard to ignore Huggable.

Only Lean Against Tree had really been watching when it happened. "The rock's opening," she yelled out.

Conversations stopped. Running children stood still. Heads turned.

The animal stepped onto the muddy ground. She wore something different to cover her hips, and a strangely colored hide covered her teats. She closed her eyes against the light, then shaded them with a hand, and she peered up at them. Right at them. What did she think of all these people here? Did she feel threatened? She just stood there. What did she make of it when one by one all the voices from the hill disappeared into the air, leaving only the breeze and the way it brushed the leaves together? She stood there for the longest time. Her solitary gaze made I pity her.

"She's as uninteresting as the rock," said Lean Against Tree.

And while one or two others began to talk, the animal must have turned, because when I looked at her again, she was stepping back into the boulder.

"Come back!" a child yelled. The voice sounded like it belonged to Lean Against Tree's son. "Come back. I am not scared of you." Then the boy ran down the hill in long strides, dodging the trunks of trees. The animal stopped in the boulder's opening and turned. The boy had slowed down, but he was at the edge of the clearing. Twenty, thirty steps, and he would be impossibly close to the animal. Why wasn't his mother chasing him? Or at least calling him to come back? The animal watched him, just standing there. If the animal felt threatened, the boy was in danger. I started to run forward, but she stepped far too close to someone, because an arm flailed out, struck her in the chest, and knocked her to the ground. She yelled, sat up, getting ready to stand when she saw that Roofer was already running into the clearing, one arm reaching around the boy's back, the other scooping up under his bottom while the animal stood there with her arm out, calling out something that I couldn't hear because now there were more than one or two voices. The animal stood there, looking up at them, and I watched them until she heard one voice, Lean Against Tree's, cut through all the other voices. "I have never visited people with so little respect. What kind of man are you? Where's your solitude?"

I walked toward the voice, moving carefully between others, and soon saw that the boy was with his mother and Roofer was walking away. The mother was walking behind Roofer, delivering one blow after another on Roofer's back. "No man where I live would pick up a woman's son. How could you? My son was fine. He was being brave."

I tried to follow them in order to mediate the argument before Roofer had to speak, but she was too late. Roofer turned on Lean Against Tree. The first blow landed on her face. The second on her shoulder. The third struck her chest. Huggable was stepping closer, the bow no longer slung over her shoulder; rather, it was now in her hand.

Lean Against Tree was raising her fist to strike back, but I grabbed hold of her arm and twisted it to make the woman drop back to the ground. She looked up at I, her shock clear upon her face, blood pouring from one nostril.

Roofer just stood there. He wouldn't crouch down and get mating close to hit someone. The woman's mouth and chin were covered with blood. Her son was crying. He ran up and hit Roofer. Roofer slapped the son away. Huggable was pulling an arrow from her quiver. Lean Against Tree was from the river's mouth, and Huggable was going to take action for her. Roofer had already turned to the woods. He walked away as if the mother and the boy no longer concerned him. Huggable was not a good shot, or she wasn't trying to be. The arrow missed Roofer, but it cut right into someone else's thigh.

An almost-a-man fell to the ground. He clutched the shaft and screamed out in pain while Huggable ran off into the woods. I ran over to the fallen almost-a-man. It was Clever Fingers, who had the scars from elbow to wrist on one arm. He, too, was from the river's mouth. The arrow was lodged into the thigh, right near where it joined the body. Blood had soaked through his breechclout, had poured onto the wet muddy ground. I forgot all modesty. She removed her pubic apron and was ready to tie it tight above where the blood shot out in tiny spasms. But when she knelt down beside him, Clever Fingers yelled at her to go away. She ignored him, but this time he struck her, causing her to sprawl to the ground.

She looked to Far Hunter, to Chest Scars, to Arm Scars, to Lean Against Tree, and none of them said a word to her or to the almost-a-man. She would not let him die, so she knelt by him again. His blow was unsettling, but it was not strong enough to unbalance her. His stay-away call was even fainter. His leg, then her hands, was slippery with blood, but soon she had the pubic apron tied tight around his thigh, above the torn puncture.

She sat a respectful distance from the almost-a-man and sang a healing song, which was of no use. He soon died.

The animal had left the clearing, and the opening to the boulder had disappeared.

Night was approaching, and each woman was gathering up her things. If a child spoke, she was hushed. No one wanted to be on the hillside when night came, and no one would return until each full moon had passed overhead. By then Clever Finger's true body would leave to find its proper solitude in the sky, far away from the world. No one would stay there that night, and there would be no fires to keep away the jackals. By the next morning there would just be skin, some meat and sinew, and bones. I did not know if she could bear to return while those bones and rotting remains were part of the clearing.

The animal was back in her boulder. Maybe she too would never come out.

The following is taken from the notebook Pauline Dikobe kept while traveling to Tienah on the Way of God.

Day 28
We are weeks into the journey, and the corridor walls rarely feature images taken from the University district of Wadi al-Uyoun. Now the images are selected from psyche-profiles, whatever will enhance tranquillity, ease homesickness: idealized deserts, moonlit landscapes, busy marketplaces, savannahs lush with green after a good spring rain.

Day 30
We have left hyperspace to make another jump in another direction. There's no evidence that we're being followed. The glare of energy that accompanies each jump can be plotted by distant astronomers, but no slazan will see this light for decades.

Perhaps it was a mistake centuries ago to remove generals from battle, to set up buildings full of people collecting intelligence to advise the generals. All those minds at work, with no direct threat to their immediate survival. They have too long to think, too long to worry about each step of a process.

So we follow a Byzantine path to a planet without name or number.

Day 33

I am tired of looking at images of slazans. I am tired of going over the shuttle and equipment.

I feel like I've lost track of the days.

What will I be like on the planet, when I'm by myself, my only companionship\ Jihad's voice sounding in my ear?

Day 35

I study one image.

It's a slazan mother and her child in an expansive park, one of many that snake through the largest slazan city that once existed on New Hope. The child looks at the mother. I am having the shuttle's intelligence compare their facial expressions with any other images of mother and children. It's already been done by other researchers, but I'm experience-developing the intelligence, giving it past experience that it can rely on when we're planetside and it has to do such searches on its own.

The image itself was taken one year before the war broke out on New Hope. I wonder if the mother and child left the planet beforehand, or if they were destroyed in the cataclysm that followed.

All I do is wonder. I do not feel the commensurate ache from their possible deaths. I want to feel something, some sense of loss. I feel nothing.

Such is the way that a researcher's heart is hardened.

Day 40

Tamr's comrade-in-arms is named Maryam. She is a thin, willowy woman who rarely speaks. She's been a second-shifter, so she's off duty when Tamr is working with me and on duty when Tamr and I have dinner, often with Jihad and Jihad's comrade-in-arms. Today the captain has shifted the roster, so different people are working together. I eat dinner with the two of them together for the first time. Whenever Tamr gets so involved with some digression, it's Maryam who reminds her of the original train of thought. Whenever Tamr forgets the end of a joke, it's Maryam who tells the punchline.

Later I ask Jihad if Maryam is anything more than Tamr's shadow.

"Sure," Jihad says. "If you want something fixed, you go to Maryam. She's the best engineer in the fleet."

I want to ask what she's doing on the *Way of God*, but instead I ask, "Why isn't she the chief engineer, then?"

"Because Maryam couldn't give orders to her own dog."

Day 45

Intellectual thought is a warm blanket, or better, a nurturing womb that can protect us from the vicissitudes of social life. Everything that happens on this ship, this self-contained village, allows me to find comfort in evolutionary thought.

The overriding assumption has been that humans in the Pleistocene gathered, scavenged, and hunted in small groups, the size of the groups expanding and contracting with available resources. It's been assumed that most humans at that time knew up to forty people well.

The ship's population is thirty-one, including me. Ten people are on duty during any one of three shifts. So the contact population is between ten and twenty, much like that in a small Ju/wa village.

But here there are no children and no men.

Here, there is rank.

But in spite of the hierarchy, there is no boasting allowed. There is the teasing to keep people in place.

But here there are cabins and veils. There are no open huts, no constant exposure to the public eye.

Day 51

I can't sleep. I'm restless. I head to the washroom. I want to splash some water onto my face, clear my head.

The door slides open. A woman is naked, standing bent over the sink, washing something. Her back is thick, her backside curving out in adiposal comfort. I think it's Tamr.

The woman turns at the sound of me stepping in. It's Tamr. She only has on her veil. In her hand is a masculine prosthesis. She turns away, obviously embarrassed.

I want to make the moment light. "After a month in space, I sure could use one of those." Then I head back to my room, as embarrassed as she is.

Day 53

If I had known the rule two days ago, I wouldn't have embarrassed Tamr, who for two days has spoken with me about everything but our little encounter.

But, as is true of most unspoken rules, no one thought to tell me.

At the beginning and end of a shift, everyone walks in and out of the communal washroom as if the room were as public as the dining hall or gym. Since there are lavatories near the bridge and the dinning hall, and a washroom by the gym, the main washroom gets little use during a shift. Today is the first day I saw a crew member enter the washroom in the middle of a shift. She knocked first, waited, knocked again, then entered.

I hadn't knocked; Tamr had not expected to be seen.

But the prosthetic she held raises questions. Did she use it on herself when desire got to be too much, or was it something she used with willowy, shy Maryam? It's not clear which comrades-in-arms sleep with their mats apart, like roommates, and which sleep with their mats together, as lovers. If it's an item of gossip, no one spreads the news while I'm within hearing.

Day 56

This evening, under my pillow, I find one, just like Tamr's. It's in a box that has been wrapped with a ribbon. I'm embarrassed to touch it. I can't ever imagining taking advantage of its form.

Is this a gift from Tamr? Or did she tell someone else, who somehow got a lock override to plant it under my pillow? Or maybe it's less a gift and more a practical joke.

Day 60

No one's said anything about the surprise under my pillow. I wait for Tamr or Maryam to say something, for

Jihad to pull me aside, for her gossipy comrade-in-arms to make some comment and snicker. No one says a thing, no one makes a joke, no conversations suddenly stop when I appear. Who gave it to me and why?

How will I understand alien slazans I've never met if I can't understand the secretive behavior of humans I have known for sixty days?

I write this rather than write up my research notes. I feel failure in the air.

Chapter Seven

The Eighth Day

Whatever alien microbes had upset the balance within his own cell structure, and whatever alien amino acids in the local food were confusing his digestive tract, and whatever reactions his body was making to the contradictory stimuli of the past days of heat, cold, and rain, all of them came to a head the moment Esoch saw the inside of the empty shuttle. He leaned against an acceleration couch, his arm hooked around the headrest, and he breathed heavily, trying to orient himself. The sheets on the bed were twisted and reeked of sweat. All sorts of instruments were strewn across a workstation. A basket as finely woven together as the nest sat empty by the bed. All the controls were lit up. Each vidscreen was on; each showed something being broadcast by one of the imaging pins: inside a shelter, near a fire, a path in the woods. Tiny lines of Arabic crawled across the bottom of each image. Back on the *Way of God*, those nights he had stayed with Dikobe, her cabin had always been neatly kept, a few Ju/wa knickknacks neatly arrayed on the tiny desk, the two mats unrolled, the blankets neatly turned down. Why was there so much disorder now?

Just ten or so days ago he had helped Pauline do a final inventory, and in silence they had gone through locker after locker, speaking only when she had named an item and its location and he had verified it was there. Thus, he knew where to find the shovel. It was perfectly clean, no sign that she had used it to dig up and refill that hole beside the shuttle. Did slazans dig graves? Had they buried her? Why would they kill her? As he walked out of the shuttle—surveying the hillside, unmoved by the reds, oranges, yellows, and seeing no one—and as he slipped blade into soil, he knew that he first should have awakened the ship's intelligence and set up a defense perimeter, but he truly didn't care. He wanted to dig away at this dirt now, he wanted to know now if it was a grave, if Dikobe was at the bottom.

He had once learned that the slazans on New Hope buried the bodies of criminals and burned the bodies of good people, the good soul being set free from earthly life. Had he heard it from a military trainer or from Dikobe? Would that idea apply to these particular slazans? Had the person in this grave done something terribly wrong while she was alive? Each time Esoch bent over, the snakelike creature back in the nest bit again and again into his belly; each time he thrust shovel into soil, metal scraped hard against palm and swollen wound; and each time he lifted out dirt, the muscles of his lower back became taut, hard, dense with pain. The sweat was more feverish than cooling, and the late-afternoon sun cast a grim light on everything. He stopped, looked up at the hillside that surrounded the shuttle, and saw no one. He returned to his effort and dug and dug, and the hole deepened slowly.

He tried to imagine who would have buried Pauline, and he couldn't. When his old name—his grandfather—had died, it had been his father and his uncle and two cousins who had buried the body in a giant anthill. In Chum!kwe a murdered woman had lain in the street for a day, her mouth open, flies swarming, the settlement director demanding that everyone see the product of their violence, then handing scrip to Bo and ≠oma to carry the body far out into the brush where the jackals would find it. After Ghazwan had died, the casket carrying his body had been shot toward the war zone, so that centuries later it could join the dust of his slain comrades.

The shovel struck something, and that something gave. He imagined it was Dikobe's head, and he sat until nausea passed. When he stood, the light-headedness had doubled. It would be better to go inside, to hook himself up to the medcomp, to have his blood analyzed and cleansed. Instead, he crouched, his head spinning now, and he carefully lowered himself to hands and knees. He reached down into the pit and scooped away at the dirt—brown, dark dirt mixed with hard blackened bits like from burned pottery. And flesh touched what metal had struck. It was a foot. A naked foot.

This time the nausea came as great waves within his belly and bowels, and he considered going to the other end of the grave and digging until shovel reached skull when it occurred to him that if the foot were a human foot, then this would be Dikobe's grave. He brushed away the dirt until he could feel skin more readily than soil. Then he cleared the top of a shin to remove the doubts that persisted, even though the feel of toe, the curve of ankle said everything. The skin was cool, leathery, inhuman, not the skin he was accustomed to, and every time he touched it, his hand involuntarily jerked back as if shocked by electricity.

And then he sat by the grave for the longest time, knees pulled up to chest, arms wrapped around legs, and he took in everything. Pauline was not buried here. Pauline could still be alive. Who had buried the slazan? Pauline? Someone else? Had she left on her own or had someone taken her away?

He counted days in his head. Twice to make sure he had counted right. Three afternoons ago Pauline—or the enemy, if he existed here—had shut down the shuttle's transmissions. Three nights ago the *Way of God* had left Esoch in a blinding flash of light. Esoch should have been here the next morning.

He finally forced himself into the shuttle, closing and locking the hatch behind him. He sat in one of the acceleration couches. It was the one he had always sat in when he had done simulated run-throughs with Dikobe. If she was alive, he was going to find her now.

"Maher," he said. It was her son's name, and the name of the intelligence.

There was no response.

He keyed in the name.

Again, nothing.

He keyed in first one message, then a second, then a third. A screen lit up, and Arabic letters quickly flashed one by one, like a row of falling dominoes, onto the screen

Please key in password.

Password? He didn't know any password. And if he guessed the wrong one, the intelligence might be closed to him for good.

Esoch let himself fall back into the acceleration couch. No wonder Jihad had been unable to get through. The intelligence was dormant, unable to communicate. Dikobe had to have done this. But was it just her own personal madness, or had there been some external threat?

He meant to sit up, but instead the dizziness overtook him.

He noticed first the dull throb in his palm, the equal pain in his gut, then the shipwrecked queasiness that eased through him like water lapping at the beach. He opened his eyes. The small screens showed night. Several transmissions from imaging pins showed fires. He should be curious as to who was sleeping by those fires, but he wasn't.

He sat up and tried to concentrate. He had to find Pauline.

He first found out that he could call up individual programs. Data would be collected, sensors would work, but Maher, the intelligence, wouldn't be there to associate one set of data with another; it would be like having eyes without deductive reasoning, language without social skills.

Esoch called up various help menus. He must have blanked out because he found himself staring. It took him several hours, but he located the program that hooked into Pauline's implant. He would use the implant to locate her position. On-screen he had a large-scale map of the area, a magnified, clear version of the maps he had on the tracking disc.

There was no blip representing Dikobe.

He whispered her name, he spoke it, he called it. Pauline, Pauline, Pauline, it's Esoch; Hwan//a, it's ≠oma. But nothing. No trace. He finally found a log of implant use. Her fifth day here. At 1638. She had shut the implant off along with everything else. It had never come back on-line.

He tried to find a record of the implant itself. A military implant couldn't be shut off. A civilian one could—privacy rights and all. But the record told him nothing.

Esoch stared at the screens, the lights, the switches. All this equipment, and he had no idea where Pauline was, or if she was even alive. And he was too sick and it was too dark to try to find her.

The medcomp was located by the bed. He kicked the basket away, watched it roll once, then totter, then spin upright. He pulled off boots, onesuit, supporter, leaving them in a pile by his feet. He leaned forward, the dizziness like an empty halo in his skull, and stared at the blank medcomp screen, the buttons, switches, and lights. He should know how the thing worked, but he couldn't remember.

He lay down, and stared at the gray ceiling. He smelled Dikobe's sour sweat, the sheet under him still damp. Here is where Dikobe had lain, here is where she had fought the adaptation sickness. And then what happened?

Each worried thought followed one right after the other, but he felt no anxiety, just the gentle approach of sleep, as if he had only been counting backward to ease his mind.

He woke in the middle of the night, the faint lights of the controls casting a glow around each shadow. The bed conformed to his back, with the same firmness of the desert sand. He felt like he was both secure and floating. The solitude he felt was tremendous, and for some reason—the buried dizziness, perhaps, or the exhaustion—he found himself lying in the hut his parents and N!ai's parents had made for the two of them in //gausha. N!ai's mother and several other women had carried her there, and she had screamed for them to let her go: she didn't want this man they had given her, and her scream was so loud that he, on the other side of the face of the huts, could hear her clearly. His friends had to drag him to the hut. And he sat outside the hut, on the male side of the fire, his friends joking with her friends on the female side. And finally he went in. Her oldest cousin sat beside her, to ease her fears of sleeping with a strange man she had seen only when their parents had visited each other to exchange gifts. He lay beside her. She lay down and cried. The cousin, a woman who always coughed, who was so thin that you could see her ribs even when the food was good and other women had skin glossy with fat, lay down on the other side. The cousin left later for her own husband. He watched N!ai, just a shadow, get up and head to her mother's hut.

The next day he heard N!ai's mother chide her: "You are too old to sleep with your mother. You are married to a good husband. He is the one you should sleep with." But N!ai protested. Her friends went off to gather or to play, and she was there, with a husband she didn't want, and she said so, shaming her mother, angering her father, who threatened to hit her, though ≠oma knew her father never would. So at night he slept without his wife, or she slept far away from him.

His older sister, Kwoba, had been married before her breasts had grown, before she had menstruated, so he had understood why she had kept running back to their mother, why she hadn't wanted a husband. And whenever he met N!ai, whenever he joked with her and found joking so easy, he was glad he wasn't so much older, nor she so much younger; he was glad that when they married she would have breasts and she would have menstruated, and he wouldn't have to lie beside her like his brother-in-law beside his sister and dream about some future night when they could make love.

When his parents left /gausha and returned to Dobe, he wanted to return with them and forget all about this marriage business. But he said nothing, and he stayed. His relationship with N!ai and N!ai's sister was kai: they could joke and play and insult the other's penis or labia without anyone getting angry, but toward N!ai's father and mother, he felt kwa, and he was to treat them with the utmost respect, rarely speaking to her father, never speaking to her mother, not even looking directly at her, if possible. With N!ai's brother there was supposed to be some kwa, which made it hard, because when he hunted with her father or her brother, there was no joking. Her father joked with his friends; her brother joked with his friends, and ≠oma found he did not know what to say, that he was quiet most of the time, that the jokes made by N!ai's sister rarely made him laugh, that he was a touch afraid of laughing, and anytime he felt angry, he buried it the same way that you buried a dead body in an anthill—everyone knows its there, but no one sees it. So at night he played his thumb piano and quietly sang his mournful songs, and afterward he slept in his hut, N!ai more and more often there, but sleeping under a separate blanket, her body distant from his touch.

One night she slept under his blanket, but she moved away when he touched her hip. Another night she slept under the blanket, and he did not touch her. Another night, and she pressed her back to him, and he found himself both full of desire, and awe, and fear. She giggled when it became clear that for all the talk, all the stories, all the play, he was quite uncertain just how to go about this.

The next morning she smiled at him across their fire, and

her father spoke to her and her mother spoke to her and he wanted to return to Dobe, where talk was easy, where he didn't have to worry about giving offense.

Here, on the shuttle, he could talk to the walls.

The Ninth Day

Esoch awoke with the vague resolution to track down Dikobe. But the resolve of the lying down is not the resolve of the standing. Once he was on his feet, his head once again felt weightless. He barely made it to the sanitary closet, and what came up was a few strands of bile and air. His whole body shook, and it tried to expel nothing, and the nausea remained, as if his stomach were full of foul matter. Shitting was equally unsuccessful and painful. He sat in the tiny shower cubicle, and the water supply ended before he had the energy to soap himself. The recycler went on, and it would take ten minutes to prep the water for another shower. He soaped himself during the second shower, wounds on belly and palm stinging fiercely, and he sat, weak and dejected, during the third. He wouldn't be hunting for Pauline today. He sat until he felt well enough to make it back to the bed and to the medcomp alongside it. It took him a while, but the medcomp was set up much like the med-kits he'd been trained to use, so soon one IV was drip-feeding him while another withdrew blood as needed, first for analysis, second for recycling.

By midafternoon the first blood recycling was finished, salve was spread over wounds on belly and palm, and Esoch had figured out what he wanted to do. He was back in the acceleration couch. The screens were alive with images. The clearing was empty of slazans. No one was on the hill. A quadruped— long legs, front knees bent—was drinking water from the stream. Hanan had liked this animal in particular.

He didn't want to think about Hanan. He wanted to find Dikobe. He re-entered the system, called up help screens, and found his way to the index of the visual record.

After reviewing the instructions he keyed in the date— thought for a moment; remembered the numbers ticking off at the lower right-hand corner of the visor—then keyed in 0330, the time of the probe drop. There were no images of Pauline Dikobe on record. He called up a composite of external images. There were none. The screen was blank. He searched for the next available image: the clearing, at night, the fires upon the hillside, each one distant from the other, the shadows that sat or slept on either side of the fire. He keyed in for a relighting of the figures, and now he could make her out, standing in the clearing itself. Pauline was wearing nothing more than the pubic apron he had made for her, and she held her arms tight to her chest, to warm herself in the night chill.

Esoch was relieved to see her. It meant she had been alive and relatively healthy while they had been so worried. She must have shut off transmission. There was no sign of an enemy. No sign of a threat. Why had she come out at night to stand alone, almost naked, in the clearing?

He searched and found the readout logs. He discovered a five-minute span for which there was no imaging. After some sorting he found the log on power usage, which graphed and displayed levels of use and sources of power. The imaging of Pauline in the clearing had been powered by the emergency battery. He backed along the graph, to 0334.21, when the power had dipped to almost the zero-line: the emergency battery activated, but not used. Here was the end of the five minutes. At 0329.08 the graph's line shot straight up a cliff, to the level of power the small nuclear reactor supplied at night. He now read the graph forward in time. At 0329.08, the level of power dropped. The reactor had been shut down: Jihad's wish. With the nuclear core shut down, the shuttle would have been harder to detect. Who did Jihad think would detect it?

He imagined Pauline in the shuttle, asleep. The sounds she'd been accustomed to, the low-level light she'd maintained, all of it gone; the sudden silence, the abrupt darkness would have woken her. The pure blackness must have been disorienting, the day's dizziness returning, everything wavering. The only sound was the whispered breathing of the ventilation. She must have tried to reactivate systems. She must have tried to contact the *Way of God*. And with everything caving in around her, she must have stepped outside, to where everything was open, where the black sky afforded a little light.

On the screen Dikobe had dropped to her knees, had fallen forward. Her fists pounded on the ground. She looked up, her mouth open, and even though there was no sound, Esoch knew she was screaming. He reversed the image to where Dikobe was walking out into the clearing. He watched her check the hillside, then look up into the sky. There was a touch of light upon her face, and she covered her eyes with a forearm. He reversed the images to where she had shielded her eyes: 0338.52. He went through the catalog of the shuttle's own eyes and chose an eye that had been positioned atop the shuttle in order to watch the contours of cloud and the shape of flight. He replayed the recorded images starting at 0335.

It was a night sky, and he strained to see a spot of light that might have represented the *Way of God* or one of the probes being dropped. Just when he thought his eyes had found them, and not some distant shimmering planet, he saw what had caused Dikobe to shield her eyes. He watched the tiny balls of light expand outward, bright red at first, then shifting to blue and sinking to nothing. Nuclear explosions. But one ball of light was much bigger than the others: a tiny, cold sun, then nothing.

He reversed and again watched these transitory stars: ballooning red, contracting blue, then night and distance. He watched a third time, as if by watching carefully he could come up with some alternative explanation, some better way to explain to himself the glint of light off metal, the *Way of God* pulling out of orbit, the blinding whiteness across his reality visor, and the sudden explosion of parachutes. Each time he watched—and he watched it a number of times—he saw the same thing and arrived at the same conclusion: a slazan warship had attacked the *Way of God*.

On the adjacent screen Dikobe was screaming at the sky, pounding on the ground. She didn't know how the captain and Jihad had worried about her. She didn't know that they had just dropped a decoy probe, that they had sent someone down to her. She screamed and pounded. The *Way of God* had been destroyed, and all she knew was that she was truly alone.

On the first screen tiny flashes of white streamed across the sky: debris burning up as it entered the atmosphere. Then: a thicker stream of white, something bigger falling through the atmosphere, burning on its way down. Esoch did a careful scan of the sky. Nothing survived except two tiny blips of light. They were quickly identified as two mapping satellites. They would orbit for years before they, too, slid from the sky and burned up in the atmosphere.

He was with Hanan. She was lying on her back; he was on his side because that was the only way they both could fit on her sleeping mat. He placed his hand under her breast, liking the warmth, the dampness of her skin. "I don't want to go down," he said. "I don't want to be away from you. Not for six months."

She smiled. It was obvious she was touched, but the smile

didn't have the warmth of someone who fully believed the generosity of the words. "Men are so sentimental. You know, I'll still be here when you get back."

At first it was impossible for Esoch to do anything. He sat in the acceleration couch and stared without seeing. Twenty-eight people were dead, many of them who hadn't known how to like him: he hadn't worshiped the god of Abraham, he wasn't Semitic enough, he wasn't a woman—he was Dikobe's boy, and that last word, *boy*, traveled back a millennia and across languages where his size, his stature, the shape of his skull, the manner of his subsistence, were all used to deny that he was a contemporary human, to deny that he was a man. And there was Jihad, who had issued his last instructions, and Tamr, who had wished God's blessing, and the captain, who had called him by his self-given name and asked if he was all right. Amalia and Viswam would never share their mats again, and Rajeev would not have to spend the night at his workstation and feign his dedication while Viswam was screwing away in the cabin the two men shared. Hanan was gone, and so were all the months he had squandered when he could have been with her.

How do you grieve?

When he received news of his father's death, he and N!ai had walked the several days back to the n!ore where his parents had lived. It was !gaa, the hot, dry season, when food was scarce and you could see a woman's ribs. When they arrived, his father had already been buried. Many different families had gathered together within easy walking distance of the Dobe waterhole. He remembered spending the cooler hours of morning and evening clearing a new village, building new huts, and transporting the few things they owned because they could no longer live where someone had died. He remembered the abrupt wailing, his mother, his sister, his aunts, and several female cousins. He sat around fires and talked with other men, and he listened to them tell stories about his father. Every time he tried to speak, he was overtaken by tears. At night he played his thumb piano and sang a mournful song he had made up: when his second child was old enough to gather with its mother, he would come to live at his parents' n!ore. Now his father wouldn't be there.

His father was now among the //gangwasi, the spirits of the dead, and soon after his death, he made his oldest daughter, Kwoba, terribly sick and tried to take her away with him so he wouldn't feel so alone and miss so much everyone he had loved. During a healing dance ≠oma's uncle had to leave his body and go after his brother and convince him to return Kwoba to the land of the living.

Later that year his mother moved to N≠ama to be near her brother, who would hunt meat for her until she remarried, so now Dobe, where he had grown, was a place where uncles and cousins lived, not parents, not siblings. One loss, and everything had changed.

In another sense nothing had changed—he would go back to /gausha with N!ai and hunt for her parents while she gathered food for him—but now it all felt different.

At Chum!kwe, nothing changed, nothing felt different. Someone died, someone got cut up and put in the infirmary, and still you lined up for mealie-meal at the regular hours, and the bottle shop opened in time for evening consumption. Night surrounded Chum!kwe like any other place, but the only //gangwasi were the ones you had brought with you.

Death seemed to change nothing anywhere else. After Ghazwan's death, after Esoch's compassionate leave, which he spent planetside, in Wadi al-Uyoun, where he saw only masculine faces that reminded him of the face belonging to his comrade-in-arms, Esoch returned to the military orbital and found new faces marching to the same old orders, following the same old schedules. It was as if Ghazwan had never existed.

But here, in Dikobe's shuttle, there was no routine to return to. He sat and he wanted to cry. He wanted to scream. He wanted to pound against the controls or upon the metal deck. But he sat and contemplated his solitude.

That evening he called up for the last recorded image of Pauline Dikobe. She was walking away from the shuttle. She wore a chameleon suit and a pack much like the one he had worn. She reached the foot of the hill and stopped. She turned to face the shuttle, raised her hand into the air, and waved, her hand sliding back and forth as if wiping clean a sheet of glass. Her face was blank, and he tried to read something into her expression. But she wasn't waving to him or to the dead crew of the *Way of God*. She was waving to a hunk of metal, her source of protection. She pulled up her hood, tapped the chin strap into place, and turned away. In an open clearing the chameleon suit was colored a light brown, the color of soil mixed with sand. But once Pauline was in the woods, the tiny sensors embedded in the suit's fabric caused the suit's colors to darken, to match the browns and greens of the surroundings. From a distance it looked as if Pauline had disappeared.

She couldn't be tracked by equipment. The suit radiated the same heat as the surrounding environment, so she was impossible to find using infrared. Radar was useless in such dense woods.

He stared at the screen, the trail empty, the day and time registered in Arabic at the bottom of the screen. She had left yesterday. Just hours before he'd shown up. If he had swum ashore sooner, if he had not stared at the wall of forest, if he had not lost his tracking disc, if only he had ignored Jihad's instructions, if only he had ignored his fears that the enemy existed on this planet and had called her on the palmtalk. . . .

A slazan entered the image. It turned to look at the shuttle, then to look up the path. Esoch magnified the image and recognized him. It was the young slazan male with the music box and bright-red hair, the one who had approached the shuttle on the second day and played the music, the one Dikobe had given a woman's name: N!ai. Esoch could feel again the same anger during those first five days when Dikobe had ID'ed each slazan individual with a Ju/wa name, appropriating the names of his life for her own purposes.

The slazan whom Pauline had named N!ai was crouching now, and it was clear that he was examining the spoor left by Pauline's boots. Esoch remembered crouching beside his father, who, with his uncle, was examining a kudu's spoor. The two men talked back and forth, using secret words for the kudu because to mention its name might give it strength, just as drinking water or drinking melons might make it possible for the kudu to urinate out the poison from the arrow they had shot into it the day before. They talked, one right after the other, the different words forming one trail of thought: the kudu was zigzagging from tree to tree to stay in the shade, so it must have passed here during the hottest part of the day, and look how it was hobbling, weak from the arrow's poison. N!ai, the slazan, looked like a solitary version of those two hunters. He rose, gazed along the trail, then followed after Pauline's footsteps.

He remembered what Viswam had said while they were in the loading dock, working on the probes: "While you and Hanan were getting some, um, rest" (the *um* was intentional, followed by a grin), "Pauline went out to lay down some imaging pins, and the redhead you liked, the one with the music box, talked

with two or three of the women, then went to follow Pauline."
So this was the second time Slazan N!ai had trailed Pauline. After the first time Pauline had stumbled back into her shuttle and
shut everything down.

Even though the images had been recorded yesterday afternoon, his body reacted to them as if Esoch had witnessed a con-
temporaneous event: adrenaline flowed, and with the chemistry
came a desire for action, a refusal to let another delay make a
difference. He stood up, grabbed his pack, and was ready to load
it with supplies from the lockers, when all of the past days'
symptoms took over again. He sat down to stop his head from
spinning, to keep the bile down. He wasn't going anywhere today. He slammed a fist against the deck, and he started to cry.

It was the ninth day of Dikobe's mission. There were 191
more days scheduled for her research. Then a four-month direct-
return trip to E donya. That made it more than a year before anyone would suspect that the *Way of God* was in trouble; how
much longer until the warship was registered as missing in action, how much longer until they sent another ship?

Pauline had told him there might not be another ship. She
had told him that ibn Haj planned to destroy the data because he
wanted no record of this planet to exist if peace was ever negotiated with the slazans. The General preferred to let the world be
rediscovered by humans after the war's end.

Now they wouldn't be back, and there was no more research to use or misuse. If Pauline had told him the truth, if ibn
Haj had told her the truth, then it could be a decade before any
human returned to this world. There was just Esoch, more solitary than a slazan, unless he could find Pauline.

Once he was calm, he returned to the acceleration couch
and called for the next image of Slazan N!ai. It was ninety-seven
minutes later. The slazan had returned by a different path and
stopped abruptly, crouching near a tree. Esoch called up a composite view of the whole clearing. There, in front of the shuttle,
was Esoch himself, shoveling up dirt, then leaning into the
grave, all while N!ai quietly watched. Almost thirty minutes after
Esoch had entered the shuttle—dizziness had probably overtaken
him by then; he must have been asleep in the acceleration
couch—N!ai walked down the hill, careful step after careful step,
as if ready to flee. He came to the hole in the ground, he reached
in, and he felt the skin of dead slazan. N!ai got up so quickly and

awkwardly that he almost stumbled back to the ground, but then he was up and running, up the hill, out of sight, out of range.

Esoch was struck by the fear.

He had never thought a slazan could feel such fear.

It was later that Esoch looked at the times. N!ai had been gone for ninety-seven minutes. Was that enough time to catch up to Pauline? If he had found Pauline, what would he have done? Why had he come back?

Esoch felt the need to pace his frustration away, but three steps to the bed, three steps back to the acceleration couch, was enough to send him to the sanitary closet, where he promptly threw up.

That evening Esoch started searching through the imagery, between the hours when the *Way of God* appeared to have exploded in the sky and when Pauline left. He wanted to know why she had gone. Maybe then he would know why Slazan N!ai had followed.

During the day, Pauline's sixth day on the planet, newcomers came to the hillside, spread across it. The readout at the bottom of the screen counted time and numbers; Pauline had not reintegrated the shuttle's intelligence, so the old-timers were not identified and the newcomers were not given identifying names.

Pauline had once told him there would be a huge crowd of curious slazans come to see the strange thing in the clearing, so Esoch was now surprised by how few actually showed up.

Slazan N!ai was there, but without his large tin piano. He talked to some, then left. Before the explosion he had always been there when Pauline had come out.

A few more slazans arrived. Several walked off into the woods, then returned. There was plenty of space on the hillside, and there was plenty of distance maintained between slazans. But when one slazan, who wore a chi !kan, called to another, phrases that came out as short barks, Esoch began to feel like there were too many people, that for slazans this was indeed an unbearable crowd.

And what was Pauline doing now? Was she sitting in her acceleration couch, counting numbers, determining why two adults could sit on either side of the same fire while two other adults remained meters apart? Or was she curled up in bed, the medcomp recycling her blood, cleaning it of alien microbes, cleaning it of the hormones that carried grief throughout her body?

And then she stepped out, and the boy ran after her, and the giant slazan male grabbed the boy. The bodies on the hillside drew close, and he had to magnify the image a number of times to see what had happened: the blows upon the giant's back, his turning on the smaller man, the smaller man falling away, the giant turning, and then the woman with the bow and arrow, and the arrow hitting someone else.

N!ai knelt beside the bleeding man, removed the breechclout, and tied it around the man's leg far too late. Esoch magnified the image several times to the point where he felt perverse. Pauline had been right. Slazan N!ai was a woman.

The dead body, once everyone had gone, looked terribly alone. No one had cried out. No one had performed any ritual. Perhaps what he had been told in training was right. Slazans had no feeling for death. There was no grief, no sense of loss. They could sacrifice man after man in this war until the very end because the dead had no one to grieve for them, no one to demand that the war mean something important.

He was relieved to watch Dikobe come out. He watched her sit by the body for the longest time. She was evidently still sick, the way she leaned forward, closed her eyes, then snapped them open as if forcing herself awake. He wasn't sure if she sat there for so long because she was contemplating this man's death or if she was too weak to do anything. He was disturbed to watch Dikobe examine the body. He told himself how few slazan bodies had been directly examined by human specialists. When she shifted his breechclout to look at the slazan's penis, he felt divided by two emotions. Curiosity made him want to look; disgust made him turn away.

He had seen images of slazan penises before while in training. A trainer explained why they were shown. "The slazan penis has a slim bone in it. It doesn't need an extra load of blood to make it erect like the human penis. Why do I mention this? The slazans are a tournament species. The men grow to twice the size of the women. If they are anything like the tournament species we have observed on three humansafe worlds, then we know that men compete with each other for the women. We also know that choice rests with the women because a smaller woman is capable of outmaneuvering a larger man. But in some species sex can be forced. Slazan men rape women who refuse them and who cannot get away. Remember this. If slazans win, they will want to show their power over us. A long history of rape will be our future." There had been a few giggles and one outright burst of laughter, but these were greeted with stares so powerful that the audience took on a look of unified agreement.

On the screen Pauline was dragging the body down the hill, taking a few steps at a time, recovering her breath, then pulling again. It was painful to watch. He couldn't understand what she was thinking. Why touch the body? Why interfere with their ways? What would they think of her for doing this? But if she didn't bury the body, she would have to wake every day, step outside, and there, on the hillside, would be a rotting corpse, its body covered with insects and stink, its meat torn apart by whatever scavengers this planet had.

He didn't want to see any more; he called up the next image of Slazan N!ai. She was standing on the hillside where the dead man had been. Standing behind her was a child, beside the child a grown person who was obviously a woman, with bloated belly and tiny breasts. N!ai cautiously walked down the hillside, as if sneaking; then she leaped into the shuttle and disappeared. Pauline returned and found her. She stepped out and Pauline said something in slazan, which seemed to shock Slazan N!ai. Neither woman saw a giant male—Esoch was sure this one was a little bigger, with darker skin and larger eyes than the one he had watched in the previous day's images—amble toward them. Esoch had his eyes closed, so he had to rerun the image and watch the blow that drove Pauline to the ground, that bloodied her mouth and caused her to lose the mouth prosthetic that allowed her to shape her mouth to properly speak pan-slazan.

While he watched N!ai carry Pauline back to the ship, it made him wonder about everything he had heard about slazans during training: they can't stand to be together, they don't like to touch unless they're mating, the women are subjugated, kept out of sight.

Slazan N!ai went to the pregnant slazan, who was holding two baskets, each full of food. She walked back and placed the baskets in the shuttle doorway, then walked very quickly back up the hill.

The enemy of Esoch's training didn't leave gifts. They killed you while you lay unconscious.

The next image of Pauline was in the camouflage suit, and he could start to imagine what had happened to her while in the shuttle. She had awoken on the shuttle floor—or had they laid her in the bed?—her face bloodied. She felt she had deserved the blow. If not for her, there wouldn't have been slazans gathered on the hillside. If not for her, there wouldn't have been the commotion, there wouldn't be a man lying dead on the ground. She went through the lockers, shoved what she needed into the pack, emptied the basket of its food, perhaps muttering to herself while she did this, the way she had muttered loud enough for him to overhear her thoughts whenever she had got angry. She would be telling the air how she should have followed her plans in the first place, how she should have left the shuttle craft far away, hiked in on her own, as solitary as any slazan.

If he left tomorrow, he would be only a day and a half behind her. She was wearing a thick, cumbersome suit. Wherever she was going, she would have to travel the way he had, around rivers, along twisting paths, always pausing to consider her next direction. After another blood recycling he should be ready. He could catch up to her. But once he did, would she come back with him?

On one of the screens Pauline turned and waved farewell.

The following is taken from the notebook Pauline Dikobe kept while traveling to Tienah on the Way of God.

Day 98

Our destination, the planet without name or number, has more and more become a part of daily speech. The crew calls it No Name. The corridor walls have started to project scenes recorded from No Name's northern forests. Gravity and air mix have been changing incrementally to match my future working conditions. Corridor daylighting and nightlighting have also been extended to match the expected cycle on No Name, whose day is almost an hour longer than the day on E-donya. As the minutes in a day increase to match our cycle to No Name's cycle, so do the lengths of the shifts. There is always someone complaining about No Name hours.

Day 100

The air smells stale. If we had been on patrol in the war zone, we would have docked with an outpost by now, taken a bit of shore leave, had systems checked, air revitalized.

"Is the circulation system out," I have heard, "or is this the way it'll smell on No Name?"

I had always assumed that grown women had left adolescence behind. Of course, I don't say that.

Day 102

We've been too long together. No one can march off

to a café to drink tea among a different group of people;
no one can pack up her bags and visit a different set of
friends; no one can change the routine habits that have
come to annoy everyone else.

Tempers are short. Comrades-in-arms announce
each other's shortcomings over the dinner table. Nothing
is too petty to mention. This is why, I say to no one,
slazans evolved a need for solitude.

Day 103

Last night Fatima and Rebecca, comrades-in-arms,
third-shifters, went at it over dinner while I ate at a
nearby table. The argument ended with the meal, and
they rose from the table in heavy silence. As they passed
by, Rebecca looked my way and smiled.

I looked away.

Rebecca's been eyeing me for a number of days,
though she has yet to say something to me that is more
than a polite greeting. The romance of the outsider.
When on shore leave Rebecca has been known to share
mats with anything that walks on two legs. Fatima's
married and claims to find spiritual pleasure in her
chastity. It would be a bad pairing if the two women did
not work so well together.

This morning Rebecca invites me to join them at
their table. "No one should eat alone," she says.

Fatima explodes, calls her a hypocrite, calls her a
dirty Jew, calls her an uncircumcised promiscuous illit-
erate, and stomps out of the dining hall. Rebecca and I
eat in silence at separate tables.

Day 105

Before the morning call to prayer, Hamida, currently a first-shift member of the bridge crew, and one
of the ship's two medics, slammed Jihad against a bulkhead during a heated moment while playing free-ball.
Free-ball is a no-contact sport. Jihad's arm was broken.
First-shifters are answering the call to prayer while I sit
with Jihad in the dispensary. Hamida sets the bone, fas-
tens the monitor splint in place. She does not apologize;
Jihad does not thank her.

During breakfast Jihad cringes and mutters,

"Fucking Hamida." The splint has just injected another dose of healing agent.

At dinner no one speaks to Hamida, not even her comrade-in-arms. Hamida stares down at her plate and touches fork to food. She eats nothing but her pride.

Day 106

At breakfast people start talking to Hamida again. Last night she went to Jihad's cabin and apologized profusely within hearing of Jihad's gossipy comrade-in-arms. So now she's forgiven, part of the crew again. She's lucky, I think, that these people believe an apology is appropriate redemption; among the Ju/wasi she'd be teased about this for years.

Day 109

The air-circulation system is as cranky as everyone else. The air now carries the faint smell of the washroom. The whole engineering-and-maintenance crew is working across shifts to locate the problem.

I try to concentrate through a persistent headache, a constant tightness behind the eyes.

I try to pay attention to Jihad. She's working with the programming, trying to figure out a systematic way to evaluate the causes of slazan violence. I try to explain how intra-species violence grows out of rights to food and rights to a mate.

"No, no," Jihad says. "It has to do with territory. If it wasn't territory, there would be no war."

I disagree, but I'm too tired to explain how humans, and perhaps slazans, aren't like dogs who piss out their territory. But at dinner I see the way everyone is seated apart, in twos and threes, the way eyes harden if you try to approach a group, as if one more person at the table will cause one more argument.

Day 110

The air still smells of piss and sweat.

Tamr and Maryam sit down at breakfast. Both faces are pale. Dark skin puffs up under their eyes.

The captain looks up from her meal. "If this ship

smells like a toilet one more day, I'll make Dikobe here the chief engineer."

Day 112

The problem is solved. The air smells stale, but the other odors are fading.

If the captain apologized, it wasn't in public. Crew members joke about toilet air.

Tamr takes it out on me. She has started calling me Chief Engineer. When I ignore that, she starts listing every slazan evil she can think of.

"You know," I say, "this behavior of yours gives humanity a bad name. Why don't you learn something from the slazans and try a little solitude?"

"Fine," she says. "Solitude it is."

Day 115

Today is the day I start the reality workshop to learn pan-slazan. I expect to find a sullen Tamr by the reality chair, there to monitor vital signs while I live out a slazan childhood. But Maryam is there instead.

At the end of two four-hour sessions, Maryam looks at me with concern. "Are you okay? Your color isn't right."

I feel terribly alone. Maryam offers comfort; she pats me on the shoulder.

I have noticed once again how empty my cabin is. I sleep on one mat. The other is rolled up, in a corner. I wish there were men on this ship.

Day 117

I have considered writing down some of the lurid dreams I have had, but just thinking about them makes me anxious. I had gone several years without taking a man to my bed. I should never have opened my arms to ibn Haj or pressed my backside against the Ju/wa lieutenant. This is a hunger you can survive, I tell myself.

Day 120

A new roster is posted.

Rebecca is first-shift bridge crew. Her comrade-in-arms, Fatima, is on second shift. Rebecca joins me for breakfast and smiles a lot.

I work with Jihad during the first half of the shift. She is amused. "You've an empty mat in your cabin," she says. "Rebecca would like to try it out. Fatima is on duty just when you two go off."

I try to change the subject, but Jihad wants to talk about mating, about sexual dimorphism, about estrus cycles. She wonders if slazans have breeding seasons; it makes sense for a solitary species who prefer non-contact. "It's biologically insecure. Every egg isn't fertilized, and every fertilized egg doesn't mature to birth, and every infant doesn't survive to adulthood. If you wait to the next breeding season to gamble on a litter comprising one child, you are taking a tremendous evolutionary risk. A regular estrus cycle would make more sense."

She nods, considers it, then maps out ways to verify, using imaging pins planted through the forest to try to create a behavioral census. I am impressed how quickly she dispels naive assumptions, how quickly she creates a research plan.

After lunch Maryam once again monitors my reality-workshop session. I come out feeling terribly alone. I say nothing for a while, wanting to bathe myself in someone else's words. Maryam shares my silence like a desire.

Day 121

After living once more as a slazan to learn their language, I am again greeted by Maryam's polite face. Afterward I have dinner with Rebecca, and I barely listen to her. I look at her face. It is attractive. She is lively. That night I look at the extra mat in my cabin, rolled up, out of the way.

I remember the first time my husband lowered his face to my thighs, how I tried to push him away. "That's got to be"—I couldn't find the right word— "distasteful."

He shook his head, smiled, and after a few moments I couldn't resist the gentle touch of it. In my mind I transformed his head into Rebecca's, and the pleasure remained pleasure. I then lowered my head, and I couldn't imagine anymore. I so badly want someone in my arms. Why this failure of the imagination?

Day 123

Jihad doesn't ask me outright if I plan to share mats with Rebecca, but she asks about all the dinners. We don't look at any of the programming; we end up talking about mate choice, about how the dynamic of male choice and female choice shapes, over evolutionary time, the look of a species, but we are really talking about why she's in love with her gossipy comrade-in-arms, why Rebecca sits down to dinner with me, and why I listen to her talk for hours about nothing.

Maryam once again sets me up in the reality couch. But this time, after the workshop, I throw up. I don't want to talk slazan. I don't want to think slazan. I don't want to be slazan. Maryam waits outside the washroom while I clean up. Once she sees that I won't collapse, she clasps my shoulder, says she'll see me tomorrow.

Rebecca finds me at dinner. She's all smiles and talk. I barely eat. She tells me how beautiful she thinks No Name will be. How lucky I'll be to get away from the ship, the stale air, the hot tempers. How exciting the work will be, how useful for humanity's future. After the morning with Jihad, everything Rebecca says strikes me wrong. I tell her I'm going to sleep early, which must have been the wrong thing to say, maybe a piece of argot I hadn't learned, because she shows up at my cabin not too long after I have dressed for bed. Her smile is tentative, her look fragile, as if she suddenly realizes she might have made a mistake, that maybe I don't really want her. I almost take her in so as not to hurt her feelings. "I'm sorry, Rebecca, I'd invite you in, but I can barely keep my eyes open."

I stare through the darkness and imagine I can see the bulkhead. Falling asleep is as likely as finding a slazan homeworld. I count the days until we return to E-donya.

Day 124

Tamr is sitting next to the reality couch the next day when I show up. I almost smile, but she doesn't look too happy. "I heard," she says, "that slazans make you sick."

I know she's trying to be funny, but I want to tell her to fuck off.

"But I have the cure," she says. She holds up a bottle of wine.

"I won't learn a thing if I drink that."

She opens the bottle. On the console are two cups from the dispensary. She pours wine into each cup, then hands me one.

"What's the occasion?" I ask.

"You didn't fuck Rebecca; you might as well settle for wine."

We end up drinking the entire bottle of wine. The words flow out of us with great ease, but even as the wine loosens whatever is tight within us, we each control the direction of our words, we circumvent talk of the air-circulation systems, we bypass slazans, we detour around the war, all to insure that words can remain a commodity, our medium of exchange; and when the bottle is empty, when it is time to leave, Tamr takes me into her arms, her embrace large enough that I feel like I'm being hugged by my mother. I tell myself not to argue with her again about slazans. I couldn't bear the solitude afterward.

Chapter Eight

The Seventh Night

By the time that Clever Fingers, the almost-a-man with scars from elbow to wrist on one arm, had died, the shadows had grown long, and the silences were terrible. The animal was in its rock, and Huggable had long since fled the area. In the confusion the woman from the waterfalls and the woman who never spoke had also left. But night was too near at hand for any woman from the river's mouth to find a place to build a fire and settle down safely for the night. Flatface invited Chest Scars to sleep on the other side of her cooking fire, and Flatface's eldest daughter invited Far Hunter. Childless Crooked invited Lean Against Tree, whom she called Brave Mother for the way she had faced a man's blows. Squawker had already left while invitations were made, slipping into the forest when no one was thinking about her, and Wisdom looked off into the distance, daring anyone to infringe upon her solitude.

Crooked was watching I, and I knew just what she was thinking: the healer had many fires, and she had a sturdy hut where she could maintain her own solitude. I invited Lightfoot Watcher and her daughter and Arm Scars and her chest-high son and knee-high son.

They walked to I's shelter, following one by one on the path, sometimes stopping because one of Arm Scars' sons ran off to chase a yellow-wings or retrieve a dropped stickyball. At one point, I had to tell Arm Scars' chest-high son not to gather flatbugs from a particular tree.

Arm Scars did not say anything to her son. Instead she turned to I, as if waiting for an explanation.

Lightfoot Watcher started naming plants for her daughter, and I appreciated the pregnant woman's show of respect.

Arm Scars' chest-high son had looked to his mother, who had said nothing, and now he was taking the bugs one by one and dropping them into his mouth.

I gestured at the gentle rise of land. "Flatface gathers from up there down to this path."

"Who?"

"The first one to invite a woman to share her fire. She has a scar on one cheek."

"You call her Flatface."

"Her mother had taken to calling her that. My mother and Flatface shared mothers."

"The tree should be notched."

"Who wants to notch trees? Each woman knows where another woman gathers."

Arm Scars told her son to leave the bugs alone, and her son insisted he was hungry. The mother pulled some nuts from her shoulder bag. "Eat these." The knee-high son said he wanted some, too. Arm Scars full-stared for the barest of moments at I, then averted her gaze. I wanted to withdraw her invitation, but the woods carried the colors of approaching night. A man called out in the distance, his exact words lost in the music of his call. I did not recognize the voice. Roofer called back his Iamhere-stayaway.

Once they had arrived at I's camp, Lightfoot Watcher and her daughter, who wanted to play, walked off to find loose firewood. Arm Scars sat at the cooking fire and asked if there was food for her children. It seemed strange to I that Lightfoot, who lived where there were few, was more respectful of I's solitude than Arm Scars, who lived where there were many. Did living with so little solitude, as the ones of the river's mouth did, make each one a little less of a person?

Almost all of I's food was eaten before night filled up the woods, and only after Lightfoot Watcher had offered to help I track a lightfoot did Arm Scars promise to go to the river and catch a number of spawning fish. The promise was not her last word. She sat at the fire, the glow making the scars in her arms look like fresh cuts, and she talked to I like each woman shared the same mother. She talked with I the same way I sometimes sat and talked with Flatface or with Talk Too Much, who it turned out talked a lot less than this woman from the river's mouth. Lightfoot Watcher had built a new fire where I had kept the waiting fire, and she and her daughter had already curled up for sleep. Throughout the dark a number of males called out their Iamhere-stayaways when each one should have been in a nest and sleeping. The noise should scare off any nightskins roaming the night. The daughter and son were cuddled up by the fire, oblivious to the noise.

Arm Scars had stopped talking, and enough silence followed that I felt it would be proper to seek her own solitude in her shelter. Arm Scars said, "You say nothing. Have I offended you?"

"No."

"You talk little, even for one who lives by the river."

In her shelter I played the gzaet, but she did not concentrate on the music. She listened to the occasional long call and its response. She waited for the cry in the night that meant injury. When a cry echoed through the woods, it sounded nothing like the one she had expected; it did not carry the heaviness of a male voice, the pitch of air that carried through a throat-sac. This cry came from a woman's throat; it was low, deep, and no wind carried it through the night; the cry was carried by the strength of its owner's voice.

I found the heavy torch. It had been made by a male from the dunes after she had set his arm, which he had broken when, dizzy from fever, he had fallen from his nest. The torch was the last of three, and the wood was black with previous use. Wrapped around the top was dried bark that would catch fire as easily as dried thatching.

She lowered the torch into the cooking fire, and the sudden blaze lit up the camp. Lightfoot Watcher was sitting up, staring into the night. Arm Scars held her knee-high son in her lap and murmured to the taller one. The cry continued. I could not recognize the voice, but it seemed to come from the direction of where Flatface and her eldest daughter lived.

The flame of the torch dwindled, but the red coals at the tip cast enough light for her to make her way along paths she knew well.

"Where are you going?" asked Lightfoot Watcher, who had already stood, her belly heavy and dark in front of her.

"A woman is in trouble."

"No," said Arm Scars, still seated, a hand upon each child. "She is not in trouble. We call her Nightskin because of that. She hunts well, and she cries out her rage."

It was Far Hunter, then—the tall woman with scars from shoulder to elbow on each arm, with the beginnings of throat pouches along her neck. She was calling out her anger the same way a man would call out his position.

"Why is she angry?" asked Lightfoot Watcher.

"The one who was killed was her mate."

I sat down and considered this because it made no sense to her. I had cried out into the night after she had lost the infant that had grown from Sour Plum's pollen, and Crooked had cried out each time she had given birth too early. But neither woman would have cried out like that if Old Sour Plum had died.

"Mates die," said Lightfoot Watcher, "mates leave. No one mourns."

"Sometimes," said Arm Scars, "mates remain. The dead man was called Clever Fingers because he could make anything. Nightskin opened herself only to him because then he would make things only for her."

"Another woman did not want his gifts?"

"No. His fingers were good, but he was still not a man."

"But if the gifts are good?"

"A woman wants a healthy child. Clever Fingers has been waiting to be a man for too long. Only Nightskin would mate with him, and now Nightskin carries a child within."

"She does not look pregnant," said I.

"She and I shared a mother," said Arm Scars. "She told me that she no longer feels desire when it comes time."

"Nightskin," Lightfoot Watcher said, her words slow and careful, "could have mated with Clever Fingers during her whole desire, but she also could have mated with a full-grown man the day she felt herself open inside for a man's pollen."

"Nightskin was lucky Clever Fingers would mate with her. Each was lucky for the other. Until today."

Lightfoot Watcher turned away, her back to Arm Scars. I felt like doing the same. I had begun to despise this woman who spoke so poorly of the woman who had shared her mother.

Arm Scars started to speak to I, who sat like she was listening but who heard nothing. Far Hunter still cried out. Flatface's eldest daughter had invited Nightskin to her hut and hearth. I could see Far Hunter sitting upright by the cooking fire, lit by glowing embers. Would Flatface's eldest daughter be in her hut, feigning sleep, or would she be comforting her infant daughter, aroused and frightened by the nearby cries?

Flatface had told I stories about the ones who lived along the river's mouth. She had told about one woman who had grown angry at another woman. The first woman had made her body feel anger as if it were desire so she could get mating close to the second woman and kill her. Huggable had lived by the river's mouth for a time. She had heard Far Hunter's threats two days ago. I wondered if Huggable could hear this cry, if Huggable understood this warning.

Far Hunter's cries eventually ceased, giving the night over to the animals to make their own sounds, their own cries of "I am here; stay away."

The Eighth Day

I, who had slept poorly, forced herself awake with the first light of morning when everything holds the color of mist. Arm Scars' smaller son was already up, humming softly and digging into the ground with his mother's digging stick. He stopped, smiled at her, then continued with his work. She walked behind the camp to the midden before heading off to where Huggable had built her hut.

She expected to find the hut and hearth abandoned, to find that Huggable had taken her kaross, her bow, and her daughter to some place far away and safe. The hut and hearth, surrounded by brush, appeared empty. The fire was smoldering; no food or arrows were hung awaiting use. One did not enter a hut without invitation, even an abandoned one, but I had lost all respect for Huggable. She entered the hut to see what had been left behind. There were several skins laid by the fire where Huggable and her daughter must have slept. There were two karosses, each hanging from a separate curl of wood. The first kaross was poorly crafted and still had patches of lightfoot fur. The second one was well made and filled with fruit. There was no meat. There was no sign of her bow and arrow.

She examined the thatching, the way the sinew had been knotted. The workmanship didn't show the care of a man who lived nearby. It had the almost-a-man quality of someone who wandered much and worked little. Why had Huggable accepted these gifts?

I was standing by the cooking fire, considering what she should do, when Huggable's daughter returned to the campsite. She called out "Healer," started to run forward, then thought better of it and stopped. She looked down toward the ground and away, like a respectful young woman should, and stood there shyly.

"You are well behaved," said I.

"I don't mean to intrude," said Huggable's daughter.

"And where's your mother?"

"In the woods still."

"Hunting longfish with arrows?"

Huggable's daughter turned away in embarrassment.

"Has she been taken by desire?"

"She wants to have a baby so I won't be her baby."

There was a yearning in the voice that echoed a yearning within I, and it made her dislike the girl's mother even more. She told Huggable's daughter to stay near the hut before she left to follow the girl's spore, retracing each step from toe to heel in order to find where her path had diverged from the mother's. Huggable could give up her solitude to whatever man she desired, but it was wrong to leave a waist-high daughter alone in a hut.

I was near the edge of a ravine when she heard Huggable's mate call out his Iamhere-stayaways. The voice was distant, but well controlled, not so loud as to create echoes, so that I could tell exactly from what direction the voice originated. The voice didn't have the deep resonance of a grown man's call, and I recognized it immediately. I tried to convince herself to turn away, to go back and take responsibility for Huggable's daughter until her mother returned. But she followed Hugger's familiar voice, each call getting louder, the sound of his pleasure evident in each noisier call.

The one and the other were near the bank of the river, partially surrounded by brush that had not been burned away this spring, so it was easy to get close enough to see without being seen. Huggable's pubic apron and bow and quiver had been dropped in one pile; Hugger's breechclout lay near it. Now Huggable was bent over, one shoulder leaning into a young tree, her arm wrapped around it while Hugger stood behind her and called out with each thrust. Then there was silence, and both breathed heavily. Huggable half stood, half leaned against the tree, her eyes cast forward as she waited for Hugger to start again. Hugger remained behind her, looking up, his head turning back and forth as he searched the brush for sign of any possible competitors. He wasn't looking very hard because he didn't see I crouched there, up the hillside. He called out his Iamhere-stayaway, and I decided to leave.

But she didn't leave. She stayed, and soon Huggable leaned against the tree and opened herself to Hugger, who once again thrust and called out. Watching this should have bothered I. She should have felt how the bark of the tree would scratch away at Huggable's cheek and her shoulder, how the tension would build in her back, and how she would find all of that painful tonight or tomorrow when it was over. But instead she could almost feel Huggable's pleasure and wanted to share in it, and it was then I realized that her time for this was not too far off.

She made her way back to Huggable's campsite. The daughter was happy to see I, and I could not just leave her. With Huggable's fishing stick they sat by the river and caught three small fish, which I cut up and let Huggable's daughter cook in the fire.

Huggable returned while I and the daughter were eating. Hugger followed her until he reached the edge of the cleared ground. Once there, he stopped. He remained standing, his eyes respectfully averted, and he would probably remain there until Huggable left. He would follow her until her desire had ended or a larger man, whom Huggable should accept, drove him away.

Huggable walked to her daughter and squatted beside her.

She eyed the healer, and I returned the gaze. Huggable's face was lined with dried blood on each cheek, and each shoulder was rubbed equally raw. She met eyes with the healer, keeping hers round, hard, and angry. "My daughter can take care of herself."

The daughter looked back and forth between one woman and the other. I averted her eyes and said nothing. No one should be disliked for the way they talked after so little solitude. But she hated Huggable now. To say so would make the hate touchable.

"My daughter can take care of herself," she said again.

"A sunskin might disagree," said I.

"Sunskins stay away from people," said Huggable.

A child who saw a sunskin would run, and sunskins chased any meat that ran. But I knew that Huggable would insist that her daughter would not run. So there was nothing to say, and I rose, the daughter's head tilting up. She could feel the daughter's eyes upon her as she left. She heard the slap, and the daughter's brief cry. She continued walking.

Only when she was almost there did she realize she was heading toward the clearing.

She expected to find the almost-a-man's body torn apart by animals. Instead she found nothing. There was no body. She had to recall where Lean Against Tree had stood, along which path Huggable had walked, before she could remember where the almost-a-man's body had fallen. The blood she could not stop had soaked into the ground, leaving a dark surface, a tiny version of where the boulder had landed. The ground was torn near the body, and she could make out lines in the wet ground where the body must have been dragged. The lines ended at the hard black surface in the center of the clearing.

Had the animal come out to take the dead man? Had the animal dragged it down into the boulder? But why? She didn't want to believe what came to her mind, but it made too much sense. They had never seen the animal eat. They had never let it out to find food. What else was the animal to have done?

Beside the rock was a place where a hole had been dug and refilled. Here is where the animal must have buried the bones after she had finished her butchering.

It was too much for I. The boulder falling from the sky; the true bodies in the night sky who grew large, changed color, and disappeared; the number of people who had come: Lightfoot Watcher's terrible request, one man and another pacing near Crooked, Far Hunter's anger and midnight cries, Huggable's strange daughter—and now this, this animal who would eat each one of them if she was hungry enough.

The dizziness came over her entire body, and she fell to her knees on the hillside. The boulder wavered before her. She shut her eyes, but the wavering continued in the darkness. She didn't know later if she had lain there a long time, but when her empty stomach had settled, when her head no longer felt the rush of water, she opened her eyes. She was still on the hill. The boulder was still there. The animal must still be in it. She had to do something, but she did not know what.

When she returned to hut and hearth, I found Lightfoot Watcher and her daughter still there and Arm Scars and her sons gone. The land had been brushed clean of all debris, firewood had been neatly piled near each fire, and fish, eggs, and greens were laid out before the cooking fire.

Lightfoot Watcher said, "The woman from the river's mouth fished and gathered the food. She said a healer as well-known as you should not go without food."

Lightfoot Watcher did not say why she and her daughter had remained. I wanted Lightfoot Watcher with her big belly to leave and to be somewhere else when she gave birth, but I's mind was more filled with thoughts about how to get the animal to leave.

In the shelter were several baskets that she had not gifted to someone else. The first had been given to her by a man who had come with a twisted and bloody hand; Old Sour Plum had crushed it with a rock. The second had been given to her by Squawker after I had stopped a baby from coming while Squawker was still nursing her son who could not yet stand. Hugger had made the basket for I, and it was too poorly made to be a gift she could give. The third had been made by Long Call last autumn when he had wanted to mate with her.

She set several of the eggs near the fire, and she cooked a portion of the fish. She placed the greens, the nuts, the cooked fish, the fire-hard eggs, and three raw eggs in the first two baskets.

"I will carry a basket for you," said Lightfoot Watcher.

"The food is for the animal in the rock."

"Do you think so much food will make it go away? Or will it want to stay?"

It was a good question, but a person's questions sometimes revealed more about herself than about others. "It needs food," said I.

"It would be better if it left. Nightskin was here." Lightfoot Watcher said nothing for a while, then: "Nightskin did not leave with Arm Scars or with Chest Scars. She told Arm Scars that she wants to stay. She said the animal caused the trouble. She said if the animal had not been here, Clever Fingers would still be alive. Nightskin said that she wants to put an end to the troubles the animal started."

I considered this for a moment. As long as Nightskin, whom I had called Far Hunter, thought the almost-a-man lay dead in the clearing, she would stay far away from the boulder. But after each full moon had passed overhead, when the true body was gone, Nightskin would return to the clearing. If she saw the body was gone, if she thought what I thought, what would Nightskin do then? Lightfoot Watcher had not asked Nightskin any questions. "A woman who threatens another woman scares me. This person scares me more."

I placed both baskets on the ground. She looked to Lightfoot Watcher, who said nothing, so I asked, "Did she say she would do something?"

"She said nothing to me. I said nothing to her. She might have looked into my womb and harmed each child." Lightfoot Watcher looked as if she had more to say, but instead was silent. "Perhaps," she said after a while, "neither you or I should give the animal food."

Lightfoot Watcher was respectful. While I thought about what to do, Lightfoot Watcher averted her eyes and told her daughter to eat some tubers.

I's mother had told I the story of the hungry woman several times, and each mother who lived near the river had told each of her children the same story.

There was one woman and another who had shared a mother. The first woman was old enough to have children. The second was old enough to mate. The three had not eaten for a long time, and perhaps this was why the first daughter had not had a child. It was winter now, and they roamed the land looking for meat. They found none. The mother died. They were so hungry that each daughter ate half of the mother. They roamed and hunted and found nothing. The second daughter died, and the first daughter ate her. She came to live by the river where there was food, but she liked the way a person tasted even more. When she tired of lightfoot or darkfur meat, she found a small child who had run away to play, and she ate her up. One by one each woman who lived by the river realized what horrible thing was happening. One woman, whom many called Steady Bow for the way she took careful aim, lost first a son and second a daughter. In her grief she took her bow and her quiver full of arrows, and she hunted down the hungry woman and shot her dead. After that no one talked to Steady Bow. No woman would hunt with her. No woman shared words with her. No full-grown man would mate with her. No one made her gifts. Each one turned away when she offered a gift. She left to live some other place where no one would have heard that she had drawn her bow on a person. It was winter when she found a place where no one had heard of a woman called Steady Bow. Snow covered the land, and she did not know what food you could find in this strange place during the winter. No one knew her mother, so no one told her where the lightfoot grazed. She died of hunger; her only happiness was her solitude.

I thought of this tale because she felt the need to retrieve her own bow and arrows from within her hut. If the animal did accept the food, if she did decide to leave the boulder and the area, it would be wrong if Nightskin was there on some distant path, waiting for her.

When I had been a waist-high child, an old man had wandered near the river. He was confronted there by an almost-a-man, a son of the woman who had given birth to Flatface and I's mother. The old man yelled at the almost-a-man to go away. The almost-a-man yelled the same. Each one stood as if planted. Then each one approached the other. Neither looked away. Neither found something of interest in the distance to walk after. The old man came mating close to the almost-a-man and broke his arm. The almost-a-man went to his mother, the healer. The healer called for each daughter. I had walked with her mother, with Flatface, and with the mother they shared until they found the old man, who faced them and stood as if planted. I watched each woman take her bow. I watched each woman hold out her bow arm and stand there as if ready to reach into her quiver and pluck out an arrow. The old man looked to I's mother and her bow. He looked to Flatface and her bow. He looked to the mother they shared and her bow. He looked to something off in the woods. He walked after it and was never seen again.

I returned to her hut. Upon seeing I emerge with quiver and bow, Lightfoot Watcher retrieved hers. I looked at the mother, her belly large enough that she should consider the coming child over other matters, and she found herself struck by Lightfoot Watcher's womanly bravery, her trust for the healer, the questions that she could have asked but didn't. Each woman picked up a basket. I walked first, followed by Lightfoot Watcher, followed by Lightfoot Watcher's daughter.

As they got closer to the clearing, the paths became large, brush that used to line the trail now trampled or uprooted and cast aside. In the distance Sour Plum called out his "I am here you are there." His voice became louder the closer they were, and I remembered the old man's threat. I walked more quickly, pulling ahead of Lightfoot Watcher, who could not follow at that pace. She heard something thud, fruit that had fallen from the basket. She slowed her pace but did not trouble herself to pick up what she had lost. Soon there was a second voice, a young male voice, a voice without resonance.

The path she had chosen brought her near to where Clever Fingers had died. It was past midday, and the brightness of the sun made everything in the shade look dark and cool. A breeze from the north carried the sun's warmth to her. Across the way, in the woods, she could see one then the other, the old man and, farther down the path, Flatface's almost-a-man son.

The sight was comical, even when seen from a distance, the sort of thing that attracted one woman and another to watch. Flatface's son was standing still, chest puffed out, yelling in his boy's voice: "I am here. I am walking." Old Sour Plum's chest wasn't puffed out; it was large with his age, and his voice had the deepness of an old man's voice. "I am here. You are not," he said, not a long call, because he wasn't challenging Flatface's son. The boy wasn't any kind of rival: no woman worth mating would mate with him, except maybe early in desire when it didn't much matter, and he had not yet become an expert at making anything a woman would want. He had ruined a lightfoot hide that Flatface had given him. Old Sour Plum wouldn't hurt him, but being a man, and an old man at that, he wouldn't let the boy walk the path as if he owned it.

Someone else was watching, too. The rock was open, and the animal had stepped out. She wore just her pubic apron and sandals. She looked thinner than before, and her limbs hung loose as if she were exhausted or sick.

I stepped back and crouched down so she might not be seen.

"The body's gone." It was Lightfoot Watcher, and she had spoken in a woman's whisper, her voice made so a hunting companion could hear but not the hunted. Both mother and daughter were crouched low behind I.

Neither Flatface's son nor Old Sour Plum had moved. First one called out, then the other, and it looked almost like Old Sour Plum might be teaching the almost-a-man bravery for the time when he finally left his mother and found another place to eat and to mate. One and the other were oblivious to being watched, and the animal seemed to be aware of that. With each call back-and-forth the animal approached the edge of the clearing, then scurried up the hill, staying close to the large trees, to get a better look. Her ability to move with silence impressed I, but the truth was that even if she had stood and waved her arms, neither rival would have noticed her.

What I noticed was this: the animal was now far away from the rock and watching Old Sour Plum and Flatface's son yell at each other while the rock sat there, open and empty. The calling could last a long time, unless a woman and another came to watch and tease, because Old Sour Plum would most likely wait until the other became tired and walked off the path. Flatface's son was as stubborn as the mother.

I knew if she stopped to think she would think like a woman who was pregnant and take no risks, so she kept low and strode as quietly as she could down the hill, halting every now and then to look up at the animal and make sure that her eyes were on the sight above and not on I's approach to her abode. And just before she broke from the woods, that last thought stopped her. The animal did live there. I was uninvited. But after the lean time of winter, a group of women would go into a cave to kill a darkfur for its meat; animals don't offer invitations, and she wanted to see the infant that suckled on the animal's teats, she wanted to see the butchered remains of the almost-a-man so she could know for sure that her thoughts had been correct, so why was she standing there thinking?

She ran toward the rock, came to the opening, and jumped in the way she might jump up onto a rock. The ground inside was smooth; she lost her purchase and fell. The inside was dark, like a cave during the daytime, but at the same moment she was aware of all the light. It was like the night sky, darkness full of lights, nice round lights, the color of true bodies, the color of blood, the color of the water, and colors that were vaguely familiar, but she couldn't name the source of those colors, not right away because along with the lights there were drawings.

There was a drawing of the inside of a hut made like you were hanging from the ceiling. There was a drawing of different paths. There were drawings of Huggable's hut and hearth. But

the drawings looked like the things themselves. And the drawings moved. And talked. Huggable's daughter asked if she could
nurse. Huggable turned her back to her daughter. The stick that
changed colors, and now this. I was so scared, she couldn't move
at all, not to look for where an infant might be sleeping, not to
look for signs of butchering, and not even when she felt the inside of the rock get darker, when she knew without looking that
someone was standing at the opening, that it had to be the animal, and when she turned, there she was, all shadow and daylight
behind her. The animal wasn't moving either. She was standing
as stiffly as I was. Why didn't the animal just kill her?

A foot swung back and fell out of sight to the ground. Sunlight caught the face and teats of the animal, whose eyes were
wide-open, whose mouth was spread in an impossible-to-read expression. She brought her other foot down and took several steps
back. If she was going to let I step out, why hadn't she earlier
made some polite noise so I would have known that she was returning? The animal said something.

It could talk.

It said the same thing again. And again. She sounded like a
child just learning to say the words she had first heard in her
head. "I am here. You are there." Could she really be saying
that? Could she really know how to speak and tell I that she
could stand here, where the animal lived, with the lights and the
drawings that moved and spoke?

The animal said it again, maybe because I hadn't responded,
and now she was certain that the animal was actually talking,
and somehow an animal talking was worse than everything in
this rock that scared her so. She moved forward, and the animal
walked back, giving her plenty of room. I could stay and talk, or
she could run for the hill. The animal had given her plenty of
room to run. I stepped down from the rock, and she became uncomfortable at how close the animal actually was, so she backed
away, her heel scraping the side of the rock. She malspoke the
pain, and the instant she did that, the animal leaned toward her.
The gesture alarmed her, and she cried out. The animal stepped
away and tilted her head as if she hadn't quite understood what
I had said.

Now I wished she hadn't cried out. Old Sour Plum must
have heard, because he was lumbering toward them at a speed
that surprised I. She didn't know if she should warn the animal
or Old Sour Plum, and she didn't really believe that Old Sour
Plum would get that close, but he already had his arm out just

about when the animal had heard the approaching man, and the animal was turning soon enough to watch Old Sour Plum's hand snake out and take hold of her shoulder. The old man turned, let loose, and the animal was lifted off the ground for a moment and fell back stumbling, never regaining her balance. Old Sour Plum called to her like a rival, "I am here. You are not," and the animal was scrambling back. But she stopped and stood up. She watched Sour Plum. Sour Plum called out again, and the animal said nothing. She must not have known how quick the old man could be, because she tried to sidestep him and instead was thrown back to the ground. Now it was terribly easy for Old Sour Plum to lean over and strike out at her. Once, twice, a third time. There was blood on the face, blood on the teats, and it was the blood that made it impossible to watch.

I pushed at Old Sour Plum. "Stop this," she called to him, her voice hard, speaking with an edge, something to be heard even by an enraged old man. "Stop this!" She struck Old Sour Plum against the cheek, then darted back just before he returned the blow.

His eyes rounded in anger, and he stared at her.

"Stop, old man!" It was Lightfoot Watcher's voice.

Old Sour Plum looked up the hill. Lightfoot Watcher had stepped out of the woods and onto the bare hill. Her one arm was outstretched, in her hand the bow.

The face of Old Sour Plum's anger changed. He had come down to save I, and now a strange woman threatened him. He said nothing. He stared I down, full face, forcing her to avert her eyes. She heard him breathe, and she expected him to say something. She drew up her courage and met his eyes.

Old Sour Plum spat on the ground at her feet, then spat on the animal and walked away.

The animal lay there, dazed, a thin sheen of blood on her body, her skin the color of wood. Her useless teats moved with each breath. Lightfoot Watcher remained where she was, her arm lowered, her gaze surveying the clearing as if looking for someone else to approach.

What should I do about the animal? She could leave her there. And if she died? Then her worries and the old man's worries and Nightskin's worries would all be done with. But I am a healer, the voice within her said. When you have to hold a body, you hold it like the body of a child or the body of an animal. This indeed was an animal, and she picked the animal up, surprised at how heavy she was, and carried her to the rock and laid her body inside it. The animal would be out of the sun and out of sight, and I would have time to return to hut and hearth and get her gzaet. Would the music work on such an animal?

She looked around, but each thing was so strange that she had no idea how to think about it. But there was no sign of blood, no sign of butchering. What had happened to Clever Fingers' body?

When she stepped back into the clearing and the sunlight, Lightfoot Watcher was waiting for her, a basket in either hand. The daughter was still up the hillside, half-hidden behind a tree.

I quickly took the two baskets and placed them both in the rock. She returned with Lightfoot Watcher to the hillside and the daughter. I said, "I am going to get the gzaet from my shelter."

"Should I stay here?"

If I asked Lightfoot Watcher to remain, what would she owe the pregnant woman later? Did she want to return and find the animal dead? "Yes. If you have no hunger to be elsewhere."

When I returned with the gzaet, its heaviness pressing against her belly, its strap digging into the back of her neck, Lightfoot Watcher rose from where she had been sitting. The daughter rushed up to I and impulsively grabbed at her hand. "The animal left while you were gone."

I looked to Lightfoot Watcher, who said, "She left not too long ago."

"Then she wasn't that hurt."

"Tell the healer," said the daughter, "about what the animal wore."

"She wore skins," said Lightfoot Watcher, "that covered all of her but her face. The skins changed their colors. And she had something big and heavy she wore upon her back."

"Tell her what happened next!" said the daughter.

"She was almost into the woods when she stopped in her tracks. She turned and looked at the rock. She lifted her hand into the air and moved it back and forth like a man smoothing out an animal skin. Then she turned again and walked off at a quick pace."

"No. When she was in the woods. Tell what happened then."

"The animal started up the trail. But before she had taken even a step, she was no more. She was gone."

"Gone?" I asked.

"Gone," said Lightfoot Watcher. "She was there. Then she was gone, as if you had blinked."

I said nothing. There was the gzaet resting in hands and

against belly, there was the rock, its entrance open, its inside dark, and there was the empty path the animal had taken. "The animal couldn't be there and be gone."

"I saw what I saw."

"It must have left tracks."

"I will sit by your instrument if you want to follow such tracks."

"There won't be any," said the daughter. "The animal was just gone. Gone animals don't leave tracks."

"Quiet," said the mother, obviously irritated by the tone of the daughter's voice. "The healer will want to look for tracks. They might be there. We will watch the boulder and the gzaet."

Several different feelings took hold of I at the same time. She was amazed that Lightfoot Watcher could know what I wanted to do. She was relieved that there would be someone both to protect the gzaet and to watch the rock. And she was suspicious of Lightfoot Watcher's intent. There were the twin lives, and Lightfoot Watcher's desire that each one should live.

Tracking the animal turned out to be easy. The shape of the spoor was different. The sandals she wore seemed to be divided into two parts that were divided by a line. The back part was larger and dug deeper into the ground. Lines like cut-up snakes pressed into each track. The animal must also have been carrying something heavy in the bag on her back; the spoor was deeper than when she had worn just a carry bag and had walked off to plant the sticks that changed colors. As before, the animal paused briefly where paths met, but she moved on, choosing another path directly. Her pace was sure and steady. There was no sign of stumbling, of uneven steps, of leaning against trees. It became clear soon enough that she was heading for the river.

The river was at its highest level, its surface the color of the leaves above, the leaves above cut into two by a river of sky. I knelt to the moist ground to try to read what had happened. The heavy sandals came off. She could make out where the bare feet moved about, where once, maybe twice, she balanced on one bare foot. Had the animal removed her skins before crossing the river?

I laid down the carry bag in which she kept the various dried herbs she had carefully wrapped, removed her pubic apron, took off her sandals. The riverbank was like clay, and it was easy to see where the animal's feet and hands had slid down the bank. The animal had gone in with ease. The water was cold, and it took I a while before she slid her body all the way down the bank. The water came up to her chest, and she shivered. Her

steps were slow. The river's current moved around her. Her feet
sank in the muck. Something brushed against her skin. The water
rose to her neck, and she wasn't yet halfway across. She didn't
want to lose the animal. The next step brought the river up to her
mouth, and even though she could breathe through her nose, she
could feel a part of herself begin to panic. Her heart was a pregnant woman's heart; she wanted to turn back, be safe. She
wanted to have a hunter's heart, but her heart wouldn't beat with
such firmness. She forced the next step even though she knew,
just as she leaned forward into the step, that it was the wrong
step. Her body fell into the water, the water slid into her and
over her. She struck at the water with her hands; she kicked at
it with her feet. Her head tilted back and her face found the air.
She fought with the water and felt herself falling back into it.
Her feet scraped against muck, she struggled harder, and she
found herself safely standing, her balance regained. She stood
there, water up to her neck, and coughed out what she had
sucked in.

   She reached the other side of the river, and there was no
sign that the animal had hauled herself up here. Once she was
out, her body dripping, she could only find the old fading spoor
of a nightskin, of several lightfoot, of other, smaller creatures,
the lightness of their pace barely pressed into the ground.

   The animal had not gotten out of the water here. Then
where? She did not want to cross the river where it was so deep,
not again, not so soon, so she followed the current, clambering
over fallen branches, walking around thorny brush, avoiding a
patch of itchleaf, never seeing any sign of where the animal
might have emerged from the water. Finally she came to a spot
near where Talk Too Much had once made hut and hearth. A
number of trees had been felled long ago, and the sun shone
down. But it was late in the afternoon, and the sun gave more
light than heat. The river was shallow here; I could see both
stone and fish. She stepped across, and followed a number of
paths, calling out as she walked near where Talk Too Much's eldest daughter lived, and later passed a stone's throw away from
Flatface's hut and hearth.

   The sun was atop the trees when she returned to the clearing. And she stopped when she could see the rock. The opening
was still there. And outside the rock was an animal. I stepped
back and hid behind a tree. The animal wore skins that were the
color of leaves in the autumn. The skins themselves looked as
thick as leaves. And they covered all her body but for her hands

and head. The sandals were dark and covered the foot and went up past the ankles. In the animal's hands was something long. It looked to be made of the same material as the rock. It sliced into the ground like a knife, and came up with dirt. This animal was digging a giant hole with ease. And it wasn't the same animal. She was smaller than the other one, with lighter skin, and hair that barely covered the top of her head. Her chest was flat; she had no teats and no child.

The animal stopped digging and looked at the hillside. She must not have seen I, because she returned to dig and dig. Finally she stopped and leaned on the digging stick with the large knife on the end. She laid the digging stick down, then lay down herself. She reached into the hole with her hand. She soon stood up and her body wavered as if she had lost all energy. She almost tripped on her way back into the rock. Did this animal suffer from the same sickness as the animal with teats?

The opening disappeared, and, not moving a muscle, I watched the rock. What was in the hole? What had the new animal felt? It took a while to work up the courage. The voice inside kept telling her that the last animal when it had been this sick hardly came out at all. In fact, it had stayed inside for more than a day. I walked cautiously down into the clearing and toward the rock. She kept her eye on the rock and was ready to run if the opening should reappear.

She reached the hole and stepped around the scattered dirt. She saw what the animal had seen. It was a person's foot. She wanted to run, but she knelt down, found she had to lie down, and then she reached out to touch the foot. Her hand shot away. She touched it with a fingertip, brushed away at dirt, felt an ankle. She brushed more dirt, felt a dead, cold calf. The feel of dead skin was overwhelming. She stood up, turned, and stumbled, then managed to run as fast as she could up the hill, and she kept running until she was in the woods and the animal in the rock couldn't see her. It wasn't until she regained her breath that she understood that Clever Fingers—his entire body—had been buried there.

Lightfoot Watcher and her daughter had been in hiding, and they quickly followed her. Each was quiet during the walk back to hut and hearth, and I wondered why the first animal had wanted to trap Clever Fingers and his true body in the ground. She couldn't find a reason. She then wondered where the second animal had come from.

What was she going to do?

The following is taken from the notebook Puuline Dikobe kept while traveling to Tienah on the Way of God.

Day 135

Only ten more days.

The days blur. We have been decelerating at one g for several days now, but I would have to look in my notebook to tell you exactly how many days it has been.

The days alternate. Fights or apathy. The preparations for approaching the planet have begun to energize the crew. Jihad's comrade-in-arms has started to talk about how this whole thing is a trap, how we'll find a fleet of slazan warships waiting for us, ready to take us and our technology captive.

What's scary is that no one laughs.

What's scary is that I don't argue with her.

I let her have her way, and she treats me kindly.

Day 142

Three days until we enter orbit.

The screen on my cabin wall is on. I keep a watch on my destination. Now there is the far-off sun and much closer is the full ball of the planet, neither of which have a name or a number, except those assigned to it by the Raman probe, facts buried deep in the probe's memory, laid away under layers of top-secret classifications and passwords. The *Way of God*'s intelligence has erased the image of all other stars to insure that no one on board can calculate our current position

in the galaxy. So in the darkness there is just this distant
ball of light and heat, and much closer this ball of blue,
inkblotted by green and brown, swirled over with white,
like the three humansafe worlds, like the world humans
and slazans once attempted to share. The unity of evolutionary forces. There is no god but God. I wish I believed.

Day 145

We are in orbit.

Tamr congratulates me. She tells me my research
will win the war. She tells me that we'll make the galaxy
safe for human expansion. I despise these words. I despise the way I let myself listen to them. I despise my
earlier promise to let this all pass. I tell her what I've
been thinking for so long. I tell her she's full of shit. I
tell her that this world belongs to these slazans. "I would
pick up everything I own and walk away from the mission if I knew for sure that these slazans would be
harmed by my research. They aren't the enemy. They
haven't killed a single human. And if God bothered to
make them at all and to give them intelligence and to
give them children to love, then he didn't do it just
to test a batch of humans in a third-rate warship."

I am surprised that Tamr does not strike me. I am
surprised that she does not storm off. I see another tor-
ment as she nods, as she reconsiders everything she's
said, and how I must have felt about half of it.

And I am weary of all that thought. I am weary of
making the social calculation for everything I say. I am
weary of realizing how little they have changed since
they met me five months ago.

I am eager to go down there.

If I am to feel so alone, it is better to be alone down
there, where solitude is expected, than to be alone among
thirty other people, where to feel alone is a failure of our
tiny society or a failure of my individual soul.

I am to go down in one hour. I just wanted it recorded somewhere, to remind myself later, that I am terribly scared. There was a surprise farewell party last
night. The tables in the dining hall had been unbolted
and moved to the bulkheads. There was music, dancing.

I danced with the captain, I danced with the executive officer. Jihad opened wine for those who drank alcohol, and she toasted me. Tamr embraced me and said arguments were just words. God measured deeds and desires. "May God go with you, for all our sakes," she said.

We don't *act* like we love each other; for that moment we *do* love each other. Those protohominids who could not feel such love, who could not be part of the group when the group came together—when each member forgot who had wronged whom—those protohominids most likely reduced their chances of becoming our ancestors.

Now, no longer feeling alone, I no longer want to be alone down there.

The following is taken from the notebook Pauline Dikobe kept during her 200 day study of the slazan foraging population on Tienah.

Day 1

I landed at midday. I sat in the shuttle. The shuttle sits in an open space that once may have been cleared by natives who had lived here, and it faces north where the clearing overlooks a series of slopes; in the distance, the blue hint of a lake can be seen. The rest of the clearing is surrounded by a concave slope, easing up into dense forest. Through the clearing, practically alongside the shuttle, is a thin stream, hardly more than a brook. The leaves facing the clearing have become transfigured, the oranges, reds, and yellows bright and supple with life. Such beauty, and no botanist to examine those leaves and explain nature's artistry.

The clearing is growing gray with evening.

End of day one.

Nothing has happened.

The locals are up there, hidden behind trees, keeping a safe distance from this giant intrusion into their lives.

I want to transmit one giant "I told you so" back to E-donya, to Wadi al-Uyoun, to ibn Haj, Ascherman, and Muneef. I should have landed far away; I should have hiked in. But there is another truth, which is this. As much as it is a mistake, I was comforted then and am even more comfortable now surrounded by the controlled environment of my anthropological hut. I can check the various screens and monitors, check the outside temperature, now a cool fifteen degrees, or the barometric pressure, or the number of natives beyond the edge of the hill, hidden by the trees, nothing more than gray figures in the twilight. There are only four now. There are never more than two or three close together, and judging by their sizes, I would guess each of those groupings comprise a mother and her young. Outside that, no one gets closer than five meters to another, except for brief moments to exchange some words, their voices so low that not even our intelligence can reconstruct what is said into anything resembling words.

Animals are already habituated to the shuttle's presence and are coming to drink from the stream's water. The slazans remain distant. In fact, they are starting to leave. I yearn for one who will stay, who will build a fire and watch over me, as if I were worthy of watching.

Day 2

End of day two. I watched animals. Slazans came to the edge of the hill to watch, only to walk away later. They are too far away, their movement behind trees making it impossible to ID them accurately in order to evaluate who is returning, who is new to the scene. None of them dare come close. Jihad talks to me incessantly, drawing conclusions at a rate inversely proportional to the amount of evidence we are accumulating. She's talking territory, threats, violence, distrust—the same old evil slazans. It's as if nothing I taught her on the *Way of God* mattered. How can someone so bright end up sounding more naive than many of my weakest students?

The animals look at once so familiar—quadrupeds, snout, ears, tail—and yet so alien in shape and color, that I wish once again we'd brought an ethologist to describe them, to watch their behavior, and perhaps now I would be able to listen to her voice offering me polite instruction of how to watch, what to watch for.

Day 3

I step out into the early-morning mist, my legs and

breasts bare. I wear a pubic apron and chi !kan, courtesy of Esoch al-Schouki, my love for one night. I am glad there are no men on the *Way of God*.

Nothing happens. I have breathed the air, and by nighttime I feel nauseous.

Day 4

I walk around. I feel dizzy. Nothing happens. The slazans watch from the hillside, that's all.

Day 5

I walk to the stream, and the good Muslim girl in me finds it difficult to unknot the chi !kan, to drop it to the ground, to untie the pubic apron. I bathe. The morning air raises goose bumps. The water feels like ice. If the slazans care, they don't express it in their conversation. I run inside to throw up.

That afternoon I walk up the slope, straight toward them. I want something to happen. I stand in the woods, alone. They have all very quietly, with the barest whisper of sound, disappeared.

Day 6

It's morning of the sixth day. I'm about to go out, to wander about my little clearing. No frightful moves today. Last night I dreamed it was daylight out and one of them came toward the shuttle while I was still inside. He carried a musical instrument I had seen in a catalog of slazan artifacts. He plays for the shuttle and walks away. Why would he come so close to the shuttle? I wonder.

I know, in reality, why none of them have.

Day 10

The adaptation sickness is almost past.

I have taken to writing down some of the more vivid images in my dreams. The slazan with the music box. Esoch coming to rescue me. If these slazans keep hiding from me, I'll need something to do.

Chapter Nine

The Tenth Day

A lifetime is what makes a successful hunt possible: an older cousin gave the young boy a bow, made from a branch and strung with twine twisted from animal sinew, and he shot grass stems at tree trunks, then, later, at dung beetles, finally at waxbills, which were plucked and cooked and eaten; he learned animal tracks when gathering with his mother, when setting snares with his father or grandfather, when playing hunter with other boys, bringing pretend meat home for girls who were pretend wives; his father fashioned small arrows for a small, sound boy, and he shot geese and hares, and sometimes joined his father or his grandfather or his uncles when they hunted for the large meat animals; he listened to stories of past hunts—step by step what the animal did, what the hunter did—growing bored and going off to play, and later coming back to listen again; all until he was given a bow shaped like his father's and arrows whose tips had been dipped in a poison made from !hwah beetle larvae, and he went out, shot, and killed a female kudu; so his father made cuts into his skin on the left side of his body and rubbed in charred herbs and animal fat and soot; and days and days later he went out, shot, and killed a male duiker, so his father made cuts into his skin on the right side of his body, and rubbed in charred herbs and animal fat and soot; now, while living in the boys' hut, where they joke about erections and tease each other for sneak-

ing off into the bush alone and without a wife, he can feel the
blued lines upon his skin that mark him ready to marry. The
marks in his chest to lift up his heart make him want to seek
meat; in his arms, to make his aim steady and good; in his back,
to make sure the game won't run away; upon his brow, to make
him see things quickly: the lines there so that when sitting by the
fire, he would look and see those blue marks and ask himself
why he was being lazy, didn't he have a family to feed, shouldn't
he be hunting?

He woke an hour before dawn to ready himself. The
medcomp had finished the second blood recycling; he felt weak,
but healthy. He showered without incident. He ate a serving of
specially cultured yogurt, and he didn't throw up. The washer
had cleaned the onesuit, and he applied the patches.

Then he had to decide what to take with him. There was no
training or tradition here, no oiling of the bow, no laying out of
arrows and checking for bent ones, no extra application of poison
on the foreshaft; here it was guesswork and good sense. He
rooted through the lockers, those that Dikobe had left neat, and
those that had become a jumble of tools and equipment. The
larger of the two med-kits was gone; he packed the lightweight
one. Both fire cones were still there; he took one. The sleeping
bag was gone; he grabbed the heat-sheet, which he had cycled
through the washer, off the top of Dikobe's bed. The needle rifle
was still in the locker, but it looked like she had taken the pistol.
One set of rain gear was gone; he took the other. She had left behind three onesuits; he was sure there had been four. There were
two torches; she must have taken the third, unless it was at the bottom
of locker three, where everything had been recklessly piled. He
also took along ten rations, twelve drink packs, and his own pistol, torch, and tracking disc. He was sure he was forgetting
something, but he wasn't sure what it could be.

Nowhere could he find the chi !kan or the pubic apron he
had fashioned for Dikobe. She must have taken those with her,
and he now had a sense that she had left here intent on doing the
research the way she had originally wanted, coming to some
place alone, like any other slazan, and setting up camp, ready to
do good, old-fashioned, outdated participant observation, as she
had talked about back on the *Way of God.* But how wrong-
headed she was! How long could she survive on whatever rations
and native fruit she had taken? She had no skills and she had no
gifts.

Outside was mist. The sun was a distant glow. He was accustomed to the carefully filtered air of the shuttle, and the alien smells of the open air struck him with a mild shock. Everything he had grown accustomed to seeing on a series of screens looked alien and misshapen.

He stepped down onto the ground, and the shuttle door followed its new programming and slid shut behind him. No more open doors and surprise visitors. He pressed his thumb against the eyeplate, more a ritual than a necessity. The door slid open. He stood there and watched it slide shut again.

He scanned the area and saw no one. The tracking disc picked up no movement. He walked to the hillside, to the trail Pauline and N!ai had followed, and he found their separate tracks. He was surprised by the clarity of the tracks, and he found in that surprise a degree of hope. Once he was into the forest, the spoor became harder to read. Two nights and numerous animals had passed by. The tracks were partial impressions; here he could make out a heel, there a toe, farther along the instep. If Pauline had been aware that Slazan N!ai was following her, she had made no effort to confound the pursuit. She had stuck to the main paths. If Esoch lost her spoor, it was easy to find it within the next meter or so.

He moved with a degree of stealth because he did not want to attract attention to himself. So his presence ended up surprising a few animals. A dense tree became an explosion of birds who flew up beyond the forest canopy. A long-legged animal— like a lean antelope with awkward legs and a pointy snout— bounded off into the woods, the landing of its hooves a rhythmic fading whisper. Small animals scurried. Insects buzzed, several alighting on him, escaping the brush of a hand and returning again.

He came to a winding river and checked the disc. This was a tributary of the main river, this was the one he had followed south to this area. Pauline's tracks stopped near the river's edge. There was a confusion of tracks, N!ai's, and all the animals that must come to drink out of these waters. Among them he found the track of a naked foot with toes he was sure were human. Pauline must have stripped down, stuffed everything into her pack, and gone into the water: the surest way to lose a tracker.

He checked the tracking disc. No one was nearby. He looked around, saw no one. Sure that he was alone, Esoch undressed, folded his few clothes carefully, and left them by the side of the river. Naked, he dove into the water and rose to the surface just as his fingers touched the other bank. He felt vulnerable getting out of the water, but there were some tracks to examine. They turned out to belong to N!ai. Pauline's were nowhere to be seen. N!ai headed north, downriver. Would Pauline have gone north, toward the river's mouth, to where slazans were more closely settled, to where nighttime fires were sometimes as close as a half kilometer apart, or would she have headed south, to find slazans who lived in greater solitude?

A loud voice carried through the woods. It started low, grew louder, then diminished. He felt like the call had been directed at him, like he had been spotted and told to halt. The voice sounded again, and Esoch listened carefully the way a child listens to thunder in a storm. The voice sounded even farther away. He dove back into the water and got out of the river near his clothes. He was still naked, but here there was a pistol within his reach.

Once he was dressed, the fabric of his onesuit now damp and clingy, he set off upriver.

Several hundred meters up, there was a tiny clearing, partly flooded by the river's high water, and there were a tremendous number of tracks. And in the cacophony of prints he found signs of a boot. He spent over an hour searching the area for the second one and found it five meters south, on a thin trail. Pauline had stepped off the trail to make her way around a rather large animal dropping.

He couldn't seem to find the next track, and he felt at a loss. This wasn't like tracking an animal for the hunt. If you found fresh, neatly carved tracks, of, say, a wildebeest, you would follow the spoor, but if a thin layer of sand had filled in the track, if insects had walked across it, if all the signs told you the animal was far away, you wouldn't bother to pursue it. The only animal you would pursue a day later was one that had already been shot and was slowly dying from the poison on the arrow's tip. He had never had to pursue an animal with such a good head start.

He almost gave up there, but he knelt at the right time to see the distinct lines of a heel driven into the soil. Her weight was on her heels for that moment, so Esoch also looked up and saw another nest right above him. He walked farther along the trail to get a better look. It was a well-crafted nest, and it was empty. Dikobe had looked up while under it; had there been some noise to catch her attention?

He found the next set of tracks easily enough, but very soon she came to another watering spot along the river, and her tracks were thoroughly mixed with all the others. Was Dikobe drinking the water, or was this her way to confuse any potential pursuit?

He screamed her name out into the woods, and he heard his voice come back. And then another voice. Deep, resonant, distant. He checked the tracking disc: nothing within one hundred meters. The voice sounded again. This time closer.

His hand had gripped his pistol before he had considered the gesture. He felt the same sense of anger he had felt when the mother had approached him. But no one had harmed him. The pistol warmed to his touch. The voice sounded again. He knew it was a long call, that there was a message in the words, but he knew no pan-slazan, not even the word for *hello*. A branch broke in the distance. The slazan was making it clear that he was approaching. Did the nearby nest belong to this particular slazan? Was he claiming his own territory?

Aggression, Dikobe had told him—one of the few things he remembered—was more display than threat. There was no violence unless the two on display disagreed on the outcome. Esoch considered calling out again, then reconsidered: it was his first call that had attracted this attention. Had the slazan heard a challenge and was now responding? A beeping sounded in his head; the tracking disc had registered movement within a hundred meters. The voice was loud this time, impossibly close. Several more branches snapped. The slazan was making his position perfectly clear. Esoch had nothing in particular to defend. The pistol was still in his hand. He could defend himself. But Dikobe had suited up and walked off to prevent such violence. He replaced the pistol on its waisthook and chose a path to flee when the slazan stepped out into the clearing. And stopped still in his tracks.

Esoch knew he should run, but something about the slazan held him mesmerized. The slazan was taller than the slazan mother Esoch had confronted, but he hadn't grown anywhere near the gigantic proportions of the one who had struck Pauline. Under his chin, along his neck, were gray pouches that hung loosely, but they weren't like the heavy extra jowls of the giant one. His skin was darker than Slazan N!ai's and the mother's, but not the ashen gray of the giant. He wore a rough breechclout that did a poor job of hiding his genitals. He carried a finely crafted bag that was bulging with things. And he wasn't moving. In fact, he now took a step back.

The pistol hung from Esoch's waisthook, a clearly felt weight. His hand was already beside it, ready to unhook it and

take aim. The slazan's round eyes widened, his head tilted, as if
trying to understand the purpose of the sudden gesture. Then the
slazan's eyes were fixed on him, and Esoch could sense the
alien's increasing anger. To stare back might display strength, but
it also might provoke even greater anger. Esoch looked away,
just for a moment; he was going to look back, but it was in that
moment that the slazan leaned down—Esoch's attention caught
by this movement—and charged forward. The trained moves
came easily. Esoch twisted out of the way, one foot still in place,
the slazan's shin catching hard against it, stumbling forward,
while pain shot through Esoch's leg, pain he ignored as he
brought clenched hands against the slazan's back, causing the
man to stagger a few steps, lose balance, and collapse onto
the ground.

A deep core of fear dissolved and filled Esoch's belly. He
knew he couldn't out-fight the larger man. The slazan rose from
the ground and faced Esoch. The slazan's eyes were dark and
watery. Esoch wanted the pistol. Instead, he stared back. He
stood like he stood in formation, at attention, rooted to the
ground, meeting the glare of belligerent trainers, any twitch or
blink a sign of weakness, and so Esoch faced the slazan with the
same stiffness, the same open eyed challenge. And the slazan
turned, took two careful steps away, turned again to face Esoch.
Esoch was still rooted. The slazan walked away.

After another hour of looking, Esoch found Pauline's spoor.
The impression was clear, just to the edge of the trail. Several
steps ahead was the clear outline of a boot with a heel, the zigzag features of its tread etched into the ground. It was the same
variety of boot he had worn; it made him feel like he was following a version of himself.

It was past midafternoon. If he turned back now, he would
make it to the shuttle before evening shadows stretched out into
darkness. But he had brought the torch and enough rations to
continue on through the night. How much of bravery was fool-
ishness, how much of cowardice the lack of conviction?

He decided to continue. This time he walked loudly; he
wasn't going to take anyone by surprise. Any calls he heard were
in the distance. Quiet, he decided, must be for hunters.

By late evening, when green forest leaves and brown trunks
had taken on a startling dark clarity, Esoch was sweaty and exhausted. His onesuit was rank. His stomach felt continually
empty, in spite of his generous supply of rations. And there was

the faint hint of nausea; he should return tonight for another blood recycling.

But he couldn't head back. Her trail was clearer than before. It went straight and sure down the middle of each path she had chosen. It was now an animal trail—there was no evidence of slazan use—and the path got thinner and thinner. She was purposely heading away from any sign of slazan habitation. The woods were denser; nothing had been burned out. Prickly branches and leaves clung to the fabric; one set of thorns, unseen until too late, ripped at his sleeve, exposing his arm.

The torch became useless. It lit up everything in front of him while darkness hovered at his sides, behind his back. Off to his left something tore through the brush; far behind him some leaves rustled, and some distant creature hooted several times and was quiet. Insects swarmed around the light, and he felt quick stings on his face and arms.

He placed his pack on the ground and dug through his gear for the fire cone. After setting the device he laid it in the center of the path and took fifteen steps back. He was able to count to twenty-three before several concise jets of flame shot out, withdrew, and shot out. Five minutes later everything in the radius of one meter had been scorched to the ground. Nearby plants sizzled in the heat, but the area had been too luscious and green for a fire to take hold and spread. The cone glowed with the shifting reds and oranges of a small fire and gave off the equivalent heat. It would have been nice to have had one of these on those nights when he had been making his way to Dikobe's shuttle.

He sat down near the cone and its wavering heat. His back cooled as the night did, the dampness making him shiver. He turned to let the fire warm his back, and he stared at the night like it was a wall. As he drifted off to sleep, he found himself imagining the //gangwasi surrounding him. There was not only his father and Ghazwan and Hanan, there was Bo and N!ai and N!ai's father and mother: people from a life he had killed off, but people who should still be alive.

He sat up, shook his head free of them, and stared out into the darkness. The nightsounds seemed to close in around him, and he felt as if there were always something just beyond the nearby brush.

How did a slazan male live alone, night after night, with this noise and their imaginations?

The Eleventh Day

The next morning Esoch awoke, his face puffy and his right arm swollen with insect bites. After finishing his morning rations, he swallowed one tablet to fight fever and another to fight nausea. Pauline had returned to larger trails, where her spoor was mixed with that of a number of slazans, but her spoor was easy to follow. At midday her spoor had led him to a swamp.

High grasses and weeds stretched up out of the muddy waters and spread off into the distance. Huge flocks of birds flew about. Insects moved in swarms. Pauline's tracks ended right where water met land, broken reeds and stalks marking where she had gone in. How do you track someone through a swamp?

Pistol, torch, and tracking disc were slipped off waisthooks, were sealed in the pack along with med-kit, fire cone, and rations. Esoch set the pack away from the water before stepping in.

The swamp was shallow at first, but the muck took hold of his boots, making progress difficult. Water rose to his ankles, then his shins. The water was cold. There was a sudden drop-off, and he almost stumbled, grabbing at reeds, taking several long strides forward to regain his balance. The water was up to his waist. The fabric of the onesuit billowed out around him, and he could feel the water's cold in his scrotum. Several green-and-blue insects flitted about his head. Something in the distance splashed into the water. He turned his head. The reeds were now as tall as he was, and he couldn't see the path or his pack. The swamp had enclosed him. Up ahead there were patches where water flowed like tiny rivers among the reeds, brush, and tangles. There was no clear sign where Dikobe might have gone, if she had walked straight ahead or turned back.

Pauline had taken the next steps, so how could he not? How could he turn and abandon her? Ten more steps: the water, cold and muddy, was up to his chest, and there was no sign that Pauline had been here. He turned, tried to retrace his path, the muck pulling at his boots. He emerged from the water several meters from the trail where he had left the pack.

He stood, shivering and miserable, there among the reeds and tree trunks, his pants drenched, water in his boots, mud squishing between his toes, and the sun shone down with more light than heat.

He emptied his boots of water and set off to walk around the swamp, wet fabric rubbing against the skin of his legs with each step. He stayed as close to the water as he could, looking for broken stalks, for some sign that Pauline had exited the swamp, and whenever he found such a disturbance, he crouched low to look for the corresponding bootprint, which he never found.

He felt like she had been purposely evading him. He kept asking himself why she would have gone into the swamp until the question became a ritual, a blank spot in his mind. A flock of birds, more like a cloud of them, flew overhead, a matching shadow flying above the ground. Several of the pointy-snouts darted away when he drew near. Some kind of deep-blue lizard scurried away and plopped into the water.

By late afternoon he had traversed a quarter of the swamp's perimeter. His face and arm were even more swollen from insect bites, and a dull itching nagged at him. The sun had neared the trees when he knew he had to turn back. How could he abandon her?

"*Pauline!*" he shouted. His voice echoed.

There was no answer. Not even a male long call in response.

"*Hwan//a!*"

Again, no surprise, nothing.

He started to head back, retracing his steps around the swamp, his eyes still searching the reeds and muck for some trace of Pauline that he might have missed the first time. He continued to call out her name. Why, he didn't know. She must be a day or so away from here.

Evening was setting in once he reached the hard dirt of the animal trail, the muscles in his back strained and sore from the humped-over search, the old nausea returning. Two days of tracking, and he had lost her. He couldn't go back to the shuttle; he couldn't abandon her.

He looked at her spoor again, traced the outline of her instep with his forefinger. Just next to this particular print was the print of a slazan sandal. He didn't think this was Slazan N!ai's print, but he wasn't sure. At this point he remembered the pair of new-eyes Pauline had stowed away after they had had the preflight inventory. "If you come down with me," she had said, "you could use these to hunt down some meat for us." She dangled the pair of glasses, one of the stems between thumb and forefinger, the clear plastic sheen catching the light, the rims thick and full of microprocessed gadgetry.

And immediately he knew everything he had done wrong, from preparing his pack to his cursory reading of this trail. The slazan footprints were also heading toward the swamp, and he wanted a clearer reading of them, a clearer sense of whether or not a slazan had been pursuing Pauline. He wanted to come back tomorrow with the new-eyes.

He used the tracking disc to determine a direct route back to the shuttle, and he set it to cause a ringing in his head every time he began to deviate from the chosen paths. He tried to plan ahead for tomorrow, but the planning seemed useless. Weeks had gone into planning the *Way of God*'s expedition, months had gone into Dikobe's preparation for her landing, and in just five days everything was gone. He tried to imagine that things would get better, but he couldn't. It was as if his body—still walking forward, stopping when the disc rang, his eyes seeking out the proper path—expected more than did his heart.

It was nighttime in the forest, but in the clearing the sky was a deep purple, on the verge of opening itself to the stars and blackness. Strident beeping sounded in his head, and Esoch allowed his training to take over: he crouched low and pressed himself against the trunk of a large tree. The beeping stopped. Whatever had moved had also stopped. He stepped up to the next tree, which brought him close enough to the crest of the hill that he could look out on the clearing.

Across the hillside, on the ridge where an arrow had killed a slazan, a fire burned, bright yellow against forest black, and beside the fire stood a shadow. For a moment Esoch felt shaken; then he calmed as the firelight cast its glows on the rough hide of the pubic apron, the tough brown skin of legs and torso. The face was impossible to see, but it was looking in his direction. The slazan must have been sitting by the fire, keeping some sort of watch, and it had stood when it had heard his approach. Who could it be?

He scanned the area for signs of another slazan, but this one was the only one. He took several tentative steps down the hill. The slazan did not move, but the dark shape of its head seemed to shift in the darkness. Esoch walked more quickly. The slazan watched. Esoch increased his pace, made it to the shuttle, jabbed thumb against eyeplate, waited for the grinding slow slide of the door, the slazan still watching from a distance, its body as still as that of a tree. Esoch stepped inside, and the door slid shut after him. He felt suddenly safe.

The rush of adrenaline drained out of him immediately.

Suddenly Esoch didn't care about the slazan by the fire nor about the slazan's purpose. He sat on the bed, his knee touching the hard metal of the medcomp. Each night he had spent in the shuttle, the medcomp had infused his body with refreshed chemistry; every morning he felt better, and every evening his condition had deteriorated. For the barest of moments he remembered dancing at Dobe after his father had died, the boiling energy in him, in the other men, in his uncle with the thin, wrinkled face, N!ai sitting by his mother, and his older sister Kwoba was terribly sick, everyone thought she would die, too, and the next morning she was better, and N!ai spoke to him as if words were honey, and everyone in the face of the huts walked about as if old animosities had been forgotten. He needed something more than chemistry to keep the memories and //gangwasi out of his head. He couldn't bear to see the spirit of his father or Ghazwan again. Esoch programmed the medcomp to induce a deep sleep. He stripped off his clothes and laid his grimy body down for another recycling of his blood.

The Twelfth Day

Esoch woke before dawn. After a shower he dressed in the cleaned onesuit, the torn sleeve still hanging open around his right arm. His face and right arm were still swollen, but the medcomp had given him something that suppressed the itching. He felt neither nausea nor light-headedness, but he felt nothing else, either. Everything seemed distant, as if his mind were disconnected from his body; the contours of the acceleration couch, the plastic of the controls beneath his fingertips, were vague sensations.

The slazan still sat by the fire, and its dark eyes were upon the shuttle as if it knew Esoch were already awake. Esoch knew that was impossible, but he could come up with no explanation for this slazan's long watch. Had it slept at all during the course of the night?

A magnified image revealed a slazan he vaguely recognized. It had dark scars along both arms, and under its neck were the beginnings of graying pouches. Esoch ID'ed the slazan as Watcher and called for previous images: Watcher sitting by a fire and talking to two slazans at a nearby fire, one with scars across its chest and the other with scars across its arm, nursing a child; Watcher calling out something to a well-breasted woman who was walking away; Watcher standing over Slazan N!ai as she tied her pubic apron around the dying man's leg. Watcher looked like a man, but he spoke only with women. He sat complacently by a fire, and the men always seemed to be restless and moving about.

On the adjacent screen Watcher sat on the crest of the hill by the fire and still looked down as if the shuttle were the only thing of importance in the world. And Esoch remembered the shock at seeing her (him?) by the fire last night, and how, for the barest of moments, before he was aware of Watcher's bare skin and the pubic apron, he had thought that the dark figure wore a uniform, that the figure had found the shuttle and had come for him.

Esoch called up the images from the sixth morning, at 0338.52—he remembered the numbers perfectly—to watch again the nuclear explosions form momentary stars against the night sky. He waited for blue shifting light to die out—he was surprised how old pain could feel fresh—and watched the traces of white that cut across the night sky. He waited for the distant line of white, like that of a shooting star, and then he watched it numerous times. Something heavy was falling through the atmosphere. He reversed the image, tried to connect the object with one of the explosions, but he couldn't. Could it have been the slazan warship that had attacked the *Way of God*? Or could it have been the slazan's lifeship? Could the warrior have survived the crash and be out there, somewhere on this planet?

Esoch gave up watching after half an hour. Whatever had fallen must have burned up during re-entry. Anything that survived the explosions and the crash wouldn't long survive the radiation. There was just he, Dikobe, and the slazans who foraged through these woods. The war had died in orbit.

He had wanted to take time assembling his hunting gear this morning. The sun had risen, and the clearing was free of mist: dew gave fresh color to the grass on the hill. According to the large-scale map, however, a storm front was approaching. He had to reach the swamp before the tracks were erased by the rain. He placed med-kit, rain gear, rations, drinking packs, and needle rifle in the pack. He replaced torch, pistol, and tracking disc on waisthooks. Then he searched through the jumble of locker three and couldn't find them—worried a moment that Pauline had taken them—but his fingertips found the plastic casing. The new-eyes were in the case. He hooked them into the computer and spent far too long setting up the programming. Once he was done, he closed them back in their case and hung the case from the fourth waisthook.

Watcher did not react when Esoch stepped out of the shuttle. Esoch faced Watcher, and the slazan did not look away. Esoch walked across the torn black ground toward the same path he had taken yesterday, and Watcher's head turned, eyes intent on his actions. But Watcher remained seated and made no other move.

Esoch was barely at the end of the first path when the tracking disc, still on his waisthook, sounded in his head. He stopped and checked the disc. Whatever had moved was no longer moving. He turned, and saw nothing. In the distance birds called to each other. Farther off insects buzzed. Something scurried through brush. Would Watcher follow him?

From then on the tracking disc was virtually silent, ringing only twice when he deviated from the general direction of the swamp. It was midmorning when he arrived. Thick black clouds hung low overhead, and thunder sounded from the east.

He placed the new-eyes over his own eyes and tightened the strap until it felt firm against the back of his head. The new eyes had been programmed to look for Pauline's footprints. Esoch had used the soles of his boots to demonstrate design, and he had the computer adjust for Pauline's larger foot. He now found a clean imprint so the new eyes could calibrate programmed expectation against this soil's reality.

At the edge of the swamp, water had sunk into Pauline's tracks, virtually dissolving them. The other tracks were difficult to read. Animals had walked through them; he, in his exhaustion, had stepped on a few. The new-eyes compensated; thin lines of white highlighted where the boot's heel had cut into ground and where the toe had made its impression; the new-eyes interpolated what was in between, and thin lines of phosphorescent yellow connected the white lines to create the full outline of Pauline's boot.

Esoch followed the tracks away from the swamp and back into the woods, taking great care where he placed his own feet. White lines got darker the deeper the print. Thick white around the toes, more interpolated yellow around the arch, the heel. The distance between the steps was more than he remembered. But it was obvious. He should have noticed it yesterday. Pauline had been running toward the swamp. Esoch turned and followed the forward momentum of her spoor. Halfway there, between swamp water and woods, whites and yellows conflicted, overlapped; Pauline's toes had turned, she had sidestepped once, then twice; perhaps here she had turned her head, tried to look back, before she had run headlong into the swamp.

He removed the new-eyes—more a nervous gesture than anything else, a desire to look at landscape without technology intervening—and held them in his left hand, while with his right hand he examined overlaying slazan footprints. A few drops of rain stepped lightly upon some leaves. He placed on the new-eyes, and focused on the slazan spoor, until he could sort out one set of tracks from another. There had been two slazans. Both had worn sandals. One set of sandals was smaller than the other. The lines of the larger sandal matched the smooth outline of a foot. The lines of the smaller sandal didn't have the fine curves, were almost graceless, as if the sandal had been poorly crafted. He followed the three sets of spoor back into the woods, then turned, to follow the tracks, step by step, back to the swamp. The wearer of the smaller, ill-made sandals had been running—her feet far apart, the toe digging in, the back of the sandal slapping at the ground, barely making an impression—moving in the same direction as Pauline when she had made her own run for the swamp. Wind rushed through the leaves now, and far away something snapped. The trail emerged from the woods—where rain fell lightly on Esoch's face—and headed down the path toward the water. The wearer of the larger sandals had walked—long, careful strides; nice, full impressions in the dirt. The back of Esoch's eyes hurt; he wanted to remove the new-eyes. He was now where Pauline had twisted to look back, then raced for the waters. Here's where the wearer of the larger sandals had taken several quick steps as if to catch up, to see what was happening. And he stopped. Here the slazan runner had stopped. Here the runner had stood, here he had shifted his feet until the back foot was perpendicular to the front one, its weight traced in thick white. Esoch imagined this slazan holding bow and arrow, taking steady aim.

Esoch removed the new-eyes. Without them he could barely make out the forward foot, and the back foot was well mixed with other prints. He looked out at the swamp where Pauline had gone. Why had she been chased? What had she done? She had a pistol. Why hadn't she turned and used it? Had she been driven toward the swamp, or was the swamp the ideal place to elude pursuit?

The rain was becoming heavier. Esoch removed the brown-

and-green rain gear from his pack and put it on over the onesuit. Then he put the new-eyes back on, the dull pain behind his eyes persisting.

The wind was stronger, and leaves rustled together with the sound of a river. And the rain became stronger until it was a downpour. The water ran down his hood into his face and soaked into his boots. The new-eyes compensated for the darkness, and everything looked like a sepia landscape, some kind of alternate world. He watched water swirl into the depressions where the slazan had stood. He was overreacting, he told himself. There was no device to date Pauline's footsteps or the slazan runner's, no method to determine if both had run down this path at roughly the same time. The slazan could easily have been in pursuit of something else, perhaps an animal that it had wounded with an arrow, one of those small, plump things that scurried through the woods and hardly left a trail. But then why had Pauline been running? Could she have heard the call of the slazan Esoch had confronted? Could she have run for the swamp to avoid him as he yelled out his territory?

Esoch was shivering. A thin line of muddy water snaked down this trail, over one of the prints, and into the swamp. Slowly the line would widen into a stream, and all these tracks would be erased from the land's memory.

The slazans' spoor showed them leaving the area, heading in the general direction of the shuttle's clearing. They did not pursue her any farther. Esoch did.

He headed off around the swamp in the opposite direction from yesterday. The ground was becoming softer, his boots sticking more readily. He walked and looked and trusted the new-eyes to record whatever he missed. The rain poured, and he kept telling himself that it wouldn't be long before he found some sign, that she would be alive. He imagined she would be under some canvas shelter that she'd tied to several trees. She had decided to rest by the swamp, away from normal slazan routes of travel. She would see the approaching figure, the flash of green-and-brown rain gear glistening with wet, and she'd know it was someone from the *Way of God*, would know from his stature, his way of walking, that it was he.

And with each break in the reeds he saw nothing but swamp, each drop of rain striking water, radiating across the surface and around some brown stalks. For once he longed for the hot, dry spring back in the reserve, when you spent half the day lying in the dry heat of the shade, awaiting the cool nights, perfect for dancing.

It had been one of those unbearably hot days when Pauline Dikobe had walked into the chu/o, the face of the huts, along with a man from /xai/xai, where she had lived since winter. Esoch had been old enough that rather than gather with his mother, he could play with other children in the nearby pretend face of the huts, where his cousin /gau tried to talk young N≠isa into lying down with him like they were husband and wife. The woman whom everyone called Hwan//a, the name they had given her in /xai/xai, was the darkest-skinned person he had ever seen. She wore clothes like the other reds who had come, like the medico who had come to cure his leg a while back, but it was surprising to hear her speak the Ju/wa language with such ease, and the way she smiled so readily had everyone captivated. Everyone talked about her smile when she was off with women gathering in one place. And everyone teased her mercilessly for the blood she extracted from every arm.

When she was introduced to ≠oma, she knelt down and smiled. She said, "I was named Hwan//a for a woman whose husband's name was ≠oma. Should I call you little husband?" Everyone laughed and joked about how she would have to gather for a husband who still hunted anthills. His grandfather, whose name was also ≠oma, said that he and his grandson could be co-husbands so there would be someone old enough to hunt for Hwan//a. On nights when he slept at the boys' hut and played his thumb piano too long, /gau or /tashe told him to go lie by his old wife and play music for her. Sometimes in the evening when she was sitting by the hut she had built for herself between the children's face of the huts and the real one, he would walk up to her, his small thumb piano cradled in one arm, and ask her if she wanted to listen to some music. She always listened, and on the oracle discs she would record the sounds and play them back. She would tell him how much she liked his music, and he would show her how he was learning to play one song or another.

His father would sometimes come to take him away. "Can't you see Hwan//a is busy. If she doesn't do the work no one can see, they won't let her stay here, and then we won't have the tobacco and metal knives she brings." And when Hwan//a told his father how well he played for such a young boy, he told her, "Don't tell him he's so good. Don't tell him that reds all over the world would sit and listen to that. He will think he is the owner of music. He will play music all day and never hunt, and if he never hunts, he will never have a wife."

He sometimes went gathering with his mother and aunt when Hwan//a went with them. A long rain had filled a pan with water; from the distance it looked like a large, shimmering lake. Since the men were in the face of the huts or out hunting far away, the women decided to bathe. He watched Hwan//a undress because he was curious about how she looked under those clothes, if everything was shaped the same way as on a normal woman's body. He had sat naked in the water; he remembered how warm it had been, how hot the sun was, compared to this constant rain, and he remembered now how he couldn't stop staring at her breasts. He had looked at breasts before, how they changed on a woman over time, but his attention had never been held the way it had been then; they were the breasts of a young woman, firm, dark, nothing at all like the hanging, comforting flesh that his young infant brother cried out for and found so readily, that his younger sister still desired, her voice sometimes loud and insistent when she accused her mother of being stingy with her breast milk. Hwan//a must have noticed his stare, because she smiled at him in a funny way and turned her back to him while she bathed, allowing him a wonderful view of her taut rear, something he knew he was supposed to be interested in, but it was her breasts that made him curious, that had awed him, and he watched them closely when Hwan//a and his sister started splashing each other, her breasts moving slightly with each swing of her arm.

The first time she undressed for him on the *Way of God*, he had carefully watched her remove her tunic, then her sinteeyen, and her breasts were not the same. They didn't hang down like a mother's breasts, but they didn't have the allure they had had when he was a child. She took his hand and placed it on her left breast, and he, uncertain what he should do with his hand there, said, "Do you remember how you once bathed with my mother and aunt and I did nothing but stare at your breasts?"

"You were too young," she had said, "to stare at breasts."

"I did."

"I remember Ju/wa men talked more about butts than breasts. You must be making this up."

When Hwan//a had lived at Dobe, his family visited /gausha only once, and N!ai's chest was still like a boy's. Years later ≠oma and N!ai had sat by old rock paintings and had giggled about the little lines drawn between the hunters' legs. It looked like she had tiny buds on her chest. On the next visit her breasts were shaped like tiny melons. Dark angled lines, like those of a zebra, had been carved into her cheeks, marking her as a woman, and her parents' siblings and cousins joked about how they should have chosen someone older so she would be married by now. When they were married, her breasts looked like those of other young women, and how he had wanted to hold them in his hands. After nights and nights of waiting to have sex with her, many of those nights spent alone (N!ai having left to spend them with her mother), N!ai finally curved her bottom toward his abdomen and let him awkwardly find his way into her. After a while she enjoyed this, and they would go out to gather alone, to be less respectful and quiet because anyone in the face of the huts knew what you were doing. One afternoon he had held her breasts and delighted in the touch. But she had taken his hand away and said, "This is for your child's food. Your food is here." Sex was called food, and he felt the thrill as she pressed back toward him, her hand reaching between her legs, finding his penis, guiding it in. Never had she wanted him to take her breasts, caress them, hold them, take the nipples between his lips, tug up gently, touch teeth to their delicacy, and he remembered Pauline guiding his hand, his head, whispering instructions, until he was in her and she had pulled her body taut beneath his, straining against him until she found release.

He knelt to examine a slazan track that the rain had not yet erased. According to the new-eyes, it didn't match any on the trail. He continued walking, the rain diminishing to a drizzle, then stopping. The skies above were still gray. Two sets of rations left him feeling bloated. He had made it halfway around the swamp and found nothing. He was going to find nothing, and then what?

It had started to drizzle again by the time the tracking disc alerted him that he had reached the point where he had ended his search yesterday. He looked around. Nothing looked familiar; or, better, it looked as familiar as everything else he had seen. He kept walking and walking, finding nothing but water and mud. The rain dripped through the canopy with maddening persistence, sounding once against leaves, sounding next against his hood. The chill of the day had sunk into his bones, the constant shivering hollowing out his emotions.

He almost didn't see the figure at first, its dark form, the way it was hunched over something in the swamp, looking much like a collapsed body. He was slogging through the swamp, water rolling away from him with each step, and he was almost halfway there when he recognized the figure for what it was: a broken-off tree trunk, rising out of the water, snapped off by some wind, the rest of its body angled away, submerged in the water. Pauline had been wearing her chameleon suit; this couldn't have been her.

By the time he had circled the swamp and found nothing, by the time the gray in the sky had darkened with approaching night, he had started to hear the song's refrain over and over: tree broken broken. He heard the thumb piano, the soft thwang of several notes carrying across the quiet night air. Tree broken broken. A hunter had gone to hunt by himself and after a long time saw another hunter. He ran to the other hunter, only to find the broken stump of a dead tree. Tree broken broken. He had sung that song over and over those nights early in their marriage when N!ai had left their hut to go and sleep like a child beside her mother.

Esoch circled the swamp twice and saw nothing. He called out, Pauline! and he called out Hwan//a! until his voice was hoarse. He finally made his way back to the shuttle. He knew that if he still had that tiny thumb piano, he would be able to play it until the bitterness sounded in the music and was carried away by the wind.

The rain had let up by the time he neared the clearing. From a distance he could see no sign of Watcher's fire. He reached the hillside and found the clearing to be dark and empty. The clouds overhead blocked out light from both moons; to the east a few stars shown in the dark-blue gap between trees and cloud. A sudden breeze from the east carried an unpleasant odor. His eyes tried to focus on the darkness of the clearing, and he knew what the smell belonged to. He had never reburied the body, and now the rain had filled the hole, perhaps soaking through enough of the dirt to allow the dead body and its stink to rise to the surface.

Esoch increased the intensity on the torch, and a shaft of light stretched from him to the black clearing floor. He ran the light across the clearing floor to the grave, and had to run it back. There, in the center of the clearing, was the body, laid out neatly, no sign of mud on its figure, the ground around it spotted. The slazan's mouth was open, as were his eyes, and dark beetles crawled over the body. Deep in the woods some animal howled.

Watcher must have dug him up, must have left him lying there. Had Watcher done it to free the dead man of the grave, or was Watcher sending a message to Esoch? Another gust of wind, and the nausea overtook him. He was on his knees and retching, everything sour coming out of him. He kept heaving up nothing but gasps of air, and he thought that maybe Pauline was the lucky one.

He didn't remember how he'd made it past the body to the shuttle or how he'd stripped and hooked up his body to the medcomp. All he remembered was lying naked in bed, waiting for the //gangwasi to come. When he awoke in the morning, he couldn't remember any of them.

The Thirteenth Day

On a number of screens he could see the body, no longer neatly laid out; nighttime scavengers had left it torn and bloody, with gaping holes in the chest, and legs and arms jutting out as more bones than flesh. Even with the air filtered and recycled, the shuttle seemed to bear a trace of decay.

After showering and eating, he loaded the memory from the new-eyes and did a search for Dikobe's and the slazan's tracks. There was nothing. Pauline had eluded everyone's pursuit. How far south would she go? Where would she settle? Is this what she had truly wanted?

Later he reviewed the images collected by the shuttle. After he had departed, Watcher had left her fire, crept along the hillside, and checked the path where Esoch had walked. Watcher also walked down the path. So Esoch had been followed, but not for long: Watcher returned within twenty minutes. Without hesitation he walked straight toward the shuttle, knelt down by the dug-up grave, and with the palms of his hands, began the slow tedious process of scraping out the dirt. Esoch watched with morbid fascination the way Watcher gently brushed the dirt off the man's body, the way he cupped the dirt up from along the body's sides, his legs and arms, to give Watcher room to reach down and lift the stiff body out of the grave.

And this is what struck him: the tremendous strength it must have taken to reach down and lift up that weight. Was Watcher male or female? All he had seen grown men do was avoid each other, except for that one moment when that man had picked up the running infant and had carried him away from Pauline. He had seen women touch their children. Had he seen adult slazans touch each other?

He called the index on N!ai and called for the moment when she had knelt over the dying man and tied her pubic apron around his thigh. Standing above N!ai was Watcher. Watcher wasn't staring off into the distance. The stance was that of one who was on guard, but she was looking down, her eyes on the man's face. Esoch couldn't help but think that Watcher was female. Were she and the dying man kin or were they mates? What else could explain the intensity of that look?

Now Esoch knew that everything they had taught him about slazans had been a lie.

All he wanted to do was sit in the acceleration couch and let this great sodden depression take over his life. He forced himself up, he forced himself to go through the jumbled contents of the lockers and reset everything in place, calling out each item to the computer until he had a complete inventory.

He had enough food to last a month.

And then what?

The *Way of God* was not due back to E-donya for over a standard year. If a second mission was sent, it would be at least another half year before it arrived here. And if ibn Haj had told Pauline the truth, there would be no second mission.

He could use the shuttle, fly overhead, try to track Pauline down using all the sophisticated equipment he had. He already knew Pauline's reaction to that. But how else was he to find her? At some point she would have to settle down; at some point to survive, she would have to ally herself with some network of slazans. The only way Esoch could find her was through other slazans.

He found the hood: brown fabric, faint electric lines, two dark round eyepieces, and a mouthpiece, part oxygen regulator, part sensory provider. When he had learned Arabic and Nostratic, he'd worn one of these. When he had gone through military simulations, he had worn something more elaborate and had sat in a sleekly designed reality couch, whose surfaces had been smudged with hours of use.

On the *Way of God* Pauline had handed this hood to Esoch. "There are two of them," she had said. "Learn slazan with me. Then you can accompany me planetside."

They had been two months away from their destination. Esoch still spent every night in the same cabin, his mat next to Pauline's, but they rarely made love. When she curled up next to him, placed a possessive leg across his legs, he felt a tremendous need to be apart. He had started to look forward to her leaving, to things going back to normal, to talking with Hanan. He had decided that he would not sleep with Hanan—she *did* have a husband to return to—he just longed for the joking and the companionship.

He stared at the hood now. If he had learned slazan, if he had gone down with her, none of this might have happened. Perhaps the slazan warrior had been monitoring her presence—she had been on the planet for five days, the *Way of God* had been in orbit for six—and when she'd shut down transmission, the slazan warrior had been alarmed, had felt he had to take some action.

Esoch was afraid of the hood. He had heard stories of diplomats who had tried to learn slazan but instead had gone crazy. He had watched it change Pauline.

But if he didn't learn slazan, he would surely go crazy. How many more days could he live without any kind of contact? He had been on his own eight days now. He couldn't bear many more. If he learned pan-slazan, if he could speak with the locals, then perhaps he could find a way to get them to accept his odd presence: he could hunt down an animal, offer the meat as a gift, anything so one of them would talk to him, making it possible to talk to another, then another, until he used their slender, solitary networks to find Pauline.

He ate a full meal. He voided bladder and bowels. He laid out mask. He laid out gloves. He set down the prosthetic device that would fit in his mouth so he could more capably make the sounds that comprised pan-slazan.

And then he considered how distant he would be from the world while learning another language. He set the alarm to go off if any slazan came down the hillside and approached the shuttle. There were four alarm lights that would blink on and off with the alarm, and he could set their colors: the military love of code. Red for N!ai. Yellow for Watcher. Green for any other slazan. And what if Pauline came back? He didn't know if the shuttle would recognize her in a chameleon suit. He set the alarm to go off if a humanoid figure with most of its body covered by fabric came down the hillside, and he set it to go off if it recognized Pauline. He chose the color blue, and the alarm was set.

The following is taken from the notebook Pauline Dikobe kept during her 200 day study of the slazan foraging population on Tienah.

Day 21

I haven't written in this notebook for days, for what is there to write? I go out in the day, wearing pubic apron, chi !kan, and sandals, and I walk the same paths, establishing a predictable home range. I gather nothing but notes, which I whisper quietly, and which are, in turn, sorted and categorized by the intelligence into material I can later go over, rearrange, and rewrite as necessary in the evening.

I watch footprints, but I don't trail them, having neither the technology nor the skill, nor wishing to appear any kind of a threat. I listen to the distant long calls of the males, and I move in another direction when any come close. I have tried to place imaging pins into trees that stand near the intersection of trails, but they are all destroyed. Jihad has transmitted to me a map of the area, highlighting where fires are maintained at night, and I have used that to track down their shelters. I approach them, making as much noise as possible, and the encampments are empty when I come to them. I never cross the circle of tree or brush that surrounds an encampment. I watch from afar. I have not been invited. I see what food they have hung out to dry, what artifacts they have made with elaborate care.

I have found elaborately constructed nests, but the

imaging pins I leave near them are destroyed. We have
a few images of an adult male climbing up a tree and
making his way into the nest. Why would a male sleep
alone, perhaps run the risk of sharing a tree with the
black-skinned predators that come out at night? Is this
his way of proving his strength and fortitude, the way
male bucks carry heavy antlers and certain birds risk
predation by showing bright colors to a potential mate?
And why would a slazan female choose strength and fortitude while her hominid sisters choose men for their
abilities as hunters, for their prestige, and for their abilities to care for their own children?

But all I have are questions.

All I have are field notes.

The result has the value of an archaeological dig.
You can make fine, wonderful guesses based on the artifacts, the layout of tools, the number of fires, the
number of food types they hang out of scavengers'
reach, but if you don't see the behavior that goes along
with it, they are nothing but guesses. Certain nights I
grow tired of field notes, I grow restless with guessing.
I think about my imaginary slazan and his music box. I
muse about who he could be and why he plays music.
Gza, I know, is a slazan word which means both music
and healing. As far as we know, both meanings are
never used in the same context, but that may not have
always been the case.

Day 33

I have a rash on my shins. Some plant waves its
greeting as I press by, and my skin is reacting to some
chemical. The medcomp has synthesized different salves.
The first two do nothing; the third one causes a sting
that still won't go away. I tell Jihad to get out of my
head, to let me cry for a while in peace. I hate these
slazans. I hate the way they avoid me. I hate the way
they take no interest in my presence. I hate them because they probably have no interest at all in the way
this pain is driving me crazy.

Day 38

Three days ago. I feign several naps near where
paths intersect. I implant imaging pins into the tree as I

rise, using the tree trunks as support. No one notices. Two days later the imaging pins are untouched.

Today we begin to collect visual information.

The first recording of a slazan is this: a lactating female with two naked juveniles, both female. The adult female stops. A second adult female approaches from another direction. She wears a pubic apron and what looks like a kaross bundled up behind her. Who made this kaross? This second adult, or someone else?

The adult female says one word. The second adult says another word. The intelligence confirms what I thought I had heard each say. They spoke pan-slazan.

Daughter.

Mother.

Both adults look directly at the imaging pin, or more appropriately, to where I had been sleeping, and the four walk off. It's three days later, and no one else has walked directly along this intersection of paths.

Now the names. The second adult, the one without breasts, was an adult female, the same stature as her mother. Issue one: they use titles rather than names. The urban slazans on New Hope used names, locations, but never did we hear titles. Issue two: I walk around like a Ju/wa woman, my breasts visible. I look like a lactating female. Do they wonder what has happened to my child?

Day 39

Just when I've grown accustomed to walking in the wilderness, my breasts bared to view, I've grown self-conscious. I have asked al-Shaykh to get someone on the *Way of God* to make a facsimile baby I can carry.

Day 42

Nothing new. It's almost as if they avoid the intersections where I have placed the imaging pins. What do they say to each other? Who tells whom?

Day 44

Today we get to watch male sexual dimorphism in action.

Through images transmitted from one of the imaging pins, we see the makings of a fight. Here, ten meters apart, are two males. Each is larger than the two females we had observed. Each has the throat patches for long calling, and each has ignored the other's loud signals. They stand stock still, staring at each other, obvious violence in their stances, in the tension of their muscles.

I feel an equal tension. Here's the violence. Here's what I came to see. My purpose in life is to calmly watch each attempt to hurt the other. One male is somewhat taller. The second male has a sleeker build, and may be capable of more damage.

The sleeker one calls out, a long loud call.

The tall one stares hard.

And the sleeker one turns and walks way.

The tall one remains silent.

When the sleeker one is out of sight, the tall one calls out, long and loud, several times. The intelligence makes out words, blurred together the way words can blur together in a song. "I am here. You are there" is the translation in Arabic. Then follow five footnotes of the specific slazan words, their denotation, and the connotations we know.

I ignore the notes. I wonder: Which one had wandered this area first? In other words, which one claimed residence? What had the fight been over? Territory? Access to a local female? It must have been the taller one's territory; most animals will not invade and force a confrontation unless they are certain of winning.

Is there a territory? The ethologist assumes yes. What makes a territory worth defending? There has to be a stable source of food, a well-defined area.

The Ju/wasi have territories of sorts, but none that they defend. An area around a waterhole is called a n!ore. Several siblings who have lived there for a while are considered its owners. Relatives through blood have access to the flora and fauna of the n!ore. But each Ju/wa, through her relations or the relations of her husband, has access to several n!ores. Since intergroup marriage is the norm, ties between n!ores are constantly created. In the desert reserve, it can rain over your waterhole one day and over your neighbor's the next. One spring can be wet and plentiful; the next can be dry and stingy. The best insurance, the best risk-management policy against such unpredictable circumstances, is to accept visitors to your n!ore so that in your time of need you will be accepted elsewhere.

The root goal of all animals is to survive in order to reproduce, and the best overall strategy is to consume as many calories as possible while expending the least possible energy. It takes energy to patrol a territory, to protect its resources. The desert reserve is an area of patchy resources—a broad expanse of dunes and dry river courses—to keep it for yourself calls for much energy for little gain. It makes more sense to know your territory, intermarry, and share your resources according to custom. However, if you decrease mobility, increase the reliability of the resources, decrease the flexibility of group identity, decrease intergroup marriage, farm, harvest, keep to yourself—then there is something to defend, something to perhaps fight a war over.

But what about the two slazan males? How big a range did the tall one have? And what did he gain by keeping the other male out?

Chapter Ten

The Ninth Day

The sun was still resting atop the trees when I returned to the hillside the next morning. She sat behind a waterberry bush and waited for the second animal to come out of the rock. The hole in the ground was still there, Clever Fingers' body and true body still buried beneath the dirt. The sun left the trees for the proper solitude of the sky. Bushytails, pointed-ears, and a longfoot all came at different times to drink from the creek. I had brought some of the food that Arm Scars had left her, and she ate when she thought of eating. Mostly, she heard the voice in her head ask her questions, and she had no answers.

By late afternoon the second animal had not emerged, the first one had not come back, and I decided to tell Flatface about her plans.

The land around Flatface's hut and hearth had been cleared of trees, for she liked to return there every spring and fall. Not far away was the hut and hearth belonging to Flatface's eldest daughter. Trees and berry bushes had grown between the two places, so each woman could have her solitude. Flatface's hut had been built by Long Call soon after he had started nesting near the river, and Roofer had built a roof as solid and as dry as the one that covered I's shelter.

Laid out alongside the walls of the hut were stones with flat surfaces. Flatface had spent the past several summers, when the river was shallow, seeking gray rocks with surfaces that had been flattened by the rush of water and sand. Then she had taken colors, mashed from different berries and mixed with soot, and with her fingers she had drawn lines that looked like things you could see. She let the rain wash the rocks clean so she could draw again and again until she had drawings good enough to consider them her wisdom. Then she would take them to the Many Huts, where she would build a hut to shelter and preserve her wisdom for any woman who was interested. Wisdom, each mother said, is easily lost. The words a daughter does not hear turns into air that no one breathes.

Flatface herself was sitting by the cooking fire and eating fish that was spread out on a clay platter. Before I had reached the charred remains of the waiting fire, Flatface, without looking up, called out, "Long Fingers, Healer, I have fruitnut and fish to eat."

I declined twice before she accepted. She sat down on the other side of the fire, taking only what Flatface placed within her reach.

"Do you come with news or stories?" asked Flatface.

"News. I leave tomorrow morning to go to the Many Huts. I have with me my bag of herbs and poultices to leave you, if you wish. I know how you listened when your mother spoke."

"But it was to your mother she gave the gzaet. Are you sure you should leave?"

I hesitated. For the first time in her life she felt like there were certain things best left unsaid. She said them anyway. "The animal has left the rock. I do not know where she has gone."

This seemed to frighten Flatface, who looked to the tree branch where she had hung her bow and her quiver.

This glance in turn frightened I, who hesitated, then continued. "A second animal has appeared. It now lives in the rock. It has not come out."

"You went back to the clearing," said Flatface. She averted her eyes, as if in shame. "How will you know if you breathe in a true body while you cut up a body?"

"I did not cut this one up."

Flatface looked at I. "My eldest daughter took whitefish to Old Sour Plum. He told her the body is gone."

"It's gone."

"Did the animal eat it? Old Sour Plum said you gave the animal a gift of food." Flatface stopped, looked away, then looked back. "Did you give the animal food so it wouldn't try to eat us?"

"No," said I, even though the words were not true. "The animal buried the body."

Flatface looked horrified, and she looked content with her horror.

"When a person dies," said I, "you and I can move. You and I can stay away from the body. The animal must not be able to move the rock. She must not understand about true bodies. Perhaps it is her way."

"It is the wrong way."

"Yes. But it is the animal's way. Now there is a second animal. Are more animals going to come? How will you or I or anyone else deal with them? Some person must have seen one animal or another. If one woman saw such an animal, she would have placed such wisdom in the Many Huts. That is why I must go."

"It is not safe to go to the Many Huts alone. Should I go with you?"

"I am sure Lightfoot Watcher and her daughter will accompany me."

Flatface said nothing for a moment. She took a rock, smashed it against the shell of a fruitnut. First she ate the fruit; then she broke the second shell and ate the tiny nut within. In

front of I rested a fruitnut, and she did the same. Then Flatface
said, "Your mother and I shared a mother. What do you share
with this woman who watches lightfoot?"

"She is full of respect and full of help."

"Her belly carries two."

I said nothing.

"You know that I gave birth to a child who gave up breath
when he was knee-high, and I gave birth to a child who gave up
breath when she still suckled from my teat, and you know that
I left them where they had died so their true bodies could return
to the night sky.

"I want you to know today that I have buried one newborn
and another. One was born too early and was unable to breathe.
She was as red as clay and as soft, and she was small enough to
fit in my two hands. Even though I shouldn't have, I held her to
my breast and I cried and wailed because this would have been
my first child. The second one was born with one leg. A man
cannot live with one leg. I buried him before he could breathe in
a true body. I wanted to hold him, too, almost as badly as I
wanted to hold the first."

Flatface had averted her eyes just enough so that I could
watch the emotions play across her face and know they were
true. But now she faced I. "Your watcher of lightfoot should
know this. We sometimes have to bury children."

I had no response, because she knew Flatface was right. She
looked off in the woods and said, "I would prefer your company,
but there is no one else by this part of the river who could heal
anyone who needed help."

"Then go to the Many Huts. But before you go, tell the
woman with the animal's teats to go."

It took a moment for I to realize that Flatface was referring
to Huggable, who, like the animal, had teats and no infant. "You
want her gone because she killed the almost-a-man," said I.

"Nightskin, the one you call Far Hunter, has spoken to my
daughter, and to Wisdom, and to Wisdom's eldest daughter, and
to Squawker. Each woman wants Animal Teats to leave.
Nightskin says she caused terrible trouble when she had lived by
the river's mouth. There will be more trouble if she stays."

"Has Nightskin left for the river's mouth?"

"No," said Flatface. "She says she will live near this part of
the river."

"There is no mother of her mother who has lived here."

"The same is true of Squawker."

"There was plenty to eat when Squawker's mother came to live near the river. There is less now after the animal arrived."

"My daughter has eaten well. Nightskin is a fine hunter."

"Nightskin does say she is a fine hunter."

Flatface looked ashamed. "Yes. She boasts like a man."

"And you accept her as someone who will live near this part of the river?"

"Since the animal has arrived, there has been trouble. I am frightened. She is a woman with strength."

"She is like a man with arrows."

"And you, Long Fingers, are you a pregnant woman who watches and waits for things to happen? The animal is still here, and nothing has gotten better."

Huggable sat with her back to the cooking fire. Laid out in front of her were a series of long, fairly straight sticks. One such stick was in her hand, and she was shaving off thin strips of wood with a hard gray adze that someone must have given her elsewhere, because no man who lived near the river worked well with stone. She was making arrows. Her quiver, which hung just outside the opening of her shelter, was full of arrows. Huggable's daughter sat away from her mother. She was removing bones from a fish whose body had been slit open. She was getting dirt all over her fingers and in turn all over the fish.

I wanted to stand at a respectable distance from hut and hearth, but that was impossible given the way it was tightly surrounded by brush and trees. "I am here," she said softly, so as not to startle, as well as to give the illusion of polite distance.

Huggable's daughter smiled, thought better of it, and averted her gaze. Huggable rose and turned. Her teats had shrunken. There was the rustling of leaves, the purposeful snapping of green limbs. Hugger emerged from brush on the other side of the camp. He stared at I with wide, hard eyes; he thrust out his shoulders, and he stood there, trying to look menacing.

"Go away, Healer," said Huggable.

Her daughter looked to I, then to her mother, clearly upset by the words.

I told Huggable that she would be leaving for the Many Huts and would be gone for a number of days. "Maybe you should leave here, too."

Huggable averted her eyes. First I thought this was a gesture of respect; then she saw that Huggable was looking to Hugger,

who took a step forward. I found herself wishing she felt threatened by Hugger, but she'd known him since he was a boy.

I said, "Maybe Hugger should leave with you."

"He won't leave."

"Then mate with others." There was the poorly built hut,
and there was the kaross lying by her hut that still had patches
of lightfoot fur on it. "You will get better things if you mate with
more."

"No."

"He's protecting you," said I, keeping her voice steady
while all she felt was increasing anger. "You fucked only with
Hugger so you could ask for his protection."

Huggable turned and walked away from both I and Hugger.
She stood, her fingers plucking at leaves, tearing them apart.
Hugger, without effect or power, leaned from one foot to the
other. He still was not a man. Solitude was something he played
at like a girl plays at hunting. Huggable continued to tear at
leaves because there truly was no way for her to respond to the
strength of I's words—to fuck, to manipulate, to promise exclu-
sive mating and a child in exchange for a difficult favor—even
people from the river's mouth must find that disgusting. But,
then, Huggable was not from the river's mouth. And there sat her
daughter, the dirtied fish laid out before her. Would she grow up
to act this way?

"When Nightskin saw you," said I, "she threatened you
with arrows. What would make a woman so angry?"

"I did nothing wrong."

"You killed her mate. That is a good enough reason for
leaving. If she kills you, she will have to go far away to live. She
will have more solitude than a woman with a child can face."

"She won't leave," said Huggable. She tore a whole handful
of leaves off a sourberry bush. "She's strong like a man. No one
can make her leave. You wouldn't understand."

"You are not safe here, then. Why stay?"

"Because I know she will follow me."

"If you leave, she will return to the river's mouth."

"Did someone tell you that? Because she told me she plans
to stay by this part of the river. She knows no one by the river's
mouth will want her back, not even the women with whom she
shared a mother."

"How do you know this?"

"I know. One woman then another told me."

"Why would they say such a thing to one who shares no mother?"

"Each did because she had to. There is no reason for me to tell you. Now go away. This is my hut. This is my hearth. You are not welcome. I have no food to share with you."

"Leave. That's all I say. Leave, so that your daughter will have a mother." I did not remain. She was ashamed of her words and the effect they would have on the girl. She heard the daughter's sharp cry, she heard the girl's quick footsteps. She turned, thinking the girl might be running to her, but she saw through the brush that the daughter was in her mother's embrace, her thin arms tight around Huggable's neck.

The forest was darkening, and I sought out Nightskin. But Flatface's daughter and Talk Too Much said they did not know where she had built hut and hearth. Talk Too Much, whom I called Wisdom to her face, went on about how Nightskin was awaiting child and how no man would build a hut for a woman who would not mate again for a long time, even if the woman was a good hunter and could provide meat. Talk Too Much also told I she would build a waiting fire where I could sleep now that it was almost dark, but I wanted to sleep in her own hut. If she did not know the paths so well from years of walking them, she might have lost her way. There was the sound of movement in the distance, and she imagined a four-legged nightskin seeking her out. She ran quickly, her leather carry bag slapping her side, until she made it back to her camp.

Lightfoot Watcher and her daughter were sitting by the waiting fire. Next to the cooking fire there was a whole sparklefish, and an array of springleaves and wetroots. I looked over to Lightfoot Watcher, who after a few words of greetings, respectfully ignored her. Her belly was tremendous. The teats were almost large enough to nurse. I malspoke her own laziness as she ate the food Lightfoot Watcher had provided. She thought of the twins and what Lightfoot Watcher had asked of her, and she found it hard to sleep that night. Every sound from the forest seemed alive with threat. If she died, who would know how to use the gzaet, who would heal those who were hurt? The fear ate at her as if it had gone days without eating.

The Tenth Day

In the morning I wrapped her kaross about her body, tying it off at the waist, and she filled it with nuts and tubers. She placed some herbs and poultices in her carry bag, and she hung around her neck several strings of memory beads, one of which had to do with the delivery of children when the mother was infirm. She wrapped her gzaet in a blanket, set it in her hut, and placed several memory beads over it, the shape of the design meant to discourage intruders.

She said farewell to Lightfoot Watcher, who in turn said that a woman should not walk alone through places where another woman might gather. I said she had disturbed Lightfoot Watcher's solitude far too often, and the other woman insisted that on long travels a woman prefers company to solitude.

Soon Lightfoot Watcher and her daughter had made their preparations, the three fires were doused, leaving coals the color of ash and the color of night, and the three set out on the journey, I leading the way, Lightfoot Watcher following from a respectful distance, and her daughter beside her. As they walked, the daughter began to enjoy her solitude, walking farther away, sometimes running ahead, other times taking a thin animal trail that ran near the main trail. She found and killed a many-legs. She pointed out the tracks of a nightskin that had walked here a night or two ago. She was bitten by a hatebug and cried for the longest time.

They came to the crest of a hill, and the shape of the land beyond was only vaguely familiar. The path now moved downhill, as did the tiny trails left by rivulets of water that had run along this path. Rain that fell on this side of the hill flowed down to a different stream from the one that drank in the rain that fell on the hill's other side. I had traveled here only when called to heal someone who was sick or injured.

I placed cupped hands around her mouth and called out, "May we walk!" She called it out several times. There was no response.

I started down the path. She turned her head to see Lightfoot Watcher following, her daughter not far behind. She was impressed by the way the daughter had given up play for the path. To have such a daughter.

Late in the afternoon they met up with a woman. She sat in a clearing where many trees had been felled. She leaned against a rock, enjoying the last touch of sunlight while an infant nursed from her teat. A naked boy ran around the rock and yelled at his mother, who occasionally watched him run.

The woman recognized the healer, who had come this way last winter when the bones in her mother's body had hurt so badly that she could not walk. The healer's music had given the mother some peace, but since she could not have music every waking moment, she went out one night to fall asleep in the snow. The healer, because she had not truly healed, refused any gift beyond the food necessary to return home.

"Where are you going?"

"To the Many Huts," said I.

"Whatever grows in the woods is yours to eat, whatever runs on four hooves is yours to eat, whatever swims through the water is yours to eat, and whatever wood lies free is yours to burn."

I offered the same for where she lived. "Whatever solitude you may still have with children is yours again," said I, ready to leave.

"Healer," said the woman, rising as one did when things were serious. "I have heard talk of a strange animal who wears strange skins. I have heard of a woman with a daughter and a son who was followed by this animal and who gave it meat and fruit so it would not kill them."

I said she would be careful, and the three left. Lightfoot Watcher thought it odd that the woman had not heard of the rock that had fallen from the sky or of the animal inside it.

"A woman from this part of the world keeps to herself. Each knows the paths and the flowers and the animals and where I live, but not much else seems of interest."

"Is there a third animal?"

"I don't know."

Before nightfall they settled in a clearing, built a fire, and ate the rest of the food they had brought with them. They had seen no one else. Lightfoot Watcher's daughter asked what the Many Huts would be like, and Lightfoot Watcher said she did not know. "My mother never did her wisdom. What worth, she said to me, is wisdom if you have to travel many days to find it and many days more to return with it?"

The daughter looked to I. "Have you seen it?"

"Yes. And once we find a lightfoot to take with us, you will see it, too. Your eyes should see it before your ears hear words about it."

The Eleventh Day

Neither I nor Lightfoot Watcher knew the area, so neither knew where lightfoot were most likely to graze. Now each woman moved as quietly as leaves caught by the breeze, but the daughter had never liked to play the quiet hunter, so she was prone to step on fallen branches or shout in excitement when she came face-to-face with a bushytail searching the ground for nuts. They followed the contour of the land until they reached a stream, and walked along the stream until they came to a clearing full of grasses. They must have been too loud, because the clearing was empty. But there were plenty of tracks. Lightfoot Watcher's daughter now took each step with greater care, and there was more quiet than before. The animal talk and bird talk became louder. It did not take long to find fresh spore, track the lightfoot, shoot several arrows into him, and track down his weakening body.

By sunset the body was butchered and the meat was being smoked above the fire. Over the course of the afternoon, several women came by, and each in turn was offered a portion of food. Except for one woman who kept hinting she wanted more, each returned half the portion she had been offered after she heard that the healer was going to the Many Huts.

That night, after Lightfoot Watcher's daughter had curled up to sleep, Lightfoot Watcher complained to I that everything hurt. I sang several healing songs, which did little good.

"These aches will stay until I give birth." Lightfoot Watcher sighed, then patted her enormous belly. "I wonder if the first one is too scared to come out."

A silence hung around the fire. The words angered I. She knew what Lightfoot Watcher was saying with such innocent words: the first one was scared of coming out and never breathing. I wanted to say that it had not breathed, it had no true body, so it could not truly be scared, that only Lightfoot Watcher was scared. But she had felt both infants kick while she had sung, and she didn't believe. And because she could not direct her anger at Lightfoot Watcher, she explained to Lightfoot Watcher her anger at Huggable, who had teats and no infant, who had killed a man, and who did not leave even though Nightskin had threatened her death.

"She should leave," said Lightfoot Watcher. "I think Nightskin would track her down."

"What kind of woman would do that?"

"Nightskin is a woman but she is not a woman."

"You mean she is ugly?"

"No. I am scared of her because she is like a man."

"She is large. She has almost-pouches under her throat. But

she is a woman. Arm Scars said Nightskin mated with the almost-a-man she called Clever Fingers. You heard her share the same words. Arm Scars said there was an infant growing within."

"Arm Scars spoke to me before she left. She told me that Nightskin was a man as well as a woman. When Nightskin was born, her mother did not have the heart to bury her."

"Did Arm Scars wish her mother had buried Nightskin?"

"She did not say. But Arm Scars was happy that Nightskin was not returning to the river's mouth."

"Why didn't you tell me?"

"It sounded like an anger story. While you were gone, she told several anger stories, and I stopped believing what she said. But this huggable woman is frightened. Say again what Huggable said to you, and you will hear Arm Scars' story even though Huggable never told it."

That night Lightfoot Watcher told her daughter a story:

There was a woman who lived near a small lake. On the other side of the lake lived another woman with her daughter. Every day the first woman could see the other one. The first one did not like this lack of solitude. She did not like the way the other one drank from the same water she did.

When her desire came, she mated with one man and another as a woman should. One night, when she felt her body open to take in the man's pollen, she became sick with hatred of the other woman. She asked her mate if he would promise something. The mate was sweaty with desire. He said he would promise anything. She asked him to destroy the other woman's hut.

A promise made while one is willfully mating close to another is not a promise to break.

The next day the man destroyed the hut, and that night and the next night and the next he mated with the first woman.

The first woman gave birth to a daughter, and the daughter suckled the first woman's teat, and the daughter grew, and seasons passed. When the daughter was as tall as the mother, she felt desire, and she mated one man after another. When she knew she was old enough to have a child, she left her mother and found another small lake to live by.

On the other side of the lake lived a woman and her son. The daughter did not like to see the woman and her son every day. She did not like that each drank from the same water as she. She felt a terrible rage.

When the daughter felt her desire, she mated with one man then with another. When her desire was strong and a man's belly pressed hard against her back, she asked him to make a promise, and he said he would. She asked him to kill the other woman.

The next morning the daughter awoke and was horrified by what she had asked. A man had no arrows, no spear. He had only a knife, and he would have to get mating close to kill. What she had asked was truly terrible.

The daughter ran to the other side of the lake to warn the woman. The woman despised her words. The daughter had asked for something horrible, and she had betrayed the man she had asked. The woman went to find another woman to help her slay the man.

When the man arrived in the clearing, he saw the daughter. Behind the daughter was the woman and another woman. The daughter told the man to go away. She did not want him to do something evil. The man wanted to turn, but each woman there knew he had made a promise. If he turned away, no woman would mate with him again.

He held his knife firm and ran at the woman he had promised to kill. The woman and the other each fired an arrow. The man was killed.

Each woman who lived near any of the small lakes was told that the daughter had killed the man. No woman shared words or food with her, not even her mother. The daughter lived long enough to give birth to a son, but during the winter she could not find enough food to feed them both. Each soon died.

"Why do you feel bad?" the daughter asked Lightfoot Watcher. "Why do you tell me such a story?"

I did not listen to Lightfoot Watcher's response. She was thinking of Huggable and her daughter. And then she was thinking about the daughter she did not have, how there was no one to watch her play the gzaet the way she had watched her mother.

When I was still small, she had watched her mother play, and she had tried so hard to memorize the order her mother had pressed down the keys. When her mother was off gathering, when she was too far away to hear, I had tried to play some of the musics. Once her mother snuck up on her as quietly as a nightskin, and she struck I for playing the gzaet. She struck her across the back, across the head, across the arms. She yelled foul, angry words. And while I sat there, crying, her body sore from all the hitting, her mother said softly, "You have to wait. You have to watch and learn. When you first touch the gzaet, you have to touch but not play. There is wisdom when you don't press down on the keys." So I listened and watched and touched the keys when her mother was gone and played the gzaet when she was sure her mother was too far away. When I was almost as tall as her mother, her mother placed the gzaet in front of I and said, "Play just the top keys. Play me a song for the ears."

The Twelfth Day

It was a hazy morning, and it seemed the sun would never burn away the smokiness. The Many Huts was no longer something you stepped into, the way you stepped into a clearing; the mist had made it a part of the forest.

I and Lightfoot Watcher and her daughter walked the outside paths of the Many Huts. In four different spots a pole—each carved from a thick, straight sapling—had been driven into the ground. At the top of each pole rested a smooth, unmarked pot that was held in place by several wooden pegs. The lip of the pot was just above I's head, and she had to use both her hands to place a portion of meat inside each one. Sometime later any woman who came to the Many Huts and cleared it of debris would take a portion.

Before a woman could enter a hut and seek out its wisdom, she had to do the same work. Lightfoot Watcher's legs hurt, and she did not feel she could bend over. She sat against a tree at the edge of the Many Huts while her daughter removed fallen leaves and branches from the gutters and the paths. I made her way along the paths, uprooting seedlings that had sprouted, all the while glancing into the shadowed openings of each hut and wondering, Is it in this hut that I'll find wisdom about the animal?

The mist rose from the ground, stretched out, and disappeared, and the sun struck the huts from above, making it look as if a sun were inside each one, or as if each were inhabited by something almost alive, a true body, perhaps, who had refused to leave the earth because it feared the complete solitude that awaited it in the sky.

The trees of the forest became a distant wall that surrounded the area, the colors of the leaves just beginning to change. I looked around, and she was surprised that the Many Huts was so big. Now that she was grown, she had thought it would look smaller than it had when she was a girl and had come here with her mother.

Each hut was as well built as the one Roofer had made for her. Trails moved in and around the huts like a winding river, so that a woman could walk through one hut and another and never be seen by another woman in a nearby hut. I considered how many women had made their wisdom, how many huts had been built, and how each hut had been made so well that a woman could live in it. What would it be like if people lived this close together? Could a woman behave respectfully enough so each person would have her solitude, so someone wouldn't let her eyes go wide and stare at someone whose eyes were also wide. She couldn't imagine it; it would be as it had been on the hillside overlooking the rock: wide eyes, strong words, and death.

Lightfoot Watcher's daughter stopped her work and knelt down on the ground. "Look here," she said. "There are tracks like the ones the animal made."

They did look like the animal's tracks. There was the straight line in the middle, and the heel cutting more of an impression than the ball of the feet. The trail was covered with these tracks; this animal had left and returned to the Many Huts a number of times. Lightfoot Watcher's daughter had picked out a very fresh track, and I traced it with the tip of her finger. It made an impression like the animal's track, but the curve was somewhat different. It could be a different animal with a different kind of sandal, but the shape of this curve had a familiarity to it.

The fresh trail led directly to a hut several steps away from them. I rose and listened. The only sounds came from the forest. She called out, "I am here. Another is here. Her daughter is here. Who are you?"

There was no answer.

Lightfoot Watcher was walking down the path now, each step careful and quiet, as if she were tracking a lightfoot. The bow she should have left behind at the tree was held in an outstretched arm. The quiver of arrows hung over her shoulder. I wanted to wave to her in some way that would make Lightfoot Watcher put down the bow. Nightskin had made threats with her arrows. Huggable had aimed her arrows too readily. I didn't like the way an arrow had changed its meaning since the rock had fallen from the sky, but at the same time, she was fearful of someone who would sit quietly in a shelter and not answer a woman's call.

I stepped toward the hut. Both the daughter and Lightfoot

Watcher matched her step for step, the mother's free hand reaching back to take an arrow out of the quiver.

I entered the hut. She did not notice what kind of wisdom was sheltered by the roof and the walls. Sitting in the far corner was an almost-a-man. He had a man's rough skin, and his throat pouches were just beginning to hang down. His skin and his hair were darker than any she had seen on a man before. She could not tell his size because he sat with knees drawn up to his chest, his hands clasped in front. His entire body was covered in skins the color of muddy water. The skins were thin as leaves, just like the skins worn by the second animal. Beside him was a large bag of the same color. His cheeks and hands had been cut and scratched; lines of dried blood looked like poorly made scars. The almost-a-man did not avert his eyes, but he did thin them so that he did not give I a full stare. He moved his head just a bit, so his half-closed eyes could focus on what stood to I's side. It was Lightfoot Watcher, the arrow in her bow drawn.

"I am I. I live near the Winding River, and I heal people who ask me to. We have come to the Many Huts to learn some of its wisdom."

The almost-a-man, the stranger who wore skins like the second animal, said nothing.

"Where are you from?"

"Far away." He spoke the words carefully, as if I might not understand. There was a strange sound to them, but they were just words.

"How far?"

"Very far. I live in a place like this."

"You live in a Many Huts?"

"Yes."

Lightfoot Watcher leaned forward and said, "Go away."

I found herself frightened by the violence in Lightfoot Watcher's voice. I wanted to use different words, but she did not know what kind of words to offer this strange almost-a-man. What Lightfoot Watcher said did make sense, and no man would dare argue with a woman sided by another woman.

This one didn't argue. He waited. He sat and waited and he cast his eyes on her, then on Lightfoot Watcher. I didn't know what he was thinking, and this was unsettling. He stared and he waited. Lightfoot Watcher had already averted her eyes, which made it impossible for I to turn her head again. She greeted his stare, first feeling respect for the Stranger, then anxiety, then disgust. He stared as if this were his hut, his place to demand solitude, and this bothered her more than the two animals who had inhabited the rock.

I said, "Go away."

The Stranger at last showed a sliver of respect. He bowed his head and looked down at his knees. Looking up at them, he had seemed defiant; now, curled up, he looked defenseless. "I would go away." There was a pause. A proper pause. His hands, I noticed, were like an infant's hands. The fingers were so perfectly shaped. There was no sign that this man had ever built a nest, shaped wood, or fought over where he could walk. His hands made him appear harmless. Lightfoot Watcher lowered the bow.

"I would go away," said the Stranger, "but I am looking for something."

Something? A man might look for food, or for a mate, or for the materials to build something, but what specific thing would a man look for that would take him to a place so far away from where he lived that no one here had seen such skins?

"There is a creature here. It walks on two legs, like a person. It shapes things with two hands like a person. It has a head shaped like a person's head, with thin eyes, a large nose, and a mouth. But it looks and acts nothing like a person."

"Yes," said Lightfoot Watcher.

I faced Lightfoot Watcher.

"You have seen it?" asked the almost-a-man.

Lightfoot Watcher hesitated under I's gaze. I didn't know why she wanted Lightfoot Watcher to lie. "Yes," Lightfoot Watcher said. "The animal has two teats like a woman who's given birth, but she has no infant to nurse. Its skin is as dark as the darkest earth. It lived in a boulder for a number of days, and then it left."

"Do you know where it went?"

"The healer tracked it, but its trail disappeared."

"Was there only one animal?"

"Yes." Lightfoot Watcher's voice sounded different. The lie was audible.

The stranger widened his eyes and looked to I. "Was there only one such animal?"

"Yes," said I.

That should have been the end of it. The animal was seen, and the animal was gone. There was no reason for the Stranger to talk further or to know anything about the Winding River, where I and Flatface and Talk Too Much lived. But the Stranger had more to say, and he did not avert his eyes while speaking. "I come from far away. Where I live there are many like the animal with teats. These animals flock together like birds in the sky. They cannot stand to be alone. They eat food like our food. They use land the same way we use land. But they breed constantly. They breed so often that their women always need teats."

Lightfoot Watcher listened with such dismay that I began to doubt what the stranger was saying. The words sounded like one of Talk Too Much's swamp stories, where the evil thing in the swamp that ate children was always described as having several terrible habits along with its taste for children.

The Stranger continued. "I want to find this animal and take her away. She should be returned to where she lives. Tell me about the boulder that she lived in."

"I was told it fell from the sky," said Lightfoot Watcher.

"Tell me where it is," said the Stranger, and he was smart enough to give eye to Lightfoot Watcher.

I, too, looked to Lightfoot Watcher, who said nothing, who did not live by the river, who had no reason to keep another male far away, who owed no favors to the healer for whom she had done much without exacting any promise in return.

"Tell me the reason you won't tell me."

Lightfoot Watcher said, "Where the boulder is there is one man and another and another."

"I am not seeking a mate. I want to find the animal and take her to where she lives."

"The boulder," Lightfoot Watcher said, "is by the lake. I can show you the trail."

"I have seen that boulder. It rests on the beach. It trails gray and blue fabric in the water. There is one deeper in the woods. I need your help to find it."

I didn't believe these words about a boulder trailing fabric. She was surprised by how readily the Stranger had met Lightfoot Watcher's lie with one of his own. Having no argument to make, she instead leaned forward. "Go away," she said. "Go away from here. If you must find the animal, find her on your own. There is no woman who gathers or hunts near the boulder who welcomes you. You now sit in a house full of wisdom. This is not a place to sleep or to eat. No one welcomes you here. No one has food to share with you. Go away."

I backed out of the hut and stood away from the opening. Lightfoot Watcher stayed where she was. Her daughter looked to one woman then the other before going to stand beside her mother. The Stranger watched this, waited a moment, then stood. The large bundle the color of muddy water had straps, and he slid his arms through them until the bundle was secure on his back. Without a word, gesture, or look, he left the Many Huts and disappeared into the woods. What would he really do if he found the animal?

Lightfoot Watcher and her daughter did not want to remain in the Many Huts, and they left for the clearing where they had spent the previous night. I remained alone, and she almost followed the mother and her daughter. She did not want to meet the Stranger again, and she was sure he would return. He did not have the hands of one who could live in the woods.

The Many Huts' emptiness was no longer peaceful; there was something very empty about this kind of solitude. There was hut after hut after hut, and it looked as if the Many Huts had been built without meaning, as a way of filling up time when one was tired of staring at something, tired of finding food, and tired of people.

She returned to the edge of the clearing where the pole rose from the ground. Near that was the first hut, and she entered it. There was a circular hole in the roofing that allowed light to enter. In the center of the floor was an earthen bowl still damp with rain water. From the large bowl, radiating outward, were small gutters to carry the rain out of the hut. There was a *tarabayza*, the word her mother had used, a word that I recalled with some ease: four wooden legs rising as high as a woman's legs, and across that a surface as flat as a cleared camp: a series of tree trunks split in half, smoothed over, laid down flat side up. Atop the tarabayza were the tools, each one made of the same material as her gzaet. Beside them were several stones for sharpening the blades of several tools. The tools themselves were old, so old that they were dented and stained with splotches, and not one had the same color as the boulder in the clearing. Her mother had said there had been more tools when she was a child, and that the tools had looked better. The tools were as old as the gzaet, as old as the knife she carried and used only for healing.

The next few huts had more tools. I went on to other huts to look for different kinds of wisdom. She saw male wisdom provided for a woman, perhaps so she could wisely choose whose gifts to accept. She saw clay laid out in such a way so she could learn how to make a pot for cooking. She saw different kinds of knots, more than she had known existed. She saw dif-

ferent styles of thatching. And she saw female wisdom. She saw
drawings upon rocks of animals and ways to butcher them. She
saw drawings of ways to hold a child as she emerged from your
womb.

There was no drawing or depiction of the animal or the
boulders it might live in. There was no depiction of any kind of
animal that was shaped like a person and flocked like birds. She
started glancing into huts, skipping huts as the day progressed
and the light dimmed. She headed finally to the older huts, the
ones toward the center clearing. The thatching had gone gray
with time, and a musty smell filled the clearing. In one hut there
were drawings with more lines and colors than she had ever
seen, but the colors were as soft as sand, and she could not make
out what was drawn. The drawings were not made on rock or
wood, and the fabric she touched crumbled a bit. In the end she
found nothing of use. A slazan woman who had seen such an animal before had never come to the Many Huts to share that wisdom.

Then she looked through the huts a second time, casting
quick glances inside each one to look for a second kind of wisdom. And she found nothing. She saw no sign of slazans who
wore skins as thin as leaves, the color of muddy water, who wore
sandals that left tracks like the tracks of the animal with teats.

She finally left for the clearing where Lightfoot Watcher
and her daughter awaited her. Lightfoot Watcher worried that the
Stranger might find them so close to the Many Huts. The daughter echoed her mother's fear. They followed the paths south until
the forest light dimmed, then found a clearing where they could
build a fire.

Now that she felt safe, Lightfoot Watcher asked questions to
the point of rudeness, and I found she had no interest in answering. She wanted to sit in quiet solitude on the other side of the
fire and concentrate on her thoughts, which rushed over her mind
like low water over rocks—there was no wisdom about the animal, no wisdom about the Stranger, each had worn the same kind
of skins, the Stranger had said he knew where the animal lived,
the Stranger was a man who came not in search of a place to
gather food or a woman who would accept his gifts and then
mate with him, but instead came in search of the animal—but
each time she could almost make sense of these thoughts and
hear a clear voice in the soft rushing waters, Lightfoot Watcher
asked another of her questions, and all sound was lost.

Lightfoot Watcher's daughter asked the question that made all thought impossible. "Do you think the strange man will follow us back to the boulder?"

The Thirteenth Day

At dawn Lightfoot Watcher said she could not gather that morning: her belly weighed too heavily. I left to gather alone knowing that when she returned, Lightfoot Watcher would have walked off with her daughter and her digging stick and found some quiet place in the woods to deliver her child. No one was in the clearing when she returned, and all she could hear were the sounds of the forest. She divided the food she had brought back, and she mashed up some smoked meat. Lightfoot Watcher knew she shouldn't have asked I to take one of the twins. Another woman could not do for her what only a mother should do. You had to take care in the way you nourished your life. If you take all a bird's eggs, there will be no eggs when you are older. If you shoot all the lightfoot in a clearing, there will be no lightfoot to hunt when you're hungry. If you take all the berries, there will be no berries to attract the lightfoot. Afterward you will always be hungry for the rightness of things.

If she had not been so weighed down by these thoughts, I would have heard Lightfoot Watcher's daughter much sooner, the quick trampling of a child running through the woods. "Healer!" she called out. "Healer!"

I stood up, expecting to hear about the child who was born.

"The baby's coming. It's out of the womb and coming, but the water hasn't broken."

Lightfoot Watcher's daughter ran off, and I followed. Lightfoot Watcher's daughter knew exactly where to run, and soon they came upon her mother.

She was crouched down, her back pressed against a smooth-bark tree, her knees bent outward, her feet firmly planted. Her pubic apron was off, and she had tied the kaross so nothing hung below her waist. Before her she had dug two holes, one for each placenta. When I knelt before Lightfoot Watcher, she saw that one hole had been dug deeper than the other. The ground was dry.

"The water hasn't broken," said Lightfoot Watcher.

"I can break it."

Lightfoot Watcher said nothing. She groaned instead. The

head was making its way out. There was a shimmering color covering it.

"May I touch you?" said I.

Lightfoot Watcher opened her eyes wide: yes.

I wished she were back at her hut and hearth, back where she kept everything. She had the ideal tool for this: long, thinner than any stick, pointed, and made of the same thing as the gzaet. Here all she had was her medicine knife. She withdrew it from her sheath. "Be as still as a rock." The head was pressing against the water skin and emerging from Lightfoot Watcher at the same moment. Lightfoot Watcher's thighs were taut, her head was back, eyes closed. Now it was like playing music; you knew what to do, you moved with ease and with speed. I pinched at the water skin, pulled it toward her, and sliced through with the knife. The waters flowed out. The infant came out with equal ease, virtually landing in I's hands.

Lightfoot Watcher looked to the healer, eyes open. "Is it a girl?"

"It's a boy."

"I will bury it."

The second child was also a boy. I stood aside while Lightfoot Watcher accepted it into her hands. It sucked in air and life. It cried and continued to breathe. It accepted its true body, and the true body remained.

The child suckled from his mother's teats after they returned to the clearing, and the daughter ran about the nearby trees with an excitement she couldn't contain. She sang one of the healer's healing songs like it was a game song.

I barely noticed this. Each thing she owned was where she had left it, but everything looked different. She scanned the ground for the three-clawed spoor of a foodgrabber, but she couldn't find one. Instead she found tracks belonging to the Stranger.

Lightfoot Watcher said, "Have you mislaid something?"

I looked up. Lightfoot Watcher's hand caressed the infant's head. She did not need a new worry. "No," said I. "There are longfoot tracks."

"We have enough meat."

"Yes." She looked at the spoor. The tracks went in the direction of the Many Huts. Why had the Stranger come here? "We have enough."

She looked through her bag and her kaross, and she found nothing different. But she was sure that the Stranger had gone through her things.

They remained there for the day. Lightfoot Watcher's daughter left with I at midday to gather for the journey back to Winding River. In the camp the infant slept or nursed, and Lightfoot Watcher had eyes for nothing else. She said nothing to her daughter, and while nursing she acted as if her daughter did not exist. That afternoon she sat on one side of the fire and told I that if the child still breathed when she returned to the Small Lake that she would give it a private name.

"What name?" her daughter asked.

"It's a name for me and my son."

Lightfoot Watcher's daughter looked away from her mother and over to the healer. I wanted to take the daughter into her arms, but the daughter needed to learn her solitude. I averted her eyes.

I left the clearing to be away from Lightfoot Watcher. She wore her carry bag, and her healing knife was in its sheath by her hip. She did not go where she first had planned. She instead followed the trail toward the Many Huts and found the Stranger's spoor as he approached their encampment and as he left. The daughter's question kept sounding again in her head; I did not want the stranger to follow them to Winding River. The afternoon light had started to walk up the trees and toward the sky. I headed toward another part of the woods.

The darkness was almost complete when she returned to the clearing. The daughter was curled up by the fire, a skin covering her body. Lightfoot Watcher stared into the fire, the infant in her lap.

"I am here," said I before she sat on the other side of the fire, "and I am cold."

"The fire," said Lightfoot Watcher, "is here to be shared."

I had no words to share. She listened to the nighttime voices and to the way the fire burned.

Lightfoot Watcher said, "Several days ago the woman you call Arm Scars told me another anger story when you had left hut and hearth."

I said nothing.

"One woman and another told her that the healer who lived by Winding River would go where a dead body lay and cut up the body to see its insides and the way they were put together. One and another woman said the healer is sure to have breathed in one true body and another and is sure to be crazed and unreliable."

The story, in part, was true. When I first had learned the gzaet's music, she would also try to learn the music and shape of a person's body. Every now and then someone she tried to heal was too sick, too hurt, too old to be healed. That night, if the person was someone she did not know, if one of the moons was bright, if the trails were absent of nightskin spoor, she would go to the dead body and learn its shape with her knife. She tied fabric around her head to cover her mouth, so she would inhale only air. It was not something she did often, and each time she did it full of fear as the forest darkness, so much darker against the moons' brightness, closed in around her. She said to Lightfoot Watcher, "No healer I know has done such a thing."

Lightfoot Watcher looked away from the fire and out into the woods. "I can understand why a healer would say what you have said. I can understand why a healer would be wise to apply her knife before scavengers applied their teeth. I can understand how the music might not touch what the fingers have not touched." She lifted the infant to her teats. He squirmed for a moment, yawned, then relaxed. "All I ask is if the one I buried has felt the blade of a healer's knife."

"No," said I, her voice harsh, because anger was the best smoke to fill the air and hide where you had burned truth into ashes.

"A woman gives birth alone. It is not often one woman knows where another has buried a child who has not breathed."

"The child," said I, "is buried and will remain buried."

Lightfoot Watcher nodded, but I did not know what the gesture meant.

That night, before she slept, I lay back and remembered the feel of the slick surfaces of tiny muscles and the way they slid along fragile bones, and she heard patterns of music in her head, songs she had played for infants who had breathed in a true body but who soon after faced death as quickly as birth: a fever burned the infant's eyes empty, skin swelled with an insect bite, an older child pushed or twisted too hard, or a pointed-ear had taken a good bite before the mother scared the animal off. Now, as she saw muscles that moved kicking legs or arms that barely reached or fingers that gripped, she heard the music differently, some of the patterns changed, and she played them over and over in her head, until she was sure she would remember them, so she could play them one day if such musics were needed again.

The Fourteenth Day

The next day's journey was a difficult one for I. She had dreamed so often of having a daughter who would gather with her, who would sit by her side and watch her play the gzaet, who would one day become healer and let I properly enjoy a woman's solitude; she had imagined this so carefully that she had forgotten how different each mother was. Of course Lightfoot Watcher would hug the infant to her, of course she would suckle him every time he cried, of course she would have much less energy for a daughter who should be learning her solitude. But her very proper and respectful daughter did not want to be forgotten like the remains of unripe fruit that's been tossed aside after several mouthfuls, hunger making bitterness acceptable to the tongue. So the daughter stayed off the path and ran through the woods, dodging around trees, shouting out anytime she saw a patch of itchleaf or saw a crawling hardbite, anything that might have once attracted her mother's concern. Lightfoot Watcher, whom I now thought of as Son Watcher, looked up the first time to say, "If you recognize it, you are big enough to stay away from it." Then she would say nothing, but she did look up each time that her daughter called out. This didn't seem to be enough, because the girl ran farther and farther from the path and called out louder and more often. The baby cried once, and Son Watcher raised him to her teat.

I worried that the Stranger might follow them, as he had followed them to their camp, so after a while she led Son Watcher and her daughter around in circles, along different paths. When they came to a shallow creek, she had them walk through the water for a good while before returning to a path. Son Watcher complained sullenly, fearful that she might slip on the creek's muddy bottom, angry that I would worry about the Stranger now that they were so far away.

The sun had left the tops of the trees and was heading for the center of the sky when they came to a clearing where Son Watcher wanted to stop and rest. Her daughter waited for the infant to start nursing before she asked her mother for food. I said she was going to gather a bit, even though they had more than enough. She walked quickly up the path, then circled away from it, using a few dark sharpleaf trees as landmarks to find the path again. She paused to listen carefully and heard nothing. She checked the trail, crouching low, tracing every person's track with a finger. There was no sign of the Stranger.

Later they came to the land where Talk Too Much's eldest daughter gathered, and they saw signs that it had rained recently. I remembered that as a girl she had tried to convince her mother to walk to the edge of a rainstorm so she could stand where it was dry and watch it rain. Having many times sat in dryness and heard the approach of rain, always a few drops first, then many, she now knew there was no place you could stay dry while you reached out to touch the rain.

She wanted to tell this to Lightfoot Watcher's daughter, but the girl never once came close to the healer, and when she was too tired to walk, she walked slowly, almost dragging her feet as if they were too heavy to lift. I wanted to tell her that this would change. The son would grow up and think more with his penis than with his eyes. He would try to mate with a woman who shouldn't open herself to him, and he would have to wander off to find some other place to gather food and seek a mate.

The ground of I's camp was dry except for several places where the shade of the trees remained all day. Before doing anything else, she stepped into her hut. The memory beads hung where she had left them. The blanket still wrapped the gzaet, and the two strands of beads crossed it in the same circular pattern. There was the spoor of at least two foodgrabbers.

Son Watcher had not set her bow or quiver on the ground. She stood at the waiting fire, looking more like someone who had come to see the healer than someone who had shared the healer's food.

"There is still food here," said I.

"It is early in the afternoon. My daughter, my son, and I will continue our journey to the Small Lake."

"You should rest."

"I am not the first woman to travel after giving birth."

I said nothing. What could she say?

"Perhaps," said Lightfoot Watcher, "you would accompany us."

"My healing is here. I have been away too long."

"Do you want to stay? You know the Stranger will come looking for the animal."

"He does not know the way. He did not follow us."

"He found the Many Huts. He can find the boulder."

I said nothing.

"Huggable is still here; as well as Nightskin."

"That may have changed."

"Let everything happen that will happen and then return. There is more solitude where I live and so there is more food. You can take all a bird's eggs and know there is another bird who still has plenty. It will be safe. And there is no healer who lives by the lake. Each woman would treat you as if once you had shared a mother with their mothers."

I wanted to say yes. She even looked to her hut and thought of what she could carry and what Son Watcher's daughter could carry. There was too much to carry for such a long journey. I averted her head no.

Son Watcher told her about each man who lived by the Small Lake, what each made well with his hands, what kind of child each helped make if you mated with him at the right time.

"I cannot accompany you," said I.

Son Watcher stood in silence for a respectful moment. "You have shared food with me and my daughter. You have played music for my son, and you made it possible for him to leave my womb. Whatever food I have is yours whenever you want it."

I said nothing, although she could have said how Son Watcher had followed her to the boulder and had followed her to the Many Huts, and how she had offered to share her twins. In her mind's eye she still could see the patted earth under which the firstborn lay.

Son Watcher, her son placed carefully in a sling within her kaross, walked off, her daughter following. There were no more words. The solitude I felt should have been welcome, but all she felt was a kind of loss.

She rebuilt the fire in her hut and played the gzaet to ease her mind. After playing a few notes and a song, it became apparent to her ears that it had been too long since she had played. She thought of the rock and the second animal and almost stopped playing. But she did not. What good was the gzaet if she could not play it well? She played until she clearly felt the simple world around her, and now she wanted to play until she could lose herself within the music and forget even that. But there was her hunger, and there was the rock, and there was Huggable.

I returned the gzaet to its place in the hut, and she picked up her kaross. She lifted it, watched it spread out to the ground, and prepared to drape it over her body when she saw the small insect holding tight to the hide. It was the color of night and looked as hard as a stone. She had never seen such an insect before, and she wondered what such an insect would find on a kaross. She knocked it away with her fingernail. She did not bother to watch the insect tumble dead to the ground or see it spread its wings and take flight.

The following is taken from the notebook Pauline Dikobe kept during her 200 day study of the slazan foraging population on Tienah.

Day 55

A small probe bearing gifts, guided down by the *Way of God*'s AI, quietly landed alongside the shuttle. Inside the probe were three insects and one baby. The insects were imaging pins attached to tiny flying mechanisms designed to look like a local bug. Maryam had designed them with Jihad in order to monitor three local encampments. While Maryam had made the six-leggers, Tamr had made a baby for me. "It's our child," she says when I look at it the first time, her voice inside my skull. "Maryam is jealous."

The baby looks like a human infant, potbelly and pudgy cheeks, and its skin is as dark as mine, its texture cool and smooth. There is a place to open its belly to load liquid and solids for it to excrete later. It has a tiny little penis, Tamr's desire to give birth first to a boy. This boy gurgles when happy, cries when soiled or hungry, and shapes his lips into a comfortable O around my nipple.

Using images I have of Ju/wa equipment, I use the stored antelope hides to make a sling to tie around waist and over shoulders. I set mosses in the sling to soak up the baby's wetness, and set the sling itself into the chi !kan, and the baby into the sling.

I start to carry him around. I stop to nurse him

when he cries. The baby makes sounds like it's suckling, but there's no grip of tongue on nipple, there are no aching breasts, no chapped nipples, no tender looks, no addictive warmth. I speak to this plastic baby, my voice pitched higher, the rhythm and flow the beginning of all music, and I find myself speaking to my own son, long gone, who's reached the age of decision now, if he's still alive.

Day 60

Having the baby has done nothing but bring back memories. No local has come closer to take a second look.

The insects brought more luck. Each has landed, and we are now recording images from three encampments. No, *encampment* is not the correct term. The slazan word best translates as *hut and hearth*. Each hut and hearth has three fireplaces. One is at the edge of camp and is nothing more than a circle of charred black ground; they call it the waiting fire, though no fire burns at any of the sites. The second is the cooking fire, which is in the center of the encampment and is kept going throughout the day. The third is located in the hut and, like the waiting fire, is nothing more than blackened ground, perhaps a dark memory of winter's chill.

Each hut and hearth receives visits from women, so far one per day. The woman, with her child or children, stops at the waiting fire and waits to be noticed. We now have slazan individuals, faces to recognize. We ID the women. We ID the women who visit them. We ID the children. I give them all Ju/wasi names—unprofessional, of course, but I'll remember them.

One woman, a slender woman with flat cheekbones, has been ID'ed as !U. Today a woman visits, and !U calls this woman Clear Eyes. For people who avoid eye contact, the name Clear Eyes destroys all our rigid hypotheses.

I keep rewatching the moments when one woman visits another. Each woman speaks to the other as food is shared while one child shouts after the other as they play.

Everything that follows is language. We are rich in data. We are wealthy with language.

What I'd give to be able to sit by one of those cooking fires and share food with one woman and another while I listen to them share words.

Day 64

Midsummer night's musings:

Close a large metaphorical hand—the invisible fingers and palm may be an appendage of the slave trade or a real-estate transaction—around a group of individuals; rip them away from their land, their knowledge, their subsistence, their daily habits; and set them down—perhaps they will tumble out when you unroll the fingers, lie there dazed before facing this new life—in a land where they don't belong; set them there with others who have been uprooted by another hand belonging to the same economic creature, and make it so they have to talk much with each other and little with those who own their labor. They will speak a language of shared words, some from one language, some from another, all with shared meanings, but without language's built-in structures: no articles, no prepositions to join phrases together, no method to mark present or past or future. Their children don't speak this pidgin. Their infant brains are geared to take in words and to structure those words with syntax, to place phrases together in ways that relate specific time and meaning. The new language, the creole, has everything the pidgin lacked in order for it to be a language, just as their parents, in their native land, had the full range and complexity of words. The human mind is sculpted for language.

And the slazan mind? Is it more finely sculpted? A man from Cairo, Egypt, on Terra would understand every word I write, but when I speak, he would strain to understand me, our different dialects, our different accents filtering out the possibility of easy understanding. But these slazans pronounce words and order their meanings much the same way as the slazans who are separated from them by generations, by light-decades, and by huts and buildings.

Words cannot be preprogrammed. The word *wadi* in Arabic is *valle* in Spanish, but could as easily be *gato*.

What sounds we choose have history, but in the beginning there is something arbitrary, when words have nothing about them that suggests at all what they refer to. Nothing about the sound *duck* creates the image of an animal with webbed feet who quacks, flies, and lays eggs. For members of a solitary species to preserve their language against drift and change, they may have to learn its music well, there may be survival value in hearing and accurately reproducing pronunciation, word order, tone, and rhythm, so that there is not a variety of accents, a deepening of sounds, a play with new words.

But why language in the first place?

Animals react to and learn from what has happened to them. Some nonhuman primates can go one step further and devise something new—fashion a stick to dig out termites, for example—on the basis of what's in front of them. Language makes it possible to discuss what has not yet been experienced, to discuss things not present in the current environment. You can plan where to move, you can look at the sky and guess the weather, you can discuss tracks or where the best food will be to gather, you can gossip about each other's behavior to enforce the morals you live by, you can tell someone her husband has slept with someone else, you can side with one woman against another, and you can convince your daughter she should marry the person you have chosen for her.

But we are accustomed to thinking of language as the rootedness of our humanity, our sociability. Did language come to slazans and humans as some sort of spark of God, a well-intended mutation, or was there truly some selective advantage in speaking? Who benefited by being able to talk?

Chapter Eleven

The Thirteenth Day

Everything was dark at first. Everything was calm. He barely felt the hood over his head, the gloves over his hands. He heard a beating heart. He heard a voice. Other voices were distant. He had gone through this twice before, first when he'd learned Arabic, second when he'd learned Nostratic, and he knew he should remain calm, that this would work only if he did not question the experience. He still wanted to grip the top of the hood and tug it off his head. The illusion went on, because now his eyes were open. Everything was patterns now, and one close pattern made a kind of sense. He felt himself focus on the pattern. The pattern moved. Its eyes widened. And so did his. Its lips moved, and he heard a sound he recognized. He wanted to listen more. He remained perfectly still and listened. This caused the eyes to stay open and the voice to continue. Remain still, pay heed, and this voice stayed with you. He loved the feeling.

His eyes could follow things. They loved to follow the face that looked down to his while he drank from her warmth. He could hold a finger so tightly. He could touch the warmth from which he drank. He loved to listen, the way her voice went on, the words she spoke, her voice so different from when she spoke to anyone else. When she spoke to another, he lost interest.

When her voice heightened, when her voice flowed, he listened to its music.

The adult, who sat in an acceleration couch on an unnamed planet, who was learning pan-slazan, who before birth had been ready to relate one thing to another, heard this music, and overlapping it, he heard a mother whisper a lullaby in Nostratic, he heard an Arab mother talking singsong, and he thought he saw his own mother's face and heard her say something, hearing the melody in her voice and not the words, his vision fixed on her smile, the brilliance of her eyes.

He stopped for a moment, but the inside of the shuttle had the sheen of stale memories.

He heard the music of sounds, and in that music certain notes, certain notes together, became familiar, became words: shoe, light, hand, milk.

He could lift his head.

He could roll over.

He could sit up and watch.

There were sounds and there were words, and whenever someone spoke to him, sounds and words were mixed lovingly together.

But for the word *no:* always followed by a string of words, their rhythm harsh, emphatic.

All he could hear were words mixed in with sounds. He felt like he should hear more, like certain words together should start to make sense, but they didn't. It was a long river of sound traversing over the few rocks that were too large to be drowned by the torrent.

He pulled off the hood, already exhausted. Any kind of reality experience was tiring; you were learning something new, you could almost feel the reshifting that goes on in the mind as it revises one or two thoughts, which in turn means it has to revise one or two others, on and on. So much easier the tranquil excitement of learning those things that deepen your sense of the world rather than change it.

He remembered learning Arabic during his first week of military training. It seemed a language grown out of sand, herding, and God. There was submission, recitation, and holy struggle. There was sin and judgment; honor, purity, and shame. The word for *burn*, as in burning wood, carried the connotation of hellfire. But he had stepped out of the reality workshop, and he understood orders, and he learned to give orders. In the next set of workshops he sat before rows and rows of marks on a screen, and marks soon became letters, which soon became words he could hear in his head, which he could type out to speak with someone who wasn't in the same place, making it possible for one's thoughts to travel impossible distances.

Learning Nostratic had been easier, only because the root of all concepts started with those first men and women who had foraged the savannah and shared language and argued over who ate the meat from the large animal they had just killed. And atop the interpolated language of foraging came the languages of the farm, the herd, the market, the city, the temple, and the court-house, all languages he had never needed before.

Words joined into phrases, which joined into notions, which joined into conversation or story or song.

Here all he had was a few words.

How was he going to find Pauline with a few words?

He ate several ration bars and felt bloated. He walked around and felt trapped. He felt an intense longing, a desperate need to be touched, and after lying with himself—his eyes focused intently on the bulkhead above so he wouldn't visualize N!ai or Pauline or Hanan or any moment that might enhance his desire—the longing still remained, accompanied by some unnameable loss. There were no thoughts to think. There was every reason to pull the hood back over his head. He just couldn't bear to do it. The fabric felt like it was full of static electricity, but it wasn't the hood. There was something charged in his body, something that made his hands shake.

He started to make sounds. He moved his lips. He stretched his tongue. The prosthesis in his mouth shifted; he could feel it pressing against the roof of his mouth, along the walls of his cheeks, and the word he shaped sounded much different from the one he had heard in his head.

He was babbling. A string of contentment, a string of sounds. He was sure he sounded like no baby a human or slazan mother would recognize.

He was trying to walk. He stumbled and fell. He tried out words. Just one or two. Floor. Then mother. The adult in him wanted to hear the word father, but it was absent. No father from work, no father from the teahouse or mosque, no father from his hunting trip.

There were faces and names.

There was the child who shared his mother.

There was the young woman who shared his mother.

There was grandmother and great-grandmother and their sons and daughters.

There was no father.

He started to hear another word. The young woman who shared his mother said it to him. It came with a lot of other words. The child who shared his mother said it to him. They said it when he wanted to nurse more. It was something he didn't have. He didn't understand a lot of the other words or the reasons why they were spoken. But he learned this word: *solitude*.

When Dikobe had gone through the experience, she had sat in a full-sensory reality couch, which had been set up in the loading dock, right next to the shuttle craft. Esoch had sat beside her, monitoring the medcomp's drip and her vital signs, her face invisible under the brown fabric of the hood, the words she was learning as inaccessible as the expressions on her face. She came out of her second session with a look he had never seen before in her eyes. She took him by the hand, led him into the shuttle, and locked the hatch, something they hadn't done since they'd first become lovers. Her embrace was so warm, and the kiss was like no other she had ever given him, not the partly open mouth, the slight touch of tongues, but a wide-open mouth as if she couldn't get enough of him, her arms locked tight as if she were trying to make him part of her own body. He had never felt so much love so intensely, and it had frightened him. She was looking to him with a soft sheen to her eyes, and she was saying something about how it was good not to be alone and how it was love that made us human, and all the while he diplomatically tried to extricate himself from her grip. The warmth vanished like a shock. Her eyes narrowed as if she were looking at him for the first time.

"Fuck you," she said. And she left him there.

In her cabin, after dinner, she apologized and explained that it was just the tapes that were affecting her.

Now their lovemaking was like etiquette, or like chemicals, something they did so they could wake up next to each other at the end of the night.

Here, in the shuttle, Esoch stared at the screens. It was night out. He didn't feel like sleeping.

A strange man who had been speaking to his mother now spoke to him. He did not understand.
His mother said, "He says you behave well."
He felt himself smile at the mother's compliment.

He tried to say new words.
No. Proper. Improper.
Each word is a short, easy syllable.
Respectful. Disrespectful.
I am here. You are there.
Hot. Cold.
Share. Go away.

He spoke around words. Ball. Bird. Mother. He tried other words with those words. Go ball. Ball gone. Here ball.
My ball.
Share words. Words are shared. Meat share.
You give away I go.

The night was cloudy, the darkness absolute. If it had been this kind of night when the *Way of God* had been destroyed, then Pauline may have taken longer to become aware of the warship's destruction, the solitude she had been subjected to; she might still have been here when Esoch had arrived.

He ate too much again and brooded, erection in hand, knowing as he felt both a touch of pleasure and an absence of desire why they called this self-abuse. He had the medcomp give him a mild sedative, and he lay in the bed, restless still, remembering how Pauline had brooded over him while going through the language learning. After that second session she seemed in control of herself. After each tape was over, she would take him by the arm to the dining hall, and she would work hard on talking with others, as if socializing was a kind of medication. But as time went on, as the language learning progressed, she grew more silent. At first she seemed to listen more often. Then she looked about, as if the words didn't make sense, as if she wasn't quite sure why one person said something particular to another person. Each night she insisted they make love, even though it was obvious she felt no desire. She refused his caresses, wanted him in her no matter how dry she was. There was no pleasure in such friction, and the pain tightened her face. "Let's stop," he said. "You want to be with Hanan, don't you?" she said, her voice soft, the tone almost friendly, all accusation located in the words themselves. He felt young and overwhelmed by the years of her accumulated pain; he didn't know if he should stop or continue; he didn't know which would lead to the greater accusation. When she reached her moment, her body stretched out under his, her hands above her head and clasped together as if she were imprisoned, she began to sob; she cried to herself and took no interest in his attempts to comfort her.

And then one day, after a long session under the hood, she said nothing at all. She looked at each person, and she looked frail, suspicious, as if about to be betrayed. That night, in her cabin, she asked him again to take the hood, learn slazan, come with her planetside. His silence was both evasion and answer. In her cabin she pulled him fiercely to her. Her eyes slammed shut, she reached her moment quickly, a brief struggle against the day's solitude, and he kept holding her, his penis hard within her, waiting for her to tell him if she wanted to rest or if she wanted him to go on. She opened her eyes, and they were dark and hard. Her palms were against his chest, and she pushed him off her, rolled from mat to floor, and crawled away from him, until she was against the bulkhead, where she curled up, arms over breasts, knees brought up to arms. "What's wrong?" he whispered, knowing no other words to ask. She said, "I want to be alone. I don't want you to go, but I want to be alone. Oh, how horrible a feeling."

In the sanity of morning she leaned into him, worked on his desire, and afterward said, "Please, come planetside with me. I can't bear six months alone. It's why the general assigned you to the mission. You're my reality check."

He had never heard her talk like this before, and he felt disappointment more than pity. And he knew then he couldn't go down. Then he would truly be Dikobe's boy. And just by refusing to put on this hood, the one he now held in his hand, he had made it impossible to join her; he had made it possible to stay up here with Hanan.

And then, like now, he wished he had loved her better.

He had once been a child who had loved a strange woman who would listen to him play the thumb piano. Why, decades later, he had fallen into her open embrace, he could not say.

He dreamed there was a heavy pounding on the door. Again and again, a loud cry of pain, a loud cry of *Let me see you.*

He stepped out of bed, in the dream, his body still surrounded by the warmth of the thermal sheet, and the lights rose to a dim lighting, and he made his way to the hatchway. The hatch slid open, and in his dream he knew Pauline should be standing outside, returning to him, but in the morning light he saw that no one was there.

The Fourteenth Day

He didn't feel much like eating after the medcomp had awakened him with some chemical that would help him concentrate. He paced the floor, considered eating as a delay tactic, held the hood, then saw that a green light was blinking. It was the default alarm; light but no sound. There had been a visitor last night. He remembered the pounding in his dream. The words. Had he heard Arabic words? He called up the appropriate image and had the comp filter the image to compensate for the night's darkness.

A slazan subadult male made his way down the hillside, carefully stepped around the remains of the dead body (which the comp graciously did not clarify), and walked up the shuttle. He pounded on the hatch. He called out. Esoch listened several times until he could make out the words. *Let me see you.* He cried out loudly, as if he wanted the whole forest to hear. Then he turned and strode away, glancing over his shoulder once or twice.

Esoch reviewed the images until he had a clear one of the slazan's face. He had the comp do a search for other images. It was the slazan who had approached Pauline after she had bathed, the one who had stepped up to her and touched one of her breasts, the one who could not face her direct stare and so sped away. Had he come to find Pauline again? Or did he want to see the new creature who lived in the hunk of metal?

The next session was impossible. There were these taut one-syllable words that fit together with the rhythm of a multisyllable word. *The girl who shares my mother* was said in the space of time to it took to say *my sister* in Arabic.

Phrases were harder. As much as he tried, something kept him from understanding prepositions and tense—whatever words hooked phrases together changed at random. They had a logic that the child or adult couldn't turn into sense.

Or maybe he couldn't turn it into sense because he kept noticing things. Here was a woman. Here was a man. The older men were seen only in the distance. You never heard of a profession, or maybe he had to wait for a later session. Mother was always there. And like the child, he started to think it proper to go off alone. She smiled at his bravery as he tottered off on his own. The girl who shared his mother was kinder to him the more he ignored her. He started to like being alone. He was disgusted with his desire to be near someone, to hold someone in a warm embrace. His own human daydreams after the session now disgusted him.

He showered, washing off sweat and the thin film of semen that was left after he had wiped his abdomen clean. The water felt good upon his lethargic body, and he just stood there, knowing he was emptying out the tank, and he thought about the lack of desire, the lack of pleasure, and the persistent need, about how he yearned to be touched, about how he felt like doing nothing but that which made him feel worse.

"Go ejaculate on yourself," was a way of teasing among those who had a joking relationship. Among those with reserved relationships, it was a terrible insult, the words implying that the other was alone, that there was no wife or lover who would take interest in him.

He was drying off when the beeper sounded. Naked, he stepped up to the console to check the screen, the red notification light blinking above it. Slazan N!ai stood on the hillside. She was wearing her pubic apron and a chi !kan for collecting. She was looking down at the shuttle as if waiting for something. If he stepped out, if he managed to utter something intelligible in her language, what would she do?

Upon reaching the crest of the hillside I saw two things. First she saw that the rock's opening had not appeared. Second she saw why. Spread out in the cracked darkness of the clearing were Clever Fingers' bones. Some meat that scavengers had not torn off still remained, and the dead eyes in his skull were open. Even though neither of the moons had presented its face, the true body should have left by now; if nothing else, the person who had dug up the body had breathed it in.

With this thought troubling her mind, I made her way to see

Flatface, who greeted her and insisted I share of the several
leaftails that she had snared. Each woman sat on opposite sides
of the fire and each cooked her own two birds. The quiet, as well
as the way Flatface kept her eyes on the fire and the cooking
bird, made it clear that things were wrong here.

"Are there words to be shared?" asked I.

"Too many. Are the pregnant woman and her daughter still
sharing your cooking fire?"

"She is no longer pregnant; and she is walking home with
her daughter and her infant son."

Flatface did not ask about the twin.

I watched the bird meat blacken near the coals.

"Childless has started mating. I have not seen my eldest son
since Clever Fingers was killed."

"Crooked wouldn't open herself to your son."

"She shouldn't. Her mother and mine shared mothers. But it
means my son. . . ." Flatface said nothing more. It was odd to see
a mother who now rarely shared food with her son grow sad
when he had to leave and find another place to gather food and
make things.

"Huggable—the woman with the animal's teats—is mating,
too," said I.

Flatface lifted her eyes to meet the healer's. "That is why
there are too many words to share. Hugger called out all last
night. It sounded much like Nightskin crying out. Perhaps it was
Hugger's imitation."

"What do you mean?"

"Animal Teats—Huggable—is dead."

I remembered the words: *I have arrows.* "Did Nightskin kill
her?"

Flatface's eyes half closed with a kind of disgust, the way
they would have if I had named someone with whom Flatface
shared food. How had Nightskin become so accepted?

"How did she die?"

"Hugger blames the animal."

"The animal is gone."

"You saw the animal leave. That does not mean the animal
has left."

"How did Huggable die?"

"No one cares."

"A woman dies, and you don't care?"

"There is one man killed, and the one who let loose the arrow then dies. She did not share a mother with anyone here."

"Was she killed?"

"I have not seen. No one I know has seen. Why ask? There has been too much wrong, and this could be the end of it. If the animal has left as you say, then Hugger will never find her, and that will be the end of it."

"That cannot be the end of it. What has happened to the daughter?"

"No one has told me."

I was too astounded to speak. Each mother told at least one tale of how a mother had died and how a daughter or son had been taken in by another mother. For there to be a death, and no woman to act; for there to be a child without a mother, and no woman to act; for these things to happen, the world must have changed in some terrible way. I finally said, "The first animal is gone, but there is a second animal. It lives in the rock now."

"That one will bring different troubles. Perhaps I really should find a new place to gather food and work on my wisdom. Perhaps you should find a new place to heal."

I finished the leaftail, chewing without tasting the meat. Leaftails were smart and hard to snare; it was a loss to chew on such meat and not care about its flavor. But all I wanted to do was leave. The woman who sat across from her spoke with Flatface's voice and looked to her with Flatface's eyes, but I felt as if this Flatface who shared leaftail with her was a different woman.

I walked quickly to where Huggable had lived, sometimes breaking into a run. It seemed all too likely that her daughter would still be there, staring at the dead body, worrying that she would breathe in the true body.

She paused outside the brush that concealed Huggable's hut and hearth. She did not know if she wanted to see this body, but still she found the thin concealed pathway and pushed back leaves and branches, making her way to cleared ground. She stopped. Almost directly in front of her was the body. Huggable was sprawled out on her back like something large had dropped her to the ground. Between her two teats was the hilt of a knife. The hilt looked like nothing I had ever seen before.

There was hardly any blood around the wound. The knife had gone in quick and sure: death had come with the blow. Huggable's eyes were open wide, her mouth frozen in an impossible to understand expression.

Someone else was in the hut and hearth. Hugger was sitting

in the opening to Huggable's hut and facing the body. He had looked up to watch I.

I asked, "Who did this?"

"I don't know."

"I was told you had blamed the animal."

"Look at the knife, Healer. Look at the hilt. It is like no knife a man has ever made."

I looked again. Something that looked like thin strips of black reed had been wound about the hilt in an elaborate design. The curve of the hilt was odd, and she tried to imagine its purpose. Huggable's killer had to get mating close to thrust in that knife. Why would Huggable let the animal get that close? Unless it had snuck up from behind? Why would the animal have killed Huggable? How could it bear being that close? The Stranger had said, *These animals flock together like birds in the sky. They cannot stand to be alone.*

"Healer," said Hugger, "you should leave. I have kept a fire to keep away the scavengers, but the body is beginning to rot. You should not be here if the true body comes out."

"You should not, either."

"I do not care. I am not sure it would be a bad thing if I breathed in her true body. Then I would still have her."

Hugger spoke so much like a young daughter who had lost her mother that I did not know what to say. She thought of the dull sheen of moonlight, her blade against dead skin, and the cloth wrapped around her mouth and nose, making it hard to breathe. She knelt by the body and gripped the hilt. The hold was awkward. She repositioned her hand. The hold still felt wrong, as if the hilt had been shaped for a hand very different from hers. Odder still, the hilt carried the same warmth as if someone had held it a long time. She pulled out the knife; there was a soft sucking sound, a bubble of blood on Huggable's chest.

I stumbled back, as if she could see the true body rising in the air. It took her a while to regain control of her breathing; then she looked at the blade of the knife. It was covered with blood, but the blood had not soaked in the way it did with certain kinds of bones, and the blade was far too thin to be made of rock. It was a very thin blade, and it had the same kind of look to it as the animal's boulder. She couldn't remember having seen the animal with a knife, but here it was. And the hilt fit comfortably in her hand. She opened her fingers. The hilt didn't look that different. She closed her hand. It was a perfect fit, like it had been crafted for her palm. She did not want to hold it. She jammed the blade into the dirt by Huggable's dead body.

"Does it belong to the animal?"

I looked to Hugger. What would he do if she told him he was right, that it was the animal's knife? "Where's the daughter?"

"She is not here."

"Where is she?"

"Nightskin heard my calls. She took the daughter."

"No one else came?"

"No."

"Did the daughter see the killing?"

"I do not know."

"Where were you?"

"I had left. I have been here day after day to watch after her. It was too much all this time nearby and no solitude. I should never have left."

"Do you know where Nightskin keeps hut and hearth?"

Near the cold springs Nightskin had set up hut and hearth in a large clearing where a long time ago Talk Too Much, Flatface's mother, and the mother of Crooked's mother had first lived after their mother had died. This past spring, I, Flatface, and Flatface's eldest daughter had burned the brush away there, so the area would be rich in grasses and lightfoot, and it would be rich in berry bushes this autumn. For now, a woman who lived there would have to walk far to find food other than fish. Her presence would frighten off the lightfoot.

The light in the woods was slowly dying, but here in the clearing the afternoon sun shone down, making everything clear. The color of the sky was deep and distant.

I called out her approach. Nightskin emerged from her hut and gestured a welcome. Huggable's daughter came running out of the other side of the clearing; she must have been playing among the few trees that had been left standing.

I stopped where several burned logs had been placed to represent a waiting fire. Huggable's daughter ran up to her, her eyes long with happiness, but she stopped short and looked respectfully away.

Nightskin said, "I have food to share."

I said that she also had food to share at her own fire.

"Share mine with me while you're here."

"I would be glad to. If you share mine some other day."

"I, too, would be glad." Nightskin laid down a strip of leather by the cooking fire. She reached near the coals and took out several pieces of meat, which she laid on top of the hide. She gestured for I to come and sit.

I left the waiting fire and turned to see that Huggable's daughter remained there. Nightskin did not look to the child or invite her to the cooking fire. Nightskin just stood on the opposite side of the fire, her eyes following I's every move. I became uncomfortable. Nightskin was watching her movements the way one watches a lightfoot. I became aware of how tall the other woman was, of the faint ash-colored patches that stretched under the chin, of the flat strength of her belly, nothing at all like the belly of a pregnant woman. Like the Stranger in the village, Nightskin did not avert her eyes. They stood like that for a moment, on opposite sides of the fire, face-to-face, their eyes halfopen so no one would feel there was anger or threat. It was as if she were a girl again, doing this with Flatface's eldest daughter, seeing who would jump back first, but there was also something about it that was not like a game at all.

Nightskin ended it by sitting down and laying cooked meat out in front of herself. I sat, and they both ate. It was lightfoot meat. By the hut, two poles supported a third pole; from that hung numerous strips of meat. Behind I, Huggable's daughter was walking around the waiting fire, singing softly, her voice as soft as a forest breeze.

"What words do you have to share?" asked Nightskin.

"I see you have become the mother to another's daughter."

"You know this other was killed?"

"Yes. I have seen the body."

"Then you saw the knife the animal left in her."

"Yes," she said, even though she wanted to argue the point. But Huggable's daughter had remained by the waiting fire and was watching her, averting her eyes whenever the healer looked in her direction. "Why have you become her mother?"

"I heard the almost a man who one and another call Hugger cry out in the night. I had been told where Animal Teats kept hut and hearth and how Hugger always stayed there. The woman one and another call Squawker came. She told Hugger to leave before the true body left for the sky. She was frightened by the death. When Hugger did not leave, she left. Who else was to take the daughter?"

"But you did not share mothers with Huggable."

"No one did. She has lived in many places."

"You despised Huggable. She shot at Roofer, but she killed Clever Fingers."

"Her daughter did nothing. Who else was going to take her? Do you want to be her mother?"

Huggable's daughter was plucking leaves off a tree. She held the branch with one hand, and with two fingers she pulled the leaf at the stem. She dropped the leaf and watched it float to the ground before she plucked another.

Nightskin said, "You are the healer. It is said that you have not felt desire for many winters. It is said that you do not have time for a daughter. Do you want one now?"

Another leaf floated, swaying back and forth across the air, and before it touched the ground, the daughter had returned attention to the branch.

"Healer?"

"My concern is that your feelings for the mother might become the feelings you have for the daughter."

"You do not know my feelings, then. I was sure that the woman who shared my mother and who stayed the night by your fire would have explained. Then you would have understood my feelings about the daughter's mother."

Arm Scars had said things to I and other things to Lightfoot Watcher. I couldn't remember how much she had believed. "The woman with scars on her arms told me that you had mated only with Clever Fingers and that you carried a child."

"Then she did not tell you that the daughter grew from my pollen."

I looked at the ash-colored patches under her chin, at the bulk of Nightskin's body, and she remembered what Lightfoot Watcher had said about Nightskin. But it did not make sense. No man cared what grew from his pollen.

While I hunted through memories for words, Nightskin stood up. "You are a healer, and you should not have to wait until I die to see this."

I also stood, but she did not know what to say to these words, either.

"It has been said that you do things to dead bodies so that you know live bodies well." She unfastened the kaross around her waist and laid it on the ground. She laid herself flat on top of the kaross. There was something about the way she lay there, back down, belly up, that made I feel awkward, as if Nightskin's vulnerability truly belonged to the healer. I looked away. Huggable's daughter was farther away now, running among some trees, as if none of what happened now concerned her.

Nightskin lifted her hips, reached behind to undo the knot of her pubic apron, then cast the apron aside. I stood there for a moment because now she remembered Lightfoot Watcher's words and why she had not believed them.

"I want you to know this now and not take a knife to it later. I want you to see that I am both man and woman."

There were labia, like a woman's, and there was a penis, smaller than a man's, but a penis still the same. The healer crouched beside Nightskin the way she would beside someone sick, careful to make sure that knees or shins did not come into contact with the sick person's skin.

"You may touch," said Nightskin.

I was split in two by her feelings. There was a revulsion, which began in her belly and moved on up to her head, and there was curiosity, which started in her head and moved down to her fingers. She lifted the penis. It was soft, and there was no trace of the thin bone that ran along the underside of a man's penis, which made it possible for a desirous newly ripened woman to mount an uninterested old man and still take in his pollen. The penis itself joined the body where the clitoris should have been. With thumb and forefinger, the healer spread labia apart, but Nightskin's legs were too close together to see anything. As if guessing her thoughts, Nightskin spread her legs, her thigh touching I's knee. I stood up and stepped away before she realized she had done so. Nightskin lay there calmly and acted like nothing had happened. She raised her knees and turned her feet out.

I wanted this whole thing to end. She could not understand how Nightskin with such ease could do what made every other person uncomfortable. Nightskin reminded her of the Stranger in the village; both did things so differently that you could no longer expect them to behave as a person should behave.

"You haven't finished," said Nightskin. Her eyes were still averted, just like every sick person turned her head away so that her eyes could not confirm that the touch was real.

The healer tried to find a position that was both respectful and secure, and instead ended up lying on her belly. She spread Nightskin's labia and saw what you expected to see where you expected to see it.

"Feel the labia where they hang down."

The healer took one labia between thumb and forefinger,

felt down along it, down to where it hung away from the body. Nestled within was something round and firm, with a layer of softness around it. She felt the other labia, which hung down but was empty.

I let go and returned to a crouching position. The penis was still short, but it was tauter now. She touched it, then withdrew her hand and stood up.

Nightskin stood up too and found her pubic apron. "If I had been dead, you would have looked longer."

I stood there for a moment, uncertain of all her thoughts.

"You understand now," said Nightskin.

"You said on the hillside that Huggable had carried a child. You said the child grew from the pollen left by an almost-a-man who shared your mother. But that wasn't true. The child she carried grew from your pollen, and Huggable buried the child before it breathed in its true body."

Nightskin turned away from her and stared off into the woods. "Each woman who lived near the river's mouth told Huggable not to allow that child to be born. No one would hunt with her. No one would share food with her."

"Why?"

"I was a woman. I hunted like a woman. I shared food like a woman. I mated like a woman. But when I was still young, I mated with a newly ripe woman. No other woman would share food with me. No woman would hunt with me. When the child was born, it was buried, although it was a girl like any other girl.

"The woman who stayed at your hut and hearth shared my mother. The woman who stayed with Flatface, and who had scars on her chest, shared my mother. Each would share food with me only if no other woman was in sight. Each talked like she and I never had shared a mother. Then the small boulder with legs fell from the sky. I destroyed it.

"After that any woman would hunt with me. Any woman would share food with me. The woman who stayed at your hut and hearth now would tell another that she and I shared a mother. Huggable came with her daughter to live by the river's mouth, and I mated with her. No woman could be cruel to me, because I had destroyed the small boulder with legs, so each was cruel to her. She buried the child and gave its milk to her daughter."

"And this was the second time Huggable had mated with you."

"Like anyone who has a child she truly loves, she wants to

mate with the same man again. She came to the river's mouth to find me."

I said nothing.

"You want to know how it was that she and I mated the first time."

"If you have more words to share."

"I have too many words."

"I am listening."

"My desire is like that of a new almost-a-man who has discovered a pleasure in his erections. The desire has not grown smaller with age as it does for a man. So when the desire became too much, I would wander off like an almost-a-man whose mother will no longer share food with him. I wander until I find a woman who will mate with me. It is a long wandering. Young women already want to mate with old men. And then it is hard to present myself as a man. Usually I end up mating with a newly ripe woman who enjoys the freshness of mating, who is still playing with her solitude and still has not lost affection for her mother's embrace."

"And you feel desire the same way a woman does."

"But no full-grown man will mate with me. A young almost-a-man or another who is in love with his erections will mate, but each man avoids me. The only exception was Clever Fingers, who was still almost-a-man even though he had lived as long as a man. I opened myself to him and only him, as Huggable opened herself to me, and so he knew the pollen was his, so he would make more gifts for me."

There was nothing for I to say. She had heard so much that she found she both sympathized with Nightskin and despised her. Nightskin was like Hugger in the way desire still controlled her, but Hugger hunted affection. He stayed outside Huggable's hut and hearth to insure there would be someone to take his embraces. This woman hunted more than embraces, as if in being both man and woman, she had taken on the worst habits of each.

I stood. Huggable's daughter was sitting near the waiting fire and tracing her finger through the black charcoal spread out on the ground. She must have noticed that the healer had risen, because she looked up, her eyes open with questions. Did she hope that the healer had come to take her?

Nightskin also stood. "I will be a mother in time. There will be a child, and this daughter will have someone with whom she can share a mother."

I was not a mother, nor would she be one soon. She could

think of no reason to claim Huggable's daughter as her own. She distrusted her own feelings, knowing they had much to do with the nature of Nightskin's genitals. She said the meat had satisfied her hunger, and walked out of the hut and hearth, stopping to pat Huggable's daughter once on the head.

"Healer." It was Nightskin's voice.

I turned.

"It is said that a healer wants a daughter to learn the music for healing. Huggable gave birth to one daughter then another. If you want a daughter . . ."

Nightskin said nothing more. She let the idea speak itself in I's mind. I had no more words to share. She turned and strode off. But the words that never once touched air stayed alive in her head.

The following is taken from the notebook Puuline Dikobe kept during her 200 day study of the slazan foraging population on Tienah.

Day 68
We place the insects in their encampment to watch them, and then the women leave their hut and hearths. They wrap themselves in their chi !kans, take their quivers and knives, and head off with their children. It's early summer. The afternoons are hot and humid. The leaves remain green throughout the day, and the lack of color feels alien. The locals have eaten out their residences. They're moving to other areas to gather and hunt while the weather's good. At least that's my hypothesis. They'll probably all get together and plan an attack instead.

Day 74
Slazans, both male and female, can move through the woods with hardly a sound, as quiet as a ghost. At other times a single slazan can be as noisy as an inept urbanite making his first hike in the woods. They break dried branches with a snap, shake green ones so leaves rustle, call out their *I am here*'s. No predator is caught unawares. No conspecific is taken by surprise.

When noise? When quiet?

Males seem to call out their I am here's at regular intervals. If they hear no response, they don't call out again. It's a tremendous act of trust, or of hubris. It assumes that a silent male won't sneak into his range and take advantage of whatever the adult male is trying to protect, whether it be access to food or to mates. Perhaps I'm missing the point; perhaps there's no problem if male territories overlap.

Females remain quiet near their own hut and hearths, but they get noisier when they approach another woman's hut and hearth. We have no images yet of male-female interaction.

What rules should I follow? I have taught myself to move through the woods, and I make little sound. I worry that I will come upon a slazan and take her by surprise; I worry that she will interpret my behavior as that of a hunter and not a potential visitor.

But if I am not seen, I may see more; I may see something our imaging pins don't pick up.

Day 77

My wanderings, nursing child in sling, yield nothing in the way of contact.

The mapping satellites have recorded night fires, so we have a census of summer encampments. Maryam is manufacturing more insects.

Day 78

Tamr has suggested that we inject an isotope tag into various locals so we can monitor where they go. Jihad, not to be outdone, wants us to gas shelters at night and take blood samples to measure the genetic relationships of the local community.

I'm glad their orders forbid them to come down and help me. If we treat the slazans differently from the human groups we study, if we draw blood without consent, then we have made a decision about how we view these people. If we observe them the same way we observe animals, we have established their position in the hierarchy of life.

"You want them to use this data for peace," Tamr says. "You give them faulty data, you won't give them enough to negotiate adequately."

I don't respond. The mark of the socially bellicose: she uses my values, values she dislikes, to convince me to do things her way.

Day 84

Today, while walking, I hear noises off in the distance. I shift my baby into the chi !kan so he won't fall out. I crouch down and creep forward, over to the crest of a ravine. Below are two woman butchering a local version of an ungulate. One arrow sticks out from its neck, another from its hindquarters.

Later Jihad and I carefully review the images of each woman. The intelligence recognizes one woman. We've ID'ed her as !U. She owns one of the three hut and hearths we have monitored. The second woman we have not seen before. She appears to be roughly the same age as !U. The intelligence does a phenotype comparison of body structure, facial features, skin coloration, and concludes that they are not closely related. Jihad wants a blood sample.

I want to know if it's kinship or the meat that bonds these two women together.

Day 85

I have watched them divide the meat a number of times.

They hardly speak a word. They know exactly what to do.

I first consider: they must be kin. Each individual does her best to insure the survival of her genes. If the cost is not too high, gene survival is enhanced if kin helps kin. One ant—two, three, four ants—will die willingly because each other ant in the troop contains the exact same genetic material. If one dies, his genes live on. One bee can die willingly because her sisters are more closely related to her than her mother. A mammalian mother will take certain risks for her immature children because each carries half her genes. An individual will take a certain risk, pay certain costs, for the benefit of her sisters because she carries half the same genes.

But if they aren't kin, then sharing takes on a new edge. Each would achieve a greater benefit at a lesser cost if they put in less effort to track and hunt the deer and butcher the meat and instead tried to walk away with the most meat. It makes the most sense to cheat and try to go undetected. But if these women will hunt together a second time, a third, then it makes more sense to share the burden, so that each will want to hunt again, so that each will trust the other.

The vampire bat who regurgitates the night's gathering of blood for fellow members of his cave has a better chance of being fed in a similar fashion on the nights when his hunt for sustenance is less than successful. The hawk who distracts the monkey so the other hawk can swoop in from behind and pluck it from the branch has a better chance of sharing the prey than the hawk who hunts alone and frightens the monkey into hiding. A Ju/wa man hunts large meat animals with other men, he trades his arrows with other men so that the owner of the meat is not always the man who fires the fatal arrow, he divides the meat along prescribed lines, so that all share in the meat, so that he may share the meat others have killed those times when the tracks he finds are old and faded, when the animals he has felled are found first by lions, when the land is so parched that the animals have gone elsewhere.

But if there is only one hunt, if the hunters never see each other again, there will be no future need for their trust, no future need to deter their deceit.

So it's not the physical environment that makes survival difficult, it's the social environment. You have to know how to benefit yourself and how to benefit others so you will have a place in their company—a whole series of instincts, a set of Darwinian algorithms, developed to navigate the dynamic ocean of such questions—to detect people who break the rules of social exchange, who take more and give back less; to repress emotions and memories that would make living with others difficult; to manipulate the opinions of others; to behave in ways that make you appear more congenial than you are; to go along with the general consensus.

What kind of algorithms guide slazan life?

What general consensus do these women share?

What enforces their need to trust each other?

My husband, who had been agnostic, Muslim, Hindu, Jew, and Christian, took our son to some religious commune on some orbital in some other stellar system, disappearing in a maze of digitized trails full of different names, different ID numbers, all for my son's own good.

Keeping a secret is an ideal in many human societies, but it is rarely a reality; large, complex societies have kept secrets only by releasing so much contradictory data that finding the truth becomes an expensive, exhausting chore.

I spent a year looking for my son, draining my credit and my credit rating. There are enough orbitals, enough different laws for where humans live, enough intelligences programmed by different needs, that it is easy to take away your child, lose your wife. There is no shared set of neighbors and relatives to turn on you, to force you to go back, to do the rightful thing. Everything is now trust.

I have this plastic baby who sucks from empty breasts so that the slazans will trust me.

Chapter Twelve

The Fifteenth Day

The one the healer called Hugger had sat two nights near the dead body of the woman whom she had called Huggable and he had called Soft Skin, and he still sat near Soft Skin's body the morning he decided to seek out the animal who had killed her. He knew he should have left the first night, after the daughter had been taken away, after he had pounded on the boulder and called to the animal to come out, but he remained near her, his throat raw from crying out. He fed wood to the fire and listened to the sound of an animal creeping around the hut and hearth.

The next morning the body lay there, untouched, unmoving. As a boy, he had thought that true bodies left so easily because the dead body was left out in the open so scavengers could tear at the flesh. If he stayed, if he protected the body, would the true body be forced to remain, would it cause her eyes to open, her lungs to lift her chest with air? First one nightwing landed on the outstretched limb of the sunset-fruit tree next to which he had built Soft Skin's hut. Then there was a second one on a nearby tree, and each called to the other. Another alighted, and the calling didn't seem to stop. One swooped down at her, and he grabbed her digging stick and took swipes at it, driving it off. Its beak had never touched her body.

She had not gathered recently, so there was little food, and hunger emptied his belly. The nightwings called to each other. A pointed-ears stuck its snout through the brush, and he swung the digging stick at it. It scurried away. He heard another rustle in the brush.

When the healer came, he wanted to ask her for food. But she looked at him with the same look each person who lived by the river gave him. It was the same look each gave the woman who had shared his mother, whom they called Squawker, and it was the look each had given his mother until she had died. And the look grew worse when he demanded that the healer put the knife back into Soft Skin's chest so the true body could not escape. The sound of it was sickening, but now the true body was safe within her.

The healer left, and his hunger grew the way he should have grown. Before her death his mother had called him Small Gray because the pouches had never grown, he had never long called the way he should have. Only Soft Skin, who'd got the same look from each woman as had his mother, a half-eyed look, which showed lack of trust, a wish that you were elsewhere—of all the women, only Soft Skin had accepted his gifts and opened herself to him.

By night his head felt as empty as his belly. He needed to walk off behind the hut to empty himself, but the moment he did that, the pointed-ears would break through. He paced the hut and hearth, fought sleep, and swung the digging stick.

He did not remember curling up on the ground, and he did not remember falling asleep. He awoke to the sounds of snarling, of feet scuffling in the dirt. There were two pointed-ears tugging at different parts of her body. Their chests were red with blood. He rose quickly, found the digging stick, and pounded at them, until, yelping, they ran off, disappearing through the brush. The nightwings called to each other from the trees, one and another flapping hard as they moved to a closer tree limb.

He stood there panting. It was too late. Her body had been opened. The true body could be gone. He could be breathing it in right now. He knew it had been useless to try. Why had he? The bloodied knife had fallen to the ground. It was the animal's knife. Not a good thing had happened since the animal had arrived. He picked up the knife and walked away.

Walking with a knife in hand, rather than in a sheath, was somehow strange. The hilt itself felt odd to the touch, but as he strode toward the clearing, it felt more comfortable in his grip. He kept telling himself that this would be for the best. It would be done, and he would leave and go elsewhere. And if he had breathed in her true body, then he might well die, which would be for the best. He had no place here by the river. Maybe he had no place anywhere.

And neither did the animal.

Esoch was thirsty. Everyone was thirsty. The sun burned away at everything. Everything but the /gausha waterhole had dried up. He couldn't remember now, only several years later, if he had been invited to hunt with N!ai's father and her brother, or if he had chosen to go out with N!ai. Some !xwa vines were growing around a gan tree, and she had tried to dig out the root, but it was deep and big. He had dreamed that night of the !xwa root, rich in moisture, and of N!ai's kindness when he dug it out and carried it back to the chu/o.

The next day, when they got back to the face of the huts, ≠oma was carrying the root, heavy with water, children running about, crying out, Dam found meat! Dam found meat! And indeed, N!ai's father and his son had come back with the meat of a gemsbok. N!ai's father told how thin the gemsbok was, how easy it was to find in the dry sand, how it had wandered alone to drink from the nearby waterhole. The arrow he had shot into the gemsbok was an arrow ≠oma had made and given him. He called out, laughing, "So Owner of Music is the owner of the meat."

And there ≠oma stood with the meat. While there was quiet talk—yes, that's the way to do it, be generous, don't be stingy—he gave a forequarter to the two hunters, N!ai's father and her brother, he kept the meat of the neck for himself, he passed a hindquarter to N!ai's mother, the other to his wife, then the meat of the belly to another relative, the flanks to another, each receiver holding out cupped hands, never grabbing, always waiting; and each person turned to cook the meat, then hand out portions to other family members. He could feel once again the way he felt his heart beat, the way he felt the painful hunger he felt whenever everyone was watching him, waiting for him to do the right thing, and hearing, behind him, N!ai's mother speaking to N!ai: "Your husband should have hunted, too. See how proud he looks."

An alarm sounded, and ≠oma couldn't understand why the shuttle alarm was sounding in the middle of the chu/o while he distributed meat. Her husband said: "It was a good arrow. It flew straight." ≠oma knew he should deny that the arrow was any good, that he should say that if N!ai's father had chosen another man's arrow, then the meat would have been distributed more fairly. But he couldn't say the routine words. He was overcome by the way N!ai's father had spoken well of him, by the way everyone had meat and was eating it, complaining only about the heat and about how little fat there was on the animal this time of year, and he watched all this and the hardness in his belly wouldn't go away, nor would the sound of the alarm.

He remembered where he was, and he remembered the proximity alarm. There was a slight surge of interest when he thought that Slazan N!ai could have returned. He walked across the deck, thinking how coffee would be nice (but that made him think of sitting across from Hanan in the ship's café), when he stopped and gripped one of the accelerator seats.

Slazan N!ai's return would be signaled by a red light. The blinking light was blue. He couldn't remember what blue meant. What had he been thinking when he programmed a blue light to go off? How long had he been alone? Maybe he should just lie down again. Whatever it was, he was safe. The image on the screen just showed the crest of the hill. He could make out where the trails met, where tree limbs had been torn down for the fires. He saw nothing. Then he remembered he had set the blue light to go off for Pauline. Where was she? Had she stepped forward, changed her mind, and gone back?

A figure emerged from the shadows and stepped out onto

the crest of the hill. Sunlight shone clearly. The tan uniform was one he had seen in so many training scenarios, but this one was ripped and stained, as if this slazan had made a long journey through the forest. Esoch remembered that he had feared that Pauline would return in the chameleon suit, that the system wouldn't recognize her, so he had set the blue alarm to go off for any humanoid figure whose body was covered with fabric. And here he was, in the tan uniform of a slazan warrior. If this was the one who had survived the fall through the atmosphere, if there wasn't a contingent of them hidden somewhere on the planet, then this was the slazan who had attacked and destroyed the *Way of God*.

The slazan warrior walked down the hill, his steps measured, calculated, as if walking through a minefield. His eyes were always forward, looking right at the shuttle, and, through lens and processors and visual reproducing, looking right at Esoch. He halted halfway down the hill, and he sat down, legs splayed, hands pressed flat to the ground.

When Esoch swallowed, he tasted bile. This was worse than when they had closed him in the coffin, worse than when he had confronted the alien forest for the first time. He had survived all of that, and now this slazan warrior was here.

He went in search of the pistol. He looked in cabinets and lockers, he fumbled through instruments and Pauline's clothes and food, but he couldn't find it. He slammed things shut, he cursed, and he looked, and the fear grew. And the fear had a recognizable form, like a flavor forgotten and then recalled: the simulated slazan who had come for him with the knife, the simulated slazan sniper, the simulated slazan who hid in the building that Esoch and Ghazwan had been assigned to take. But those were simulations. Ghazwan had not died in battle.

But here he had cause, here he had training, here he had fear, and he couldn't find the gun. He stopped. He thought. He looked at the screen. The warrior sat on the hillside, perfectly still, eyes forward. Why was he here? Where was his weapon? What did he want?

Esoch then remembered: the patched onesuit lay crumpled by the bed. The pistol was still on the waisthook. His hands were so jittery that it was hard to get dressed, and the pistol grip felt awkward in his hand. The slazan warrior still sat on the hillside. What was Esoch going to do, dive out there and shoot the enemy?

He said names. Hanan Salib. Amalia. Viswam. Rajeev.

Sarah Karp. Rachel Stein. Alifa al-Shaykh. He forced an image of each one into his mind, he tried to remember an event: Tamr and Jihad arguing with Pauline. Sarah Karp standing at Hanan's doorway. The captain and executive officer going over the plans with him, Jihad sitting by her desk, calling up whatever maps the captain ordered. Esoch tried hard to conjure them up, to conjure up some degree of hatred. Where had it gone? Just a few days ago—how many had it been?—he had grasped hold of his pistol and aimed it at the slazan mother.

Why couldn't he hate well? Hanan was dead; here was her killer. Esoch could set the hatch to open, lean forward as soon as there was space, and fire several quick shots. The slazan warrior would have no idea what hit him.

The slazan warrior sat there. Hands flat on the ground. Legs splayed. An easy target. His uniform was dirtied and torn. His head was down for a moment, then raised. Esoch could see his exhaustion, wondered if the warrior could also suffer from adaptation sickness. He had come this far, he had sought out this shuttle craft.

Where was his weapon?

Esoch slid pistol back onto waisthook. Another alarm light started to blink. It was the green one. He thought, remembered: green for the locals. He or she wasn't visible yet. What would she think when she saw another slazan, someone just like them, but dressed in the clothes they had first seen on an alien?

He took the four steps to the hatch, but he didn't hit the open button. If the warrior intended to kill him, if the warrior was successful, then he had just captured a human artifact, complete with a wide range of human technology. Both sides destroyed everything before capture; there was to be no trade-off, no learning, no given advantage.

The scuttle controls were the easiest to find. The paranoia of war. It was absurd to think he was doing this. But there was the enemy. Esoch could stay in here and wait and wait. The enemy would be out there. If he left, Esoch would be trapped. There would be no way to walk the forest again without worrying about ambush. He set the scuttling mechanism.

He was given three options.

The ship could be scuttled if a person misused a particular control module. Or it could be scuttled if a person used certain controls without keying in the correct password. He imagined Pauline returning and using the wrong control. So Esoch chose the last option. Time. If the hatch did not reopen within a certain period of time, the ship would scuttle itself. The hatch was keyed to open to his fingerprints and to Pauline's. It wouldn't open for anyone else.

The comp asked for a time frame.

How long should he expect himself to be out there? Half an hour? An hour? What if the warrior captured him and led him away? If the shuttle exploded while he was gone, then his entire connection to humanity was gone.

He decided. Two complete local days. No, a little more. Let it go off at midday, when the sun was directly above. He had to calculate the figure in standard hours; then he keyed in the number. An hour before midday a loud siren would go off, just once. Minus two minutes the siren would go off again, and it would not stop its wailing until the shuttle had—he couldn't let it explode here. He reset the whole mechanism, expecting as he keyed in the instructions for the warrior to grow bored, to stand up and leave. Now the shuttle would take off, and once it had escaped the planet's gravity and left the world's orbit, it would explode in space, leaving the people here safe.

Now it was time to confront the enemy.

I awoke with the dawn. She had slept by the cooking fire, having given over the hut to Flatface's almost-a-man son, who was lying there asleep, three fingers on his right hand missing. He had been sitting by the waiting fire when the healer had returned, his hand swollen, pus oozing from the wounds. Crooked had mated with Newcomer, the almost-a-man who had been following her, and she had mated with Tall Enough, Newcomer's older rival. Flatface's son had tried to mate with her, and she had refused. He tried to force her, and she turned and bit off one of his fingers. Newcomer came to her defense, and in the scuffle Flatface's son lost two more fingers, and Newcomer had one of his ears torn up. Flatface's son had spent two days walking and sleeping in solitude before he could face the healer.

She had played music to calm him, she gave him water mixed with herbs to drink, and she played music again until he slept. Then, careful to touch him as little as possible, she cleaned the fingers and rubbed on a salve made from crushed short-stem leaves.

In the morning he was still asleep. She played for him again, but it was hard to concentrate. He should not have tried to mate with Crooked. Now one woman or another would worry that he might try to mate with the healer, Flatface's eldest daughter, or Flatface herself; now Flatface would have to ask one woman and another to help force him away from the river if he would not leave on his own. After she finished playing, she checked his hand. There was too much pus along the finger stumps, and she didn't know if music and salve would be enough to save him.

She went to gather more shortleaves, and her mind walked over the things she should do. It was good to think about healing and about nothing else. But when she returned with enough shortleaves, she found Squawker standing by the dark spot of her waiting fire and Flatface standing by the opening to her hut, looking in on her son.

"I am here," said the healer.

Each woman turned to her.

"I am here," said Flatface. "I am sorry to walk where I have not been invited. It has been many days since I have seen him."

"I am here," said Squawker. "I shared words with Flatface, and she said I should share the same words with you."

"I am listening."

"There is a strange person living by the river. He is an almost-a-man with patches on his neck. What is truly strange about him are the skins he wears. They are thin. They cover his entire body. All you see are his hands and his head."

The Stranger from the Many Huts had made it to Winding River. How had he found them? I asked, "Did you speak with him?"

"I had no words to share. He was so strange that I hid until he passed by. Where is he from? What would he do here?"

The healer looked in on Flatface's son, who was breathing like one asleep, not like one taken by sickness. She looked to Flatface, who had taken several steps back out of respect. "The Stranger," said the healer, "will be looking for the animal. I am going to the clearing."

"And my son?"

The healer widened her eyes for Flatface. "He lost the first finger trying to mate Crooked. He can sleep with his pain."

She walked off, expecting one woman, then the other, to follow her. Flatface followed her first.

Esoch had left the speech prosthesis on the workstation by the acceleration couch. He rinsed it off, placed it in his mouth. It pressed against the palate, rubbed the insides of his cheeks. Would the warrior understand a word Esoch said?

The blue light above the screen still blinked; the slazan warrior still sat on the hillside. A green light above another screen blinked, but the slazan who had set off that alarm had remained hidden in the woods. Esoch placed soft palm against hard plastic; the pistol still hung there. He gripped, pulled, aimed, then, secure with the ease of the gesture, returned the pistol to the waisthook. He inhaled and exhaled several times. Controlling his breathing did not control his heart, which he could feel hammering away at the inside of his chest. He could die of fear here or face the enemy, and the thought calmed him. Thumb pressed against eyeplate.

When the hatch slid open, the warrior did not stand. His face moved slightly, so that his eyes met Esoch's. Was this a sign of trust or distrust? Esoch couldn't remember. The stare made him uncomfortable. Was that from the experience, his training, or his upbringing? The warrior's body had gone taut, as if he were readying himself to move. Esoch clasped his hands in front. He wanted the warrior to see the pistol; he wanted the warrior to see that he wasn't anxious to use it.

Esoch stepped down. The warrior remained seated. One bird called out, and another bird answered. Water in the tiny brook washed over rocks. The hatch slid shut behind Esoch. There was no place to hide. He should have reprogrammed it so the hatch remained open. The sun was unduly warm, and he began to sweat.

The warrior had not spoken, only averted his eyes. A respectful gesture? Was he giving Esoch the opportunity to speak first?

Whatever he said, Esoch wanted it routine, polite, customary. He said, his speech slow and halting, the speaking prosthesis rubbing against the roof of his mouth, "I am here."

The warrior looked at him differently; the lips turned downward, the eyes narrowed. The warrior didn't trust what he'd just said; or was Esoch merely seeing human suspicion on a slazan face? "I am here," the warrior said, but his next words made no sense. Several of the words sounded familiar, but there was no meaning at all.

"I have words to share," Esoch said. What he really had were questions, but he didn't know how to say that. "I share words slowly." He looked to the warrior. Would his words mean what he wanted them to mean?

The warrior averted his eyes again, directing his gaze up

into the forest. Why had he said nothing? What was he waiting for Esoch to say?

Esoch tried again. "I share words as well as a boy who is only as high as his mother's knee."

The warrior focused his attention on Esoch. He opened his mouth as if to speak; then he stopped. A branch snapped, followed by the sounds of running feet. Esoch looked to where the warrior was watching. A slazan had taken several steps down the hill and had stopped. He was staring right at Esoch, his head tilted. Esoch almost had the sense that the slazan had expected to see something else. It took a moment, but Esoch recognized him. It was the one who had pounded on the shuttle craft hull the other night, the one who had touched Pauline's breast.

Then he was running down the hill, his feet pounding and sliding a bit on the hillside soil. His running was awkward; no, rather, it was the way he held his hand. One hand, his left, he was holding away from his body. There was something metallic in the hand, but Esoch could not make out what. It was clear now that the slazan was running toward Esoch, but Esoch could not understand why. He could make out the metal thing now: it was a knife. While he stepped back to find the shuttle's hatch shut, he wondered where the slazan had got a metal knife; at the same time he couldn't help but see the warrior stand up, reach behind his back, his hand returning to view with some kind of pistol.

The word Esoch heard in his mind was *trap* even though a conspiracy between these two slazans made no sense at all, and training took over, his hand gripped his own pistol, the warrior fired a round, the sound like a sharp clap of hands, and, too late, Esoch realized that it was the slazan with the knife who had been struck, who was falling to the ground, because Esoch's pistol was already aimed, his finger already pulling the trigger. A harsh whisper, and the warrior's leg fell out from under him, his body dropped to the ground. The warrior cried out. He shifted his body on the ground, tried to move so the hand that held his weapon was freed from the weight of his body. Esoch knew what he was thinking. He swung around, his thumb hit the eyeplate, but the hatch was opening too slowly. The warrior by now had turned enough to free his hand from under his fallen body and raise the gun. The hatch was open now, but he had no time to hide. Esoch aimed his pistol and pulled the trigger and he heard the sudden quick explosion, the clap of hands, something hard against a leg, his body falling, the hull of the ship cracking against his back, his back sliding down against the metal, the ground rising hard up against him. Everything flashed white. He tried to sit up, but his eyes closed instead. The last things he felt were the ground against his back and the pistol in his hand. The last thing he heard was the door above him sliding shut.

When I, Flatface, and Squawker reached the hillside, each woman saw something horrifying. Squawker saw Hugger's body lying in the middle of the clearing. His chest looked like someone had started a fire there and then had wiped everything away but the ashes. I saw the Stranger lying almost curled up, in the strangest of positions; she didn't know if he was alive or dead. Flatface saw for the first time the second animal and the destruction that surrounded her. The sunlight made everything look so clear.

Flatface and Squawker didn't know what to do. There were Clever Fingers' remains in the clearing and the possibility that his true body could still be there. I couldn't stay with them. She ran to Hugger first, but speed had not mattered. He no longer breathed. There was a dark hole in his chest, and a few speckles of blood had broken through. It was as if his chest had been baked the same way as the ground. What could have done that to him? In Hugger's left hand was the knife that had killed Huggable.

She crouched by the second animal, who was still breathing, a slow, raspy breath that came out in different lengths, more like a musical pattern than like breathing. I looked for a moment at the dark lines cut into her forehead and between her eyebrows, much like the scars the women from the river's mouth wore on their arms or chest. The second animal's leg was twisted, the legging had been burned, and the skin had been burned, the same way as Hugger's chest. In her hand was something hard, made out of the same material as the surface of the boulder. I removed it and placed it in her carry bag.

The Stranger's side and his shin were both the color of blood, but the blood wasn't flowing out the way it had from Clever Fingers' thigh. The Stranger's breath was hardly visible or audible. Had so slight a wound almost killed him? In his hand was something shaped very much like the thing she had taken from the second animal's hand. She removed this one, too, and placed it in her carry bag.

Flatface and Squawker's curiosity must have overtaken their fear of breathing in a true body, because each woman was now making her way down the hill. I returned her attention to the Stranger and the second animal. She carefully looked at each of their wounds. She wanted each one at her hut and hearth, where she had her herbs, where she had her gzaet. She did not want to leave them here to breathe in Hugger's true body.

I stood up and said, "I will share a generous portion of the next lightfoot or nightnose that I kill to the one or other who will share their strength to carry each of these to where I sleep."

Squawker was still standing by Hugger, still looking down at the darkness of his chest. She exhaled loudly; she had been holding her breath. "Did the animal do this?" Her voice was soft, hard to hear, and she instantly closed her mouth so as not to take in a true body.

"Look," said Flatface, who stood there nervously, looking anxious, "this is a different animal. Its color and size is different. Only the shape is the same."

Squawker took a look at the second animal, then back to Hugger, as if there was nothing about the animal worth looking at. She exhaled. "Did this animal do this?" She firmly closed her mouth.

"Of course," said Flatface. "A person wouldn't do this."

I was surprised by her own anger. "A person wouldn't do this?" She walked, clean, hard strides, around Squawker and stopped at Hugger's sprawled-out hand. She crouched down, pried open the fingers, and lifted the knife. The blade still had Huggable's blood on it. "What was this doing in his hand? What do you think Hugger was trying to do?"

Squawker looked away no. Flatface looked to the ground.

"Hugger thinks the animal killed Huggable. Hugger wanted to put an end to the animal."

Squawker said, "Watches Everything may have angered each of you with his embraces. But he never harmed with words. He never harmed with blows."

"He remained by a dead woman's body," said Flatface. "He must have breathed in the true body. The true body wanted the animal dead, not Hugger."

"I will share my strength," said Squawker. "I do not want another person to die. But I will not help move the animal."

"The animal," said Flatface, "should be left here to die. Then there will be no more trouble."

"Yes," said I, "there will. The first animal left. Not much later the second animal arrived. If this animal dies, there will be another. Then another. And then another. These animals are able to do things no person here can do. They wear things that disappear. The hilts of their knives change shape. They have rocks filled with drawings that move. I share this idea with you. I heal this animal. I don't ask her to share food with me. I don't ask her to give me a gift one of her mates has made. I ask her to go back to where she lives with others like her and to tell them not to come here. If we have one more here, we have more trouble and more death."

Flatface looked hard at I. "How can you talk of sharing gifts and food with an animal? You talk about this animal as if you were talking about a person."

"This is a person who is not a person. She has two legs. She has two arms. She has one head. And she has something that burned inside Hugger's chest until he died. She is not like a lightfoot. She is not like a nightskin. If she dies, I and you and you will see more like her. Do you want that? Do you?"

Squawker could only stare at Hugger's dead body. She said nothing.

Flatface looked away no, but she didn't return her gaze to I. She kept looking far off into the woods. "We need another woman to help."

Esoch didn't know how long he had been lying outside the shuttle, or if he was truly still alive. He opened his eyes for a moment. A slazan face looked down. Esoch closed his eyes, then opened them to look again. The slazan had bright-red hair, unlike any other. It was Slazan N!ai. Why was she looking down at him? Wasn't there something wrong about staring so long into someone's eyes? He averted his gaze, and the gesture caused pain to fill his entire head.

Sleep was easier.

So he slept, but it was the kind of sleep where the hard ground underneath could still be felt, where the direction of dreams slipped away from his control.

He saw N!ai. His N!ai. Her eyes were bright. She smiled coyly. Three scars angled across each cheek, giving her the beauty of the zebra. He reached up to trace each one. Above her head was the canopy of a //gxa grove. Beyond that was the bright light and hard heat. He remembered why they had come here, even though the grove had been well picked already. "We should go," she said. "We have gathered so little. My sister and my brother will joke endlessly about this."

"You are my wife. Husbands and wives go away to do these

kinds of things. What's wrong if they joke? When your sister marries, you will joke with her about the same things."

"My sister will ask if I was getting food or making music. She will tell me music won't fill my belly or end my hunger. I am tired of that joke. You should be tired of it, too."

Esoch felt the familiar feeling sink into him, the same sulky resentment. But N!ai hadn't said that at the //gxa grove. Why was he remembering it wrong? N!ai had said that much later, during !gaa, when the sun burned away at everything, when he had whispered to her that they should find some food to eat together out in the brush. It was then N!ai had refused to go with him.

Something grabbed hold of his shoulders, something grabbed hold of his thighs. He felt himself lifted off the ground. The pain in his leg was immense. It bore into him like something large and hard, expanding to take over every place where he felt nothing.

He tried to open his eyes. He tried to cry out. He wanted to tell them to leave him here. There were things in the shuttle that would fix him up. There was a program counting down the time, and he had to turn it off. He was being carried. He knew that. Were they carrying him off to his death? Is this what they had done to Pauline? He tried to open his eyes again, and that was the last thing he remembered, except for the pain, which seemed to follow him into unconsciousness.

The not-a-person—the second animal—was carried by the healer and Flatface, the Stranger by Squawker and Flatface's eldest daughter. Wisdom followed carrying the eldest daughter's infant. Following behind her were Flatface's other daughter and her waist-high son.

Flatface's eldest daughter held the Stranger under the shoulders. Squawker held him by the thighs so as not to take hold of the wound on his calf. The eldest daughter observed that Squawker's butt was so close to the Stranger's crotch that she had better be careful that the Stranger didn't think she was announcing her desire. "I'm still giving suck to my daughter," said Squawker. "My teats are heavy and there is no desire."

The eldest daughter said more, but I didn't hear it. She had her arms under the not-a-person's shoulders, and her weight was beginning to pull I down, the pressure of her head uncomfortable against I's belly. Flatface held her by the thighs, and every step seemed to cause the not-a-person's blackened leg to swing, her body to squirm. I could imagine the pain she felt.

And while I watched the awkward leg, Flatface started to ask out loud the questions she must have carried in her mind. "This not-a-person is smaller than the other. Its skin is lighter. It wears different clothes. Is it the same kind of not-a-person? It has no teats. The other one had teats. Is it a woman? Maybe it would be better if it was a man. Maybe a woman not-a-person is more violent than a man."

"The woman not-a-person did nothing violent."

"She killed the woman you call Huggable."

"She had no reason to."

Flatface said nothing.

"She had no reason to kill Huggable, did she?" I's voice was louder, and Squawker and Flatface's eldest daughter stopped talking in order to listen. Flatface still said nothing. All I could see was death. Hugger lying there, the knife in his hands, his chest the color of night, with spots of blood. The Stranger lying distant, a strange object in his hand. The not-a-person lying by the boulder, a strange object in her hand. Blood flowed from each body. What horrible thing had happened?

No one said anything more. Each walked on, weight pulling down on arms.

Flatface's son was not there when the four reached I's hut and hearth, nor had he left any gift behind. Several foodgrabbers could be heard scurrying away. I and Flatface laid the not-a-person down in the shelter. Her wounded leg slapped against the ground, and she groaned. I crouched low, reached out, and with fingertips touched the leg. Flatface had been watching, but seeing the healer touch the not-a-person like a mother touching a sleeping child, she could do nothing but leave the hut.

I didn't look up. She repositioned the not-a-person's leg so that the wound was not touching the ground. The leg moved in two different ways. The not-a-person groaned again. Her eyes didn't open. Sweat covered her face. I touched first the blackened skin. The not-a-person groaned. I felt along the leg, pressing as softly as she could so she could feel through the burned fabric. The leg was broken. It was broken as neatly as dried wood broke; there were no slivers or sharp points of bone that she could feel. But she had no idea how the leg bones of a not-a-person were shaped. If she set the leg and tied wood to it, would the leg heal so this not-a-person could walk again?

She stepped out of the shelter. Squawker and Flatface's eldest daughter had laid the Stranger by the cooking fire. "I would like him in the hut," she said.

Flatface's eldest daughter leaned forward to grab the Stranger's shoulders once again. Squawker did not move. She said, "Each would be too close to the other. The Stranger deserves his solitude."

"If it rains on him, will he deserve his death?"

Flatface said, "We can take the not-a-person out."

"Each will sleep on the other side of the fire. I will play music for both of them. I need them close together."

Flatface's eldest daughter started to pick up the Stranger. "You don't share a mother with him," she said to Squawker, "so let's do what the healer says."

Squawker's eyes went wide with anger. She looked straight to the healer as she passed by. She walked out of the hut almost as soon as she entered, and with no words to share, she walked away and disappeared into the forest. Flatface's eldest daughter stood awkwardly in the opening of the hut and looked to her mother, then to the healer. She opened her mouth to speak but said nothing. She walked over to Wisdom, took the infant into her arms, and left. Wisdom said nothing to the healer. She followed Flatface's eldest daughter.

Flatface remained, her daughter and son standing by the waiting fire.

I said, "You have words to share."

"I have words to share, but I feel that I will say certain words and you will hear different ones."

"I have always listened when you have spoken, but today I have two injured ones who need care. I will listen tomorrow if the words are ones which you can still share."

Flatface looked to the hut's opening. "Each of them must have played a part in Hugger's death. Why heal each one? If one will live on its own, let it live. If it dies, let it die."

I wanted to say that she was a healer, that her mother had healed, that her mother's mother had healed. But such words would only make Flatface more angry, so I respected the older woman's solitude and remained silent. But silence meant there were no kind words that made it possible for Flatface to leave now and return tomorrow. I realized that she didn't long for such words.

Flatface must have sensed the change because she stepped forward and lightly touched I, her fingertips running across I's collarbone. "Your skin is softer. It must be your time." She withdrew her fingers and softened the look in her eyes. "Long Fingers, mate this time. Have a daughter. If you had a daughter to worry you, you wouldn't be so worried about what goes on in the clearing."

The words were soft and kind enough that Flatface could leave.

She examined the Stranger first. There was a wound along the side of his belly, but there was hardly any blood coming out. The same with the wound across his shin; it was much like a deep groove had been cut into him. There should be more blood from such wounds.

His breath was ragged. She placed palm on forehead to feel what music couldn't. The skin was clammy. His eyes snapped open. He wide-eyed her. She was already rising to step away from him when his arm struck out. The blow did cause her to lose her balance and land on her behind, but the blow itself hadn't been hard at all. The blow had been as weak as his breathing. The Stranger wasn't terribly wounded. He was sick with something, and he was dying.

She didn't know what to make of the not-a-person. Was her skin too warm? Was sweat for her the same as sweat for a person? How fast should the heart beat? Was the odd breathing normal? The not-a-person let out a soft sigh, and the fabric around her crotch darkened.

The Stranger had turned his head to watch I. He said nothing. I couldn't leave the not-a-person like this. With the wounded leg, she couldn't remove the leggings. She withdrew knife from sheath and slowly cut away the fabric. The blackened skin around the break was surrounded by skin dark with the color of the setting sun. A scar ran down the calf of the uninjured leg. She removed everything up to the not-a-person's waist. She saw that the not-a-person was a man. Once the leggings were off, she covered his body with an animal hide. She walked out of the shelter, but her mind's eye saw little else but the not-a-person's penis.

She set the gzaet in front of the hut's opening. She played several childhood songs, ones her mother had played to calm her, but the notes came out sour, as if her fingers had forgotten them. She stopped. She was very aware of the Stranger's maleness; she kept seeing him enter Squawker from behind as she held his thighs and carried him here, the comment made by Flatface's eldest daughter now a vivid daydream. When she played another song to take her mind away, she saw the not-a-person's penis, and when she played another song, she saw Nightskin's. She lowered her hands to the lower rows of keys to play music to cool the desire, to make it possible to concentrate, and once she could concentrate, she played music for the Stranger to try to ease his breathing and cool the very different fever that journeyed through his body.

Esoch heard the music, the very distant music, and he heard the closer music of his thumb piano. He sat in the shade one hot !gaa day, where the shade was cooler than the sun, but not much, and waited for the coolness of night. He pressed his thumbs against the keys, and the sound was clear. It didn't jangle like the thumb pianos he and others had made with metal they had traded for at the reserve outposts. He heard again a song he had found, one note that sounded so right after the other, and he played it and played it, glad that the sun scorched the land so that no one would call him lazy for not hunting today.

And the distant music got closer, louder, and his own music became harder to hear, until all his notes were confused by a jangle, by something that couldn't be called a song, that didn't have much of a pattern, or did it? Several phrases sounded with terrible familiarity. But he had never heard such phrases before. They sounded again, and he heard the mother from the experience. *I have food to share,* the same singsong of slazan mother to slazan child, he was hearing it now, then it became something else and it was again a jumble of sounds.

He forced his eyes open. Above him was a thatched roof. It was shaped like a cone. Through the opening he could see blue sky. He tried to lift his head, but that hurt. He listened to the sounds. Who was playing? Was it Slazan N!ai? He tried to lift his head, but the pain was worse this time. Something moved nearby, to his right. He turned his head, and the pain wasn't so bad. Near him were stones surrounding the remains of a fire. Across from that he could clearly see the face of the slazan warrior. The warrior's eyes were open, and he was looking back.

This was too much. He let the pain overtake him; he let the sweet blackness return.

I saw music more than anything else, but when she heard the soft scraping of ground as the not-a-person moved, she lifted her eyes from the music. The not-a-person's head was turned to its side. She stopped playing the gzaet and walked into the hut. The not-a-person's eyes were closed. The Stranger's eyes, however, were open, but they had a glazed look, as if he were half-asleep. His skin looked dark, feverish still. She smelled something that hadn't been there before. She had tried to release the Stranger's body of the fever, and all she had released was shit.

"Can you clean yourself?" she said.

The Stranger looked away. I wasn't sure if he meant no, or if he was hiding his eyes from the embarrassment.

The healer said, "Music won't clean your behind."

"Your music won't do much," he said.

"May I touch?"

"No."

I started to walk away.

"Healer?"

She walked back and stood by the Stranger's feet. She looked to his forehead, not his eyes.

"I can't clean myself. I can't ask you to clean me. I have nothing to share."

"May I touch?"

"I won't strike you."

"Remember yourself as a child. This was done to you as a child before you loved your solitude."

"I am not a child."

"I know."

The Stranger kept his eyes averted. The leggings were connected to the shirt, as they had been on the not-a-person. The Stranger could not sit up, so she had to do what she had done with the not-a-person. She sharpened the knife on her stone, and she slid it up the inside of the leggings, surprised at how easily the blade cut through the skin. Even so, the Stranger still groaned with each jerk of his body, and she did her best to move slowly. Along his legs were tiny welts, hard and the color of blood. They were a bit larger than the bites of an earbuzz. She closed her eyes, made the image of the insect, then the look of the bite, then the look of these bites. The memory came back to her, and she went to the wall and took down a string of memory beads.

She felt along each bead, feeling for shape, looking at color. A newborn, who had sucked from his mother's teats only a few times, was brought to I's mother—when I watched everything her mother did—and her mother had tried to play music for it, but the welts did not disappear; the newborn's skin darkened the

way the Stranger's skin darkened, and he died. Another few
beads, another memory, an older child, with bites like this, who
sweated, who listened to the music and was fine. Might there be
no earbuzzes where the Stranger lived, and might the Stranger be
like a newborn, ready to suffer from whatever it was in the bites
that made your skin rise and itch?

She returned to the Stranger and the leggings were whole
again. It was as if she had never cut through them. She left the
hut, walked back and forth, her heart striking at her throat, and
considered leaving. She could pick up the gzaet, her memory
beads, and head for Small Lake, where Lightfoot Watcher and
other women would welcome her.

She placed her finger against the blade of her knife. It was
still sharp. In the hut again, crouching by the Stranger, she sliced
the leggings, cut away at them, taking advantage of the ease with
which the skins parted. She tossed the remains at the hut's wall
and didn't watch to see where they landed. She didn't want to
see what the skins did.

She cleaned him with water, taking longest with what had
stuck to his scrotum. She found herself looking again at his penis, the way it lay smoothly against his belly. She finished her
task, covered his body, and hurried away.

"Healer."

His voice stopped her. "What?"

"Where I come from, no one uses music the way you use
music. Healing is different."

I said nothing.

"Near the clearing is the bag that I wear on my back. Inside
it is the healing I need. Get it for me. Inside are things I can
share with you."

She said nothing. How could he have something to cure a
sickness he'd never had before? Or was this a sickness he understood and she didn't?

"Everything of mine is yours if you will get the healing."

What could he have that she wanted?

"If you don't, I will surely die."

That was something she didn't want.

When both were asleep, she made her way to the clearing.
She didn't like the thoughts that came to her mind, so she
thought about the not-a-person's broken leg and considered what
to do.

She came to the hill that overlooked the clearing. The

pointed-ears were nowhere to be seen. She rattled some bushes, and the nightwings flew into the sky. Hugger was meat and bones. His mouth spoke to the sky. His eyes had been plucked out.

She had to look hard. There were few signs of the Stranger's spoor, and she kept thinking that she should hurry back. One of them might have awakened by now. She found the bag among some young berry bushes that would offer their fruit at the end of the summer.

It was the color of muddy water, and it seemed larger than she remembered it. She placed one fingertip atop it, pulled the fingertip away, then touched it again. Fingers glided over the smooth softness; it felt like the well-worn skin of an animal.

She lifted it up, and its weight took her by surprise. She almost dropped it on her foot. He had carried this until this morning, sick as he was. How did he have the strength? Or did he have some special healing that made him strong? The idea was an odd one, one that she didn't want to believe, but she had seen enough to believe that each of these injured people could do anything but heal their own injuries.

But down in the clearing were Hugger's remains, and she knew that there must be more than healing in this bag. She wanted to open the bag and see what it contained, but search as she did, she could find no opening. There were no strings to tie one piece to another. Worse, there were no seams, no sign that one part of the animal skin had been attached to another.

Perhaps it would be best to leave the bag here. But how could she leave it? If he didn't get the healing, he said he would die.

It took her a while to figure out how to slide her arms through the straps of the bag, and once she did, the weight caused her walk to become a stagger. She wanted to walk quickly, but she felt as if she were carrying a lightfoot over her shoulders. It became only slightly bearable when the part of the bag against her skin, over time, seemed to mold itself to the curve of her back.

A long call sounded through the woods. I stopped, and she listened. She didn't recognize the voice, but it was the deep-throated call of a grown man. Someone new was wandering near the river, perhaps seeing if a man who always built his nest in the area would call back to question his presence. No one called back. The man called out again. The call was near. She liked the deep music of his voice. If she wanted to look later, she knew it would not be hard to find where he had stopped to build his nest.

Each was still asleep when she returned. She played some music to calm the desire she felt, but when she stopped playing, she once again thought about looking for the man who had been calling nearby.

She also thought about the two objects in her carry bag. One was the color of the boulder. The other one was the color of sun and of the sky; that one had been held by the Stranger. She picked it up in her left hand. She did not know how to hold it, nor did she remember how the unconscious Stranger had held it. She tried to hold it in a number of ways, until she found one way that made such sense that she called herself stupid for not gripping it that way sooner. And soon the part she held became comfortable in her hand. Just like the hilt of the knife.

Fear overcame curiosity. She did not want to know any more. She carried the bag and the objects to behind the midden. With a thin digging stone that had been gifted to her mother, she dug a hole. She placed both objects into the hole and buried them. Nearby was a seedling, a softleaf she had planted to let grow high enough to make a new bow. It marked for her where she had dug the hole.

In the hut each one still slept, so she left to gather food. She wanted fruitnuts and flatleaves, but most of that had been picked away, and she did not want to offer sourleaves or flatseeds, of which there were plenty, because they were food she would eat only when she was hungry. One snare held a roundtail. She cut the carcass loose and placed the body in her kaross. Some meat would be good.

She made her way to where she, Flatface, and Flatface's eldest daughter would gather. The paths through this part of the woods led neither to the river's mouth nor to Small Lake, so it should still offer more food than other parts of the wood. I sang several healing songs, a way she had of recalling patterns to play, the voice in her mind reminding her that she had to play something to heal each one, and since she gathered where one woman or another might also gather, she every now and then took hold of a branch and snapped it.

Someone else was also snapping branches, and the sounds came closer. I considered turning back; she did not want to see Flatface again today. Instead it was Flatface's eldest daughter, whom I used to call Clear Eyes. She carried her infant with her, who was kept by her side in a sling that also rested in the kaross. The child was making sounds, so as she walked, Clear Eyes used her forearm to lift her up and help her mouth reach the nipple to suck.

"I am here and gathering," I said to her.

"I am here and getting a sore teat," said Flatface's eldest daughter.

Each walked, moving at a distance, but in the same direction, eyes stopping whenever they came to something worth picking. Each knew the area well, so when one turned, the other knew what leaves or roots the first was looking for.

"After I left your hut and hearth," said the eldest daughter, "I heard a stranger call out, and this afternoon I saw that he was building a nest between where you and I live."

"I heard him, too."

"I saw him. He is large and well-shaped. Since Long Call's death, we have missed having another pair of hands living nearby. And perhaps he can offer a woman in desire something more than his hands."

"Did someone say something to him in passing?" I asked. "Is that why he is building his nest so near to where I gather food?"

"Is there another who gathers around here who does not give her teat to a child?" She looked to the healer with round, friendly eyes. "My mother once told me that a man who is a stranger is the best if you want to enjoy what you desire."

"Your mother will also tell you that a stranger is the worst if what you desire is a child."

"But when the desire is still early, isn't it best to enjoy?"

"It is good to enjoy." In her body she could almost feel how long it had been since she had felt such enjoyment. Such a strong feeling embarrassed her, so she said nothing.

"Perhaps he will stay and father many girls."

"Maybe he should have nested near Crooked."

"Childless has stopped mating. She shared food with me and said she mated with each male from another place who came to see the boulder. She is sure she is pregnant."

"She will have to wait to see."

"She is very hopeful."

"She has been pregnant before."

"Perhaps if the one inside her is fed well and perhaps if Childless lets a good healer play good music to encourage the one in the womb to stay this time, then I might have to call her another name."

"There is said to be such a good healer far away from here."

"I know there is a good healer who lives close to me. When I was a child and she was a child, I used to hold her close and look into her eyes. I didn't think that such a girl would become a woman who tried to heal an animal who killed a person."

I stopped tugging at the root in the ground. She stood up. Clear Eyes continued to pluck at leaves, as if she had said something about the nature of the rain or the moisture of the soil. "I heal anyone who can say 'I am here; you are there.' "

"Then why," said Clear Eyes, still not looking, "do you heal the animal?"

"Because," said I, hesitating a moment, considering if she wanted to utter the lie that had taken shape in her mind, "he can say those words."

I had expected a reaction. Clear Eyes said nothing. The baby girl wanted to suck again, and Clear Eyes stood up to maneuver the child to her teat. She walked over to a nearby tree and used her flatrock to scrape some woodeaters into her palm. She ate those, then moved on to gather more, moving away from I, without any kind of word, just as when she had left I's hut and hearth. I could have followed, but she did not. She watched Clear Eyes walk farther and farther away.

Esoch awoke to distant pain, to the malaise of lying in one place for too long, and to the sound of digging. The sound wasn't one of metal slitting dirt, but that of something hard scraping at the dirt. He listened, felt himself fade into sleep, hearing N!ai's digging stick jam at the gray compacted sand around the giant !xwa root: fibrous, tasteless, but filled with water. It hadn't rained in days. She tired and passed the digging stick to him, and he continued, clearing the sand around the root. His throat was dry. His body was coated with sweat. Soon the spring rains would start, soon the pans would be filled. But now it was hot and dry. While he dug, N!ai talked about going to N≠ama to visit her older brother, who was married and had two children. Her father had heard the waterholes weren't so dry, that animals had meat on their bones. They had each been making beads from ostrich eggshells, shaping them into gifts to give when they arrived at N≠ama. "The thumb piano would make a good gift to my brother."

"I will make him one."

"The one you make will sound good when played by your fingers. My brother will play well only if he has one that makes good music on its own."

He said nothing. He had heard this before. If he said nothing, if he made another gift, if he made a nice one, no one could say he was lazy or stingy. He worked well with his hands, and he knew his arrows flew straight, that the two or three thumb pianos he had made played well.

And he thought it was understood. He took a long time to choose the right wood, to twist the sinew, to trade for the metal keys. N!ai's mother took some dried meat and some //gxa nuts she had saved and gave them to N!ai to give to him. She no longer complained about him to her daughter. And N!ai smiled at him when no one was looking, and if the nights were cool enough, she pressed her backside to him in their hut, and he covered their body with a chi !kan.

A shadow crossed above him, N!ai was gone, the world sounded empty. He opened his eyes. He heard footsteps—he had to pay close attention because the footsteps were distant, their whisper fading. Beside him the warrior slept. His chest moved; his breathing made no noise. It was easy to close his eyes again.

Esoch eased himself from sleep. Listening first. There was no music. There were birds calling. One set, no, two sets of animal paws probing the camp. He listened to them scurry about and knew they were small creatures. He opened his eyes, and it was harder to listen. The back of his eyes hurt. He lifted his head again. The pain didn't explode, but it felt as if the back of his skull had been deadened by some numbing drug. The sky seen through the hole in the roof was perfectly blue. He felt as if he was being watched, but when he turned to look, the warrior was staring straight up at the hole in the roof.

Esoch did the same. They were lying side by side, divided by a burned-out fire. Part of him had expected to be dead. But he was lying in a large thatched hut, along with the slazan warrior. A group of slazans had carried them here. How long ago? How long until the shuttle lifted off for orbit?

The warrior said something. Esoch almost looked to him, but he remembered to keep his eyes facing the sky.

The warrior said it again. Two words.

They weren't slazan.

Nor Arabic.

Nostratic.

They meant: true people.

They meant: human.

Esoch said, in slazan, "I am here."

"You are there. Your words aren't. Let's speak Nostratic. You do speak Nostratic?"

"Yes."

"My mouth is not shaped for human language. Can you understand me?"

This time Esoch removed his mouth prosthetic and set it on his chest, on the leather blanket that covered him. For the first time he became fully aware of more than the core of pain in his left leg; he became self-conscious of the way the leather rested upon the skin of abdomen and thighs, the way it touched lightly upon his penis, of the oily sweat between scrotum and legs, of the thin layer of stink that coated his inner thighs.

"Can you understand?" the slazan asked.

"Yes. I speak Nostratic." He hadn't spoken it in ages, but the words came to him.

"My craft was destroyed by your warship."

Esoch did not know what to say. He did not want to reverse subject and object, not yet, not until he knew what the warrior wanted.

"You say nothing," the warrior said.

"I was not there."

The warrior was silent for a moment, perhaps contemplating the wisdom of discussing what had taken place in orbit. "On the closer of this planet's two moons is a starship. It is the ship that brought me to this planet. It is berthed in an underground cavern so it would not be detected." The warrior was silent for a moment. Then: "Tell me what I have said so I know we understand each other."

"Your ship is on one of the moons. Your shuttle craft was destroyed. You want to return home."

"No. I want to live. I am dying of some local disease that I am not immune to. The medicine I take compensates for the debilitations it causes, but it does not cure. There is equipment in my ship that will let me live. Tell me what I said."

"You are dying. There is medicine in your ship. You want to use my shuttle craft to get to your ship."

"I want the shuttle craft for you and me to go to my ship. I want to share resources. If you get me to your ship, you will save my life. I will take you to the edge of human space and save your life. You could not live out your life here among slazans. You need touch like a child needs touch, and you are not a child."

Esoch was silent. The warrior hadn't mentioned Pauline. Did he want the slazan to know that there was a second human on this planet?

"Tell me what I said."

"You want a deal. I take you to your ship, you take me to human space."

"You think I will kill you?"

"My shuttle craft is a prize. I am a risk. For months I would be in your ship."

"You are a soldier?"

"Yes."

"Then I am always the enemy. That is why you tried to kill me even though I tried to save your life."

Esoch remembered: the warrior pulling the weapon from behind his back, the local slazan, a hole burned into his chest, falling to the ground.

"The primitive," the warrior said, "was coming for you. He held a knife. He meant to kill you. I shot him. You shot me. You did that because you are a soldier."

Esoch tried to see it all over again, but he couldn't exactly remember it. The slazan had reached behind his back. The local had been running right toward Esoch. The warrior's hand appeared, fist clenched, a weapon in it. Had the warrior been looking to the local, had his weapon been aimed in that direction, or was he just reimagining it that way, making the memory conform to what the warrior had just said?

"You have no words to say. I am the enemy. But think on this: I need you to live. You need me to leave this world. If you let me die, you will be here for the rest of your life."

The following is an undated entry taken from the notebook Pauline Dikobe kept while studying the slazan foraging population on Tienah.

In the history of hominid evolution, the history of hierarchy and violence forms a U-shaped curve. Nonhuman primates who live in groups establish easily observable hierarchies—with the alpha male and the alpha female at the top, while other group members establish various alliances to achieve what the alpha might oppose. Over time there are a number of challenges and responses, overtures and reconciliations, as the hierarchy is worked out.

Among foraging cultures the hierarchy disappears.

Then, during the course of cultural evolution, it reappears. As populations grow side by side, as free-ranging movement becomes limited, people must intensify what they can get out of the land. They may domesticate a fruit or a grain, then include its harvest as part of their seasonal gathering. The more they depend on domesticated animals or crops, the more the ad hoc decisions of foragers can only lead to open conflict. Now some form of leadership makes sense. It might be a headman, someone popular for generosity and thoughtfulness, someone who might lead a massive hunt or encourage by example, by harder work. But when it comes time to invest in weirs to catch fish, in irrigation projects or large-scale storage of crops, the headman becomes a big man, someone who can boast of his abilities, someone who can, with his allies, organize a feast that will outdo all other feasts. The contributions to the feasts become contributions to chiefs, who are hereditary big men, who organize the farming, or the irrigation, who collect food as a kind of tax while, at the same time, fulfilling the obligation to be generous, to insure that everyone eats and no one starves. Because at this point any unhappy individual can still vote with his feet, can still walk off with his family to live with kin living under someone else's more generous, more considered guidance.

At some point there is no place to move. The ones who build the roads from farmland to market, from village to city, the ones who set up the irrigation works, and the ones who collect the taxes to fund this all are no longer chiefs and family and advisers, but kings and armies and priests, for agriculture is efficient enough that not all have to dedicate their life to daily subsistence. There are now great works of art, great works of writing, great developments in thought, and there is tremendous poverty.

And the curve of the U swings back up, with greater strength, as hierarchy is no longer determined by daily encounters but is enforced by heredity, mandated by law. The nature of violence has changed. No longer is violence solely the product of anger, the reach for the arrow or knife. As groups compete, violence becomes something encouraged, trained for, as one group may have to force another group out of adjacent land to guarantee a sufficient supply of food.

But when the state comes into fore, war is no longer waged to force a competing population from the land, but instead is waged to add another population and its land to the state. Violence is now a mechanism of government, a means of competition, a means of social control.

Alongside this, foraging life looks like a paradise from which we were expelled when we bit the forbidden fruit of cultivation.

The Ju/wasi are ruthlessly egalitarian. Meat from a big kill is always divided. The animal is not owned by the hunter who shot it, but by the owner of the arrow. The hunter who has killed the animal does not boast. He returns to camp to say he has found nothing of value, that it's probably not worth going out to get what he shot down. The hunters cutting up the meat complain about the lack of fat, how old the animal is, how the meat will barely fill the belly.

The Ju/wasi talk and talk. They talk about what wasn't properly done. How the meat should have been divided up. How a gift was not generous enough. They tease each other mercilessly. But when there is anger, the talk can heat up, insults can fly, while others step in, ready to work out the problems, to talk out the anger before the fight comes to blows, before one man might grab his poisoned arrows.

Such constant vigilance is required in order to fight the primate trend toward hierarchy, the trend toward violence.

One thinks of the last few centuries, the struggle to define community and culture and the individual; the human need to create a group; the human need to be your own headman—forager egalitarianism, buried in civilization's castes and classes, struggling to make its way up into the open air.

But that's too romantic. In the century when each country preached liberty, 50 million were killed in wars and 120 million were killed by their own governments. While we struggle to remove the violence from our own lives, we transfer the need, we sublimate it into the psyche of the state.

And the slazans? As we try and fail to re-create our egalitarian past, what do they struggle to re-create: the control of masculine violence, to limit it so it's only just the protection of territory? Is that why the captured slazan warriors have been men? And who sends out those men? Who cooperates to plan the slazan strategies of war?

If humans withdrew from slazan space, announced the war was over, would the war end? And knowing that possibility, could human governments ever take the risk?

Chapter Thirteen

The Fifteenth Day

When she was younger and had first felt desire, she had hunted men the same way her mother had hunted lightfoot. She was thoughtful in the hunt, careful in the approach, and passionate in the success. And as you can hunt a single lightfoot only once, so she consumed one man's solitude only on one occasion, and then she sought someone else. She ranged farther than she usually did when gathering, farther than when hunting, because she had no interest in opening herself to an almost-a-man who had just discovered that his penis did more than rain upon the leaves. Her mother turned away from her. A daughter with child would be too busy offering her teat to concentrate on learning music. There was no child the first time, nor the second, and during her next desire she had to run from a man twice her size whom she didn't want, and during the desire after that she was not quick enough to evade the blows and embraces of an almost-a-man who had trailed her for several days.

By then she had taken an interest in the music her mother played, and certain afternoons, while her mother gathered and was too far away to hear, she played, liking the act of playing more than she liked what she heard or what she felt. Now that she cared for the music, I's mother taught her the patterns to play to reduce her desire, and I played them with greater and greater insistence. When I's skin turned soft, her mother mixed water with bitter leaf and the juice of a thin stalk and gave it to I to drink. The bleeding came after a few days, and the desire was gone. Each time after that, I drank the bitterness and played against her desire, and she did not mate again until her hut and hearth had been made. Once the desire came, she mated with Long Call and she mated with Roofer, and then, when she felt that slight release insider her gut, like the snap of a twig, she mated only with Sour Plum, who had given a daughter to Flatface and to Wisdom's eldest daughter. It had been a son, and it had died before her belly had become full with him, before her teats had begun to grow from her chest. Thereafter, she drank the bitterness and played the music. On one occasion and another, the bleeding waited and the desire sounded louder than the music, and each time there had been pleasure and no pregnancy.

This time she had gathered no bitter leaves or stalks, nor had she played against her desire with any insistence. So the desire started between her legs and filled the rest of her the way smoke fills a hut and never seems to leave it. She wanted a child; more than anything she wanted a daughter.

The man—the one Clear Eyes had told her about—called out twice as the forest darkened and the shadows in the clearings lengthened, and he snapped branches to make his location clear. Roofer called out once, but his voice was distant. Old Sour Plum's voice went unheard. A woman—Flatface? Clear Eyes?— might well have told the man that I had reached desire. Not only did he make a lot of noise for a man new to the river, he also had built his nest in a sturdy old tree that grew well within the area where only I gathered.

He was a handsome man, half again taller than she. His eyes were round and clear. His hair had the soft color of freshly fallen leaves. There was a scar across his chest, another along his forearm, but there was no other sign of injury. He said nothing while she looked at him, and then he raised his hands into the air and spread his fingers. Each one was there, and each digit on each finger was there, and each finger had the well-rounded shape of those who worked well with materials.

"I am new to these woods," he said, "and I have made nothing for you."

The truth of those words gave her pause. She had not seen the skill of his work. He had not roamed through these woods, so no one knew how he reacted when he came close to a woman or another man. Desire now seemed like such a foolish thing to have brought her here.

"I have nothing for you," she heard herself say. "I have not hunted in days."

"I have no hunger for meat."

She did not know what to say, and she thought perhaps words were best shared between one child and another or one woman and another. Without averting her eyes, she placed her carry bag on the ground, then removed her pubic apron.

The pleasure she felt flowed along all the paths her desire had dug open. The man, whom she thought of as Made Nothing, was quiet, and he skillfully held himself so that only his thighs touched the back of her thighs, his abdomen touching her rear, and in the quiet of the forest, with so little of his body touching hers, she could concentrate on the feel of his penis inside her and on the pleasure it gave her. He finished before she could, and she did not want to have the desire fill her again during the darkness of night, whispering inside her head all sorts of foolish things she could do. The second time there was less pleasure. He was less skillful, and he started to call out his own pleasure, as if he wanted even the waking nightskin to know. But soon the old feeling came back, rose in her like the river during a storm, and she reached down to take hold of where they joined and to move her fingers until the pleasure filled her and broke her open.

Then it was done, and it seemed unimportant. She became very aware of Made Nothing's body, his closeness to her. The woods around had become dark. There were words one might say, but she left without saying them.

When I returned to hut and hearth, Huggable's daughter was standing near the waiting fire. She was staring down at the blackened log as if she were staring deeply into a blazing fire; she gripped her arms and shivered. She kept looking around her, but somehow she didn't see I until the healer had stepped from the woods. Her hands fell away, her eyes opened wide, and she rushed to the healer like a child to a mother, but she stopped herself and respectfully looked down.

"I am here," she said.

"So you are."

"I have words to share." She said the words with a kind of eagerness, as if she were trying something new. She was still a girl, and here she was acting like a woman.

"Where is Nightskin?"

"She is where she sleeps. She told me to come because I was the one who saw what was seen."

"I have food to share while you share your words."

Huggable's daughter followed I to the cooking fire, but she did not want to sit down. She kept looking to the hut's opening, now as dark as the surrounding woods, as if a true nightskin lurked in there. "Is it safe here?"

"It is safe. Neither one will stand up soon." She handed the daughter some sweet stalk. "Eat, then share."

Huggable's daughter ate so quickly that I gave her own share to the child, who ate that with the same greediness. While the girl ate, I walked to the hut. She listened for their breathing.

She gave the daughter more food, then built up the fire. "Each one is asleep," she said.

"I heard voices," said the daughter.

"Voices?"

"One"—she gestured to the shelter—"spoke to the other, and the other spoke back."

"What was said?"

The daughter looked to the ground as if she had done something wrong. "I heard words, but I did not understand the words. I was too scared to get close. Nightskin said the animal might be dangerous."

"But you did not run away."

Huggable's daughter sat up proudly. "I have words to share."

"Share them."

"I went running too far in the woods." She stopped, tilted her head, and looked up. I could almost see her choose her next words, lose patience before saying with a rush, "I found the body of the first animal."

She didn't understand the words. They were too unexpected. They couldn't be true.

"Healer?"

"You found the body?"

"I was thirsty. There is this hole with water. I thought the water would be cold. I ran to it. The animal was floating there. All I could see was its back."

"Her face was in the water?"

"Yes."

"And she did not move?"

"No."

I felt some unnameable loss. She saw the first animal, the first not-a-person, her pubic apron on, her teats smooth and dark, standing outside her rock, stepping back to let I come out. *I am here* she had said. What could I have done differently that the not-a-person would still be alive?

"Healer? Do you think she died because she killed my mother?"

"No." She heard the anger in her voice. Why did everyone expect evil from each not-a-person?

"But my mother hunted her."

I added more wood to the fire. Sparks flew into the air. The surrounding night became darker. "Your mother hunted the not-a-person?"

"She saw it when it left the clearing, and she left me behind so she could track it. She told me it would make Nightskin happy again. My mother and another woman tracked it. They lost the spoor, but a man told my mother and the other woman that he had seen the animal swimming in the river. They found the spoor again and tracked the animal to the swamp. My mother . . ." The daughter stopped and averted her eyes. The tone of voice changed, as if she had started to tell a new story. "My mother chased the animal into the swamp, and the other woman shot an arrow from behind the bush and hit the animal in the arm. The animal turned, and all it saw was my mother. That's why the almost-a-man stayed by our hut and hearth. My mother was fearful the animal would come for her. My mother said that the animal stood in the swamp and just disappeared, like it had never been there. My mother was scared it would come back, and it did."

"Were you there when the not-a-person came back?"

"I was playing. I was a stupid girl and I was playing. I heard my mother scream and came running back. And . . ." She stopped saying anything.

I could find no words. The girl gained control of her breathing and stared at the fire, saying nothing more. "It is too dark out," said the healer. "I will share my fire, and tomorrow you can return to Nightskin's hut and hearth."

Huggable's daughter turned her face to I. Her eyes reflected the colors of the fire. "But you should come with me. That's what Nightskin said. You should come with me to see the animal's body."

"Nightskin said that?"

"Yes. An old woman had told her about the second animal. Nightskin said that you would need to see the first one to heal the second one. She was right, wasn't she?"

"Why didn't Nightskin come to share the news?"

"She said you would like the words best if I spoke them."

"She was right."

It was soothing to stare at the fire's bright coals, the color of blood bright against the hot darkness. A few flames walked back and forth across the larger log, but these would lie down soon if she did not add more wood. I wanted to know what kind of woman would send a girl out alone in the woods.

The ground was hard, nothing like the reserve sand that accepted the body. He wanted to sleep, but a dull restlessness, a kind of frustrated current of energy, traveled his entire body. He wanted to get up, but the dull pain in his head sharpened when he lifted his skull from the ground. Through the opening in the roof, he could see a small part of the night sky. The stars were clear, tiny bright embers, as bright as they had been in the reserve. Why had he left?

Could he blame it on !gaa's heat, which never let up? At midday the sun was so hot that the sand burned the feet. It was best to seek shade, to dig a hole, urinate in it, and then cover yourself with sand to keep the sweat inside your body. You gathered in the morning or before sunset, and often you carried a branch with leaves to offer the slightest of shades. Everyone had grown tired of eating roots that were bitter, others that were tasteless, but meat animals carried little meat on their bones, their ribs sticking out as a person's ribs stuck out.

People argued, and while everyone who lived in the face of the huts might come together at a dance, while everyone might feel good about living together, the heat remained, and the arguments started again. One night N!ai's father wondered out loud if his wife was seeing another man. He then said he had seen her go off in the bush, and he had seen Debe's footprints follow hers. Others said he was wrong. Others said he shouldn't say such things about his wife. Others said he shouldn't say untrue things about Debe. But still he accused Debe of screwing his wife. He yelled at his wife. He yelled at Debe. "I'm going to get my arrows!" he shouted, but men had already grabbed hold and pulled him away. In urgent voices they told him that he didn't really want to kill Debe; they reminded him of the time old //koshe had shot arrows at a rival and hit someone else by mistake. He wouldn't want to kill someone who had done nothing wrong. Debe was angry, too, fuming and shouting, and several other men had taken him, pulling him away to cool his heart.

≠oma had watched in quiet, dreadful awe because he hadn't

known his wife's father was capable of such anger. And as his daughter's husband, who was to be respectful, it was not his place to pull one man from the other.

The next morning no one in the face of the huts spoke more than necessary. There was a terrible quiet. N!ai's parents had been making gifts in preparation to visit their son and his wife's parents far away in N≠ama, where perhaps there would be more water and better food. So now, after last night's fight, they gathered together what they owned, preparing to leave today rather than later, probably to stay at N≠ama until Debe and his family had forgotten the argument, until it had become a joke, a way of chiding N!ai's father the next time his anger burned like the sun.

But N!ai's mother still suffered from her husband's insults. She saw that ≠oma was gone, and she went to look for him. She found him burying his thumb piano.

"Daughter," she said to N!ai before they left the face of the huts, "why did your husband bury his thumb piano? Won't he want to play it when we rest?"

N!ai looked to ≠oma, and he saw how she wore the same look of betrayal that her mother had worn when her husband had accused her of screwing Debe.

N!ai's mother said, "Why did he promise you the piano so you could give it to your brother? Why does he hoard his piano like a lion hoards his kill?"

He wanted to shout at her, but he respectfully avoided her look. He looked to N!ai instead. "Wife, I made this thumb piano for your brother." He held up the one he had made from wood and sinew. "This one is ugly and plays poorly, but it is not old and battered like the one I play. This one would make a better gift."

"Your husband," said her mother, "does not know what a good gift is."

All talk in the face of the huts stopped. A woman called out from her hearth, "Cousin, you shouldn't talk that way about your daughter's husband."

She turned on the speaker and said, "How should I talk about someone who is so lazy and stingy? How should I talk about someone who would rather play music than hunt meat for his wife? How should I talk about a man who brings back !xwa root when my husband brings back gemsbok? You tell me, cousin, how that thumb piano he plays every night looks more battered and old than that one he made from the poorest of roots."

"It *is* battered, old woman," he cried out. He ran to it, dug it up, muttering to himself, the anger building because he did hoard the thumb piano, the anger building because of all the things he couldn't say to his wife's mother, all the jokes he couldn't share because he hunted with his wife's father and his wife's brother. He walked back to the face of the huts, the thumb piano in his arms. He stood by the large stones where men sat while making arrows. "See how battered this is," he shouted, and he heaved the thumb piano down, and it made a terrible sound. He regretted the sound the moment it was played, but still he picked the piano up and threw it down again. And he stood there crying, "See how battered it is, you old, greedy woman? See?"

There was talk and talk and talk. They were telling her she shouldn't have spoken like that to her daughter's husband—why would he want to stay and hunt for a woman who spoke that way?—but even more were talking to him, asking him how he could have done that, how could he be so stingy, did he think anyone could own something forever, didn't he see how hard his heart had become because he had owned the thumb piano for too long?

He told them he was not wanted here, that he was too stingy, too hard-hearted, and he left, he walked away, but they were grabbing him, the woman whose husband was named ≠oma was calling him husband, those whose sons were named ≠oma were calling him son, those whose brothers were named ≠oma were calling him brother, and they were pulling him back, warning him about the lions that would eat him up if he left, reminding him about his wife, whom he had to hunt for so her body would glisten with fat once the rains came, who would one day give birth to children, who would need the meat he would hunt.

So he left with his wife's family, and he listened to N!ai's mother speak in harsh whispers to her husband, who glanced up at ≠oma with an almost apologetic look before he told his wife to hush. They stopped that night. N!ai's mother placed a large stick into the ground to represent where her hut would be, and N!ai placed a stick where theirs would be. Fires were built. N!ai offered him roots and gwa berries, but she did not speak to him, as her mother had not spoken to her. N!ai went to sleep beside her mother, and her mother did not send N!ai back to her husband. So he lay there and stared at the stars and imagined other possibilities until he was sure everyone was asleep. Then he rose and left. He would play music for the foreigners, and he would live like a male lion who did not have to share. He expected a lion to take him that night, but none did.

Two days later it rained just long enough to clean him of his sweat. The next day the land was touched with tiny specks of green. Later that day he stopped himself and looked off in the direction of N≠ama. He imagined what N!ai would say to him. What her mother would say to her sisters and her friends. He imagined all the stories they would tell. How they would never let him forget.

But still he stood there and stared while it began to rain, while the sand sucked up the water with a hiss, while roots drank in what water they could; and he imagined how quickly N≠ama would be surrounded by green, how tonight they might dance all night long, so what did he expect at Chum!kwe that would be so good, why hadn't he turned and gone back?

There was no going back now. Not unless he believed the warrior. A starship. Hidden on the moon. Just waiting. Ghazwan and Hanan were dead, Pauline was missing—why was it he who was being given the chance to escape? Perhaps he could get this slazan to talk with the local slazans; perhaps they would help him find Pauline. But would the warrior take two humans back?

The slazan warrior slept. Esoch said "I am here" several times, but the warrior did not respond. How would he mention Pauline? If nothing else, he wanted to ask the warrior how long they had been here. Was this the first night or the second?

He wanted to know if tomorrow was the day, or if it was the day after that when the shuttle would rise from the clearing and up into the skies, where it would detonate, disappear into blue nothingness, the remaining debris scratching invisible lines beneath the midday sun.

He wanted to know if the slazan warrior was truthful. Could people who lived a life around solitude afford to lie? Did honor mean something more than words? Or would the slazan take him captive the moment the shuttle had docked with the slazan starship? The slazan could return home with the prize of recent human technology and a human prisoner to spare. Or would the slazan murder him and remove all risk of betrayal?

Perhaps he should betray the slazan first. Then he would have the slazan starship. And then what?

Esoch had to keep telling himself that Hanan was dead.

And next to Esoch was a shadow. His breathing had grown worse, raspy and short. Before night had stolen most of the colors away, Esoch had noticed how different the warrior's skin

looked, how dark it had become. The warrior's body had begun
to stink of shit. It was hard to connect this man in his imagination with the one who had fired the weapons that had ended
Hanan's life.

Esoch wanted to hate him.

The Sixteenth Day

In the morning the healer came and cleaned each of their
bodies. Esoch watched her, and she kept her head turned so he
could not see her face. The hands moved with tremendous efficiency. He wanted to apologize. He wanted her to know how
ashamed he felt. He didn't know why he should feel this way.
His leg was broken, and there were no bedpans. But each spread
of wet cloth between his buttocks, around his testicles, came
away with shit and dignity. He wanted to say something, but
what few words in his repertoire would have any meaning to
her?

She played music after that, stopping once to say something
to another slazan. The other one's voice was higher-pitched, like
a child's. Was the healer also a mother? Then the music resumed,
mostly jangle, but he started to hear some patterns. The warrior's
eyes were closed. If he had wakened this morning, he didn't
show it. But as the music played, his head shifted back and forth
as if he were negating something.

The healer walked in and stood for a moment at their feet.
She left then. He heard two sets of footsteps head away from the
hut. The other one spoke, and the voice was distant.

He was alone now. What was he supposed to do?

The sky above was perfectly blue.

He listened to the warrior's ragged breath. He wanted to
ask: Why did you come into orbit? Why did you attack? But the
warrior's eyes were closed. He breathed. He would stop breathing. His death would make everything easier.

The body floated as if it had been hung there. I, who stood
at the edge of the spring, had to watch closely to see the body
at all. What it wore had become the color of the water. I could
make out the lines of the back, where the legs hung from the
body, where the black hair of the head drooped away at the other
end. The bag it had worn on its back was gone.

I had walked here with Huggable's daughter, all the while
hoping that the first animal—the not-a-person who had worn the

ugly kaross—had been lying in the spring, her head on land, her mouth and nose open to the air. I had known Hugger since his mother had first come to the river and had set up hut and hearth with a knee-high girl and an infant boy. Why did I now feel a greater loss than when she had seen Hugger lying upon the blackened ground, something black and hard burned into his chest?

Huggable's daughter stood by her side, but she did not look to the spring water. Her eyes were turned up to watch I's face. I expected her to ask something, if the not-a-person would kill anyone else, but the girl said nothing.

Nightskin stood nearby, her left hand grasping a large limb, torn from a tree, most of its branches broken off. She held it like one might hold a staff and stood there firmly, as still and as strong as the piece of wood she held.

She had used her stone knife to shape it last night so the healer and she could pull the body ashore. Nightskin had left one branch on so that end of the limb curled round like a hook. She now lifted the limb off the ground, reached out with it, and snagged the body with the curved end.

The body did not come easily. It rolled in one direction, then the other. And soon Nightskin, who had stood with such dignity, now moved her feet this way and that, leaned forward, pulled back, and Huggable's daughter had started to giggle, when the body unexpectedly rolled over, and its face rose from the water, its eyes open and blank. Huggable's daughter cried out and ran to hide behind a thickbark tree.

All the questions the girl had asked I on the journey here came back. Why can't the body be left there? What about the true body? What if it can be breathed in? Maybe it would be better to leave her body there. There was plenty of water to drink elsewhere. A leg was a leg; why couldn't the healer fix the second animal's leg without looking at this animal?

But I wanted to see what the body was like.

She wanted to know what a not-a-person was.

And Nightskin, unlike anyone else, understood that.

Huggable's daughter was now and again peeking from behind the tree when the body hit against the bank and while Nightskin and the healer struggled to get the body onto the dry ground.

Then it was on the grass, and what it wore now became the color of the ground, the colors of mud and grass, and Nightskin stepped back. It was surprising to see Nightskin so scared.

The not-a-person's mouth and eyes were open. The eyes looked more like those of a fish than those of a person. The skin was wrinkled, and it had become the color of ashes. The stink of death soon chased away all other scents.

Nightskin said, "I will take the daughter back to hut and hearth. I have food to share if you are hungry later."

"I have food to share for all your help."

Huggable's daughter did not argue when Nightskin took her away, leaving I alone with the body. The sounds of the forest surrounded her. The sounds went on as if nothing of importance was happening here in this tiny clearing around the spring.

She removed her medicine knife from its sheath and set it by the body. She took several steps back. She placed the bag on the ground. Her vest followed. On top of that she placed her pubic apron. It was easier to bathe than to make new clothes. From her leather bag she took out one of the pieces of cloth she had traded for, and she tied it around her face. Her lips and nose were covered. She could breathe, but she hoped once again no true body could enter like air through the cloth.

To start was harder than she had imagined. Like the other bodies she had cut open, it belonged to someone she did not know. The woman had not shared food or fire with her. But so much of the past days had been controlled by this woman's presence, that I felt like she knew this not-a-person—this woman who'd worn a plain, ugly kaross—even though she had only been given the opportunity to say three or four words.

I touched what Ugly Kaross wore first. The skins were smooth to the touch, but every now and then you could feel a thin line that ran along the length of what she wore. I found where the arrow had struck the arm, where the blood must have been spilled. It did not look like the kind of injury that could kill, but a lightfoot could be felled with a lesser shot. At the waist were several pouches. She pulled at the tops, and each pouch came open. One had something black and shiny as a rock; in its center was something flat that looked like water. Was this the object Ugly Kaross had looked at while walking along the paths she didn't know? Another pouch had an object just like I had found in the second not-a-person's hand. She placed this one in her carry bag to bury by the first one. On the other side of the body, one pouch held something small and round. I placed it in her carry bag. The last pouch was shaped like a sheath to hold a knife, and it was empty. Had this sheath held the knife that killed Huggable? Had Old Sour Plum and Flatface been right about this woman, this not-a-person, this animal?

It did not take long for I to find out how the skins came open. The eye could hardly see it, but when she tugged at the neck, the whole thing came undone in a nice line from neck to loin. But the body was too stiff to twist her arms out of the skin, and this made I wonder how long had it been since the animal, the woman, had died. How had she ended up here in this spring?

I cut away at the skins. The body, even dead, the skin wrinkled, the muscles of one arm gouged by an arrow, was something to look at. The shape of the legs, of the arms, the look of the muscles and how they showed you the way they were used, all gave a body beauty. You could only stare and admire such beauty when the body was dead.

And this body, this body like none she had ever seen before, had its own kind of sense. It struck I almost with a force, like a strong wind that halted you in your tracks, how similar and how different this body was. I could not help but reach out and touch one of the teats, then press it. It was solid. Not the solidity of muscle, more like the firm softness around the waist and buttocks during the fall, when food seemed to ripen faster than one could eat it. The teat was not just a sack of milk that would shrink away once an infant stopped nursing. These teats remained.

And there were the genitals, which were covered with hair, which was odd. The lips were shaped differently. They were thinner and did not seem to hang from the body. She did not touch anything else.

She could spend all day looking at the body, but there was the leg to consider first. What were the bones like? She went back to the carry bag, took out her stone, and sharpened the knife.

The warrior still slept.

Esoch forced his head up, the pain along the back of his head returning, making everything inside him waver, awakening the reciprocal pain in his leg. He wanted to see the clearing where Slazan N!ai had built her fire. The land was bathed in light. He laid his head back, the hard rock of pain dissipating into a vague mist. The sky above was perfectly blue. It had to be close to midday. If this was the second day, then it was too late.

The slazan locals had to have carried them here, so they couldn't be too far away from the clearing. The warning siren would be loud enough that it should sound like a distant wail. Once he heard it, he would know that he was stranded here forever.

He waited and heard nothing.

Through the hole in the hut's roof he watched a large white cloud float overhead, eclipse the sky, then float away, trailing blue behind it. He wondered where Slazan N!ai was, why she'd been gone so long. Could there be some council of slazans deciding their fate? The one who came at him with a knife must surely be dead. Someone would want retribution.

Time passed. The warrior slept. The light shifted.

It had to be past midday. He hadn't heard a siren. He had one more day to make it back to the shuttle.

It was close to midday when I was finished. The sun shone through the break in the canopy and lit up the grasses where she had worked, where the blood had spread like a darkness around the woman. High up, leaves had started to change colors. I looked at the woman's face and wondered what thoughts had gone on behind those eyes. It was then she saw the darker marks on the woman's dark neck. This skin bruised like a person's skin. I touched fingertips to throat. It was easy to find it, shaped like a tiny tree trunk, where a person could feel herself swallow. I touched along the length of the throat, felt it again, thumb on one side, fingertips on the other. She could trace where it had been crushed.

What I felt was so enormous that she had no words to describe the emotion that fell through her like a rock through water. First Clever Fingers. Then Huggable. Then Hugger. And now this not-a-person, this woman who had worn an ugly kaross. Who would get mating close to the not-a-person and kill her?

I bathed in the river. She took handfuls of mud and pebbles to scrape away the blood on her body. She had always thought that a person was worth healing just because she was a person, and now she wondered if that was no longer true.

In the distance she heard Old Sour Plum's long call, and she found herself paying attention to the up and down of its music, to where in the woods the old man might be. All this blood, and desire still persisted.

She wanted to think of other things, thus she made it that her mind's eye did not see corpses, but instead saw both a bone and a broken bone. She saw muscles around each bone. She was already building the splint, knowing it wouldn't be much different from the splint she would have made before she had seen the body. But her mind was thinking music, patterns, of reaching out into the not-a-person, now knowing more about what to listen for in response. She knew what music to try to play. Did the not-a-person know how to listen?

There was a roundtail caught in one of her snares. It wasn't much meat, but it was some. Another snare had caught a pointed-ears, who was still struggling to escape. I, who had no love for pointed-ears, left it to hang there.

Flatface was waiting for her at I's hut and hearth. Flatface did not stand by the cooking fire as she did when she called to I and I was still in the hut. This time Flatface stood by the waiting fire.

I did not know how long Flatface had been there. Perhaps she still wanted to share the important words she had spoken of yesterday, or perhaps she wanted to know if I had mated with the man who had built a nest nearby. But now important patterns were playing through I's head, and she wanted her fingers upon the keys. She wanted to set the splint and play the music.

"I am here," said Flatface.

"I am here, too. You came with words to share."

"Yes."

"I have words, too. The not-a-person is dead."

Flatface said nothing, and I knew what words she had to share.

"Huggable's daughter said her mother had hunted the not-a-person. She said that another woman was with her and fired an arrow at the not-a-person. You went with her and shot the arrow."

"No. The woman you call Huggable shot the arrow."

"Did you then track down the woman and kill her?"

Flatface looked away no. "Huggable and I had tracked her to the swamp. She fired at the animal after it had gone into the swamp. Then the animal disappeared. We could not see it. Huggable grew fearful. I was scared, too. The animal disappeared, like it hadn't been there. We returned to the river as quickly as we could."

"Why?"

"What are you asking why about?"

"Why did you hunt the not-a-person?"

"The animal. We hunted an animal. Nothing had gone right since its boulder fell from the sky. Huggable had been waiting for it to leave the clearing. She thought all her problems would end if the animal was gone. She had asked for my help when she saw the animal leave. The tracks were easy to follow until they came to the river. We headed south. We thought she might go to where there were fewer people. We lost her trail, but we ran into a man who had seen her. She was in the river and trying to come out. He had heard of the animal and was scared, so he pushed her back in. Huggable and I followed the river until we found the tracks where she had emerged. We followed the tracks until we found her near the swamp."

I heard the words, heard what they meant, but she couldn't help but turn away. Flatface could speak to her back.

"Healer," said Flatface, "it was an animal. And we should have tracked it down. It later killed Huggable. If it hadn't died, it might have killed me."

I wanted to say something. She wanted to say how the hilt of the knife had changed shape, how things the Stranger had held also changed shape. But she couldn't say this without making up her own lie. What the woman had worn had a sheath. The sheath was empty. Had she lost her knife? Or was Flatface right? Had Ugly Kaross killed Huggable?

"Healer, you act like one who has no words to share."

"The not-a-person had done no evil. It walked out of the rock. That is all. One, then another, did the evil. A woman hit Roofer. Roofer hit the woman. Huggable shot an arrow at Roofer, and the arrow killed someone else. Why hunt the animal?"

"A small boulder with legs landed near the river's mouth. It did many strange things. The boulder with legs was destroyed, and nothing evil happened at the river's mouth. Here, by the river, the boulder stayed. The animal in it stayed. Look what has happened."

"So you listened to Nigthskin." I faced Flatface, her eyes wide. "So you want to impress Nightskin. Is that why you hunted an animal who looks more like a person than an animal? Is that why you shot an arrow at her? Do you want Nightskin to share her meat with you? Do you want to share words with her? Do you like the feeling of safety? Destruction didn't start with the animal. It started when Nightskin arrived."

"You share words, Healer, but they are full of envy. By the river's mouth she destroyed the small boulder. Here the larger one falls from the sky. The animal comes out, you play music, you watch, and a person dies. You follow the animal, and you lose its trail. You go to the Many Huts and find no wisdom. And another person dies. You will make sure the second animal lives, and another person will die. Yes, you are the healer. No healer would help a wounded pointed-ears, but you will heal the animal in your hut, and you will make the Stranger lose his solitude by lying close to it. You are the healer. You are used to how another listens to your voice. You want each set of ears to hear only your words. Nightskin might have better words. You say what you say for no good reason."

I could not think of one specific thing Nightskin had done that could be truly called wrong. I could think only of Huggable's daughter, shivering and hungry by the fire. She could think only of Nightskin's search for mates, the easy way desire came to someone who was no longer a newly-ripe woman or an almost-a-man who had just discovered his erections. She could think only of the way Nightskin had offered her a dead body. She wanted to tell Flatface about Nightskin's genitals, but she wanted to say that only to poison Flatface's feelings. And how could she say anything, when Nightskin had made it possible for I to do something that Flatface would find terribly wrong? It was then that I knew that she was behaving just like a woman from the river's mouth. I could accept Nightskin only when she had done something so important that I had no choice but to share food and words with her.

Flatface had no further words to share. She spoke no soft words this time. She averted her eyes, then let her feet follow what her eyes saw.

For a while I could do nothing. She stood there and remembered everything she had done. What could she have done differently?

Esoch couldn't decide which was worse, the sharp pain in his right leg or the dull coating of pain along the back of his head. He had rested too much to sleep, and all the energy in his body asked for movement.

The voices he had heard, the ones that had awakened him, had stopped just a while ago. How solitary a species was it if two of them could go on talking at such length? How much of what he knew about slazans was propaganda? How much was misunderstanding?

The light in the hut diminished; there was the sound of movement. N!ai must be standing in the entranceway. Esoch wanted to raise his head but couldn't. The warrior said a word.

Esoch could make out the sound *gza*, which meant medicine, in the sense of something that heals, but the other sounds slipped around him.

"I am here," N!ai said.

The warrior said more. The sound *gza* again, then a word for carrying—or was it the word for bag?—followed by the word for back.

N!ai said no. The words came out. She spoke more slowly than the warrior, but the sounds still came out too quickly.

The warrior spoke again, enunciating his words more carefully. Esoch did not know if this was because he was trying to control his anger or if he thought N!ai was too stupid to understand, but the words had to do with gza in a bag he wore on his back. He used the word *die*.

N!ai said nothing. Esoch wanted to raise his head, see the expression on her face. She spoke then: the words *death*, *destruction*, the foul version of a word that meant *to hug*, the word *death* again, then the word *no*—no medicine, no bag, no more destruction.

The warrior spoke, using the word *music;* no, not music, some other word built around *gza*.

The last time N!ai had spoken, there had been a tension in her voice, much like the way her voice and the other voice had sounded when they had talked to each other. This time her voice was quiet. Esoch felt like there was defeat in the voice, but how could he tell? "I will play," she said, the word *play* being the word used when one talked about playing music. It was also the kind word for *touch*, as in a mother touching a child.

The warrior used another word for death. It was the compound verb, *make death.* Did that mean to kill? Had he threatened to kill Slazan N!ai? No, he had used the word for *me*, the object, not the word for *I*, subject. Had he said that N!ai would kill him?

There was more motion outside. Esoch forced his head up this time, and it felt like a block of pain supported his head, holding it up off the ground. But he could make out N!ai in the afternoon sunlight. She held the tin piano in her arms. She set it down tenderly, and she sat behind it. The music sounded. She started with a simple pattern that she kept repeating. Esoch lowered his head back to the ground. He imagined himself with his thumb piano. That tune he could play on his thumb piano; at least he could capture its rhythm. He imagined what keys he would touch, in what order, at what length, but the pattern had become complex, complex enough that he couldn't find a pattern at all. He had lost the logic of the notes. Then for a moment he had it again. Was he hearing a slazan mother speak? He listened again to the voices he had heard during the language experience—he listened again and again to the mother's words—and he now could make sense of the last two visitors. Slazan N!ai had spoken this morning with a woman, and last night she had spoken with a girl.

He looked to the warrior, whose head turned to face him. There was a different kind of look in his eyes. Esoch thought he saw despair, but the set of the eyes and mouth made it look so much like contempt. The warrior spoke in Nostratic. "She has the medicine. She won't give it to me. I will die."

"I am unable to move. My leg is broken."

The warrior looked to the roof. "She's primitive. She thinks music heals. I will die."

She thinks the music heals. So that is why she brought it down to the shuttle and played it. It wasn't a superstitious exorcism. If you try not to touch with fingers, you touch instead with sound. He thought of the trance dances, of the men who had learned to control n/um, how the boiling energy would rise through their bodies, and how they would pull out the arrows of sickness shot at their bodies by the spirits of the dead or by God; nothing at all like the medical ward where machines had read his body and recommended his diet, nothing at all like the planetside hospital where they had laid out Ghazwan's body, surrounded by machines with all their readouts and nonmelodic beeps.

The warrior did not believe at all in the music, so it would do nothing for him. Esoch knew nothing of the music, and so what could it do? Music, like trance dancing, couldn't knit together a broken bone. He wasn't going anywhere soon.

Tomorrow, at midday, the alarm would sound.

I had heard them speak, and though she had tried to ignore that fact while she played for the Stranger, she found the thought of it overtaking her later while she made preparations to heal the not-a-person. She used a stone knife to shape the wood for the splint and thought about how softly they had spoken, how she had been unable to hear their words. She cut strips of leather to tie the splint and wondered why the Stranger would speak more with the not-a-person than with her. She touched fingers to the keys of her gzaet, never pressing down, never playing, just trying out the patterns she might play once the bone was set, but she kept losing the trail of her thought. The not-a-person could do more than force out a word or two. He could speak, and that was truly upsetting.

When she returned to the hut, two splints in one hand, leather thongs in the other, she found the Stranger sleeping fitfully, his body rocking back and forth, much like an infant struggling with a bad dream. If there was no improvement by tomorrow, she would have to dig up the bag.

The not-a-person's eyes were open. He was watching her watch the Stranger. He averted his eyes when she knelt by him and laid wood and leather by his injured leg. He continued watching her. She let her eyes meet his. "Do you have words to share?"

He looked up at the roof. "No," he said.

I left the hut, and she stayed outside for the longest time. She did not understand how one word could affect her so strongly. But it was late. Night would soon wean the day of its light. Yesterday's tension had returned to her genitals, and she wanted to leave and return before the woods were hungry with darkness.

She stopped in the opening. His eyes were open. She told herself to act like a woman, and she stepped forward. How would he react when she touched him? The Stranger had said these people liked to touch. She knelt down by his leg. She spoke slowly. "I have words to share."

He said something. She heard his words over again in her head before she knew he had said, "I am listening."

"Your leg is broken. Do you understand? Your leg is broken."

He said nothing for a moment, then: "My leg is broken."

"I am going to put the bone together properly and then tie it in place with a splint."

"I don't understand."

"I am going to put the two parts of the bone back together. I am going to tie the bone in place with a splint." She raised the strips of leather and the pieces of wood so he could see them.

There was another pause, then: "You are going to tie the leg so it is together back."

"You don't have to say what I say."

"Good."

"It will hurt."

"I know."

"It won't hurt as much later."

"I know."

"May I touch you?"

He said nothing.

This worried I. Maybe the Stranger was wrong. Maybe they didn't like to touch. Or maybe when they spoke like a person spoke, they came to like solitude the way a person did. She said again, "May I touch you?"

Another pause.

I worried more. Should she ask a third time?

"Yes," he said.

Esoch raised his head to watch. The dull pain felt like increased pressure. His head felt light. Maybe he shouldn't watch. Her arms stretched out. Her skin looked softer than he remembered. The red of her hair was fading into a dull brown. Her fingers took hold of the blanket and made several folds underneath, then set it again down on his thighs. Her fingers reached out again, and he readied himself for the pain.

He watched her touch his other leg, tentatively, at first, as if she expected some electric jolt, though of course she wouldn't know what electricity was. He watched her face and tried to read the look of concentration or the look of anxiety. And maybe he had seen enough in the language experience to understand that her expression contained a mixture of both.

He had to lie back down again. He could only feel the way her hands clasped his healthy calf, how they pressed around it, how fingers probed the contour of muscle and felt for the way muscle met bone. He thought: this is the first human leg she has touched. This is how she learns how to set it. But tomorrow he would not be able to walk back to the shuttle and disarm the self-destruct.

But the rushing thoughts seems less and less important as her fingers and hands touched his leg. He tried to count to himself how many days since he had swum ashore from the coffin, how many days it had been since another's skin touched his. He remembered Hanan tracing the scar along his leg. The sensation nourished something deep within his body, and he let himself give away to the feeling.

She said something. He made out the words *touch*, *other*, and *leg*. He readied himself.

The pain was excruciating.

When she stopped, he felt the concise pressure of the splint and heard her rise, he found he was relieved. He lay there, faint, and he found that the solitude had made his body perverse: he yearned against all logic for her to reset the splint; he was willing to accept that pain, if only her fingers would touch his skin again.

I fed the cooking fire, and she began to prepare the food. While she skinned the roundtail, placed the meat on the coals, and pounded leaves into a swallow paste, she thought about the not-a-person and the easy way he had accepted her touch. She liked the freedom she'd had to truly feel the shape of his leg, to feel how that compared with the dead skin, the dead muscle of the leg she had cut open. She respected his strength. He had ground his teeth and tensed his muscles, but he had said nothing when she had tied the splint. He only let out a long, terrible sigh once she had left the hut.

But, still, what was she to think of one who accepted touch so easily, of one who had no solitude worthy of respect? Why did she feel differently toward this creature than she did toward Hugger? Perhaps it was because she had never seen this one touch another, but once or twice she had already imagined the woman alive and mating with him. She was surprised how the vision stayed in her mind, like the memory of something she had seen. When she thought of the mating of two nightskins or two lightfoot, it was like thinking about making an arrow or removing bones from a fish, but when she thought of this not-a-person mating with another, it aroused feelings she wanted to forget.

She brought the food to each one, setting a portion first in front of the sleeping Stranger, setting the other portion beside the wakeful not-a-person. He watched her crouch down, he watched her place the food in front of him, he watched her rise, and she was sure he watched her leave. She was stepping over his legs to get to the opening when he spoke: "I have no thing to share."

She stopped. She did not know if she wanted to face him. "Can you make the boulder move?"

"I don't understand."

"The rock the first"—she searched for a word that would not be offensive—"one of you came in. The rock you lived in after she left. Can you make it move?"

"The one who left. Do know you where she is?"

What would he think if he knew? "No. She left, and no one has seen her."

He made some kind of sound she didn't understand. It was a low sound, mournful. She turned to look at him. He had turned his eyes toward the wall, as if he could see something there. "What I call you?" he said.

At first she did not know how to answer the question. She said, "One or another call me Healer."

"Healer?" The word sounded truly strange coming from his lips.

"Yes."

"One or another call me . . ." It was two sounds, but it was not a word she knew.

"It makes no sense."

"Yes. No sense. Call me No Sense."

"No. It is not something to be called."

He said nothing.

She wanted to ask about the rock again.

He stared at the wall, then said, "Healer. I need to urinate. I don't want to urinate myself again."

She had chosen the wood from which she would shape crutches, but they were still not made. She looked at him, considered what it meant to lie there in his own urine. She told herself that it would be like touching a child, like handling an animal. She walked up to him and held out her arms. His hands grasped hers. They were strong, firm hands. The blanket fell away, and his injured leg leaned against the ground, and he cried out. Then she had his arm around her shoulder, and she stood straight up, his body rising with her, the foot of his injured leg rising from the ground. He breathed heavily. She was sure he wanted to scream out in pain. She led him outside the hut, and in the sudden overflow of light she could look down and make out how soiled his skin was. She hated having this body so close to hers, his skin rubbing against her skin, his weight pulling across her shoulder. She was tempted to let go of his hand. They walked away from the hut to the closest tree.

She should have averted her eyes, but her curiosity was too strong. She remembered Flatface and the way she had watched when each of her children was old enough to walk away from the hut and wet the ground on their own; she remembered how Flatface watched, as if this were something new to be seen. Now she watched him take his penis in his hand, and she watched the liquid fly out in an arc to leave its marking upon the tree.

While going through the slow, painful process of leading him back, she thought of having him lie down in the open. It would be easier to play the music for him then, but she recalled the woman floating in the cold spring waters, the gouge in her arm, the bruises upon her throat. No one would enter her hut. No one would attack him there.

Once she had laid him upon the fouled ground and had covered him with the blanket, he said again, "I have no thing to share."

"The rock," she said. "The rock you live in. It came from the sky. Can you make it go back?"

He looked at her, as if trying to understand what she wanted.

"Can you make the rock go away?"

"Yes."

"Will you?"

"Yes."

She did not know what to say.

He said, "There. Carry me. Will leave. Now."

"When you can walk."

"Now. Better. Carry me."

She looked away no. "Later. When you can walk. And then the rock will be gone."

"Yes."

His voice was a falling off, but he had said it himself. The rock would leave. All the problems would be gone. She touched the food she had laid out for him. "I share this food with you. I have more to share if you are still hungry. I will play music for you, and when you can walk, I will take you to the rock."

She left him to his solitude.

Standing in the clearing, she felt like she could still feel his arm around her shoulders, his hip against her hip. The whole thing suddenly repulsed her. She wanted to be away from here, away from this not-a-person, away from the Stranger. She wanted to be pregnant, she wanted to have a daughter, and she wanted a daughter so that she would never have to heal again. But if she could heal the not-a-person, if she could heal No Sense, then the rock would be gone.

The healer started to play.

Esoch had propped himself up on his elbow, in spite of the pain that coated the back of his head, and tried to eat the mashed food. It was easy to swallow, he knew he needed it, but the nausea was almost unbearable. He lay back down and listened to the music. He recognized a few of the patterns. They had become familiar enough that he considered them songs.

Was she playing music for him?

And what if it could heal him? He had to make it to the shuttle by midday tomorrow, and she had said, if he understood her properly, that she would not take him until he could walk on his own.

But how could music, on its own, heal?

He thought of his ruined thumb piano and how little it had accomplished. Perhaps her tin piano would help a sickened slazan who expected it to work, but the music wouldn't touch him. Where he had grown, the healing happened when women clapped and sang well, when men danced until the n/um boiled in them.

The healer had started to play a new song, and the rhythm of it reminded him of the rhythm of the dances, of women clapping and singing. He raised his hands and clapped, trying to remember the rhythm of the claps, the songs the women sang when the men started to dance.

I started by first playing the top two rows of keys. She played songs her mother had sung, songs Flatface had sung to her when her mother had gone away to heal someone. She started slowly, each pattern clear; then she played faster, letting notes flow into the others like rushing water. She slowed again, and she started to play the patterns she had thought out after cutting apart the woman's dead body. She wanted to hear how they sounded, to hear how her fingers played them. They did not sound as good in the air as they had in her head, so she changed them. She played the new patterns, made more changes, then played until they came to her easily, until she had changed them enough that they sounded akin to the patterns as she had first imagined them.

He remembered: when his sister Kwoba married /ontah, when she menstruated for the first time, when he killed his first antelope, when there was tension in the air, when many were gathered near the waterhole, when two groups had come together and something unnameable was in the air, or when his sister Kwoba was terribly sick not long after their father had died, a group of women have built some fire and have begun to clap and to sing and soon they sit in a circle around the fire, and the men have put the rattles on their feet, and they have started to dance through the circle, around the fire, their feet hitting ground, digging into sand, everything easy at first, stops and starts, bantering and teasing, then the clapping and singing growing more energetic under the night sky, darkness closing in, the fire lighting faces and hands, the clapping, the feet, the rattles, the singing, all, enthusiasm growing.

Now that she was happy with the patterns, she lowered her left hand to the lower keys and pressed down lightly, feeling for the resonance. She looked at the not-a-person, at Broken Leg, and she concentrated the music on him. The resonance felt wrong. She changed several of the patterns she played, felt for the resonance, and it was worse. She returned to a simple song, something to keep her fingers busy, while in her mind she tried to listen to him, to hear his voice, and once she heard it—the way he had said, "No sense. Call me No Sense"—she played out the rhythm of it, and the resonance was not so harsh.

But now she heard what she had been concentrating too hard to hear in the first place. He was clapping. She returned her fingers to the top keys, played a simple pattern, and listened to the way his palms came together, a teppity-teppity-tep, that wove about through the air like a flathead wove its way through the brush. She played until she had matched the rhythm, then tried to find a melody for it. It was an ugly melody, but when she played it on the lower keys, the resonance was smoother. She hesitated, unsure how to play such ugly sounds, yet continued because music and healing were not two different things.

He thought of circles when he remembered the dance. First there is the fire, built in a circle of sand, around which every other circle completes itself. The circle of women surrounds the fire. The men dance through this circle and around the women, their feet imprinting another circle. There is the circle of children and young men and women who are watching. There is the circle of small fires where those who are tired and who do not want to clap or dance can sit and watch. Around this is the darkness of night, of the bush, and waiting there are the //gangwasi, the spirits of the recently dead, who are attracted by the music, who long for the kin they have left behind, who want to make them sick to have them come with them so they will not be as lonely in the land of the dead. Around that is the horizon, a distant dark circle separating earth and sky, and encircling them are the stars.

And the dance has gone on, from the fading of light to the clarity of the stars. Male feet pound the ground in rhythm, male bodies are coated with sweat, their eyes like smooth crystal, and the men shout out, gu tsiu, gu tsiu—pick it up, pick it up, and the women's voices and handclaps have a new energy, a louder rhythm. An older man, his father's uncle, falls. Several other men move over to him, help him sit up, rub sweat into his body.

Soon he stands, his body trembling, and he walks over to Karu, and his hands touch her shoulders. He trembles, he gurgles, he shouts. He pulls the arrows of sickness from her, and he moves on to N/ahka, who is sitting next to Karu. They clap and talk to each other while his uncle lays hands on N/ahka, then on the son in her lap. He moves from person to person. /gau's n/um has boiled and he has entered !kia, his body trembling, his eyes glassy. He places a hand on ≠oma's back, another on his chest. /gau calls out. ≠oma's uncle is now standing pulling sickness from N!ai. Next to N!ai is his mother, next to her is Kwoba, whose eyes have a different glassy look. She has burned with fever for several days, and people have started to say she might die.

For a moment I cannot concentrate. She feels her desire more intensely. There is a sweet tension from the depth of her stomach to where she can open herself for a man, and she starts to play music that will once again help herself forget this desire, forget herself, remove her body from the world until all that remains are her fingers, the keys, and the music, when she feels the soft break inside her, like the snapping of a leaf off a bush, and she knows that tonight she will have to choose wisely who will be her mate if she wants a daughter, and once again she plays the music, tries to feel the music, tries to remove the sky, the surrounding trees, the cooking fire, the ground, her desire, the feel of the earth against her bottom, her feet, until she feels only the music, the way it journeys to him and back to her, the way she tries to ease him open so the blood flows the way it should, so that sweetness inside is released and pain falls away the same way pollen and dust fall away from leaves when the rain arrives after a long spell of dryness.

He remembers his own dancing. He remembers lifting each foot and stamping down hard, the way the foot hits ground and the feel of it journeys to where spine and head met. He remembers the rhythm, moving with the claps, the rhythm of the feet, stamp and step forward left, stamp right, stamp and step forward right, stamp left, the /khoni wrapped around his leg from ankle to knee, the many dried cocoons brushing against his legs, the little stones in them rattling, adding to the rhythm. His breath quick, sucking in the smell of smoke, the lightness of his head, the growing of the pain in his gut, the sudden wall inside and the fear of continuing, of the pain, of perhaps going too far and losing his soul. And his uncle is by him, rubbing in his sweat, snapping his fingers, shooting arrows of n/um into him. He is ready.

He trusts his uncle. He trusts everyone. The clapping is right. The songs are right. He is part of everything. The fear is still there, and he keeps breathing, he keeps stamping, and he can feel his own n/um, the pain in his belly, the heat of it boiling inside him, the shivering on the outside, the way it rises through him along his spine, until it is everywhere, in his feet, along his hair. Everything spins around. The people are small, distant. The tree tilts. He runs to keep balance. He runs until someone takes hold of him and leads him around, and rubs the sweat off his body while his blood boils, everything is fire, and he places his hands on someone, ready to heal.

The music touched the leg, and she played out the pattern, the rhythm first, then the melody, and tried to match it to the shape. What she felt in return jarred, so she changed the music, starting slow, like her first careful touches, then quicker, as if taking hold, then moving in, until her mind's eye can see bone touching bone, marrow touching marrow, blood flowing through its own rivers, playing so that the body would ease into what it should know how to do, so the body would not fail the person who lived in it, so the body would not rob a person of his solitude, making him too aware of his pain, the pain taking away his chance to gather, to mate, to shape things with his fingers and his hands, to avoid what should be avoided, to be aware of the world in order to walk through it with the solitude of mind that makes life bearable.

He remembered the way the dance changed, how he rests by the fire, how he gets up to move his feet, but it is more like walking than like dancing, the clapping without energy, but now the women start to sing better again, now they clap more loudly, with a rhythm that makes sense to the legs, and now his feet dance to such clapping, and now the men dance again, and in some the n/um begins to boil again. Hands reach out. /gau's world tilts and he plows his head into the fire, and his two brothers pull him out, his father talking to him. Someone else in !kia runs off into the bush, then back. Another man stands on the other side of the fire. He, too, is in !kia. He pulls sickness out of a child. ≠oma's uncle is leaning over Kwoba, his muscles trembling, his body rigid; deep in !kia, he calls out, then falls to the ground unconscious. Another uncle and his mother and his grandfather are sitting by him, rubbing his sweat, talking to his ears while his soul leaves the body and travels into the sand. It goes through a long underground river to another place on earth. There he climbs a thread higher and higher, heading toward

God's place, when he meets up with !xam—≠oma and Kwoba's father—and !xam is carrying Kwoba's soul in his arms. His uncle tells !xam that Kwoba still has to live, that she has a child who is still nursing and another child who clings to her and is scared of men she doesn't know. !xam says he misses his daughter, that he can't bear to be without her. Let her go back, his uncle says. She will be up there one day, but it's wrong to take her away while she still has children and a life to live.

And their father lets Kwoba go, lets her go back with her uncle, who comes awake back in the camp. Kwoba's face is drenched with sweat. It looks like the fever has broken. And he wants so much to be like his uncle, but he can't see the sickness he pulls, he can only pull it. He can enter !kia, but only for a while, because he fears the deeper pain, he fears dying as his uncle has, he fears losing his soul. And around him are his father and Ghazwan and Hanan and N!ai and N!ai's father, and N!ai's mother, and Pauline, his own //gangwasi, not all of whom are dead, and he tells them to go away, he listens to distant music that seems to coat his body, to seep into his body, and he tells them to go away, that he wants to watch his uncle, who is standing again, ready to dance again, because the sun is rising and this is when the dancing is at its best, this is when everyone wants it to be good because the dancing should always end with everyone excited and together.

And now there was just music. She listened, and the ugly sounds she had played for Broken Leg now seemed less ugly. There was a strange sense to them, the beauty of a distant land she had not seen, and she felt her fingers press keys with their own logic, she interwove the patterns of his music and the music she had always known, and she played and played, slowing down, the river becoming a stream, becoming a brook, becoming drops of water sliding along stone, across leaves, slipping into the ground. She played until one finger and another alternated keys, and the music was quieter and quieter, like rain at the end of a storm, then there were the last few drops, then there was silence. And she began to hear once again the birdcalls, the insects, the breeze in the leaves high up, and the crackle of the dying fire behind her back.

He remembered the sunup, the heat, a woman throwing sand onto the fire, people heading back to their huts or to find shade, children asking for food, a baby's short cry and the offering of the mother's breast. He remembered laying his palm on Kwoba's forehead, her skin cool to the touch. He lay upon the ground, aware of the alien sounds around him, how the music had stopped, how nothing in the camp seemed to be moving, and he wanted badly now to go back.

He wanted to dance again, while other men danced, while women clapped, he wanted to learn to better bear the pain of n/um, so that when he entered !kia, when the energy boiled in him, he could reach out and see clearly the sickness he pulled, until he could clearly see the //gangwasi out in the darkness, until he could climb the thread up to where the Great God lives, to argue with him, to ask him to pull out his arrows of sickness so someone could be well, to promise that they would love better and share better so that the person who was sick was wanted, or to say why that person could not be lost to them, not yet. He wanted so much that was impossible that an unbearable sadness filled him, like no sadness he had felt before. He opened his eyes. The sky above could not be seen. There was the whiteness of a cloud above. The late-afternoon light had a certain clarity about it. He raised his head, and it didn't hurt at all.

The following is taken from the notebook Pauline Dikobe kept during her 200 day study of the slazan foraging population on Tienah.

Day 153

The days are getting shorter. Late summer heat. The leaves are green throughout the day, and I miss springtime's wealth of color.

Each morning I walk the same trails through the forest to make my presence predictable. Today a subadult slazan male awaits me at an intersection of one of the trails. He stands there, watching me, then looks away. I stop the moment it becomes clear he won't move from the path. What would a slazan woman do?

Then he turns away. He walks off, but just before I can consider this one more lost opportunity, he stops after several steps and casts me a backward glance. He does this several times. I decide to follow. He walks up one path and down another. He stops every now and then to pick some food, and he eyes me, then the infant in my chi !kan, while he slowly nibbles away at berries or leaves. I keep my distance, only walking when he walks, never staring. I wonder if he'll take me anywhere special, show me anything new. I follow him for an hour before he runs up a trail and away.

Tamr says, "He's just another coy male."

Jihad says, "He's playing with you."

Day 156

It's the fourth morning I have followed him. Today he waits until I arrive; then he leads me along for three hours before running off.

He never does anything when I follow him; he no longer gathers food; he just walks, once in a while looking back to see if I'm still there. It's like he's a lonely adolescent, just filling time.

Jihad tells me the intelligence has picked up a pattern. The subadult male stays within a single watershed. The only hut and hearth in the watershed belongs to the adult female we've ID'ed as !U. Is this !U's son?

Does this watershed form a range? Does !U's range overlap with other ranges? When !U's (supposed) son becomes an adult, does he leave her range for others? Does he walk across several watersheds as we have seen other slazan males do? How far away will he go from his mother?

Day 158

Today he appears with a young female, somewhat smaller than he. She has come to !U's encampment on a number of occasions. Sometimes she brings food to share; usually she takes what !U offers.

Together with the subadult male, we repeat the same process. I follow them and watch them exchange glances, an exchange that surprises me. At one point the female turns to face me, widens her eyes, and then lifts her pubic apron—surely an obscene gesture—before dancing away and running off. The male calls something unintelligible—perhaps it's the slazan equivalent of *hey!*—and runs off after her.

It is this very social exchange of glances that holds the mind. Why do relatively solitary creatures use language, why do they have the self-conscious intelligence that created human society?

There are plenty of theories about how competition with another species may have been the engine that drove the development of intelligence. Slazans have the opposable thumbs and binocular vision of tree dwellers. Had they stepped from the trees to the ground like the apes? Had another slazan primate species also taken to the ground? The presence of one species would have set off a dynamic in the other, a leaning toward enough co-operation and sociability to provide the necessary edge to properly exploit the environment and enhance repro-ductive success. The other possibility is that there existed at the same time a completely different species of animal who was evolving toward intelligence, creating an arms race in intelligence, forcing slazans to give up whatever solitary behavior necessary.

But each theory implies that at one point or an-other, slazans had to rid their environment of remaining competitors, a kind of innate genocidal impulse. In spite of all wartime efforts, in spite of all propaganda to the contrary, that notion is unconvincing.

So what force drove the machine of evolving intelli-gence?

Day 163

I'm sitting against a tree nursing my plastic son when my coy subadult male appears and walks up to me. I find myself rising, as if we will enter conversation. "I am here," I say.

He tilts his head to one side.

I hold the baby in my arms. Its lips have fallen from my nipple. It has not nursed the requisite time, so it starts to whimper.

The subadult male looks down at the baby. I look from the baby to him. What is he thinking?

Before I know it, he has taken the child from my hands and has disappeared into the wilderness. I run, I scream, and I almost catch up. But he is gone.

I shut down the shuttle, cut off the voices from the *Way of God*, and scream out my solitude. The baby was plastic. It had no life. It was a ruse. It was stupid to have called it by my son's name.

Day 164

I can't get up.

I don't mourn for plastic.

I think of the General—ibn Haj's superior—the one who looked like my younger sister's husband, whose charms resided only in his looks. I know how he will see things. He will be blind to all the conversations we have recorded, all the words slazan women have shared. He won't see how !U and the other woman divided up the meat. He will see the subadult male, the way he stole the plastic child. The General will see a murderer of babies, and he will see all the justification he needs for the war effort.

Day 165
Captain al-Shaykh offers to cut the mission short, bring me back up. There's nothing more we'll learn in a month. I refuse. There's so much more I need to know.

Day 166
I take my walk, and he is there again. He doesn't walk away. He approaches with a piece of wood. He lays it in front of me and backs off. I ignore it, and I ignore him until he has left. Then I pick up the wood. It is crudely carved, shaped like a tiny flute. I raise it to my lips and blow. The tone is soft, like a whisper.

Jihad says, "It doesn't make up for a kidnapped baby."

"Dead baby," I say.

Day 167
Today he brings a basket crafted from dried reeds. The basket contains freshly ripened summer fruit. Not a single piece is bruised in any way.

Day 168
Today the gift is a knife, finely shaped from bone. The wooden hilt, however, is as crudely made as the whistle.

Day 170
After a day's absence he reappears. This time he has brought what appears to be a belt, with a sheath for the knife. It is not at all well made. I hold it in my hands and look at it. He steps forward and runs his hand over my shoulder. I step back and look up. His eyes are intent on me. He steps forward again. His hand presses against pubic apron, and I stand there, held by curiosity and surprise, as he firmly curves his hand along my vulva.

I drop the belt and flee.

* * *

The gifts were mating effort.

Why he thought he could mate with me, I don't know.

But I know the age-old game: kill another male's child, then mate with the freshly receptive female and conceive a child of your own.

A woman would have to develop an effective counterstrategy to safeguard her children. The hominid strategy was to choose solicitous males, ones whose kindness was its own kind of mating effort, a measure to insure, but not guarantee, the life of your children. But ancestral slazan woman, who preferred solitude, would not have chosen sociable mates, mates who would feed their children in the dual effort to propagate their genes and be allowed to mate once again. They would have preferred large, aggressive men who could survive, men who would maintain their solitude. But how to preserve their children against infanticide? Like lions, they could mate with a number of men, so no male would risk destroying his own child. But that would not be enough. Slazan males new to the area would still have a motive for infanticide. Slazan women needed something more. The woman who had intelligence—the woman who cooperated through language—gained an edge and had more children who survived to reproduce.

I have no data to support the idea; I have only intuition. But I believe that slazans did not compete with another species, nor did slazan groups compete with each other. The engine of change was the need for women to cooperate with each other against solitary but powerful men.

Day 185

Al-Shaykh does not want me to be far from the shuttle, especially after the incident with the subadult male. Still, I stuff a change of clothes and other gear into a pack. After a moment of hesitation I add the pistol. I head for the village site thirty kilometers away.

And I return both enthusiastic and depressed. I have sneaked up on a couple mating, and I used an imaging pin to record the moment. I came upon a male soaking reeds and twisting them together to make one of the elaborate nests, his attention focused so intently on the work that he never seemed aware that I was watching. And I have walked through the village.

The number of shelters is amazing, over fifty. The paths wind around in serpentine fashion, just as in slazan cities, so people can be close by without being seen. Each shelter contains some kind of artifact. The older huts contain extensive paintings. I think of them as structures of knowledge, cultural knowledge made evident. It seems odd for primal utopians, purposeful hunter-gatherers, to maintain such a tradition. No; *maintain* is the wrong word. Hence, my depression. There are signs of evident decay: runoff ditches filling, scattering of leaves, grasses, and shrubs sprouting up between huts.

Near the village are fruit trees. A round, beautifully red fruit that contains a soft yellow pulp. It takes a while to notice among the disarray of time—the fallen trunks, hollowed and lined with moss, the new shoots vying for sunlight, the immense quiet and shade—but you do become aware of how all the trees of similar age are arranged in rows. Orchards. I now look through images of other overgrown clearings, and we record signs of what may have been agricultural plots several generations ago.

These slazans are not primal utopians.

They are a failed agricultural colony.

They know how to hunt and gather because there are pan-species psychological mechanisms that recognize the behaviors necessary for this way of life, just as the children of those who speak a pidgin end up speaking a language.

Why did I so badly want them to be like the Ju/wasi?

There is no special purity to being a forager. I forage through the images of their lives—the data I collect—with the same care a medieval army foraged a conquered town, taking in hand gold, food, and women.

Day 186

I remember now what the General said over dinner. He wanted me to prove the obvious, that this was a failed colony. It was the justification to open this planet to human habitation.

Day 190

I have resumed my walks. I don't see my suitor, my surrogate son's kidnapper and murderer. I dream about an adult male who follows me, who takes interest, who wraps his arms around me. I awake, frightened and aroused.

I imagine returning to the *Way of God*, and the thought of the tiny corridors and the press of people leaves me feeling a similar ambivalence.

Day 192

I see my suitor today from a distance. He is using one hand and an elaborate stick to dig into the ground. The other hand hangs at his side. He grunts. He stops. The arm he isn't using hangs at an odd angle.

He turns, sees me, and walks off quickly, as if my presence poses some threat.

I examine the images that evening. His arm is broken, perhaps in two places. A digit is missing from his small finger. His face has several cuts. Who did this to him? Why? Was it done with the same calculation with which he took hold of my plastic child, or was it the result of a fight, the striking out in anger, the escalation of some conflict over territory?

I have watched—several times—images of !U telling Clear Eyes she has little to share. !U places three strips of meat before Clear Eyes in a show of generosity. In !U's shelter, covered by a blanket, is meat she hid this morning.

Why the deception? By giving away little and claiming it is much, does she hope to increase Clear Eyes' generosity when !U should visit her? And does Clear Eyes detect the cheat? Does she too feign generosity and save her food for closer relations?

In each human transaction an individual has to decide to do what is in her own best interest: to invest in the relationship, to invest in the group, or to invest in the self's own needs. Conscience becomes our tool to preserve reciprocal arrangements, guilt to keep us within society's norms, and anguish to remind us of our own persistent desires.

But as we deceive, so our conspecifics search out

signs of our defection: the look in our eyes, the stance of our body, the sound of our voices. Thus we develop our abilities at self-deception—for how can we give away our own deception if we are not conscious of it? In times of illness we overdo our injuries and gain extra attention. We feel desire and denounce philanderers. We attack others for our own flaws. But we also repress memories of being wronged so we can continue a relationship. We see another's generosity and not the calculation behind the altruism. We enjoy the romance of courtship and ignore our simultaneous calculations when securing a mate. We question what other individuals do, but we adopt the common cause.

The common cause is the war.

We live in a culture of war.

And culture is as strong as our own individual desires—why else would young men and women, who have no children, willingly go off and die? It's the greatest of evolutionary mistakes, the sure sign of culture's ultimate strength over the gene.

The state, to its advantage, can combine our ability for self-deception and our willingness to die for our genes; it expands the genetic family into the human family; it plays marches to synchronize our moods before it sends us off, hand in hand, our consciences pricked, then spurred forward: to feel hate and call it devotion, to feel murderous and call it bravery, to feel love for your comrades-in-arms, for your shipmates, for your battalion, for your cause, and call it love for all humanity. And only when you struggle forward, risking your own life to save the life of someone you barely know from enemy fire, only then is there any truth to it all.

Chapter Fourteen

The Sixteenth Day

It was late afternoon, just before the sun hid behind the distant trees. Broken Leg was sleeping, or at least pretending to sleep. The Stranger had soiled himself again. She cleaned him, all the while noticing how hard and swollen the bumps on his legs had become. With each touch he twisted his head back and forth, and she wasn't sure if his body was rejecting her touch or if her touch brought pain.

She left the shelter for the river, where she bathed. To be alone, to feel the rush of the water, to listen to the sounds surrounding her, all of this made it feel like solitude was something she had lost. Here, on her own, the slow way desire crawled through her again was a pleasure in itself. She felt alive because she was alone.

He lay there and listened, surprised at how comfortable it was to listen. The pain in his leg radiated from the break and no longer felt like a pain that had infected his entire body. His body was clothed in a thin layer of sweat, his abdomen and thighs dirtied by the residue of waste, but he no longer felt like the dirt was layered through his soul. He sat up, and he did not need to lie back down again.

He could not believe what he so urgently wanted to believe: that the simple playing of music could have done this for him.

Even if music could heal, even if the playing of notes could act upon emotions so that the brain released the proper hormones, activated the proper synapses, how could this creature alien to everything he had known have played the notes a human brain would understand?

Evening was approaching, and so he had tonight and tomorrow morning to convince Slazan N!ai to show him the way to the shuttle. By midday tomorrow it would be too late.

While thinking these thoughts he became aware that there was no music being played. Nor was she moving about the encampment doing whatever chores she did when she did not play music. Slazan N!ai must be gone. And when she returned, he couldn't call her Slazan N!ai. It was a scientist's label, the ethologist naming the observed animal so it can have some humanity, some quality that earned it a degree of empathy while the observer cataloged what it did to whom. This woman was called Healer. Esoch looked at the slazan warrior, who was still lying there, his skin darkened and blotched, his eyes half-open, and Esoch wondered what the warrior was called.

The warrior, it turned out, was awake. His eyes opened all the way, and Esoch politely averted his gaze. He heard the warrior's voice. "You can sit up now."

"Yes."

"Can you stand up?"

"No. I need"—he did not know the Nostratic word for crutches—"support."

"The healer had my pack. In it is medication I need. Without it I will die before I reach the ship."

"The healer is gone."

"I am the enemy. You want me to die."

Esoch expected the warrior to go on, to remind him that the warrior's starship offered his only hope of salvation. But the warrior said nothing more. It was only then that it occurred to Esoch what the warrior might be thinking: that the human's hatred was so intense that Esoch would rather remain alone on this planet than see the slazan live. "What are you called?" Esoch asked.

"You could not pronounce it."

Esoch held up his prosthetic. "I could try."

"I would not want to hear you try."

"What do I call you?"

"Call me according to your thinking. Call me Enemy."

"Should I call you Warrior?"

He made a sound. Like hearing a word in a language you are beginning to learn, then translating it, Esoch recognized the sound as laughter. "Is each slazan a warrior?"

Esoch's thoughts were confounded until he became aware of what the slazan meant. "Then why are you here, if not because of us?"

"Because of you? How could I be here because of you?"

"Then why are you here?"

"This is a slazan colony. Why should I not be here? Why are you here? Why is there a shuttle craft on this planet?"

"The shuttle came with a woman who was to study the slazans here."

"And she studied them for science or for war?"

Esoch did not know what to say. Pauline herself hadn't known.

"I, too, am a scientist. There is one here at all times to study the ones who live here. My rotation had just started. My replacement will not arrive for a number of years. When your ship came into our orbit, I grew scared that you would discover my own ship. I decided to meet you in orbit and make contact."

Esoch repeated the words. He could feel the death in his own voice. "Make contact."

"Yes. Your warship fired. I had no choice but to fire back."

"What kind of scientist are you?"

"What kind of scientist was the first one you dropped down here? She came in a warship. It is a war. My ship was armed."

"How do I know?"

"How do you know your ship fired first?"

Esoch nodded, realized that a nod was a gesture, not a word, and said, "Yes."

"It shouldn't matter. I approached them. I was the threat. They fired. But you want to trust me. You want to know that I didn't lie to you. I have no proof. You think I fired first? How does that put me in the wrong? This is a slazan world. A human warship enters orbit without permission. Would it be wrong for me to fire? Wouldn't it be foolish not to fire?"

"Why do you argue when there's nothing to argue?"

"Because you are quiet. Which means all the arguments go on inside you. You have words to share, but you share them only with yourself. You say nothing, so how do I know I can trust you? In six months you could learn how to fly an alien starship. You could take it from me. You could kill me. You could return home to humanspace with a slazan ship. How do I know you won't do that?"

"You don't."

"Then we each have distrust to share. I can die and you can stay here forever. I can live, and you can live. My life means much to me. I cannot betray the person who saves it."

"Why not? Why not get my help first and later remove the risk of betrayal?"

"If I betray you, then you have reason to betray me. If you blow up a satellite, then I should blow up a satellite, and it should be over. If you take something of mine, I should take something of yours, and it will be over."

"It sounds good, but it is just words."

"You think I will kill you because I can. But I am not human, and I do not think that way. Have you studied animals?"

"Some."

"You know that an animal may threaten another of its kind. If I know you're stronger than me and if I back off, nothing happens. If you know this is the land I use, you back off. There are fights only when each doesn't know exactly where the other stands, when each doesn't know who is right in that situation. So if I have a weapon, it's only to show you that I have my claws, that I have my fangs, that I have my display of power so that you and I can leave each other alone."

"Slazans have done more than display weapons."

"Of course. Because once a human has something, he has to use it. If he has an erection, he has to mate. If he forges a sword, blood is drawn. If he builds a bomb, a city is exploded. You are the ones who cannot be trusted. You are the ones who fire first, who call the destruction self-defense, and who are astounded when the other side returns fire. You want the first word and the last word, and you leave no words to be shared."

"You have made each human evil. You give me an argument for which there is no response. You have the last word, it seems."

"No. The healer won't give me my medicine. I will die. All the final words will be yours."

I desired no one but the one she thought of as Made Nothing. I desired his strength. I desired the pleasure she had felt the night before. But I also desired a daughter, and there was no woman to ask if Made Nothing's pollen made daughters or sons. Old Sour Plum had sired Squawker's daughter, and each of

Flatface's daughters, as well as Talk Too Much's eldest daughter. I knew this only because a woman would tell another woman such things while they shared words during a hunt or while they shared food. The words would be uttered in a low hunter's voice, a sound that barely carried, so no man would know which child came from his pollen.

Talk Too Much had told every young woman how she had once mated with only one man. She refused another man who had given her many gifts. When the infant was born, a fine daughter, the other man dashed the infant's brains out against a tree. It is best, Talk Too Much always said, to mate many; then each man is happy, and a woman's pleasure can be as varied as the food she eats at the end of the summer.

I found Old Sour Plum building a new nest. He was working by the river, where the paths were clear of debris and dotted with animal spoor. She had made hardly a sound and had stopped a polite distance away, so she could stand by a tree and watch him work. The reeds and branches were soaking in the water, held to shore by netting made from dried sinew that one woman and another had given him. His body was rigid with concentration, and his hands moved with a slow tenderness and care as fingers twisted reeds through an intricate design. She was both amazed and amused that this lumbering old man held so much skill in his fingers. In her heart she felt like a mother watching a daughter tracking a lightfoot or a son shaping clay with his hands. The rest of her body was warm and impulsive, and she wanted to be drawn in by Old Sour Plum's strength, by the shape of his muscles, by the sureness of his stance. But when she thought of this strength, all she saw was his arm lashing out and Ugly Kaross hurled to the ground, her face bloodied.

She walked away and approached again, this time reaching out to snap one branch, then another. Sour Plum called out, and she responded, so he would know the sound was not made by another man. This time he stood with his back to the half-finished nest. He held several reeds in one hand. They looped over his palm, and he looked at them like something he had just discovered there.

I looked to him, then averted her gaze. Beyond her own desire, she felt nothing. She said again, "I am here," and stepped forward.

Old Sour Plum stepped back.

She hadn't expected that reaction. She had thought his old

age wouldn't matter when she approached, the sheen of her skin soft, her intent obvious. She took several more steps.

And he stepped back again.

The evening air was warm, but she felt cold. She could not move. She did not know what to do. She wanted her feelings to be stronger.

"Go away," he said. His voice was low, with no trace of kindness.

She walked up to him with the intent to reach out, to convince with her fingers.

He turned on her, his lips stretched back, his teeth bared. His eyes were wide and hard. Then the look was gone and he backed away from her and turned his face away. "Go away," he said.

She did not leave. She did not want to stay.

"You tell a woman to aim her arrows. You heal an animal who kills. Go away. Go. Away."

The sky, when it could be seen, had lost its color. In the clearing, where it had all started, the color of sunset splashed along one side of the woods. Across the darkened ground was a number of bones and the buzzing of insects.

Roofer's call sounded nearby, so it was easy to find him, but he did not hold still for her. He saw her, and walked away. She called out to him. He kept walking.

She almost headed to where Made Nothing had built his nest yesterday, but she worried about the son that could result from such a mating. She worried about how Roofer and Sour Plum might react if Made Nothing decided to stay near the river and make gifts for the elder daughters who would soon mate again.

She returned to her hut and hearth. She removed the blanket from the gzaet. She wanted to play it. She wanted the notes to sound and to distance her from everything in the world. But there was the Stranger with his ragged breath. There was the not-a-person with his broken leg. She began work on the crutches. She shaped the wood with her stone knife and stopped often to use stone against stone to sharpen the knife. It was getting thin and brittle, and she would need a new knife soon. She worked and she worked; all she could think about was the two of them; all she could feel was her desire.

A voice called out from the shelter. It was Broken Leg.

"Healer," said the voice a second time, and she had to listen again to the sounds in her mind to understand what he had said.

"I am here," she said.

"The other one . . ."

"What about the other one?"

What he said was a jumble.

She should stand up from her work. She should go to the opening. She should kneel by him and listen to what he said. She couldn't bear to be that close. Her knife slid along wood; another shaving fell to the ground. "Say it again."

He spoke more slowly, but only several words were clear: Healing. Dying. Needs.

How much destruction waited in the Stranger's bag? "You don't understand what you ask."

The jumble of words again, the three words that were clear: Healing. Dying. Needs.

I's anger surged through her like a kind of pleasure. "If I hear you, I know you're there."

"Healer."

I could not believe her own anger, nor did she fight it. "I don't want to know you're there. I don't want to hear you."

"Healer."

"I don't want to hear you. I want to be alone. I don't want to know you're there. Take your voice away. Take your voice away."

Broken Leg said nothing more. I worked and seethed. She despised their presence. She despised herself for feeling this way. She despised the desire that perched inside her and reached up to her belly and clutched her heart and made it hard to think about anything else but about how these two were here, how she had to worry about them, how they had made the rest of her life impossible.

She could not bear to be this way. Before she knew it, she had wrapped her kaross around her as if she were going to gather, and left hut and hearth. She knew where she was going, but she did not think about it in words that her mind could hear.

It was night. Tomorrow morning he had to find a way back to the shuttle.

"I heard what you said to her."

Esoch did not know how to think of him. It made sense that he had been here long before the *Way of God* had arrived. But for what purpose? Was this a military outpost? Was he a kind of lookout or guardian? Or was he a scientist sent here to study these slazans, an enthnographer like Pauline, who had studied slazan foragers to better understand slazan nature. Whichever he was, he spoke too much for a slazan. No wonder his superiors had exiled him to a place as far away as they could send him.

"She won't get my pack. She's afraid of more destruction."

Esoch thought of Pauline, who was out there heading south, most likely. He said, "I told you a woman came down in the shuttle. I did not come down with her. I came down in a decoy probe."

"I know," the warrior, who might well be an ethnographer, said. "I saw the probe where it had washed up ashore."

"The woman who came down left for the south before I got the shuttle. You need to help me contact her."

"You want me to find her?"

"I want you to talk to the locals. I want them to ask others. I can't leave her alone on this planet."

"There was a girl here last night. Did you understand what she said to the healer?"

"I barely remember the girl."

"And the woman who came today?"

Was it worse to say they spoke too fast or that he didn't try hard enough, that despair had made it all so difficult?

"It is not good news."

"What do you mean?" Esoch already knew what the warrior would say. He didn't know if it would be a lie.

"The body of your companion was found. She is dead."

Esoch looked away. The warrior must be lying. He didn't want to deal with two humans. Pauline had to be alive. If only he had left the beach sooner. If only he hadn't lost the tracking disc. If only if only if only.

His fist hit the ground. He clenched his teeth. He would not scream out, he would not cry, not in front of the warrior. Pauline had to be alive.

"How did she die?" he asked later. The hut was dark. The sky above was dark blue easing into black.

There was no response.

"Did they say how she died?"

"Yes."

He must have been waiting for Esoch to ask. He had left Esoch alone, had allowed him to lie there with his grief and his solitude. Was such respectful silence to be considered sympathy or calculation? "Tell me," Esoch said.

"Two of them hunted her down. An arrow hit her. She escaped the pursuit. She was found dead by the girl."

"They hunted her?"

"Two of them did." The slazan's voice grew softer. "They were afraid of her."

"What had she done to frighten them?" he asked, even though he suspected the answer.

There was no response.

"Why would they hunt her down like an animal?"

Again, nothing.

Esoch turned as much as he could without causing his leg to hurt. He reached out and touched the slazan's body. There was no response, no reflex against his touch.

He listened carefully. The slazan was breathing. His breath was soft, but consistent. How long would the slazan live?

Esoch lay back and tried to make himself comfortable. He knew of two slazans who had died since Pauline's arrival. What did the other slazans think of Esoch? Were the two who had hunted Pauline equally scared of him?

The healer's absence now frightened him.

As she made her way through the darkening woods, I told herself she wanted a daughter. In her mind's eye she saw Huggable's daughter, and in her mind's ear she heard herself explain again how such a daughter had come about, reminded herself that everything wrong with the daughter had been in the milk she had suckled, not in the seed or the soil.

The cooking fire in Nightskin's hut and hearth had been well fed, and flames raised their arms higher than a person's head. The hut, the poles where meat hung, the daughter's curled-up and quiet body, were all well lit. The trees nearby were the color of soil, between them blackness filled up the hollowness like dark water.

Nightskin rose to her feet the moment I stepped from the woods. She approached I in easy strides, and she made no greeting. Her hand reached out, and fingertips brushed I's shoulder. Her touch was as light as a breeze. "Your skin is so soft."

I's body was trembling, but she did not feel cold at all. Her belly was empty. Her thighs were moist. She shouldn't do this. But Huggable had done this. A young woman far away had done this. The daughter was lying so still that I watched her until she was sure the daughter was breathing. Nightskin had not moved, but I could hear her breath. Nightskin's words were quiet ones, ones that disappeared with the rustle of leaves. "Do you have words to share?"

"No." I turned and walked away from the clearing, into the woods. In the distance, away from the light of the fire, everything was the color of ash, and night had not yet drowned the land. Firelight cast its light on one side of the trees, and there were the dark clouds of their shadows flickering against the nearby trees.

I removed her kaross and bunched it up, placed it against the tree, and leaned her shoulder into it. She stretched out her fingers behind her, undid the pubic apron, and heard it land upon the ground. She lowered her back, raised up her bottom, and closed her eyes. She had no interest in looking back to watch Nightskin drop her pubic apron, nor did she wish to watch Nightskin's penis rise from between her labia, even though she now saw it all very well behind her closed eyelids.

Nightskin's hand was against her bottom; she could feel the knuckles, the pressing in, as the woman's hand led her penis to where I had opened herself. I felt her own breath suck in, the recognition of pleasure, the feeling of skin within her, and she pressed out, her desire wanting to take as much in, another part of her, the part that formed words in her head, wanting something very different.

It was not long before Nightskin stopped thrusting, then pulled out of her. A new moistness against her thigh explained the reason. I had what she wanted, but her desire left her bent there, her bottom moving about. Nightskin touched her back. I felt herself straighten up, and she moved away to another tree.

"Healer?"

"Stay away. Just for a while."

"You have so little solitude."

I felt herself nod.

"I understand. You are never alone now. And here I am, much closer than you want someone to be."

I liked the way Nightskin understood what she felt. I looked to the other woman's naked body, but the fire was behind her, and she could see nothing.

"I can make myself a fire at the edge of hut and hearth. You can sleep by my cooking fire or in my hut. You can have all the room you want to be alone."

I walked to the shadow that spoke. Her hand took the soft

penis, and she ran her fingers around it, letting go when she felt
the rest of her, then touching again, the skin soft, no sign of the
thin bone on the underside, the amazement when it remained
thin, but seemed to rise, expand, harden.

I leaned against the tree, the kaross between her shoulder
and bark again. She planted her feet firmly and again sucked in
her breath when she felt the other's penis become part of her.
She pressed out, wanting as much of it as possible to be in her,
she pressed hard against the other's thrusts, and she tried to think
only of the other's penis, of nothing else, because the pleasure
was good; it was good to be away from hut and hearth, it was
good to be away from the two who lay there, it was good to feel
such rare sensations run through her. Nightskin's fingertips ran
along her back, hands caressed her face, her forehead, hands
placed themselves firmly at the base of her neck, fingertips resting on collarbone, gripping so Nightskin could pull hard, thrust
into her, the pleasure coming out as sighs.

"So good," I heard herself say. "So good to be here and
away from everything."

"You want your solitude back," said Nightskin.

"Yes." Saying it carried its own kind of pleasure, its own
desire.

"You want the Stranger gone," said Nightskin.

"Yes."

"You want the not-a-person gone."

"Yes."

"Do you want me to make them gone?"

"Yes."

It was with these words she felt the sensations that had been
building in her flow through her, and she reached down, pressed
hard. She said yes, yes, yes, and felt with each blow where penis
joined vulva, and a great release shook her body. Her face
slapped against bark. The kaross fell to the ground. And everything felt wonderful for that moment where there was pleasure
and nothing else.

Then everything was fragile. The bark was rough on her
skin. Every shift in breeze caressed. Nightskin stood behind
her breathing hard. I could still feel Nightskin's hands upon her
shoulders, the fingertips upon her collarbone, and she was shivering, her belly empty, but there was no expectation. Nightskin
was all shadow, and I hated herself, hated her desire, hated everything that had brought her here.

Nightskin touched her shoulder again, and I tried hard not

to flinch. Nightskin said, "By tomorrow night you will have your solitude back. If your desire is strong again, we can share the heat by your fire."

I let herself nod. She knew what Nightskin was saying. She knew what she had asked Nightskin to do.

Nightskin accepted that I had to return to her hut and hearth. "As long as each is there, you do have to be there," said Nightskin as she looked through the wood she had stacked for something that would act as a firebrand.

I headed back to her hut and hearth, the forest dark, I relying on the number of times she had walked these paths to find her way there. She listened to the night's many sounds and half wished a nightskin, the kind with four paws, would leap out, take hold of her in its jaws, and put an end to it all.

She kept feeling Nightskin's hands around her neck, and she kept seeing Ugly Kaross, her body floating in the cold spring water. She kept seeing the empty sheath, which might once have held a knife. She kept seeing the neck, the bruises there. She had tried so hard not to think about those because she had been sure it had been Flatface, who'd had so many words to hide, who had been so vehement that Ugly Kaross was a threat to everyone. But it hadn't been Flatface. It had been the fingers around her own neck that had done it. If Ugly Kaross had not stepped out of her rock at the wrong time, Clever Fingers would still be alive. If it hadn't been for Huggable's terrible aim, Clever Fingers would still be alive. Huggable must have told Nightskin about tracking Ugly Kaross to the swamp, how she had been struck with an arrow. Nightskin must have stalked the swamp, waiting for the wounded woman to emerge. Now could Nightskin have kept her anger burning for so long? And after Ugly Kaross was dead, what then? Had Nightskin gone to Huggable? Had she desired Huggable's embrace? Had Huggable refused her? Or had Huggable taken her in, making it so easy for Nightskin to wrap her arms around Huggable's chest.

But why did she want to believe this? Why did she want to think this of Nightskin, the one who had accepted that I sliced knife through dead skin to look at the shape of muscles and the arrangement of heart and stomach? Why did she imagine this of the one who had just given her so much pleasure? Of the one who had promised to return her solitude?

Because Nightskin had asked the questions that had allowed I to ask for two more deaths.

Now, she was scared, walking through the night, a glow of
fire perched at her side, because she knew that Nightskin had
discovered a taste for death, a desire to set things right. She
knew Nightskin would do what was asked of her. She could
warn the Stranger. She could warn Broken Leg. But that would
betray her words. Because she and Nightskin had been mating
close when she had asked. This is what she had wanted.

And one other image stayed in her mind. When Nightskin
spoke to her. When Nightskin said they could share I's fire tomorrow night, I had looked over the other's shoulder, had seen
how the fire had dimmed, had seen the daughter sitting up, head
facing in their direction. The daughter had been watching.

I did not try to sleep when she returned to hut and hearth.
She touched the cool surface of the gzaet. She checked the sleeping figures of the Stranger and Broken Leg, their bodies just
shadows in the faint light cast by the coals between them. She
picked up the memory beads, fingered their shapes, took them
out by the cooking fire and looked at their colors, and let them
remind her how best to make a set of crutches. She was a healer.
If this pregnancy took, she would have a daughter who was a
healer.

I fed the cooking fire, she set the pieces of the crutches in
front of it, and she began to work. If Broken Leg could use them,
if he could stand without too much pain, then he could leave before Nightskin ever showed up. I still had to think of a way to
save the Stranger, whose ragged breath sounded in the quiet. As
long as he breathed, she had to worry for him as if he might
breathe forever.

He was awake when the healer returned. He saw her look in
on them, watched her take out strings of beads. He heard her
footsteps, he heard wood strike wood, the crackle of sparks, and
he saw the shadow of flames rise high against the hut's wall. He
strained to hear what she was doing but could not make out the
whisper of sounds.

The pain in his leg was held in tight by the splint, and it
flowed through him like ink spreading through water. Tomorrow
morning he would have to convince her of many things: to get
the ethnographer's medicine, to lead them back to the shuttle.

And then what? Fly away to the moon? Board the slazan's
starship? What would General ibn Haj think if Esoch came back
early, having dropped the enemy off at a nearby star?

Would he be better off staying here? A lone alien among a population of loners. What kind of survival was that? And what more destruction would happen if he remained? But if he went with the enthnographer, if the ethnographer kept his promise, then Esoch could go back home. To survive all this and still stand at the edge of the reserve, to still fear the taunts and jeers, to still imagine N!ai's bold angry eyes. There had been nothing for him anywhere.

He wasn't like Pauline, who had left home for the University. He wasn't like Hanan, who had left her marriage for the stars. They had moved with purpose, and their destruction had been like the arrow that had hit the slazan man, something their decisions didn't account for, but he had left the reserve full of anger and empty of intent. The thumb piano was destroyed. He made no music. Since he had left the reserve, all he had manufactured was death.

But if he made it to the shuttle, if he left with the ethnographer, if the ethnographer took him home, if he made his way to the reserve, what about Pauline?

What if the ethnographer had lied about Pauline's death to keep things safe, to deal with only one human?

He couldn't leave Pauline alone on this planet.

The following is taken from the notebook Pauline Dikobe kept while the Way of God *returned from Tienah to E-donya E-talta.*

Day 3

I walk and pace and speak; I watch the lines scroll out on the screen; and I wonder how long they will let me keep these words.

I say this because I want it to be part of the record, if I get to keep this record. The shuttle returned to the loading dock. I got out. The shuttle door slid shut. It won't reopen. The intelligence has shut down. All the data has been closed off, confiscated. A pretimed message appeared on the captain's log. I am officially relieved of my post. All my work and data belongs to the military now. The General has his research. He has aggressive male slazans. He has a slazan who commits infanticide. He has a slazan who cheats a companion. And he has his failed colony.

And ibn Haj, who gifted me with a slazan knife, who moved so well in my embrace: he smiled well, and he lied even better. Captain al-Shaykh told me he had thumbprinted the order.

Day 5

I expected Jihad or Tamr to justify ibn Haj's action. I expected them to argue that I was soft on the slazans, that I couldn't be trusted to bring back the material untouched. I expected them to be more loyal to their beliefs, more loyal to the humanity they served, than to whatever sense of friendship they felt toward me.

But Jihad has made numerous attempts to use the ship's intelligence to get at the data in the shuttle. She claims the captain is—off the record—aware of her attempts and has done nothing to stop her.

Tamr has twice tried to get the shuttle door to unlock.

All for nothing.

Day 7

I had longed to witness the Garden of Eden.

I had hoped my foraging slazans would be primal utopians.

I had hoped to find this place where every contradiction of life was well managed.

I find that I yearn for some way of life that would create a human who would accept her own self-contradictions, and in doing so she could step out of our evolutionary past like some fragile, winged creature emerging from her chrysalis, the broken shell lying there to be consumed for her own nourishment.

So I look back to my foraging Eden, so that today's problems are like original sin, our reason to struggle, to make us worthy of God's better judgment. When one male confronts another, testosterone and adrenaline escalate, angers flare. When males hunt, testosterone remains even, the mind remains cool. We take the anger in our hearts and stalk our enemy like hunters. I coldly consider ways that I can dig up truth they have buried, how I can make sure these slazans are not one more victim of the war.

Aggression makes individual survival possible. Morality makes survival in groups possible. And somehow that makes for necessary evils, and those evils make for necessary goods. I tire of this balancing act between evil and good, between self and community, between my interests and your interests and our interests; the wars continue, we breed one failed society after another, and we long for Eden, struggling to create what we truly never had.

Chapter Fifteen

The Seventeenth Day

The woman who called herself Nightskin did not move. She stared at the river of sky that ran between the treetops, and she watched the clouds float from one side to the other. The daughter tried to make fire from coals and only got coal dust all over her face. She cried. She said she was hungry. Nightskin just looked up and tried to ignore her. There was only the sky and her. The daughter went off to find wood, to find leaves to eat. Had her mother taught her which leaves were safe to eat?

When Nightskin had said the words last night, they had been easy to say. The passion had run through her. The words had been right. The idea had been right. Nightskin remembered a night when she had lived near the dunes. She had been with the woman she called Soft Bottom, who was later called Huggable by one woman and another. The wind had been chilled that night on the dunes. Soft Bottom had come to Nightskin for warmth, and she had called out *yes yes yes* just like the healer would call out years later. After giving birth to a daughter, Soft Bottom came to the river's mouth, looking for Nightskin's warmth. When Soft Bottom gave birth to the second daughter, one woman and another from the river's mouth made Soft Bottom bury the infant before it could breathe. So Soft Bottom headed south to live by a sunset fruit tree and mate with Rival, who one and another called Hugger and who now was dead.

Nightskin thought of the story her mother had told her, about the one who had killed the woman who ate children. The woman who killed her had to leave hut and hearth, and she died alone in the winter. I did not bury you, her mother had said. Remember, I did not bury you.

Nightskin considered leaving this hut and hearth and finding another place to live before the growing child within her started to show. She would also have Soft Bottom's daughter, who would help her when the infant inside her was born. She could find a place where no one would have heard of how the second animal and the Stranger had died, and each woman who lived there would share readily with a new woman who could hunt well, and then she would not die like the woman in her mother's story.

But she did not want to leave the river. She wanted each woman to look to her with the same respect Nightskin had seen in the face of each woman who lived by the river's mouth after she had destroyed the small boulder with legs. But here she did not want each face to look at her with the kind of respect that hid obvious fear. The woman the healer called Flatface had told Nightskin that she wanted to throw rocks at the boulder. The next animal, the one who would come after the second animal, would see this and know it was not wanted.

Nightskin had asked: what if the next animal came and had nowhere but the boulder to live? Perhaps they should make the insides of the boulder a poor place to live.

Flatface had had no answer. Nightskin could not tell the old woman how she had sat on the hillside, how she had watched the animal go in and come out. She had seen where he had placed his hand to make the entranceway appear. When the animal was gone, Nightskin, too, had placed her hand on the round surface the color of crystal. The boulder had not opened to her. If she had the animal's hand, if she pressed it to the round surface, then they could go in, then they could destroy whatever was inside the boulder. When the next animal came, it would find another animal's hand lying on the floor, it would see the destruction, it would be sure to leave, and no animal would ever return here again. If Nightskin could make that happen, then she would not have to leave, and each woman would look to her with respect and awe.

Still, the thought was easier than the action. A giant white cloud stretched from one line of trees to another and didn't seem

to move at all. The ground against her back was hard. To kill
from a distance was an act of cowardice—it was unwomanly. To
kill bravely meant getting mating close. To get mating close and
to kill were equally disgusting.

Death had to come with surprise: the animal alone, emerging from the swamp, stumbling more than walking, head turning
this way and that, confused, her lips speaking words, asking for
help. Or death had to come with anger: Soft Bottom refusing to
mate, preferring the rival almost-a-man who made nothing well,
turning her back, walking away. But to think out death, to plan
it as a woman plans a hunt, was something even more terrible.
She wanted to hate the second animal, but she couldn't. The second animal had done nothing. She heard her own voice: *You
want the Stranger gone. You want the not-a-person gone. Do you
want me to make them gone?* And she heard the urgency in the
way the healer had said *yes, yes, yes yes yes* while she held the
healer from behind, feeling herself inside the healer, ready to do
anything she asked, to make for some desire, some need for
those words to be more than air, which vanished like a breeze
that touched you and was gone. She imagined the animal's chest
gouged open, the Stranger's throat cut where he breathed and
bled, and she imagined the healer opening herself to Nightskin,
taking her in, enjoying the pleasure of the freedom that only
Nightskin could bring.

She knew such a thing would never happen. She knew the
healer would despise her. But still she saw the healer open to her,
she saw the two dead bodies, and she kept the pleasure she
would feel rushing through her, waiting release. She rose from
the ground to get what she needed.

Esoch imagined his return. He imagined the circle of huts,
a fire in front of each one, the voices back and forth, some
women talking to each other from their hearths, several men off
making arrows, another group of men standing around a man
who was throwing his oracle discs into the air to see where they
would fall, several children running around the center of camp,
tossing a melon back and forth; and N!ai rising from her parents'
hearth, rising from beside her mother, turning in his direction,
her eyes upon him, alone, no other man, no child in her arms,
and he lifted his arm to wave, and her arm too made its way sky-
ward, a smile, radiant in the early-morning light, taking her face,
making him welcome.

And Esoch opened his eyes because it was too good to be true. Everything had the bright sheen of the early-morning gray, a dusty hue, like something old and forgotten. In the desert reserve he would have seen the sun rise, he would have a secure sense of how long it would be until the sun touched the center of the sky and erased all shadows. If he didn't make it to the shuttle today, he would never return home.

Esoch sat up. The slazan was still breathing. In this light his skin was sapped of color. Esoch looked at the slazan's fingers, scraped and dirtied; they still looked like the fingers of someone who did not work with his hands. Perhaps the slazan told the truth; perhaps he was an ethnographer, not a warrior.

The fire between them was nothing but coals, orange and gray, faint heat against the morning chill. Alongside Esoch were what could only be crutches. The craftsmanship was crude, nothing like the nests he had seen, or the bows, or the straight accuracy of the arrows. There was the one long leg, and affixed like the top of the Nostratic letter *T* was a bar of wood where he could rest his armpits. Lower down were two small stumps, where he could press down with his hands. A hole had been bored through the main leg, and a rounded stick had been jammed through. It took him a while, and a good deal of pain, to figure out how to rise. And then he stood there awkwardly, wearing the upper half of his onesuit, the rest cut off from the waist down.

He eased himself out of the hut. The dimensions of the crutches had not been well calculated: his hands barely reached the grips, and cross pieces jammed into his armpits.

The fire at the center of camp was nothing more than gray heat. The healer was curled up and sleeping soundly, her hair almost as brown as other slazan hair, just a few traces of red. Behind her a leather blanket covered something, the tin piano?

"Healer?"

She didn't move, and Esoch feared to wake her. She had been up most of the night, and he did not want her exhaustion to foul her mood, to have her speak to him the way she had last night. He needed her cooperation.

The morning was fresh, the sun not yet visible above the trees. Esoch tried to believe there was enough time.

He heard water flowing nearby. Here was a way to present himself well before the healer, not as some half-naked creature with skin caked with shit. He maneuvered himself toward the sound. Thirty-two agonizing swings forward on the crutches, each landing on his right leg, jarring the left and renewing the pain. But the water was clean, clear. The area where he stood had been cleared of vegetation, and the slope of the land eased into the water.

Movement behind him, a rustling in the leaves. He tried to swivel around, panic making the movement hard and urgent, and he almost fell in the attempt. A tiny black animal scurried off at the sound of him. It wasn't a slazan. No one was hunting him. Maybe the ethnographer had lied. Maybe no one had ever hunted Pauline.

It took longer than he had imagined to undress the upper half of his body and make his way, on crutches, into the river. There was the constant fear of slipping, of the splint being damaged, of the way his leg had been set undone in such a way to make the pain unmanageable. But the flow of water itself, the chill of it, was tremendous. His stance was precarious. His attempts to splash water onto his face with his right hand were feeble. But the water flowed around his chest, and he could feel the way it flowed about his thighs, around his abdomen. He took a crude, childlike pleasure in giving up his wastes to the river and knowing that all of it, all of it from the past two days, would be carried away with the current. He emerged from the water covered with goose bumps, his whole body shivering, his whole body clean. He would return to the healer with nothing of the past days' stink.

But the healer was still asleep.

The sky above was a clear blue. The air was cool, and he shivered. It was still early morning. The sun had warmed nothing. He had hours, he told himself, hours. How many hours would he need to convince the healer to help them?

"Healer," he said. His voice was a whisper. Why such fear? he asked himself. He spoke her name a second time, louder, then a third.

I heard her name and did not recognize the voice. The hard ground was comfortable. The chill air pushed all warmth to the core of her body, and she clung to the warmth. She did not want to uncurl her body, she did not want to get up, but the voice kept calling. She just wanted to sleep. She became aware of the rawness in her hands from shaping the wood, the stickiness along her thighs from last night's encounter, the stinging along her cheek and her shoulders. It was then that she remembered

Nightskin and the terrible promise I had exacted from the other woman.

She opened her eyes and saw Broken Leg standing at a respectful distance. He looked as if his body had collapsed upon the crutches. He was naked, but he showed the proper modesty. He bunched up the remains of his skins—I was amazed how small so much skin could become—and held it over his groin. He now seemed more naked than before, and she became more aware of the penis hidden behind the skins. Only a woman feeling desire, thought I, would think about the penis of a not-a-person.

"Sit down," she said. "I have food to share."

Broken Leg stood there, as if thinking. The dark lines, scars, that marked off one arm had also been cut across his chest.

I realized that he did not know how to show his respect by politely refusing. Or perhaps he did not understand. She said, "I have food to share. Sit down."

She watched him struggle to find a way to sit. A breeze caused leaves to whisper; she heard something behind her move. She turned; saw nothing. Nightskin would soon be here. Nightskin would not turn away. If she warned Broken Leg, then he might kill Nightskin, making I the true killer.

The bunched-up skins fell to the ground, and he was naked again. His healthy leg was bent, and he was holding the injured one still above the ground. He lowered his bottom closer and closer until he could not help but fall back, his bottom slapping hard against the ground. The muscles on his face tightened; she was surprised how easy it was to read the pain upon a not-a-person's face. He grabbed the skins and spread them over his lap.

She gathered what food was left in the hut and hearth, set aside a portion for the Stranger, and returned to the fire. She placed half of the food down in front of her. She leaned forward with the rest. Broken Leg cupped his hands and held them out before her. It was an odd gesture. She laid the food out in front of him. His hands were at his sides, as if he had never held them out, the sudden movement much like the jerky movements of a child learning to be respectful, the incorrect gestures or words quickly and awkwardly changed.

Broken Leg ate slowly. I did not touch her food. She felt no hunger at all. In her mind's eye she saw what she had not truly seen—Nightskin's belly near I's bottom, the penis rising from Nightskin's vulva, the hard skin easing into her. She closed her eyes against her vision, but her mind refused to close itself, and she still saw Nightskin press against her, she still heard her own voice say yes yes yes: yes, she desired her solitude.

She placed the rest of her portion in front of Broken Leg.

Broken Leg looked at the food. "It is yours," he said.

"Eat."

He placed half of the portion in front of her before eating the rest. While he ate, she found her stone knife. She sat before the fire and pulled the leather cover off the gzaet. "I will make you something to cover yourself."

He looked to her.

"Clothes," she said. "I will make you clothes." She slid fingers over her own pubic apron.

"Make it I can," he said.

She considered this. She had wanted to make one stay-away gift after another to insure that he would stay away once healed, but she also wanted to see how much craft was in his fingers and hands. It wasn't until she had pulled the knife from its sheath that she stopped. *They flock like birds in the sky.* Perhaps a not-a-person would not consider it evil to kill someone while mating close. She handed him the knife anyway. Next she handed him the leather. He spread it out across his legs, touched it carefully, drew invisible lines with his fingers. He unsheathed the knife and examined that. He did not even look at her.

Esoch began to cut the leather with the knife and found it difficult. He vaguely remembered the shape of a breechclout, the way a knife eased through a duiker's tanned hide, but here, so far away, the memory did not come to his hands. The healer had moved away from him and had started to play the battered tin piano. For a while all he could do was stare. He had never been so close to it. The metal was dented, stained with years and years of use since this woman's ancestors had settled here, but the keys were spaced so evenly, the music so clear and precise. It no longer jangled, no longer sounded alien; it was as if the music's logic made sense to him, even though he liked little of what she played. He wondered about the source of the piano's technology, if it used some kind of ultrasonics to achieve its medicinal effect. And while he mused, he returned to work, hacking away at the leather, blunting further this stone knife so he could wear something and not feel so naked, so aware of his penis, his balls, his vulnerability.

He had to lie down and struggle to get the breechclout

under his butt, to tie it firmly so it wouldn't slide down his hips. It was then he was overtaken by a terrible urge to pee.

The healer pointed the direction to go. He swung on the crutches—twelve agonizing swings—to where he had heard the healer do her business. The stink wasn't as bad as he had feared; it was as if the insects took care of the worse of it, buzzing as they did around the remains of shit.

It was only two swings back and he recognized a different kind of disorder among the midden's own disorder. There was a place where the earth did not have its own undisturbed flatness, its own random tangle of new growth. Is this where the healer had buried the slazan's pack?

I played on while she watched Broken Leg return. The breechclout was well made, though oddly cut. She should have made one for him. He struggled to sit close to the fire. He crossed his arms and held himself as if he were cold. The day had taken on some warmth, but the not-a-person still shivered. Perhaps they flocked together for warmth.

When would Nightskin come?

"I have words to share," said I.

Broken Leg turned his face in her direction but respectfully eyed the ground.

I found that she could not tell him about Nightskin, about last night's promises. She said, "You come from very far."

"Yes."

"Does the Stranger come from very far?"

"I don't understand."

"The one in the hut. The person. Does he come from the same place as you?"

Broken Leg said nothing for so long that I was certain he didn't understand. Then he said, "Yes. I and he come from same the place."

"How many days does it take to walk there?"

His answer came out as a jumble of words, and only after he finished did she realize that he hadn't answered the question. He had said something about healing.

"Say it again."

"The one in the hut." The next words were blurred, something about healing, about the ground. She realized he had found where she had buried the Stranger's bag. "Die he will. Needs he the healing."

"I will play the gzaet for him soon," said I, even though she already knew her music would do no good.

Broken Leg raised his eyes to meet hers. He spoke slowly. "Where live I and the one in the hut is played healing. Have I a tiny gzaet." He pushed down one finger on each hand as if playing music. "So tiny it one finger and one finger needs. But make it only sounds. Only sounds." He stopped. Somehow, on his face, she could see that he struggled with words in the same way he had struggled to rise and to sit. "Only sounds. No healing. Tiny gzaet I play to bring together people." He took his hands and hugged himself. "Hands use I to hug. Tiny gzaet sounds use I to touch. But sounds, no healing. Use we other healing. In bag."

"No," she said. She stopped playing and stood. She walked over to the hut and looked in on the Stranger. She could not hear him breathe, but she could see his chest rise and fall. She heard the not-a-person move about, she heard the crutches knock together, scrape against ground. She knew he was standing again. She turned to face him.

"His healing," he said. "Dig it I from the ground."

"No."

Broken Leg looked to his feet for a moment, then raised his eyes to meet hers. "The rock," he said. "Healing have I in the rock. Me take to the rock."

"I will play music for him."

"Dies he. Dies he."

What was she to say? She feared leaving the Stranger alone, for what if Nightskin arrived? But she would lead Broken Leg to the rock. "Will you make the rock go away?"

He spoke slowly. "Give I the one in the hut healing from the rock. Then take I the one to the rock. Then will be gone the rock."

I looked to the Stranger in the hut. Each choice was a bad one. Her quiver and bow hung from the sturdy limb of a smoothbark tree. She took down arrows and bow, though she knew she could never use them.

Esoch followed the healer. He should have been paying attention to the trails she took, but all of his attention was devoted to using the crutches. He finally got the hang of it, standing on his right foot, placing crutches in front, leaning forward, then swinging through, right foot landing, left leg feeling the jar, the pain augmented more than he could have imagined. His stomach and bowels loosened, his head felt empty. The healer did not walk quickly. She stopped constantly, glanced over her shoulder to see where Esoch was, then continued on. He tried to look for landmarks now, some way to make sense of the trail, but he found himself watching the healer, the way her back moved, the way the pubic skirt hid her buttocks, the quiver of arrows bouncing against her back, the bow strung over the other shoulder. She was not hunting; why did she need bow and arrow?

But soon he had stopped thinking about that. Soon he had stopped noticing landmarks. Soon he had stopped noticing the pain. It was amazing how easily the human mind could adapt to the utterly foreign; perhaps this was the root of all mass evil: you were a forager when need be, a drunk when need be, and a soldier when need be, and all the private fears that made you unique remained quiet and buried inside. At what point did the need-be's change you forever? Could he ever be a Ju/wa again, could he ever again fit into the difficult pattern of sharing and complaining, talking and arguing? He longed for the communal dance; did he long for the sweat and the dryness of hunting during the summer, the freezing-cold nights, the too-many children who died before they were weaned? Maybe he was better off saving the ethnographer's life and seeing if that mattered enough for the slazan to let the human live. Maybe there were answers there.

But what if the ethnographer was lying to begin with?

He rehearsed the words a number of times in his head before he spoke them to her back.

"Healer?"

She slowed. "What?"

"The woman." He did not know what words to use.

"What woman?"

"The woman in the rock. The woman who was there before me. The one who walked off into the woods."

"What about her?"

"The other one said she was dead."

"What?"

"The other one told me she was dead."

The healer stopped and turned. Esoch stopped. His injured leg throbbed. Without movement the pain seemed to double. The cross pieces dug into his armpits. The healer said nothing.

"Healer?"

The words came out too quickly. He heard the words *left* and *no see*.

"The one in the hut told me different."

"The one is sick." The healer's eyes became hard and round. She did not look away from him. The stare made him uncomfortable. He did not know what it meant. The healer spoke very slowly, taking care with each word. "The one is sick. He says things. The woman is gone. No one has seen her."

Esoch looked to the ground. Dirt looked like dirt. He considered the possibility that the healer might lie. She would not want him to know that Pauline was dead, that one of her own had hunted her down. She would fear losing his trust if he knew a slazan hand killed Pauline. She didn't know how badly he needed to get to the shuttle. "Healer?" he said.

"The woman is gone." The healer turned and resumed walking. Esoch had taken several swings forward when she stopped again. "Will you share words?"

Esoch stopped a second time. The pain was hard, like his leg had been cast in metal. The sun could be seen through the canopy. It didn't look like it was too high up, but how long until it reached the center of the sky? What could he do? The polite reply came readily. "I have words to share."

"What happened between," and he lost track of the words. "Between?"

"You and"—she used the word that meant someone from another place—"and"—she used the foul word for giving a hug. Who was she talking about? She repeated the words. She meant Esoch, the ethnographer, and, with growing apprehension, he realized she meant the one the ethnographer had shot at, the slazan local who must have died. "What happened?" she asked again.

She had a right to know; he didn't know if he should tell her.

Broken Leg said nothing, so I spoke again. "The almost-a-man I called Hugger was attacking you. He had a knife. He was going to kill you. Did you kill him?"

I had to ask it a second time before Broken Leg said, "No. The one other did."

"The other one?"

"Yes. The other one." Now that he had the word right, his pronunciation was harder to understand.

"How? How did he do it?"

Broken Leg said nothing. He hung there on the crutches, and she became aware of the tautness in his neck, the strength he was using to hold himself up.

I said, "The other one held something in his hand."

"Yes. That is what killed"—and the word *Hugger* sounded more like *hug-hug.* "Throws the thing in hand something like fire. Hard fire."

If she hadn't seen Hugger's chest, I wouldn't have accepted this. And even though she accepted it, part of her did not believe it. "And the other one threw fire at you?"

"Yes."

"Why?"

Esoch knew that until now the story had him as a victim. Victims aren't very threatening in stories. He didn't want to be threatening.

"Why?" She asked again.

"I thought he was going to throw fire at me. The thing in my hand throws"—he thought for a moment—"tiny arrows that hurt you because they fly so fast. I shot one at him." He repeated himself twice, trying different words.

"Why would he throw fire at you?"

Esoch was first surprised how readily he understood the healer. He was also surprised at how willing he was to answer. He wanted her trust. He wanted no stories the ethnographer could later betray.

I did not know what she would hear. She listened for, and expected, a lie. The words were confused again, like those of a child explaining something only a grown woman could understand. Broken Leg said there were ones who the other one lived with. There were ones where he lived. She didn't understand the next bit until he said it again with new words. It sounded as if those who were like Broken Leg acted the way a mother with one child and another will act, which is together. And what was more difficult to understand was that Broken Leg talked as if the ones with whom the Stranger lived behaved the same way. He talked about many as if all those ones together could behave like one person. She tried to imagine it like he was talking about only two people. One person, being many ones, and one not-a-person, being many of those. And each one tried to use the same land as the other. And one disagreed with the other. Then there was something about the disagreement.

"What do you call that? What is the word?"

There was no slazan word he knew. So he used the Arabic word, which was the language in which he had first learned the appropriate vocabulary. *Qital:* warfare.

She said it. It sounded nothing like the Arabic. "What is it?"

He already realized that he couldn't explain warfare, not in any way that would put the shoot-out into a meaningful context.

"And because of this"—she used her version of the Arabic again—"you threw arrows and the other one threw fire?"

He could read the look of horror on her face. He didn't know how he recognized it. Or maybe he just expected it and knew how to read whatever expression appeared.

The healer slowed her speech again. "If there was another one like the Stranger, and if there was another one like you, then the two would have ki-taal."

Esoch understood each word, but he was unsure of the meaning.

"If another and another like the Stranger came, and another and another like you came, then the ones like the Stranger would want the ones like me to help them."

Esoch felt everything sink through him. She understood what an ally was. She understood the nature of this war. She didn't know about space travel, about the immense distances, but she knew that if more like the ethnographer showed up, she would be expected to fight with them. How horrifying to her would that be?

She was speaking again, this time quickly, about going back. Esoch was certain that it was fear he saw on her face. She was scared of this war, and she was scared of what he might have in the rock.

Esoch watched her walk back down the path. He looked in the direction where they had been headed. Would this path lead them to the shuttle? If he could get there on his own, everything would be fine. The self-destruct would be shut down. He could synthesize some amphetamine that might do the trick for the ethnographer.

"Come on," shouted the healer.

She had stopped to wait for him.

He headed off for the shuttle, along the path they had been taking. He moved as quickly as he could; his left foot touched the ground, and the pain he felt seemed to fill his body. He didn't hear her come after him, nor did he watch her overtake him. The pain subsided, and there she stood in front of him.

What now? She had asked all the right questions. She knew what war was. She would try to stop him. Without her help he would never make it to the shuttle.

He followed her and tried to think of a way to regain her trust. Before the ethnographer died. Before the shuttle lifted off.

In the distance a slazan male called out, his voice a long, high-pitched echo carrying through the woods.

*   *   *

Nightskin first shared words with Flatface, who then left her hut and hearth to share the same words with her eldest daughter, who would go to share the same words with Squawker while Flatface spoke with Many Wrinkles, whom the healer called Wisdom. While the same words spread from woman to woman, Nightskin did not go directly to the healer's hut and hearth; first she made her way to the clearing.

The sun was breaking from its embrace with the trees when she stepped on the hillside. Spots on the boulder shone back the light like small, tiny suns. Across the darkened ground lay what scavengers had left. Insects huddled together over what little meat remained on Rival's bones. Some other bones had been picked clean, and she did not know which of those bones had once belonged to Clever Fingers and which to Rival. Although there had yet been no full moon, Nightskin could not believe that a true body remained in the clearing. She had told Flatface that the clearing was empty of everything but the rock; she knew no woman would come to the clearing if they saw where the eyes had been plucked from Rival's skull and the half ear that still remained.

Nightskin walked down the hill and over to Rival's skull. The stink was terrible. What she planned to do was worse. No woman would take meat from the hand that did what she planned to do. Nightskin felt herself tremble, even though the outside of her body was as still as a rock. She felt the same anxiety she had felt the night she had come to the hillside to sit by a fire, to wait for the animal to leave so she could go down and dig Clever Fingers out of the ground and allow his true body to escape. She remembered lying at the edge of the hole she had dug, her arms extended, pulling wet clay and dirt away from Clever Fingers' face and chest, and she wondered if the true body had already come free, if it had pressed against the dirt, trapped, trying to escape, if it had flown into the air the moment she had cleared away the dirt, if she had breathed it in. That would explain why she was now capable of reaching through a cloud of insects to pick up Rival's skull, slick with the saliva of other animals, why she could carry it to the edge of the clearing that overlooked the lake, and why she could toss it down the hill and watch it bounce and roll until it disappeared into the brush. Would it matter much if she breathed in Rival's true body as well? She gathered more of his remains and did the same. She carried the bones that had been picked clean, and she told herself that they had belonged to Clever Fingers. She tried to see the way his hands had held the knife that had cut the leather for her kaross, the way the fingers had tied the beads to the fringes. But the mind's eye would not see what she wanted it to see. All she saw were bones tumbling down a hill. Soon the clearing was the clearing she had described to Flatface, empty of everything but the boulder.

Nightskin tried to wash her hands in the brook. She scrubbed them with dirt, but the hands still felt like they touched Rival's skull. She made her way toward the healer's hut and hearth and stopped when she saw, far from the trail, several moonleaf plants. She chewed on several, taking in the bitter taste, waiting for the calm that followed. She thought again of Clever Fingers' body beneath the ground, and she blamed the animal. She remembered opening herself to Clever Fingers, who was now gone, and she blamed the animal. She built her hatred with the same care a woman builds a fire that is meant to last through the night.

She was chewing on another moonleaf when she heard voices. She crouched low, as if she had heard a lightfoot. She moved slowly, keeping herself near trees, until she was close enough to see that it was the healer and the second animal. The animal was on crutches, and all he wore was a breechclout. He looked almost like a boy just before he started to grow into a man.

The healer turned and walked. The animal soon followed.

This is when Nightskin heard Old Sour Plum's long call. This is when she began to follow their trail.

I was relieved to find the Stranger still lying there. Nightskin had not yet come, and what was she to do?

The Stranger breathed like the air was thick, and when she lifted the blanket, she saw the bumps had hardened. His skin looked like that of the infant a day before the infant had died.

Broken Leg leaned forward on his crutches. His face was layered with sweat. His eyes had darkened. "Healer," he said. "Let me the bag have. Let him the healing have."

I felt the hardened bumps. Her music had done nothing.

The healer's silence, Esoch assumed, was the silence of guilt. She didn't want the ethnographer to die. But the pack contained things she feared. The shuttle contained things she feared. She was right to fear those things. He searched for words. If he didn't say the right thing, then the ethnographer would die, and Esoch would remain here for years, if not forever.

"Healer," he said again, "you have shared your music. I said I would share something. I can make the rock go. I can take the"—he searched for the word that she had used—"the Stranger with me to the rock, and the rock will leave."

The healer looked up at him. "The rock will go. You will go. The Stranger will go. You will not come back."

"Yes." The moment he said it, he knew it was a lie. He knew that once he had saved the ethnographer's life, he would come back, and he would stay until he found Pauline or Pauline's body.

"Stay here," she said. She stood up and edged around him. "Stay here."

He waited. He listened to her move out back. He listened to her dig. He listened to her grunt when she lifted up the pack. He waited, knowing that he had to earn her trust. Without her trust they were never going back to the rock.

The healer dropped the pack in front of him, not out of malice, he quickly realized once he took hold of it, but because of its tremendous weight. Just three days ago the frail slazan now lying by the gray ash had carried this to meet him, to work out a deal.

Esoch searched for a way to open it and found none. It was perfectly sealed. "I need a knife."

I handed him the stone knife and backed away. Broken Leg touched the tip of the knife to a topmost corner, and like a mouth opening, a line emerged around the edges, and the top rolled back. Broken Leg, too, seemed surprised, for he leaned away from the bag, wobbled on his crutches, while the whole bag toppled over like a felled animal. The things in it rolled out. Broken Leg said a word she had never heard before. It didn't even sound like a word, but he said it several times.

"Healer," he said, "help."

She looked at the pile of shapes that had rolled out onto the ground. Broken Leg could not just bend over and pick them up. She did not even want to touch them. The shapes were strange, as strange as anything inside the boulder.

Broken Leg spoke quickly, and his words were poorly formed this time. The only word she could understand was *die*. She knew who was dying. She knelt by the spilled things. Broken Leg pointed. She touched something. It felt like the skin of a live animal. Broken Leg spoke, pointed again. She picked up the thing next to it. "Yes," he said. It had the shape of a small carry bag. She handed it to Broken Leg.

Esoch almost dropped it. There was something about it that felt like the skin of an animal just after it had died. He knew what it was, remembered the nature of slazan biological mechanics. Dikobe's knife hilt had been based on the design of a slazan knife that had been traded to humans during the ten years of first contact. He didn't use the healer's stone knife this time. He pinched a corner, and the organic box opened. It was still unnerving to watch, but he was ready for the way everything slid open, the faint sucking noise that went with it.

He couldn't be sure if this organic box was a med-kit or not. There was an array of what looked like clay balls, but they were rubbery, warm, and alive to the touch. And in the corner were two brown things that looked like bloated leeches.

"Healer," he said. "I need him awake. I don't know how to use this healing."

Nightskin now stood at the edge of the hut and hearth. Healer had walked into the hut. The animal leaned on his crutches just outside the hut's opening. He wasn't looking about. He was oblivious to everything but what was happening inside the hut. Healer must not have told him. It would be easy to sneak up on him, easier than sneaking up on a lightfoot, whose ears were always alert to the strange sound, the snap of a twig, the whisper of the brush. But Healer was inside, and Nightskin wanted her outside, in the clear, safe from any harm. Nightskin would wait until Healer went off to gather or to fetch water, but already now one woman and another would be gathering stones, would be heading toward the clearing. She could not keep each one waiting. But if Healer came out and left the two alone inside the shelter, then maybe that would be the best moment to carry out what last night's desire had promised.

Esoch hardly understood a single word the healer used when she touched the slazan's face, when she shook his arm, when she pinched one of the hardened swellings on his leg. The slazan breathed. His skin was sapped of all color that came with the flush of blood.

The slazan's eyes opened.

The healer said something to him.

He shifted his head and looked to Esoch. He spoke in Nostratic. "Do you have the medicine?"

I watched Broken Leg tilt his head forward. Something dropped out of his mouth and into his hand. It was the same color as his tongue. He raised his head and said something to the Stranger. The Stranger spoke at length. One man speaking to another. At length, like one woman talking with another. And using words that I had never heard before. Were these different kinds of words. Were there special words for ki-taal? Do you share those words when you weren't throwing fire or shooting tiny arrows at each other?

Following the slazan's instructions, Esoch lifted the darker of the two leechlike creatures out of the open med-kit. It had already ingested the medicine ball. The slazan had prepped it so he could take another dose after their meeting. The creature was hard to hold, not because it moved, but because the slime of it was repulsive. He tried to look calm. He wanted the healer to think this was totally normal. "Healer. This has to be placed in the crook of his arm." With his other hand he tapped the crook of his own arm. He raised the creature. Then gestured again. "The animal will give him the healing."

The thing Broken Leg held looked like one of the bloodsuckers that clung to any child who thought the nearby swamp was a place to play. I swallowed her own spit once, then twice, tasting bile at the back of her throat. She stretched out her hand, palm facing up. The creature was not as slimy as she had feared. There was a quiet warmth to it, as if it were hibernating. Something stung the center of her palm. She lifted it from the back with her other hand, fumbled, almost dropped it, before she could place it in the crook of the Stranger's arm. He let out a loud sigh. His body visibly relaxed. He started to sleep again.

I's hand still stung, and there seemed to be slime across her palm. All she wanted to do was wash it off. She rose. She walked out, leaving Broken Leg and the Stranger, and headed across the hut and hearth and down toward the path and stopped. She had seen something, or had heard something. And she didn't want to leave anymore. She turned and saw her: Nightskin. Nightskin, too, had stopped. She was waiting to see what I would do. Whom should she betray?

"Go away," said I.

The healer's words were firm. The healer's skin was still soft with desire. Nightskin wanted to turn, but she couldn't. The women would soon be gathering on the hillside above the boulder.

"Go away," the healer said, and Esoch understood the

words this time, heard that they weren't ritualistic or directed at him. He started to turn, which suddenly became difficult, placing the left crutch out, trying to swivel on it. He sensed the presence of someone else, wondered who she was.

And there, standing at the edge of the encampment, stood Watcher, the large woman with the gray patches on her neck, the one who had built the solitary fire, who had watched Esoch leave for the swamp, and who, while he was gone, had dug up the body Pauline had buried. Esoch knew why she was here. Three slazans were dead. The second human was still alive.

"Go away," said I to Nightskin. "There is no need. The Stranger and the not-a-person are going to leave. They are going to leave in the rock."

Nightskin looked at I, and I could tell that Nightskin did not believe her, that the other woman thought I was lying in order to save each one she had tried to heal.

Nightskin had taken knife out of sheath. She said, "You asked this of me."

Broken Leg must have understood. His gaze shifted from Nightskin's knife to I and back to the knife. Why, he must be thinking, why all this trouble in order to die here? I's quiver of arrows was hanging from the limb of the softbark tree directly behind Nightskin. The stone knife she had given Broken Leg was on the ground beside the bag. The healing knife was in its sheath, at her side. I had never used that knife for anything but healing and the cutting of dead bodies.

Nightskin walked forward. Broken Leg swung his crutch out at her, and she stepped away to avoid it. She held the knife out in front of her. Broken Leg tried to move back, but he stumbled over the Stranger's pack, fell back, the crutches dropping in different directions, his bottom, then his back, hitting the ground, accompanied by a cry of pain.

And that's when I took several quick steps, just as Nightskin took her several steps, raised her knife, and I pushed her away. Nightskin stumbled back, regained her balance. Her eyes were wide, her look hard.

"If there will be death," said I to Nightskin, "then I have to die first."

Nightskin stood there, knife clenched in fist.

I stood there in front of the not-a-person, her hands empty.

Broken Leg groaned softly behind her.

"Go away," said I to Nightskin.

Nightskin sheathed her knife. "You asked for them to be gone."

"I said they would leave. There has been enough death."

"You said there would be another animal after this one."

"I said so to Flatface. I said so to Squawker. I said so to Clear Eyes. I never said so to you. I have no words to share with you. This is my hut and hearth. Kill me or leave."

Nightskin said nothing. The knife rested in its sheath. I waited for it to come back out. I waited for Nightskin to do what she had promised. But Nightskin turned and walked into the woods. She did not stop at the edge of hut and hearth, she did not turn to look back. She was gone. I listened to her footsteps, listened to her snap branches, until she could hear Nightskin no longer.

I's body began to tremble. Nightskin could return as quietly as she had the first time.

Esoch watched the healer stand there, and he watched her listen to sounds in the distance. It was when she went for her quiver, slung it over her shoulder, that he felt it was safe to get up. He did not believe Watcher had backed down, and he wanted a weapon now. Watcher could hide behind a number of large trees, waiting for them, poised to leap and strike. Or could she really have left? Could the words of the dying slazan have been more than rhetoric: were humans the ones who had to have both the first and last word?

It was a wailing like nothing I had ever heard before. The strength of the sound was like the wind that had sounded of many waterfalls when the rock had fallen to the clearing. This sound came from the same direction, and I felt the same fear take hold of her.

Broken Leg looked to the direction of the sound, but it didn't seem to frighten him. The Stranger was sitting up and looking in the same direction as Broken Leg.

Then the wailing was over, and the fear refused to leave her.

Esoch watched the healer walk over to her tin piano, set down her quiver of arrows and her bow alongside it, and start to play something that sounded alien, tranquil, and calming. The alarm had frightened her.

The ethnographer fed a medicine ball to the other creature and set it in the crook of his other arm. "Is that a warning?" he asked.

"There are thirty minutes left."

"And then?"

"Two minutes before midday another alarm will go off. At the end of the two minutes the shuttle will take off. When it leaves the atmosphere, it will self-destruct."

The ethnographer said nothing, his silence an accusation.

"We have to go," Esoch said.

"I cannot leave my pack."

"We have to go."

"Go. Disengage the self-destruct. Or modify it, if you think I am the enemy."

Esoch manuevered himself to where the healer was playing the tin piano. "I need to go back to the rock."

The healer stopped playing, but she did not look up when she spoke. She asked something about the Stranger.

"He is still weak."

"You and I can't leave the Stranger here." She said something about skin of night and returning.

"Skin of Night is what you call the one who"—he didn't know any word he could use for *attack*—"who was here?"

"Yes." The healer almost said something more, but she returned to playing the tin piano.

Inside the hut the ethnographer was already standing, his motions slow and careful. Esoch looked to the sky. The sun was almost overhead, filling the healer's clearing with light. Leaves were taking on their oranges, yellows, and red. He wanted a chronometer of some sort, some way of knowing exactly how many minutes were left. The feeling deepened when the ethnographer removed what was left of his onesuit and searched through his pack for another.

"We have to go," he called out in Nostratic.

"You can't stay here."

The healer looked up at the sound of the words, but the ethnographer said nothing. He bent over the pack again. He pulled out one, two, three sections, which he assembled quickly into a rifle with a needle-thin point.

"Who is that meant for?"

"Anyone who tries to kill us."

Pauline had a pistol. She could be dead. Esoch knew why. "Can you kill one of your own kind?"

"They're not my kind."

And then Esoch was certain that this slazan was a warrior and not an ethnographer.

"I'm ready," said the warrior.

I listened to the words she did not understand, but their meaninglessness did not matter. What mattered was the long object the colors of the sky and the sun that the Stranger held in his arm. She had never seen anything like it before, but she could guess its purpose, and its size made it threatening. Maybe Nightskin was right—maybe there was no other way to insure the safety of each one here.

"Healer," said Broken Leg. "Will lead you us to the rock?"

If the Stranger had asked, I would have said no.

"If take us you to the rock, will be we gone. Will be no others. Take us."

I gestured to the long object in the Stranger's arms. "That objects stays."

"No," said the Stranger.

"I stay then."

"Healer. Soon will be a loud sound. Sound it louder than a baby's cry. Will sound it will from the rock. Will sound it loud for a short time. Then will come out fire from the rock and will lift the rock into the sky. If there not we, we will stay."

I gestured again. "That thing stays."

"I can lead us there," said the Stranger.

Broken Leg looked to him. The Stranger said something in those other words. The Stranger walked off. He took the correct path. How did he know? Broken Leg remained for a moment, looked to her. Did he have something to say?

"Am not I healer. Played I once music."

He looked away and struggled to follow the Stranger's path.

I waited until they were gone. She then took up her quiver, slung it over her shoulder. She slung the bow over the same shoulder. She set off on the path to the clearing.

Esoch and the warrior moved noisily through the forest, several meters apart. The cross pieces of the crutches bit into his armpit; the handgrips dug into his palms. Swinging forward each time, his left foot jarred, and each time the pain jolted through his leg and up through his entire body. He kept telling himself that he would make it, that the pain would be over once they reached the clearing, that he would soon be hooked up to the medcomp. Yet he still wanted to stop. He still wanted to rest here, lean into his despair, and allow the shuttle to leave. Then he wouldn't have to worry about finding Pauline, if she was alive, or spending months in space waiting for this warrior to be honorable or to betray him; how much did he want to rely on slazan nature? Was there one, singular slazan nature? Which human enemy would he trust with such a deal? Which human would he betray?

The warrior stopped ahead. At first Esoch thought the slazan was waiting for him to catch up, but once he got there, he saw the warrior's chest heave, the moisture that coated his face. "We have enough time," the warrior said. "Fifteen minutes" And he set off.

The next time the warrior stopped to lean against a tree. His whole body sagged, as if it would fall if the tree hadn't been there. "We still have time," he said. He didn't say how long.

Esoch wanted to rest longer. His armpits, the palms of his hands, were rubbed raw. The pain in his leg had become immense. He knew that in any moment he would throw up, and the minute he did, he would collapse in exhaustion. Holding in the nausea was like holding in himself.

The warrior tried to walk quickly, but it was now easy to keep up with him. The voice in Esoch's head counted each large tree they passed, as if he knew the exact number until they reached the clearing. He couldn't believe they could travel this slowly and get there in time. All they truly had to do was get inside the shuttle. It didn't matter if it lifted off, if it headed for space. There was still time to cancel the sequence. But still, the next time they stopped, the warrior against a tree, breathing heavily, Esoch knew they wouldn't make it.

They came to a small clearing where the path branched off three different ways. The warrior chose the middle path. Esoch hoped he had made the right choice. He breathed, he swung forward, he endured the pain. And then—up in the shuttle, in the day or so it would take to get to the moon—what would happen if the warrior insisted Pauline was dead? What if he refused to wait for Esoch to find her? Esoch kept moving forward, he tried to see into the months ahead, the slazan honoring his word to take Esoch to humanspace, so that one day he would walk back into the desert reserve, and there would be N!ai, waiting for him, with her own last words.

The leaves ahead took on the same translucent coloring as the leaves at the top of the canopy, and the forest seemed to open and swallow up the light. Ahead there were voices. Ahead there was a dull sound, like something heavy being dropped. The clearing was not empty. Esoch stopped, uncertain what awaited them, uncertain if he wanted to confront it. The warrior kept trudging on. He stopped, looked back. "There isn't much time," he said. He walked on.

Esoch placed the crutch tips in front, swung his right leg forward, felt himself and all his pain arcing over the crutches. He followed. He saw no other choice.

I followed, too, surprised how close she could get without their noticing. She did not understand how either could keep going. The Stranger, who started at a brisk pace, was soon walking like a shot lightfoot who had bled away all her energy, and Broken Leg kept jumping forward on his crutches, though the pain should have felled him long ago.

After the agonizing slowness of following them here, they approached the clearing. She heard voices. One woman. Silence. Then another. The sound of voices, but not the words. One woman had gone to another, and each had found a purpose in coming to the clearing, the same as one woman asking another to hunt, or one woman asking one then another to help force an unwanted man away from the river. No woman had come to her. She almost turned away with that thought.

The warrior had stopped just where the trees at the path ended and the hillside began. Esoch stopped at his side. He was panting. He could feel the sweat. A breeze chilled him. An insect buzzed near his ear. The warrior moved sideways until he was at a more respectful distance.

One by one, women and their children looked up to them. They were standing in the clearing. Esoch counted: five adults, a veritable crowd of slazans, spread out on the blackened ground of the clearing, all on the hatchway side of the shuttle. By each woman was a pile of stones. The talking had stopped for a moment. Then one whispered to another. They didn't seem sure about what to do. It looked as if they were waiting for something, and it hadn't been for Esoch or the warrior to appear.

The warrior pointed the rifle in their direction and started to walk down the hill, small, careful steps. He looked straight at the shuttle, as if ignoring them would make them unimportant. Esoch was no longer sure if he wanted to follow. After the first slazan had died, Pauline had walked off, alone, to make sure no one else would die. When she had been chased into the swamp, she had not used her pistol in self-defense. And here were more slazans, with stones, and he feared them and felt for them at the

same time. The warrior called after him, told him to hurry, his rifle aimed right at the slazans in the clearing.

A voice called out. The warrior stopped and looked. Each
woman turned to look in that direction. The older children turned
to look at the same time. Only then did the tinier children swerve
their heads. Esoch followed the direction of their eyes like arrows.

I heard Nightskin's voice call out, and she ran until she
reached the hillside. There was Nightskin, across the way, standing on the same path where the first not-a-person had walked off
and disappeared. The midday sun shone down upon the entire
clearing and hillside, the colors of the leaves bright, but
Nightskin stood there with such firmness in her stance that it was
almost as if there were extra light that made her so clearly seen:
the strength in her limbs, the gray flaps of skin under her chin,
the brightness of her eyes.

I looked at who stood upon the blackened ground. Flatface
stood there with her daughter and her waist-high son, but her
almost-a-man son was gone. Nearby was her eldest daughter,
Clear Eyes, whose infant daughter slept in her kaross. Wisdom
was there as well as Crooked. And there stood Squawker, who
had shared a mother with dead Hugger, and in one arm was her
infant daughter sucking her teat, and beside her was her knee-
high son.

First Squawker, then Clear Eyes, turned their attention from
Nightskin to the Stranger, who was walking straight toward the
boulder.

Nightskin called out, "Throw the stones at them."

Clear Eyes looked to her mother. Crooked looked to Wisdom.

Nightskin called out, "Don't let him get to the boulder."

Squawker reached down for a stone, and the Stranger lifted
the long object in his arms. Squawker didn't even get the chance
to pull the stone high enough to start a throw. Whatever the
Stranger had, it did not throw fire. A visible but small hole shone
in the area between Squawker's teats; then the blood in her collapsed into the hole, and she fell to the ground atop her daughter,
who cried out once and was silent.

"No!"' Esoch yelled, and he tried to jerk himself forward,
tried to use the hillside to gain momentum. The warrior was too
far away. The boy—the dead woman's son?—rushed at the warrior. "No!" The same happened to him: the hole, the blood, the
body upon the ground.

Nightskin called, "Stop him!"

And the Stranger turned, raised the long object, and everything stopped, because the boulder's cry had started. It was a high-pitched, loud wail. The sound circled around and around, and I's ears hurt. One child after another put hands to ears.

Broken Leg was halfway down the hill. He was following the Stranger. Atop the hill, Nightskin was pulling an arrow out of her quiver. The Stranger was by the closed opening. He turned and shouted some of the unknown words to Broken Leg, who, almost at the bottom of the hill, had stopped.

Something had struck Esoch in the arm and had sent him spinning toward the ground, the good leg hitting first, then the broken leg, and then the sudden pain. He looked to his arm. He looked at the shaft of the arrow, at the feathers, at the trace of blood where the arrow was embedded in his skin, but it didn't seem real, it didn't cause any pain at all. He didn't know how long he sat there listening to the siren, listening to the warrior call out to him.

Esoch rose up, the pain in arm and leg immense, and he saw that, standing before him on the blackened ground, were the women. One or two had stones in their hands, but they looked around as if confused. They should be running. They should be scared. But the sudden death, the sudden noise, must have been too much. They stood rooted to the black ground. And when the shuttle lifted off, they would be burned to death. He didn't know if he had time to make his way to the shuttle, to get inside and shut down the engines.

"Hurry!" the warrior shouted. His voice was barely audible above the wailing of the siren.

Esoch didn't move. He too shouted. "Go away!" Could they hear him? Could they understand him. "Go away! There will be fire! The rock will burn the ground with fire!"

"Hurry!" Esoch saw the warrior's mouth form the word, but he didn't hear. He knew what he must be saying. The siren's sound was increasing in pitch.

"It's too late!" he shouted back. Then to the women: "Go away."

He heard a voice shout it behind him. It was the healer's voice. But the women weren't running. They were moving like a reluctant crowd.

The warrior had fired his rifle at the shuttle. A blackened hole was where the eyeplate had been. He reached in with his hands. He was going to try to manipulate the electronics of it. He would rather die trying to get in the shuttle than live here.

Esoch wanted to lunge forward, make it to the shuttle, open it for him. Instead he lunged on his crutches toward the women. He would swing a crutch at them. He would frighten them away. One woman lifted a stone. It missed. The second one, thrown by someone else, hit his wounded arm.

I was running down the hill toward Broken Leg when the stone struck, when he fell a second time. "Go away!" she shouted. "There'll be fire!" Each woman looked to Nightskin, as if she had the proper words, before they looked back to I. And it was following this gesture that I saw Nightskin remove another arrow.

I stopped at the bottom of the hill. Her bow was tangled with the quiver, and she had to remove both from her shoulder. The quiver fell. I imagined she heard the rattle of the arrows over the sound of the rock's loud cry. Nightskin's second arrow struck the ground, missing Broken Leg. By now I had her bow and an arrow. Nightskin saw what was happening. I had her arm stretched back, the two fingers taut. Nightskin held on to her own bow, stepped back once, then twice, then three times, until she had disappeared into the woods.

Esoch twisted his body to see that the shuttle door wasn't sliding open, that the warrior remained there, his fingers fast at work, when the alarm stopped and the first jets fired. The initial heat struck Esoch to the ground. Soon all the jets would fire. Soon there would be nothing. And hands took hold of him. Fingers reached under his arms, then arms curled around. And he was half up, half dragged. He could hear feet hit the ground, the puffing of breath, and then all the jets fired. A force threw him down. Red shone behind his eyelids. A weight of a body leaned over him, covered him. And that was all he would later remember.

The fire was gone as quickly as it had started. I, who had thrown herself atop Broken Leg, now rose. The rock was high in the sky, pointed upward, then shot off like an arrow. She couldn't help but watch it. She heard voices behind her. She didn't listen to what words were said.

It was only after the rock could no longer be seen that she noticed that she stood well away from the blackened ground. It was only then she noticed how a pain had attached itself like a new skin to the back of her legs, to the length of her back. Broken Leg was stretched out on the ground, eyes closed. His broken leg was twisted against the splint. The skin on his leg, the color of muddy water, had turned the color of the setting sun. Underneath him the grass was now more white than the color of grass, as if it, too, had considered burning. The darkened ground was no longer cracked with lines of mud or scuffed with footprints. It was as flat and dark as the night. The Stranger, Squawker, Squawker's daughter, Squawker's son, were nowhere to be seen. Lying just outside the ring of black was Clear Eyes, one leg and one arm darkened, groans uttered from an unconscious body. What terrible pain it must be if she could feel it when she was not awake. The child in her kaross started to cry. After I touched Broken Leg's back, felt the rise and fall of his breathing, she stepped over to Clear Eyes. Flatface was there, lifting the eldest daughter's infant to her withering teats. The crying stopped while I looked over the burns on Clear Eyes' body.

While doing so, she looked up once. She expected something else to happen, to hear the sound of the rock again, to see something large appear in the sky and return. But the sky was the sky. The clouds were the clouds. The sun shone. She couldn't believe the sky was so empty; it was like nothing had ever been there that could have dropped to the ground.

Flatface knelt by Clear Eyes and looked to I to save her daughter's struggling life.

The rock was gone. Its leaving had made nothing better.

Chapter Sixteen

The Days After

All he felt was pain. All he heard was music. When there was music, there was less pain. He didn't want to wake up. He didn't want to find out he was alone, on this world, still alive.

The morning after the boulder left, one woman and another and another entered Nightskin's hut and hearth near the springs. Nightskin sat by the cooking fire and looked up. The daughter saw the women and ran into Nightskin's arms. Each woman unslung her bow and pulled an arrow from her quiver. Nightskin did not avert her eyes, nor did she move.

Afterward, no woman told another, not even a daughter, what she had done.

For days everything was the same. I healed the burns on one child and another, and there were gifts. There was music. There was Broken Leg's fevered talk in strange words. There was Clear Eyes' low moans and slow death. And there was talk. Wisdom talked. Crooked talked. Flatface talked and talked, for now she was a mother to her daughter's child, who would eat food that Flatface chewed and passed to her, but who still reached for Flatface's withering, empty teats.

Flatface was the one who told I about Nightskin, about how

she had abandoned her hut and hearth, taking her kaross, her bow and arrow, and Huggable's daughter.

I's hut, the one she had lived in since her mother had left for the south, carried the stink of the Stranger and of Broken Leg, so I tore it down, fed the thatching into the hut's own fire. Afterward she lay Broken Leg in the same place he had lain before, but this time the air carried away the smells.

The night after the rock had left, she mated with Made Nothing, who had built his nest between where I and Flatface gathered, and the next morning he built for I a small hut, much like the one a woman would build for herself and her child when she went out during the summer to gather summer's plentiful growth. The shelter was good for keeping her gzaet and her strings of memory beads dry when it rained.

The night after that, she mated with Roofer, after Old Sour Plum turned her away, and the night after that she mated with Roofer, then Made Nothing, less out of desire and more to make them feel that her desire had lasted longer than it did. If the pregnancy took, she knew it would be a child opened from Nightskin's pollen.

Broken Leg had slept the rest of the day the rock had left, opening his eyes only once, and I feared he would die. It seemed wrong that after so much had happened, nothing of those days would remain, that everything would be lost. She played like she never had played. She mashed leaves mixed with water to make a salve and rubbed it over his skin and Clear Eyes' skin as if each were an infant and touch came easily. The second day he opened his eyes twice, said nothing, and closed them again. The next day he opened his eyes, took water, ate mashed fruit, and said nothing.

Another day he opened his eyes and sat up. This was the day he spoke. This was the day all the talk over the past three days had come to. Because I wanted him to live by the river. I shared words with Flatface and with Wisdom and Crooked. She told each woman that the ones like Broken Leg touched the way a mother touched an infant, that they flocked like birds, that they used their hands to embrace rather than to push away. Each woman wanted him to leave. Each woman said he should live somewhere else. Before, I's words had been weak, and each woman had listened to Nightskin. Each had turned against her. If words had been shared, if each had given her a chance to speak, then Broken Leg would be gone, no woman would have gone to the clearing, no child would have been burnt in the rock's fire, and Clear Eyes would still be alive.

Now I's words were strong. Each woman listened to her, but in all the talks no one mentioned Squawker, her daughter, or her son. It was as if the mother, who long ago had brought with her a daughter and a son, had never come to the river, had never lived here. Broken Leg had tried to save women with whom he had shared nothing. Perhaps if he had known Squawker, he would not have forgotten her so readily.

He did not remember most of his dreams. He knew he dreamed of N!ai, and he knew he dreamed of Hanan, and in each they seemed farther and farther away. He dreamed he made love with Pauline, he thrust, never finished, and lay there along the curve of empty desire.

When he was half-awake, he half thought. He thought of the warrior who could well have been an ethnographer. He kept thinking that he could have made it to the hatch, that he could have opened it, that he could have canceled the code, and no one would have had to feel the full hot blow of the launch rockets. He feared waking because he feared knowing who had died.

But he did open his eyes, he did eat, and out of sheer boredom, one day he sat up. The healer was playing music, and perhaps that's what made sitting up possible. He looked to her, then respectfully averted his gaze. He heard the rustle of her pubic apron as she rose, and heard her footsteps approach. He couldn't help but look, and he watched her sit next to him, the tin piano in her hands.

She said something, none of which he understood. He shook his head, a human gesture that she wouldn't understand. "I don't understand," he said.

I almost didn't repeat her words. She reconsidered. She said, "You are one who touches. No one here touches. No one here could live where one had to touch. You cannot live well when you cannot touch." She lifted the gzaet, aware of the solid weight of it, and placed it before him. "With music you can touch."

Esoch wasn't sure he understood the words she had spoken, but the battered tin piano in front of him said everything. The metal, the keys, the internal workings, had been handed from person to person since the first colonists had arrived, as the healing dance had passed from generation to generation, leapfrogging from one generation of actual Ju/wa to a generation of re-created Ju/wa. There was something terrible about all those generations, about the things they demanded. And this feeling—the articulated thoughts wouldn't develop for days—made it difficult for Esoch to want this. He would rather touch with nothing. He would rather be away. He would rather walk off like Pauline had and find whatever might exist elsewhere in this land. But he had nothing else to share, and sharing was survival. He groped for words and found ones that did not satisfy, but they were the only words he had: "I will play."

I heard the words, mispronounced, but spoken in the proper order. She watched his fingers lightly touch the keys, and she respected the wisdom of the hands that did not yet press down.

The following is taken from the notebook Pauline Dikobe kept while studying the slazan foraging population on Tienah. This entry was made a week before her departure, on the night she had finished a five-page sketch, which later became the rough outline of the novel she wrote on the return trip to E-donya E-talta.

Somewhere, if he is still alive, there is a young man named ≠oma, who was once called Owner of Music. He most likely has married, and if his wife has given birth to several children, he would be living among the people of his father's n!ore, if his father is still alive or if the ties with his father's family are still strong. The little thumb piano given to him by the medico when he was still a child has probably exchanged hands a number of times, an especially valued gift, so good for giving, and if he misses it, he misses it with the same pang we all miss something valuable that we lost during our childhood. Somewhere else there is a young soldier who calls himself Esoch al-Schouki, who was Ju/wa once, who fashioned me a chi !kan, and who one night shared my loneliness and called me wife. Maybe he has told someone why he left the reserve; maybe there was some guilt that he still harbors, or maybe a dry spell about his waterhole made Chum!kwe seem like a worthwhile risk. While in that outpost between a world where meat was shared and another where meat was sold, he may well have drunk too much, and he may well have seen more fights within the space of days than he had seen over the course of years, and he may well have witnessed the flash of a knife. Perhaps he had joined the mili because he had almost killed someone in a fit of rage, or, more likely, he had grown discontented with the wealth of dust and the rations of mealie-meal. By now he has been re-assigned a comrade-in-arms, and they would be working together, preparing for the day when they invade a slazan homeworld.

Somewhere on this world there may well be a healer, but whatever technology came with the original colony is gone. Somewhere else, light-decades away from here, there are slazans with a technology equal to ours, and they are fighting a war with us, a war that makes less and less sense as I have watched their distant cous-ins at work. The violence I imagined for them hasn't happened; why did it happen seven years ago when hu-man and slazan shared a world?

Here I write in a shuttle full of data, data that will be examined by intelligences and anthropologists and military specialists, to be used to do the effective violence that will end the war or to find the proper words to share that will bring some kind of peace. I know that I won't be the last human whom Clear Eyes or !U or !U's son and daughter will see, and I wonder what will hap-pen to them as more and more humans come to colonize and to study.

The *Way of God* orbits this world, and they are pre-paring for my return. I am still alive, and they still exist. Perhaps it would be better if they had been destroyed, if I had died, and this anthropological hut had flown apart into nothingness. There would be no return mission, this world would be buried deep enough in the wealth of classified data and these slazans could live for a while longer without knowledge of our distant war, the idea of which may disturb them now, even though, in the end, they would take to battle as readily as any other slazan who has gone to war. Whatever is wrong about the way they live, they deserve better than what we will give them.

Still, in a week I will return to the warship, the war-ship will return to humanspace, and what will happen will happen. What's right and proper is anyone's guess; what's right is just words.

Acknowledgments

Ethnomusicologist Daniel M. Neuman, Alice Harlow, Katie Baker, Damian Kilby, and David Hartlage offered important commentary on a much shorter, much earlier version of I's story. Damon Knight and Kate Wilhelm convinced me to scrap the entire story and start anew.

Geoff Landis, Steve Swiniarski, Brian Yamauchi, Andre Williams, and Jay Williams offered commentary and answered questions. Bonita Kale, Maureen McHugh, Mary Turzillo, and Sarah Willis offered commentary and discussion beyond the call of duty. Kevin Ho and Veronica Lee answered medical questions. Vickie Wright, Becky Thomas, and Joe Heinen provided last minute help. Lou Aronica offered important early suggestions, Ralph Vicinanza went to bat for the novel, and Jennifer Hershey has been more supportive and helpful an editor than any writer could ask for. Lise Rodgers was an impeccable copy editor. Karen Fowler saved the day, as usual. April Stewart-Oberndorf gave her usual, impeccable editorial support. Andrew reduced the trips to the attic when he asked me if I'd take a break.

Meg Lynch, who in 1992 was assistant to Irven DeVore, of Harvard's Department of Anthropology, introduced me to the work of John Tooby and Leda Cosmides, to *Current Anthropology*, and to Irven DeVore and Terry Deacon's printed course notes on Human Behavioral Biology. For the creation of the slazans, I am indebted to primate research by Frans de Waal, Birute Galdikas, J. C. Mitani, Peter Rodman, and Barbara Smuts. Greg Laden suggested that the slazan social scale might be larger than is perceptible to humans. The evolutionary description of slazans is drawn from Chapter 3 of Melvin Konner's *The Tan-*

gled Wing. My ideas on human physical and social evolution are shaped by Konner, Marvin Harris, Robert Trivers, and *The Adapted Mind*, a collection edited by Barkow, Cosmides, and Tooby. For territoriality, I relied on Elizabeth Casdam. For language evolution, I turned to Derek Bickerton and Steven Pinker. The idea of a U curve in human evolution belongs to Bruce Knauft. Some readers of the above material might start looking for genetic explanations for human behaviors that are more adequately explained by environmental factors. Richard Lewontin's engaging *Biology as Ideology* should be read as a necessary corrective.

My primal utopians' re-creation of Ju/'hoansi culture is based extensively on the work of anthropologist Richard Lee. The statement by the Ju/'hoan informant on pages 122–123 is not a fictional creation, but rather words spoken by ≠omazho, a Ju/'hoan healer, to Professor Lee. A full explanation of the context for those words can be found in Lee's very fine *The Dobe Ju/'hoansi.* The education of a hunter section relies heavily on Lee's presentation in *The !Kung San: Men, Women, and Work in a Foraging Society.* I have also relied on Marjorie Shostak's *Nisa: The Life and Words of a !Kung Woman.* The description of the healing dance is based on accounts by Konner, Lee, Shostak, Megan Biesele, Richard Katz, Lorna Marshall, and the film *N/um Tchai* by John Marshall. Marshall's film, *N!ai, the Story of a !Kung Woman* is the source of the epigraph by ≠oma Word. Other work by the above, as well as the work of Patricia Draper, Elizabeth Marshall Thomas, and Pauline Weissner, has shaped my understanding of Ju/'hoansi culture when there was enough land to support gathering and hunting as a way of life. All errors and misrepresentations are mine or Pauline Dikobe's.

Author's Concluding Note

Since the early 1970's fewer and fewer Ju/'hoansi have been able to sustain themselves through gathering and hunting. Their land has slowly been taken away by others. The Ju/'hoansi and their culture persist, but in new circumstances, facing new, difficult challenges. Anthropologists who had worked with the Ju/'hoansi established the Kalahari Peoples' Fund in Botswana and the Nyae Nyae Development Foundation in Namibia to help the Ju/'hoansi create new lives. For example, with such help, the Ju/'hoansi in Namibia formed the Nyae Nyae Farmers' Cooperative, which went on to write a dictionary, and Nyae Nyae children are now learning to read and write in their native language. In both countries, wells have been dug, gardens started, and corrals built for small herds of cattle. If you would like to offer financial support for these endeavors, contributions can be sent to:

Kalahari Peoples' Fund (Botswana)
c/o Dr. James Ebert
3100 9th Street, NW
Albuquerque, NM 87107

—and—

Nyae Nyae Development Foundation of Namibia
P. O. Box 9026
Windhoek, Namibia
      (or)
c/o Cultural Survival
46 Brattle Street
Cambridge, MA 02138

ABOUT THE AUTHOR

CHARLES STEWART-OBERNDORF is the author of *Sheltered Lives* and *Testing*. A graduate of Dartmouth College and the Clarion Writers' Workshop (1987), he lives in Cleveland Heights with his wife and eight-year-old son. He teaches English at University School and is at work on his next novel.

Come enter the remarkable worlds of

DAN SIMMONS

HYPERION

The Hugo Award--winning novel of a daring interstellar pilgrimage. ____28368-5 $5.99/$6.99 Canada

THE FALL OF HYPERION

The adventure continues in this gripping sequel.
____28820-2 $5.99/$6.99 Canada

ENDYMION

A stunning return to the world of *Hyperion,* and the birth of a new messiah. ____10020-3 $22.95/$31.95 Canada

THE HOLLOW MAN

One man's anguished mental journey through omniscience.
____56350-5 $5.99/$6.99 Canada

PHASES OF GRAVITY

An astronaut's magical search for meaning upon returning to Earth. ____27764-2 $4.95/$5.95 Canada

PRAYERS TO BROKEN STONES

A brilliant collection of short fiction.
____29665-5 $5.99/$6.99 Canada
